Sky Coyote

Kage Baker

AVON · EOS

AVON BOOKS, INC.
An Imprint of HarperCollins*Publishers*
10 East 53rd Street
New York, New York 10022-5299

Copyright © 1999 by Kage Baker
Cover illustration by Tom Canty
Inside cover author photo by Tom Westlake
Published by arrangement with Harcourt Brace & Company
Library of Congress Catalog Card Number: 98-16833
ISBN: 0-380-73180-0
www.harpercollins.com

First Avon Eos Printing: March 2000

AVON EOS TRADEMARK REG. U.S. PAT. OFF. AND IN OTHER COUNTRIES,
MARCA REGISTRADA, HECHO EN U.S.A.

Printed in the U.S.A.

WCD 10 9 8 7 6 5 4 3 2 1

To George H. Baker,
who once spent a very long afternoon
trying to read *Hiawatha* to an impatient four-year-old
so she'd have some sense of his ethnic heritage,
this book is respectfully dedicated.

Sky
Coyote

Chapter 1 ✆

YOU'LL UNDERSTAND THIS story better if I tell you a lie.

Well, a myth, anyway. There was this god once, the Greek god of Time. He was a cruel old bastard and he ate all his children as soon as they were born. Zeus, the youngest son, managed to escape; when he grew up, he came back and ended the rule of Time by killing his father. Then he cut him open and set the older children free. King Time is dead; long live King Zeus.

In the twenty-fourth century, a research and development firm proudly appropriated Zeus as its corporate logo when it developed a method of time travel.

The method didn't quite pan out, though. Traveling through time is prohibitively expensive, and there are certain crucial limitations. For example, you can't go into the future, only backward into the past, and forward again to your point of departure in the present. Another problem is that history cannot be changed. Period. It's the law.

However, this law can only be observed to apply to *recorded* history . . .

So the discovery wasn't a total loss. The company altered its logo slightly and became *Dr.* Zeus. They were able to make a nice profit looting the past by collecting "lost" works of art and arranging long-term investments. They loaded a database with every event in recorded history and found they still had plenty of uncharted past to move

1

around in. They realized that if the past couldn't be changed, it could at least be manipulated to Company advantage.

But who were they going to get to do the actual manipulating? Traveling back in time is rough, if you do it the cost-effective way without extra buffers. Twenty-fourth-century agents bitch about it constantly, and demand extra pay. Fabulously rich corporations never seem to have enough cash, paradoxically enough; though you may really *need* to send that man back to deposit a certain sum in a certain bank on a certain day in 1806, you're reluctant to do it unless you've got a guarantee it will pay off in six figures. And how many times do you want to lay out money to send people through? Isn't there a way to cut costs on this?

Dr. Zeus got its answer reviewing another failed project: immortality.

Technically it's possible to make an immortal person. It is not commercially practical. It only works on infants or little children, not middle-aged millionaires; and since middle-aged millionaires are the only ones who could afford to pay for the process, it's sort of a loss as a market item. In addition, the chosen babies must meet certain stringent physical requirements, and endure years of surgical alteration and training. Not even the most determined millionaire parents, once they knew what it entailed, would put their little Gloria or Donald Jr. through such an ordeal.

So, you can't sell immortality. On the other hand, if you're looking for Company agents who will work loyally without health insurance and never, ever retire . . .

They sent a team back to Lower Paleolithic times. A permanent base was established; equipment was shipped back, too. The original team went about collecting little Neanderthals and Cro-Magnons. These kids were then implanted, augmented, amplified, fortified, hopped up, switched on, tuned in, and thoroughly indoctrinated. They were given the whole harvest of human knowledge and culture from the other end of time; the books, the music, the cinema. They grew up, these *superüberkinder,* and when the last nasty mortal tissues had been well and truly excised, the base technicians handed them the keys to the lab and said: You take over. We're going home.

So, see what was accomplished with just one round trip? You don't send your agents back and forth through time; you recruit them at the beginning and let them walk forward through time in the ordinary way. Outlay for the project was kept to a minimum, and now Dr. Zeus had immortal operatives working for it, strategically placed at every important event in history. Of course, they were promised a golden future when they finally *got* to the future. Though that hasn't happened yet . . .

And the immortals made more immortals, though not in the usual way, because they had all been very carefully sterilized; suitable infants were selected from the mortal population and processed at remote bases inaccessible to marauding primitives. More bases were built, more secret Company projects were inaugurated, and the fix, as they say, was in.

Dr. Zeus ruled the world. Covertly, of course.

By now you've probably got a mental image of these immortals. You're only mortal yourself, and the idea of a deathless, perfect race makes you uncomfortable—and maybe just a little hostile—so you imagine them intellectual and emotionless. Stuck up, too. You're probably thinking they all look like vampires or superheroes, tall and steely-eyed, the men with bulging biceps and the women gorgeous in a chilly sort of way.

Well, you're wrong. The truth is, they look just like you, and why shouldn't they? They used to be human beings.

Chapter 2 ⬿

THE YEAR IS 1699 A.D., the place is South America: deepest jungle, green shadows, slanting bars of sunlight, a dark rich overripe smell. Jaguars on the prowl. Orchids in bloom. Little birds and monkeys making continuous little bird and monkey noises in the background.

And here's the Lost City in the middle of the jungle: sudden acres of sunlight and silence in the middle of all that malarial gloom. Red and white stucco pyramids. Steps and courtyards and avenues, straight as a die. Straighter. Really impressive architecture out in the middle of nowhere. Gods and kings carved all over the place.

And here's the intrepid Spanish Jesuit, our hero. You couldn't mistake him for anything else. He's got those little black raisin eyes Spanish priests are supposed to have, but with a sort of twinkly expression the masters of the Inquisition usually lack. He's got the black robe, the boots, the crucifix; he's short—well, let's say "compact of build"—and is of olive complexion. Needs a shave.

He approaches cautiously through the jungle, and his cute little eyes widen as he beholds the Lost City. From somewhere within his robe he produces a square of folded sheepskin, and opens it to study a complicated design penned in red and blue inks. He seems to orient himself, and proceeds quickly to a wall embellished with scowling plaster monsters whose terrifying rage seems to keep even

4

the lianas and orchids from encroaching on them. He makes his way along the perimeter, then: ten meters, twenty meters, thirty, and comes at last to the Jaguar Gate.

This is a magnificent towering megalith kind of a thing of red plaster, surmounted by a green stone lintel on which two jaguars are carved in bas-relief, upright and rampant in fighting poses, with eyes and claws inlaid in gold. Nay, but there's more: no actual gate occupies this gateway, no rusting bars of iron, oh no. Instead a solid wave of faint blue light shimmers there, obscuring slightly the view of the fabulous city beyond. If you have *really* good hearing (and the Spanish Jesuit has), you can just perceive that the blue light is humming slightly, crackling, buzzing.

And what's this in nasty little heaps around the base of the gateway? Lots of fried bugs and a fried bird or two, and—gosh, the Spanish Jesuit doesn't even want to think about what that blackened and twisted thing is over there, the one reaching out with a skeletal claw to the blue light. Probably just a dead monkey, though.

Peering at the detail of the pictographic inscription that runs up one side of the gateway, the Jesuit finds what he has been searching for: a tiny black slot in the face of a parrot-deity who's either beheading a prisoner or fertilizing a banana plant, depending on how good your knowledge of pictographs is. After observing it closely, the Jesuit reaches into a small leather pouch at his belt. He brings out an artifact, a golden key of strange and unkeylike design. How did this Spanish Jesuit come by such a key? Did he read about its fabled existence in some long-forgotten volume moldering in the libraries of the Escorial? Did he track its whereabouts across the New World, following a long-obscured trail through unspeakable dangers? Your guess is as good as mine. Holding his breath, he inserts it into the slot in the parrot-god's beak.

At once there is a high-pitched shrilling noise, and the Spanish Jesuit knows, without being told, that someone has been alerted to his presence there. Maybe several someones.

The blue light falters and blinks out for a second. Seizing his opportunity, the Spanish Jesuit leaps through the gateway, moving remarkably quickly for a man in a long cassock. No sooner has he landed on the pavement beyond than the blue light snaps back on, and a mosquito who was attempting to follow the Spanish Jesuit meets a terrible, though not untimely, death in a burst of sparks. The Spanish Jesuit breathes a sigh of relief. He has gained entrance to the Lost City.

Making his way through this awesome pile of arcane geometry, he finds a shaded courtyard where a fountain splashes. Here are tables and seats carved from stone. He sits down. There's a stiff sheet of calligraphied parchment lying on the table. He leans forward to peer at it with interest. A shadow appears across an archway, and he looks up to see the Ancient Mayan.

Again, this is a guy you identify immediately. Feathered headdress, jaguarskin kilt, silky black pageboy bob. Hooked nose and high cheekbones. A sad and sneering countenance, appropriate in a member of a long-vanished empire. Is this the end for the Spanish Jesuit?

No, because the Ancient Mayan bows so his green plumes curl and bounce forward, and he inquires:

"How may I serve the Son of Heaven?"

The Jesuit looks down at the parchment.

"Well, the Margarita Grande looks pretty good. On the rocks, *with* salt, okay? And make that two. I'm expecting a friend."

"Okay," replies the Ancient Mayan, and glides away silently.

Boy, I love moments like this. I really enjoy watching the illusion coming into sharp contrast with the reality. I imagine the shock of the imaginary viewer, who must think he's walked into a British comedy sketch. You know why I've survived in this job, year after year, lousy assignment after lousy assignment, with no counseling whatsoever? Because I have a keen appreciation of the ludicrous. Also because I have no choice.

Chapter 3 ᏄᏇ

So I'm sitting here waiting for the Mayan guy to come back with our cocktails, and I'm understandably a little jumpy, because I'm meeting someone I haven't seen in, oh, a while, and we didn't part on the best of terms. When mortals are nervous, their senses are heightened, they notice all kind of little details they're ordinarily unaware of. Imagine how it is with us.

Like I notice: the sound of tennis balls, far off, rebounding. Leisure. The sound of toilets flushing, wow, think of all that expensive plumbing. The smell of the jungle isn't any worse than, say, a terrarium in bad need of a cleaning, and it's pretty much blocked out anyway by the dominating aromas of this place: colognes. Antiperspirants. Cultivated flowers. Refrigerated food all nice and fresh. I can even smell fabric: starched napkins and tablecloths and bed linens, and not one spot of mildew on anything, and this is in the tropics, yet.

As I sit marveling at the luxury of New World One, she comes into range. I pick her up about twenty-five meters to the right and two meters down, steadily ascending, must be stairs beyond that arch. She's moving at four point six kilometers an hour. I hear the footsteps on the staircase now, and through the arch I see her rising: head, then shoulders, then the white brocade of her gown.

She paused on the top step and looked at me.

7

She'd been one of those Galicians with white skin and red hair; could have passed for an Irishwoman, or English, even, until you saw her eyes. They were black. They had a hard stare, an expression of . . . *disdain* is too mild a word. Disgust, that's it, whether at me or the world or God, I could never tell.

But it had been a long time, and maybe she'd even forgotten about what's-his-name. I took a deep breath and smiled.

"Well, well. Little Mendoza." And I stood and summoned every ounce of belief in the scene we presented. Father confessor extends welcome to young noblewoman.

"Jesus Christ," she said.

"No, sorry," I replied. "The robe's got you fooled."

"What a little pudding face you have with your beard and mustache shaved off."

"I missed you too," I said gallantly, gesturing to a seat. After a moment's hesitation she approached and sat down, and I sat too, and the Mayan very providentially brought our cocktails.

"You got my transmission, then." It's safe to begin with the obvious.

"I did." She arranged the train of her gown, not looking at me.

"So." I leaned back after the first sip. "Been a long time, hasn't it?"

"One hundred and forty-four years." No, she hadn't forgotten about what's-his-name. "Since Portsmouth. I'm taller than you are, too. I wonder why I never noticed that before."

"You're wearing high heels."

"Could be." She raised her glass and considered it. She was being too much of a lady to bite the lime, but she did lick the salt.

"I like your ensemble. Bonnet *à la Fontagnes,* isn't it? Boy, they really keep up with fashion here, don't they?

That's the exact style they were wearing in Madrid when I left."

"I should hope so." She sneered. "You think courtiers fuss about their clothes? Hang around here a few years."

"If I remember right, you used to like new fashions."

"Less important now. I don't know why. I'm very comfortable here, actually. Sanitation, good food, peace and quiet. Nothing to disturb my work but the social occasions, and I manage to get out of most of those."

"So you don't party much?"

"I hate parties."

I reached out and took her hand. She looked at me in swift surprise. Then she relaxed and said, "You're back with the Church again, obviously."

"Have been. I'm about to change roles."

"Really?"

"Yes. Yes, I died heroically in an attempt to carry the Word of God to a bunch of Indians who weren't having any, thank you very much. Even now faithful Waldomar, my novice, is telling Father Sulpicio why he was unable to recover my arrow-studded body from the jungle. Anyway, I've just hiked in and I haven't even reported for debriefing yet. Can't wait for a shower and a shave."

"I would have thought you'd go for them first."

"Wanted to see you." I shrugged and had another sip. Her eyes narrowed slightly.

"What exactly are you doing here, Joseph?" she inquired. This time she bit the lime. "If you don't mind?"

"Recuperating!" My eyes widened. "I've just come from ten years as part of a Counter-Reformation dirty tricks squad in Madrid, doing stuff that would make a hyena queasy. Then I had a sea voyage here, which was *not* any kind of a luxury cruise, and two weeks on a stinky jungle trail. I'm a little overdue for a vacation, wouldn't you say?"

"Overdue for a shower, anyway."

"Sad but true." I looked into the bottom of my glass. "What does one do to order a second round here?"

She waved a negligent hand, two fingers extended. The Mayan appeared from nowhere with two new drinks. He went through the whole business with the new napkins and the old glasses and swept away. I stared after him. "What does he do, stand there just out of sight listening to us?"

"Probably." She raised her glass. "So after your vacation you're going back out into the field?"

"Well, yes, as a matter of fact."

"Going to play with politics at Lima?"

"No. They're sending me up north."

"Mexico? What on earth are you going to find to do up there?"

"Farther north than that. California."

"Ahh." She nodded and drank. "Well, you'll enjoy that. Great climate, I'm told. On the other hand—" She looked up suspiciously. "Nobody's *there* yet. No cities, no court, no political intrigues. So what could you possibly . . ."

"There are Indians there," I reminded her. "Indians have politics too, you know."

"Oh, Indians." She gestured as dismissively as only a Spaniard can. "But what a waste of your talents! They're all savages up there, Joseph. Who did you offend, to draw an assignment like that? What will you do?"

"I don't know. I haven't been briefed on it yet. The rumor is, though, that Dr. Zeus is drafting a big expedition. Lots of personnel from all the disciplines. Big base camp and everything. No expense spared."

"And you're probably going to go in there and collect little Indians for study before they're all killed off by small-pox."

"I wouldn't be surprised."

"You slimy little guy." She shook her head sadly. "Well, best of luck."

Chapter 4 ᘓᕲ

I GOT A guest suite, and I showered, I shaved, I was brought a fresh clean set of tropical whites and decked myself out in style. I left the long heavy wig on its wooden head; I like fashion as well as the next guy, but you have to be realistic sometimes. And the rest of the getup felt swell after my Jesuit mufti: silk knee breeches, gauzy shirt, frogged coat with cuffs you could conceal a dictionary in, let alone a scented hankie or an assignation letter. The heels on the shoes gave me some height, too. Oh, to be able to parade around Barcelona in this suit. You know what priests really miss? Not sex. Style. I admired myself in the mirror a few minutes before going off to report in like a good little operative.

Guest Services turned out to be located right off the lobby of my pyramid, so I didn't even have to step outside. This was good, because even with the air-conditioning on I was sweating by the time I stepped into the director's outer office.

It was lush with pre-Colombian art treasures and potted orchids. A big revolving ceiling fan moved the damp air around. High vaulted windows looked out on a walled garden where long shadows stretched across a brilliantly green lawn, and a turquoise pool of chlorinated water shimmered. No piranha would have lasted five minutes in there.

There was a receptionist's desk of carved mahogany, but

no receptionist. Okay. I looked around and picked up a copy of *Immortal Lifestyles Monthly*. Its glossy cover stuck to my fingers. Pulling them loose made a creepy tearing noise, and from behind a doorway a polite voice inquired, "Yoohoo?"

"Hello? Is the director anywhere around?" I called in reply. A few seconds later the door was pulled open and an immortal guy peered out. He looked at the vacant desk with a slight frown of annoyance.

"I'm so sorry," he said. "I can't think where she's got to. You'd be—?"

"Facilitator Grade One Joseph, reporting in."

"Ah." He reached out and shook my hand. "Good to see you. Guest Services Director Lewis, at your service. Please come in."

His inner office was a little cooler than the outer one, but I noticed he wasn't bothering with his wig either; it drooped from its wooden head on a corner of his desk, with his tricorne perched rakishly atop it. Next to that was a commissary take-out box containing the remnants of a salad and next to that a jade cup half full of cold coffee, with a film of cream streaking the surface. The rest of the desk was in snappy order, though, neat little stacks of brochures arranged by size and a keen matching inkwell-and-quill-stand set of Ming dynasty porcelain. A desk calendar told me today was November 15, 1699.

"Please have a seat. Would you like something cold?" he suggested, bowing slightly in the direction of his liquor cabinet with its built-in icebox. I nodded, mopping my face with one of my crisp fresh handkerchiefs. It promptly wilted. He brought us a couple of Campari frosties and sat down behind his desk. He was wilted, too. Lewis was one of those fragile-looking little guys who could have understudied for Fredric March or Leslie Howard. Limp fair hair over a high-domed forehead with hollow temples, deep-set tragic eyes the color of a bruised violet. Determined chin, though. We swilled down our Camparis in grateful unison.

"Ah." He set down the glass. "Equatorial or not, we don't usually have such heat at this time of the year. You hiked in on foot, too, didn't you? I daresay you're ready for a bit of rest and rec after *that* ordeal."

"I sure am, if I have the time," I said indistinctly, crunching ice. "Do I have the time, before this next job?"

"Let's just see, shall we?" He turned, and a terminal screen rose up smoothly out of a groove in the polished surface of his desk. He unfolded a keyboard and tapped in a request. Little green letters ran across the sea-blue screen. "Well! Here's your file. Oh, my goodness, you're one of our more experienced operatives, aren't you? *Look* at the missions you've been on. So you're the man who preserved the cave paintings at Irun del Mar?"

I thought back twenty thousand years. "Yeah," I admitted. "Long story, actually. They were my father's paintings."

"That's wonderful." Lewis looked, impressed. "That's in the south of France, isn't it? Or is it northern Spain?"

"Neither one, back then. We were the people who became what you'd call Basques."

"*Those* people." Lewis leaned his chin in his palm. "Gosh, that's fascinating. I was stationed in the south of France myself for a couple of centuries and I always meant to go down there on holiday, but the work just never let up. You know how it is."

I nodded. The irony of being immortal and having all the time in the world is that you never really have any time, because there's so much work to do. Except for the occasional layover at places like this, of course. Lewis turned to the screen again.

"Let's see. Quite a distinguished field record throughout prehistory! Then it says you sailed with the Phoenicians, worked in Babylon, you were a priest in Egypt, a politician in Athens, secretary to a Roman senator, brief period as a legionary, three hundred years in Gaul and Britain . . . Why, we came rather close to meeting one another there. That's where I was recruited. I was supposed to have been a Roman."

"Supposed to have been?" I tilted my glass to get the last ice.

"Well, half Roman. By that time, everybody was half Roman and half Gaul or Visigoth or one of those people. There weren't any more Roman Romans." He gave a brief sharp smile. "In any case, my mother abandoned me in the spa at Aquae Sulis. Or so I've been told. Thank heavens a Company agent came along before somebody drowned me like a kitten."

I nodded in sympathy. Lots of us started out that way. He leaned forward and resumed his perusal of my personal history. "And then you served in Byzantium—my, I wish I'd been able to see it then. I was stuck in Ireland, of all places. Did you ever meet the Empress Theodosia?"

"Yes. Evita Peron but with class. Nice lady."

"*Really.* And then it says you put in some time working with the Idrissid rulers in Morocco, then back to Byzantium for the Crusades, and then to Spain. You've been with the Church, in one capacity or other, ever since. Worked under the Inquisition, did you?" Lewis raised an eyebrow.

"Yes, and you know what? The pay was crappy. Somebody was making money out of all those persecuted heretics, but it wasn't me," I told him.

He shook his head, his turn to look sympathetic. "And here's your recreational data . . . say! You're a soccer man? It says here you played on the base team when you were stationed in Andalusia. The Black Legend All-Stars."

"I'm short, but I'm fast." I grinned, setting my glass on his desk.

"Oh, how I *wish* you were going to be here a little longer," Lewis mourned. "We've been trying to introduce soccer and get our own base team together. We had jai alai matches with our Mayans, but they insisted on killing one another afterward. Nasty business. Well, we do have tennis and croquet, if you enjoy either game."

"I'm a tennis man, too."

"Splendid. We have marvelous outdoor courts. Oh! Oh! Here we are, here's your next posting. Six weeks away. Well, you're in for a grand time. You'll be able to enjoy the annual 'Saturnalia, Christmas, Yule, Whatever' party. There's also the Grand Fin de Siècle Cotillion on New Year's Eve as we swing into yet another new century. You'll just make that one," he told me. "Your transport's scheduled to leave the next day."

"It is, huh?" I looked regretful. "Maybe I'd better miss the dance, then. I hate catching a flight when I've been partying the night before."

"Oh, I wouldn't recommend doing *that*." Lewis looked at me mildly, but there was a barely perceptible warning in his tone. "It's the Big Event of the year. There'll be no end of hurt feelings if you don't attend. Our present administrator (also known as the Incarnation of Kukulkan Himself) is most particular about complete participation by base staff and guests in his little entertainments."

"Uh-oh. It's like that, is it?" I shifted in my seat.

"Awful. Cheer up: the food's good, and most of us manage to bail out by one A.M. Just stay away from the mescal punch. His own recipe, unfortunately." Lewis shook his head. He leaned forward to look at the screen again. "You're scheduled to meet with the big, excuse me, with Base Administrator Houbert at half past ten tomorrow morning. Formal brunch in his receiving salon. He'll brief you on your mission to Alta California and provide you with all the access codes you'll need. After that your time is largely your own until your transport arrives. Social rituals apart, of course."

"Okay. What kind of social rituals?" I inquired, casting a longing gaze at the icebox. Lewis took the hint promptly and got up to fetch another round.

"Cocktails every four P.M. precisely. The administrative staff are obliged by tradition to observe cocktail hour at the Palenque Poodle, but as a guest you're free to swill where you will." He handed me another cold one. "I can recommend the hotel bar just across the lobby. Great stock of gins, and their wine cellar is really quite decent. Let's see, what else? Sunday brunch is a must, at any one of the four excellent restaurants available for your dining pleasure, and I must say eggs Benedict combines remarkably well with the breathtaking view from the topmost terrace of a pyramid, but one *is* expected to sort of circulate from table to table chatting with other diners, and that can become tedious after a while. Personally, I never manage to get all the way across the restaurant without at least one sausage rolling off my plate."

"Maybe I'll set a new fashion and eat in my room." I considered.

"Out of the minibar? Lots of luck. You'll be interrupted at least three times by well-meaning Mayans wanting to know if you forgot to make a sedan chair reservation." Lewis sighed and let the screen slide back into its hidden place. He opened a desk drawer and drew out a sheaf of papers.

"Here's your guest information packet with access codes for the base map." He slid it across the desk to me. "Green entries are the different departments, red entries are eating establishments, blue entries are recreation and entertainment areas. We have a first-class cinema that's presently hosting a late-twentieth-century film noir festival, which ought to interest you. You're a Raymond Chandler fan, according to your file."

"Dashiell Hammett, too," I told him.

"You're in luck, then: tomorrow's program features all six versions of *The Maltese Falcon.* Here's your key card for the gymnasium machines and shower lockers. This is your flyer describing social events for the upcoming month. Your physical measurements have been forwarded to our Wardrobe Department, and a complete set of morning dress, evening wear, sportswear, lounging wear, and personal linen has already been delivered to your dressing room. Your tastes in literature and music as noted in your file have been installed in your suite's entertainment center. A bottle of Sandeman Analog Oloroso has been added to your liquor cabinet. Have I forgotten anything? I don't think I have, but God knows I'll be here if you've any further questions." Lewis drooped back into his chair.

"Long tour of duty?" I asked.

"Seven hundred years," he replied wearily.

Chapter 5 ✆

New World One wasn't such a bad place, really.

That was what I was thinking to myself as I strolled through the Grand Plaza next morning on my way to the Palace of Kukulkan.

I mean, spacious—? Acres of wide-open gardens and lawns, huge old rubber trees, broad avenues with hardly a soul in sight. Every so often I'd pick up the pounding of steady purposeful feet and duck into an arched portico or behind a big flowering bush to watch as a sedan chair went by with a lot of nodding green plumes and magnificent coppery muscles moving smoothly under it. In it there were always immortals like me, usually riding alone, staring out with set features as they were jogged inexorably to some other sector of this paradise.

I got to Kukulkan's palace just fine on my own, accessing the data on my base map. It was something to see, all right. A snow-white stucco ziggurat covered with more dragons than Grauman's Chinese Theater, rising huge out of the middle of a small artificial lake. From the front portico a waterfall cascaded down over green copper steps; visitors presumably had to wade up to the front door with shoes and socks in hand. That was assuming they could get across the moat in the first place. I didn't see a bridge. But wait, there was a kind of gondola thing moored amid the lily pads at one edge. Somewhere just out of sight, I knew, a tragically dignified Mayan prince awaited my least command to leap into action and ferry me across.

We aren't really supposed to exploit our paid mortals this way. In fact, the Dr. Zeus offices in the future have a real horror of just this kind of thing going on. We're the servants, never the masters, and God forbid we should behave in such a way as to even suggest we don't know our place.

Only problem is, the mortals in the past just adore surrendering themselves to a higher power. It's embarrassing, sometimes, the way they go on. We pay really well, of course, which may have something to do with it. Anyway, it always makes me uncomfortable to have some poor mortal slob throw himself at my feet and do the O Great White God bit, especially as I'm more sort of a little brown god.

But, hell, how was I supposed to get inside? I took off my tricorne and scratched under my wig, wondering what to do.

"You must be the important guest he's expecting at his midmorning levee," said a voice from the general direction of my right knee.

I looked down and saw a tiny black child, five at most, wearing white satin breeches and a scarlet coat. Not a mortal; he was one of our neophytes, so young he was still undergoing brain and skull surgery, to judge from his heavily bandaged head. The mass of white wrappings looked just like a turban. The rest of his costume must have been designed with that effect in mind, to judge from his pointed slippers and the pink cake box he was carrying.

"Tasteful, isn't it?" he observed sourly, acknowledging my stare. "You're early."

"I won't be if I can't get up to the front door." I nodded in the direction of the moat.

"Scared of slipping on the steps?"

"It's not my idea of a dignified entrance, anyway."

He gave a snort of impatience. "Come on," he said, and I followed him around the side and through a dark tunnel of purple flowers trained over an arbor. We emerged at another face of the ziggurat, one with an ordinary-looking door set back in a recess. A small pirogue drifted on a rope at our feet.

"Give me a hand," he instructed, and as I lifted him up, I realized he really was just a baby, light as chicken feathers, with a baby's domed brow and wide eyes. He perched on the prow, balancing his cake box, while I found a pole to move us across the moat.

"How come you're not in school?" I inquired as we drifted along.

"This *is* school," he replied disgustedly. "I'm an executive administrative trainee. Houbert's supposed to be giving me valuable insights into running a base. This morning's lesson seems to be What to Do If One Runs Out of Marzipan Petits Fours When One Is Expecting an Important Guest for Brunch. I hope you like the damned things."

"Hey, I'll eat anything. Sorry he made you run around like this."

"That's okay." He shrugged his little shoulders. "This semester's almost over. Next semester I'll be sent to study with Labienus at Mackenzie Base. I've heard he's a *real* administrator. Then, next year, I'm scheduled to go to the Low Countries and learn field command from Van Drouten. *Then* I'm going on to Morocco. That's where I want to work once I graduate. With Suleyman. Do you know him?"

"The North African section head? Yeah. Worked with him under Moulay Idriss. Nice guy."

"He's working for Moulay Ismail now, with the Sallee corsairs. He recruited me." The baby's eyes were wide for a moment, and for just that moment he looked his age. "We were on a slave ship, and m-my, my mortal mother, died. Suleyman was there in chains too, pretending to be one of us, and he looked after me then. But he had his pirates lying in wait! He had them board the ship and free everybody! He took me away with him and sent me to the Company. I was aptitude-tested and scored extremely high in leadership capabilities. That's why my augmentation is proceeding at an accelerated rate, you see."

"I'd wondered. Neophytes aren't usually sent into the field this early." We bumped gently into the coping on the other side, and I fished around for the mooring rope. "How old are you, anyway? Four?"

"Three," he told me proudly, and held up his arms to be lifted out of the boat. "I guess they need good administrators these days. If Houbert is typical of the best they've got, they *really* need me. I won't work here, though. I'll be in Africa. With Suleyman."

"You've got it all planned, huh?"

"He's the best there is in his field," the kid said proudly. "I've been reading his file. Talk about a celebrated record! I want to model my career on his. He gave me my name, you know. Latif, that's what he called me when he was taking care of me. I don't remember what I was called before. Anyway, the Company's really going to need good African operatives soon, with all the history that's going to happen over there."

"Well, Latif, I hope you get your chance." I stepped onto the coping beside him, and we made our way to the door, which turned out to be the entrance to a fairly ordinary elevator. Latif put down his cake box long enough to press the button. I looked at him thoughtfully. Smart, confident kid, despite his size-10 case of hero worship. Probably with a brilliant future ahead of him, too; Suleyman had an eye for good recruits. Why hadn't any of my recruits ever thought I was a hero? I'd certainly believed the operative who recruited me was God Himself, I'd been so grateful to be saved from those screaming people with stone axes. But Mendoza hadn't liked me much even before that business with the Englishman, and it wasn't my fault the guy got himself burned at the stake. You'd think she'd show a little gratitude now and then, considering what I'd saved her from.

On the other hand, how much gratitude had I shown to

old Budu, the guy who recruited me? I hadn't exactly been there like a loyal son when he needed me, had I? So maybe the problem is simply that I'm a slimy little guy, and that's life.

Chapter 6 ❧

WHEN THE ELEVATOR doors parted, we were greeted by a blast of recorded music—sounded like Mozart—and a wave of heavy incense smoke. And I mean heavy. Blue clouds of it.

"Oh, shit, he's set fire to the copal again," muttered Latif. "He's through there. That's his morning levee room. I'm just taking this off to the kitchen. See you later."

I took a moment to adjust my wig, set my hat at the proper angle, and shoot my lace cuffs. As I did, a querulous voice called:

"The *stairs*. You didn't come up my stairs. That's part of the whole experience."

"Sorry," I responded, following the voice through the outer room to the door of the audience chamber. I looked in.

It was a very nice room, everything green and white and gold, with snaky Mayan stuff all over the walls. At the far end an enormous philodendron looked ready to eat the two jaguars that lolled half-asleep beside its pot. Slightly nearer, a golden throne encrusted with jade commanded my attention. Or maybe it was a jade throne encrusted with gold. Anyway it was a hell of an impressive piece of furniture. Too bad the guy perched upon it looked like J. Wellington Wimpy.

"Joseph." He rose slowly to his feet and took a couple

of majestic steps down to meet me. "Joseph, at last. This is the one we've heard so much about." He seized my hand in both his own and shook it up and down. "And I am merely Kukulkan the Divine Feathered Serpent, or I may be Director Houbert. I would prefer to be less the god-bureaucrat and more the artist; but one can't have everything, even here." Standing up, he had a little more dignity, because he was pretty tall for one of us, and beefy with it too. The white robe and golden sandals put you in mind of classical statuary. I wondered what possessed him to wear that feeble-looking little red mustache and skimpy beard. Oh, of course: he was supposed to be Kukulkan on Earth, the feathered serpent who was believed to appear as a white man with a red beard. Maybe the Mayans found him convincing.

"You really ought to have braved my stairs, you know. There are a whole series of theatrical effects triggered if you tread in the right places. Bursts of flame. Armored automata. Cascades of flowers. I spent decades working out the mechanisms," he told me.

"Gee, I wish I'd seen. I was helping the kid bring your bakery order up, though."

"Ah, little Latif." He smiled fondly. "Isn't he a charming child? One seldom sees them out in the field so young, but he does have extraordinary potential. Such a shame he can't stay longer! Off to the harsh new worlds beyond our ancient walls. Everyone's leaving, it seems." He sighed and shook his head.

"Are they?"

"Oh, yes. Inevitably. Our revels here are nearly ended, you know; cloud-capped palaces and gorgeous illusions will melt away quite, before the end of the next century. All this splendor abandoned to the spider and the worm." His eyes grew moist with sorrow.

"Ah, don't take it too hard. You know the Company isn't going to leave all this stuff. They'll have tech crews ripping out the gold and packing up the furniture years before we ditch the place," I said cheerfully. "You can set up your trick staircase in the next outpost. I hear Canada's got some great scenery."

"A frozen wasteland." He shuddered. "Don't even speak to me about it. How I envy you your time in California." His eyes brightened. "*Speaking* of which, I've arranged a little entertainment to make your briefing more interesting. And I'm being remiss! Naughty me. I haven't even offered you coffee. Shall I make it up to you?"

"Sure," I said, guardedly, because he had a little secret smile on his face. He looped his big arm through mine and waltzed me across the room, straight toward a bare wall. Just as it seemed we were about to smack into it, the wall swung away as silently and swiftly as if it were a curtain instead of plastered mortar. A neat effect, I had to admit. Too bad I was an immortal with an immortal's senses, because of course I'd heard the mechanisms and counterweights going off when we crossed a certain section of tiled floor; but it was almost as good without the surprise.

Beyond was his dining room. There was a long banquet table loaded with great-looking food on gold-and-jade service; coffee was steaming, orange juice was freshly squeezed, and peaked napkins were set at three places, one of which was occupied by Latif, who looked bored and impatient. The only problem was, table and chairs appeared to be suspended in midair over a pool, and there were piranhas flitting back and forth in the water.

Director Houbert stepped back to watch my reaction, his little smile spreading below his little mustache. I felt like punching the guy; I really wanted breakfast.

Now, Sam Spade or Philip Marlowe, whose adventures have kept me company on many a lonely outpost over the centuries, would have said something really snappy here to deflate the big balloon. I've never yielded to the temptation to emulate my literary pals, though; immortals can't afford to make enemies. Especially of other immortals. So I tilted my tricorne back and grinned, the picture of foolish admiration.

"Boy, what a conundrum! You designed all this yourself, didn't you?"

"Surely *you* can solve my puzzle," he crowed, his little eyes twinkling. "You who've served in such fascinating places and epochs. This should be child's play for you. I've read your file, you know. You're quite a celebrity. Come now, show some of the mental dexterity that saved you from the Pictish headhunters!"

Jeez, he *had* read my file. If there's anything more uncomfortable than meeting a fan, I don't know what it is. Maybe being eaten alive by piranhas. Latif met my eyes and started to open his mouth. "Don't you dare tell him!" cried Houbert. Latif shrugged and poured himself a cup of coffee. I could just jump across, but I'd land smack in the middle of the cups and saucers and epergnes et cetera, smasho.

"Well, let's see." I scanned the room. The fish were real, all right, and so was the water. I groped in my coat to find something to toss in, and brought out a little ball of wadded-up silver paper. It barely touched the surface before it vanished in a boiling mass of nasty little fish. Okay. No glass panel covering the pool. I scanned again and on impulse switched to infrared this time. Bingo!

No solid sheet of glass, but a kind of transparent ferro-ceramic path to the table, no more than a half meter wide and set just a fraction of a centimeter below the surface of the water. Step off a centimeter to either side and breakfast would be on me, if I were a mortal. Thanks to the highly visible temperature differential between the transparency and the water on infrared, though, I ran no risk of feeding the fish. Boldly I stepped out on the unseen path and marched across it to the table, kicking out of my way a couple of overeager piranhas who jumped at my shoes.

"Oh, well done!" Houbert applauded. "Splendid!" He came bouncing after me, and I could see Latif watching him, wondering whether he'd slip, but Houbert got safely to his chair and rang a tiny golden bell. I tensed for more theatrics: he was only summoning a trio of Mayans, who prostrated themselves on the threshold of the room. "You may serve now," he told them.

The poor bastards couldn't see the path like I could, but they must have known it was there, because they came in coolly enough and proceeded to wait on us. Great food, if deliberately weird: the eggs were pink and green and the orange juice was from blood oranges, which Houbert drank with a smirk from a golden sacrificial vessel. The Mayans whisked his napkin open for him and dished out his Franco-Mayan cuisine with reverence and patience, as befitted the Father of Heaven.

"Do you like our regional variant of *oeufs crocodiles*? These fellows can prepare anything if they're shown how once. Try the *pommes de terre Quetzalcoatl!*" Houbert leaned across to push a golden platter in my direction. I lifted my hand, but a Mayan had anticipated me and scooped a big starchy mass onto my plate.

"Swell," I affirmed. "You know, you've got quite an unusual setup here. I can't remember when I've been at a base with such, uh, flair."

"Well, of course we've had a long time to develop everything." Houbert looked pleased. "I daresay we've been the premiere research facility for a good three millennia. That's what makes it such a pity . . . But we won't speak of it, no, we absolutely mustn't. I warn you, I sob like a child when I contemplate the future."

I looked at Latif, who nodded gravely and rolled his eyes.

"Sorry to hear that."

"I was hoping—if it isn't presumptuous—you've been to such fabulous places, lived in them, worked in them, passed effortlessly as one of their denizens. How did you bear it? You saw Rome in all her splendor. Byzantium, too. How does one cope with the inevitable death of all that beauty and elegance?" Houbert looked. at me beseechingly.

"Well . . ." I bit the end off a croissant and chewed slowly, giving myself time to come up with an answer. "It wasn't all like that, you know. There was a lot of garbage and disease and starvation, too. Maybe that's it, you know, sir? You see the bad with the good long enough, and by the time a change comes, you're ready to welcome it. No more gilded carriages in the streets, but no more crippled beggars either. Sometimes it's a good idea for weeds to cover a place."

"I see your point." Houbert looked disappointed. "But in that case, there's really no analogy possible, is there? For of course we have no crippled beggars here. No ugliness, no injustice, no hunger. Only perfection. No reason for the hypothetical gods to take their revenge on us."

I nodded and stuffed the rest of the croissant in my mouth, but I thought privately that I'd seen some perfect pleasure gardens go up in flames too, and sometimes it seemed like a good idea at the time. Not that I've ever been the one with the torch, of course. That's not my job; I'm what Dr. Zeus used to call a Preserver, not an Enforcer. But, then, nowadays nobody even remembers that there ever were Enforcers, except for really old operatives like me.

"I suppose one learns not to care," mused Houbert, spreading mango jam on a helping of teosinte polenta. "After all, however many palace revolutions one flees, there's always another palace somewhere. For us, at least. The charm of the new continually soothing away regret for the old. Do you not find it so?"

"Sometimes, yes."

"And of course we immortals must above all things cultivate our sense of enchantment." Houbert spooned a massive glob into his mouth, and jam dripped into his beard. One of the Mayans deftly and immediately napkined him. "That's one of the things, the *truly* important things I've been endeavoring to impart to our little colleague here. Life is ours, eternally; whether a gift or a curse is largely up to our own efforts. Boredom is a dreadful thing to carry through the centuries. One must preserve one's sense of wonder at life. One must make it a grand continual game, full of rapture, revelry, and surprises."

He had a point there. You do have to play certain mind games to keep from going nuts. A good sex life helps, too.

"Your problem, sir, if I may speak plainly," said Latif, "is that you don't have enough real work to do."

"Child, child, how can you understand?" My god, tears were actually standing in Houbert's eyes. "There is *endless* work to do. But if you don't find a way to make it delightful, what do you face but ages upon ages of drudgery? We must retain the freshness and capacity for enjoyment of childhood—qualities that, I regret to say, you do not seem to possess in any great quantity."

Maybe watching his mother die in chains had something to do with it. Latif snorted and tossed a bit of javelina sausage to the piranhas, who made it vanish.

"And you really must learn to appreciate these things, child, or life will be the dullest eternity of bread and water you can imagine. If you *can* imagine," Houbert pleaded. "Nobody can face eternity without dreams."

Actually dreams can be a problem, but I didn't feel I should butt in at this point, because, except for the raving excess, I agreed with Houbert. It's just that not everybody has to prance around in a perpetual Disneyland to have a good time, and when you enforce whimsy with an iron hand, nobody enjoys it.

"Well, sir, I'm doing my best to understand you," Latif told him. "I'm wearing the costume. I play the games. What you don't seem to get is that I've got a *purpose* here. Purpose can be fun, too. I've had plenty of style, but I'd like some substance now, thank you. I want to learn about managing people. I want to learn about command decisions. Okay? I now know how to arrange a diplomatic banquet and brunch for a real live field agent who's actually been out in reality and done things with it. I know all about providing my subordinates with magic and mystery and fun. It's the problems I want to learn about."

"My child, my child, won't you find out about the problems soon enough?" Houbert raised his hands to heaven. The Mayans misunderstood his gesture and stepped in with hot towels, one for either hand. "But I know what it is. You're young. And who is so impatient to be perfect as a youthful operative, still in the process of sloughing off his imperfect mortal flesh? Look at you, your augmentations have barely begun, and yet you can't wait to leave your flawed humanity behind. So eager to be the perfect machine! If you'd only listen, *this* old machine could warn you that the day will come when you'll learn to savor that humanity. Playfulness, irrationality, sheer nonsense for nonsense's sake lend a dimension to life we immortals need, need desperately. How else can we endure the centuries rolling over our heads and the horrors they bring?"

"Baloney," muttered Latif.

"Well, he can't really appreciate your point, sir, because there aren't any horrors here, are there? There aren't even any problems." I took on the voice of reason. "This is a five-star vacation resort compared with some other places I've been, kid. You'll get your chance to wade in trouble up to your neck, believe me. Enjoy the hot showers and the flush toilets while you've got 'em, because for the next two hundred years or so they'll be few and far between. Take your time. God knows you've got time."

"When we stop playing, we die emotionally," sniffled Houbert, waving away Mayans.

"Oh, I don't know if I'd agree with that." I looked at Latif. "But take your fun while you can get it, that's what I always say. Your friend Suleyman, for example. Boy, the laughs we had in the souk at Fes! He had complete control of the political situation the whole time, dispatching reports and coordinating intelligence, but did he neglect to hang out by the pool in the evening with a couple of cold ones and a good book? Nope. You learn what you like, and you make sure you always have enough of it, so you can work as hard as the Company needs you to."

"He reads?" Latif asked in an offhand way. "I wonder what he likes to read."

"Poetry," I informed him. He looked shocked. "No, seriously. I mean, what would he want with adventure stories? With *his* life? And philosophy is mostly crap when you live forever. No, he likes great poetry."

"You see?" Houbert cried. "What is life without poetry?" Latif ignored him, but I could tell he was thinking about it. I looked at the Mayan waiters.

"What do you think, guys?" I inquired. It was their turn to look shocked. After a moment's hesitation, the one with the most green plumes in his headdress spoke.

"Well—we think the Son of Heaven must, in every respect, agree with the Father of Heaven."

"Oh, I do. But what do *you* think? You think all this pleasure chasing and show business and incense is a good idea?"

"Of course. You're gods. These things are fitting for You."

Boy, if the front-office mortals in the twenty-fourth century could hear this.

"You think maybe we ought to tone down our style a little? Live more like you do?"

"Why would You want to, Son of Heaven?" The Mayan looked appalled. "Look how pleasant it is here. Can You imagine any of us wanting to go back and live in the world of men? We were made to live in blood and flames and shit. We have escaped these things because we were Your chosen ones, and we would very much prefer to stay here with You. But if You were to go down to that other world and suffer as men do . . . what kind of god would do a thing like that? It's not appropriate behavior, You see."

"But a god might have work to do there," pointed out Latif. "Important work, like running things. Anyway, you don't really believe we're your old gods, do you?"

"Certainly." The Mayan looked faintly offended. "You may not resemble the gods we were led to expect, but You neither age nor die, You reside in the ancient places of our fathers, and You work miracles on a daily basis. That is quite close enough for us. Miserable wretches that we are, we take pride in knowing that we serve such splendid masters. The Father of Heaven always takes great care to behave in a suitably godly way, and I could only wish some of His children would follow His example a little more."

"Thank you, best of slaves." Houbert sighed happily and clasped his hands together on his stomach. "You see, child? *They* understand. We require pomp and circumstance. We require pageantry and ritual. There is a certain touching beauty in the way mortals instinctively grasp this about us when we ourselves deny it."

Latif's response was brief, explicit, and to the point. I looked brightly from one to the other; I hadn't enjoyed brunch like this in a long time. Houbert winced profoundly. He turned to me, pointedly ignoring his apprentice.

"Well, here's a perquisite of divinity you won't turn down, I daresay." He gestured hypnotically, and a drop-dead gorgeous Mayanette came gliding into the room, bearing a golden tray of jade vessels. I thought he was talking about the girl, but as soon as she was close enough, I caught a scent that grabbed hold of my nose and yanked me to my feet.

"Jesus, what IS that?" I yelped. It was all I could do to keep from grabbing the tray from her. She dimpled and leaned low to place it before us, giving me a spectacular view of cleavage I had absolutely no interest in at that moment. A blue mystery of aroma was coiling from the spout of an urn, a smell of every sweet deal in life, every sure thing, and every winning ticket. Latif clenched his little fists and looked away. Houbert's smile was like the sun in splendor.

"Theobromos, my friend. A little more complex than the

formula to which you are accustomed, however. This, you see, is the original recipe. This is the sacred beverage our dear Mayans reserved for the incarnation of God on Earth Himself alone. *And* for grownups." He turned and blew Latif a Bronx cheer.

"I hope your teeth rot," said Latif gamely, and poured himself another shot of java. He couldn't stop himself from adding four lumps of sugar, though, I noticed. But my attention was yanked back to the sacred vessels as Miss Mayan Universe poured me a cup of something smooth and rich and dark as any sin I'd heard confessed in three hundred years of faithful service to the Church. She held it out to me balanced on both her palms, and her smile of invitation was as tender and reverent as though I were her god, just her special god, the one she dreamed about.

Our mortal masters designed us to be pretty much resistant to intoxicants, you see; at least, the ones they knew about. Alcohol is pleasant but provides no more than a mild buzz, and the big nasties like cocaine and opium do nothing for us at all. How surprised (and horrified) they'd been to discover that *Theobroma cacao* interacts with an immortal's nervous system in a totally unique manner.

I accepted the cup from the girl and breathed in deeply. "Holy smoke" was all I could say. But the first sip unlocked my tongue and all my senses, and I won't even attempt to describe what it was like, because you'd just moan and toss on your pillow all night from unbearable envy. No kidding. You really would.

Our masters were envious enough; the stuff will be illegal anyway in the twenty-fourth century, on the grounds that it's fattening and contains refined sugar, but it never has that effect on *them*. There was talk about forbidding us its use, at the very beginning; wiser heads prevailed, though.

"Houbert, you are one swell host," I gasped. He quaffed from his exquisite jade cup and beamed upon me. How could I have thought he looked like Wimpy? Charles

Laughton in *Rembrandt,* that's it, he was a dead ringer for the guy.

"You won't find this little specialty at the commissary, I think." He raised his cup to the Mayans. "My kitchen does have its own secrets. Notice the bouquet! How many complex alkaloids, how many extracts of certain rare orchids can one perceive? You'll find the range of perception varies, but in this morning's brew I believe there are—" He took another sip and inhaled judiciously. "Let me see, I detect five distinct perfumes. Would you say? But perhaps it takes a rather longer acquaintance with the God in the Jar to become proficient in judging such matters."

How was he managing to express himself so elegantly when he'd had a snootful of this stuff? I was lost in admiration for him. Latif sipped his coffee and watched us critically. I turned to look at him and felt like crying out of sympathy. Imagine not being able to drink this yet! I wanted to tell him something to console him. Any minute now I would, too. As soon as I remembered what the other thing was I'd been going to say.

Only, how could I talk and interrupt such beautiful music? How the hell was Houbert doing that with his voice, perfectly counterpointing the Gounod in the background? What was he saying, anyway? Whatever it was, it was sheer poetry. It brought tears to my eyes. Had I thought he looked like Charles Laughton? Was I blind? Ronald Colman in *Lost Horizon,* with the voice to match. The enchantment just kept coming, too, because Latif's voice rose like a little temple flute:

"Well, I'm certainly learning important things this morning. Not one, but two millennial creatures of infinite experience and knowledge reduced to drooling idiots before my eyes. I simply can't wait until I grow up."

"You're just jealous," retorted Houbert, but I thought it was so funny, I started giggling and couldn't stop. I had become a flooded house, and about a hundred little Josephs were running around in my bloodstream frantically trying to bail me out. Damn. The buzz was wearing off. There it went. My internal chemistry revolted and dumped a few toxins to teach me a lesson. Suddenly I needed sugar.

"Where are those petits fours?" I wanted to know, and a Mayan with a cake plate was at my elbow like a devil after a soul. I took a handful of tiny, poisonously bright cakes and wolfed them down. Houbert had receded in dignity again; he was about at Peter Ustinov in *Spartacus* now. Hadn't there been a point to this feast of fools, anyway? Oh, yeah. "I was supposed to have a briefing of some kind, wasn't I?"

"Oh, that," said Houbert dismissively. "I assume the ever-so-efficient Lewis provided you with most of the mundane facts. As for the classified material . . ." He began to smile again. "I've set you another little test. Your access code strip is here, within reach. To find it, you have only to use the imagination and ingenuity that stood you in such good stead when the High Priest of Dagon tried to have you stoned!"

Chapter 7 ⚬ଠ

IT TOOK ME about two days to recover from Theobromine poisoning, but after that I had a swell vacation. I watched a lot of cinema. Played a lot of tennis. Watched serene Mayans putting up holiday decorations to which they had absolutely no cultural connection. Ate many tasty meals at the several excellent restaurants provided for my dining pleasure. Went to three holiday parties and won a door prize at one of them (bottle of aftershave). Looked up a number of old pals I hadn't seen in centuries. They hadn't changed at all (big surprise!).

Also, I accessed the code strips relating to my upcoming assignment. They gave me a lot of research material to integrate and store in my tertiary consciousness. They also gave me a duty I was not looking forward to.

I was returning my racquet to the Mayan attendant one afternoon when I was dumb enough to ask, "How do I get to the Botany Department from here?"

He looked over my shoulder and whistled. I turned to see four big Indians swerve in my direction and set down the sedan chair they had been carrying. "The Son of Heaven wishes to go to the Botany Department," he told them.

"Okay," they replied in unison, and before I could say a word in protest, they had done a neatly synchronized dip and the attendant had picked me up bodily and shot-putted me into the passenger compartment, so smoothly the other passenger wasn't even jostled. "Well, hi there." Mendoza smiled at my discomposure. "Happy Solstice Season."

"Hi." I braced myself as the chair was lifted, but it rose smooth as anything and just flew off. You couldn't have known there were straining mortal muscles or a drop of mortal sweat connected with the motion in any way.

"Don't you find this just a little embarrassing?" I asked her, struggling to get comfortable.

"I used to." Mendoza yawned elaborately. "Nowadays I just say what the hell and ride. It's easier than arguing with them, and they find it so fulfilling."

"Fulfilling?" I looked down on the nodding plumes.

"I think they enjoy debasing themselves. What else is there for them to do around here, after all? They're decadent. We're decadent. Everybody's decadent at New World One. Here, have some Theobromos." She proffered a bar with an ironical gesture.

Irony or not, I accepted. Enough time had passed since that fatal brunch for me to be able to look at the stuff again, and besides, even with the ordinary formula, New World One has the best you can get anywhere and you never, never turn it down when it's offered. Nectar and ambrosia, baby. I leaned back in the chair and felt my spirits rise.

"Yes, this is an amazing place. Kind of confining, though, isn't it?"

"Is it?" Mendoza raised an inquiring eyebrow.

"All this manicured luxury, I mean. I'll be glad to get out in the field again, personally."

"That's right, your California trip." She looked out idly at the passing scenery. "Fun with Stone Age people. Have you found out more about it?"

"I've had some briefing, yes."

"How nice for you. Why were you going over to Botany?" Such a cold black stare she had.

"Oh, just to look over one or two things connected with the job," I lied.

"Hey!" Her eyes suddenly came to life. "You can see my work."

My heart sank. "Gee, that would be interesting," I lied further. "So you've got a garden or something? I didn't think you worked with any actual green plants anymore."

"I do compilation and analysis of other operatives' field specimens, but everybody's allowed some private projects. And look, here we are at Botany! Come on." She fairly leaped from the sedan chair before the bearers had set it all the way down.

"Happy Holidays. We must remind the Daughter of Heaven to remain within the conveyance until it has stopped moving," one of the bearers informed her in aggrieved tones.

"Yeah, yeah." She waved a hand, not looking back. I followed her, thanking God she wasn't something like an entomologist.

Botany was less a pyramid and more a toppled megalith, long and low. We went through it past the labs and offices and out into the back, where a vast field was surrounded on three sides by pink stucco walls. I had figured on a greenhouse or something, which was kind of a silly expectation in the tropics. Under the open sky grew fruits and vegetables of obscene size, enough to fill the salad bars at the many excellent restaurants available for my dining pleasure and then some.

"Now, get a load of this." Mendoza hitched up her skirts and led me across the rows to a double line of green stalks. "Look at these big guys."

"You're still fooling around with maize?" She'd been doing that back in 1554.

"I could never quite give up on it. It's so beautiful, see, but the stuff is worthless as a food staple. Well, nearly. Compared to soybeans or oats or wheat. Far less nourishing. And the bigger and more golden you make it, the less food value it generally has, even when you develop high-lysine varieties. But look at this *Zea mays* and look at these primitive varieties over here, these are cultivars that were abandoned because their yield was low or they were difficult to hull, and look at the oldest one here, teosinte," she said it like a saint's name. "If you analyze its genetic structure, you know what you find?"

I was afraid she was going to tell me. She did, too, for the next forty-five minutes.

". . . so one day, one fine day when I've perfected it, this specimen's descendant will leap from the stalk, rip open his husk, and yell, 'Here I am! Supergrain! More nourishing than a speeding ear of triticale!' And it'll all be my work." She fondled the golden tassels with such intimacy, I had to look away.

"But you haven't limited yourself to maize, have you? If I remember right, you used to be a real whiz on all the New World grains and other related stuff."

"Oh, sure."

"Like for example, you'd know about the kind of grain the Native Americans in California eat."

"Well, they don't eat grain up there exactly, their main analogous staples are acorns and chia——" She broke off and swung around to look at me, terrible suspicion in her eyes. "Why, Joseph?"

"No, no, I've got good news. Trust me. You remember back when you were just out of school, when you filled out a certain form PF215?"

"Personal Goals and Preferences," she responded, and then her mouth fell open and stayed that way. "Ohhhh : . ."

"And you *said*, I mean, you know, it was you who filled this thing out, you did your best to convince the graduation board that you ought to be sent to the New World to work on its flora in remote areas, because you were this super expert on New World grains, and——"

"No! No, no, no! That was in 1554!"

"And you've been drafted for the California project, and that's how it is, babe."

If any of those giant zucchini had connected, I'd have been seriously bruised.

Chapter 8 ᔐ

AS YOU MAY have gathered, Mendoza is not the kind of woman to waste time on petty things like forgiveness. But somehow she rose above her inclinations enough to let me download the briefing material she'd need for her assignment. Maybe it was the fact that it was that festive time of year when old grudges are put aside, mistletoe is hung, the smell of gingerbread and Yule logs perfumes the air, and slaves get to whack their masters on the head with inflated pig bladders. Maybe it was the fact that she really did love her work more than anything else (or anything at all). Anyhow we saw more of each other as the century rolled through its final days, assembling our field kits and swapping bits of information that might prove useful on the job.

It was Mendoza who pointed out to me that observing our Mayans would teach me absolutely nothing about the Indians we were going to work with, just as studying Swedish farmers would teach me nothing about Turkish soldiers. Different continent, different nation, different culture, different experiences. It's a point non-Americans tend to miss, and what did I know? I'd been based in the Old World all my life. Well, most of my life. I had all those access codes to clue me in, though, and I was an expert in no time.

So, though you couldn't call our relationship cordial, we wound up going to the Grand Fin de Siècle Cotillion on New Year's Eve together.

"Wait here, guys, okay?" I hopped nimbly from the sedan chair as soon as the Mayans set it down. The lead bearer inclined graciously. I tossed him a couple of drink tokens by way of a tip and went into Botany Residential, adjusting my wig.

"Hokay, Natasha, honeybunch, your ride is here," I called cheerfully, ringing the buzzer.

"You're early," Mendoza told me, opening the door long enough for me to step inside. She turned and went back to packing a garment bag with what looked like fifty pounds of white silk petticoat. She herself was all dolled up in ballroom best, absolutely the latest Paris fashion rendered in tropical-weight cream shantung, though she hadn't yet put on the elaborately heeled shoes (higher than mine) of Italian calfskin. They were lined up neatly by the side of the bed, next to her field kit and duffel.

"I'm always early. Catches people off guard," I replied, looking around. The place was emptier than a hotel room, though she'd been living in it for over a century. She'd packed up, but the staff hadn't yet been in to vacuum, so there were dust rectangles on the console where her field notebooks had been and two dust outlines on the wall where pictures had hung. From a hook dangled a single strand of spangly holiday decoration. It had broken when she pulled it down and was too high up the wall to bother with. "Boy, I hate moving during the holidays," I said sympathetically. She shrugged and zipped the bag shut, subduing all those waves of silk.

"I passed the Grand Ballroom on the way over here," I continued. "Brother! What an engineering stunt *that* is."

"Isn't it?" She sat on the edge of the bed and fished around for her shoes. "Whole thing goes up like a hallucination in twenty-four hours. You haven't even seen the inside yet. That's his big specialty; Houbert earned his first credits designing portable field shelters like palaces. He's a genius, under all the aesthete crap."

"I guess so!"

"Not that I'll miss him." She pushed her feet into her shoes and stood up, looming over me. "Let's get out of here. Revelry and merriment await us."

Chapter 9 ❧

WHETHER THEY DID or not, I was sure impressed by the Grand Ballroom. It looked real, and permanent, until you got close enough through the traffic jam of sedan chairs and saw that the whole massive thing was just a white tent—though on a scale that made Barnum and Bailey's biggest effort look like a field bivvy. Carved cantilevers ten stories high circled around the outside, gleaming with gold leaf, and scarlet pennants fluttered from the dome, and the whole business glowed with interior lighting like a fairy castle.

"Wow" was all I could say. Mendoza clambered out of the chair ahead of me, unimpressed.

"Come on. I want a drink."

We joined the milling throng and flowed inside with everybody else, where I had the shock of discovering that this was a two-level tent. On the ground floor were a bar, hatcheck booth, retiring area, and kitchens, all gorgeously appointed in a central chamber. Around the perimeter ran a couple of long sloping ramps leading up to the second floor, curtained in swags of sea-green satin. Gaping, I followed Mendoza as she beelined for the bar, and soon we were on our way up the ramp with a margarita each and so many other immortals, you couldn't hear yourself think for all the subvocal chatter.

I thought that what I'd seen so far had been pretty neat,

until I got upstairs. The ballroom itself was floored with a vast and gleaming expanse of polished teak—over cork, to judge from the pleasant bounciness of our steps. The ceiling was held up with gilded palm trees and winked here and there with tiny electric stars. From the center a mirrored ball hung, revolving above rose-pink lights, throwing spots of light that swam slowly like fish around the walls. There was a bandstand full of white-jacketed musicians tuning up; a placard of gold script on a blood-red background announced that they were KING PAKAL & HIS PARTY BOYS D' POPUL VUH.

A few immortals drifted on the dance floor; others were sitting at a bank of tables on a kind of mezzanine, near the buffet table. I made for the food first, like the old field operative I am. Mendoza teetered along after me, sipping from her margarita.

And was that a spread! Great hors d'oeuvres and other little crunchy things. Nothing as substantial as cold cuts or dinner rolls, but what it lacked in solid food, it made up for in imaginative presentation. I remember a big pyramid of chicken salad paprikaed all over to look like our red stucco central residential complex. I remember Mayan hieroglyphs sculpted in liverwurst. I remember a scowling Mayan warrior profile bas-relieved in tomato aspic, with a bulging hard-boiled egg for its glaring eye. Green vegetable pâté had been piped in for the head's trailing quetzal plumes.

But the desserts! Let's skip the obvious stuff like the pineapple gondolas and the *gateaux pyramides*. Let's skip the little dishes of salted nuts and chalky mints. There was Theobromos in abundance like I've never seen in my long life: layered into cakes, whipped into creamy mousses, waxily coating fresh strawberries and candied fruits. There was Theobromos cream pie three inches deep, Theobromos cheesecake decorated with Theobromos bonbons, Theobromos roses on sugar stems, bombe Theobromos filled with frozen Theobromos ganache, Theobromos tartufos rolled in chopped Brazil nuts, and a whole lot of lively and obscene little figures made of plain, solid, highest-grade Theobromos. *And* champagne. Boy oh boy, what would our mortal masters say if they could see all this?

Over the buffet was strung a bannered message in gold script: WE ARE THE BRIGHT ASCENDING BUBBLES IN THE BLACK WINE OF MORTALITY. What the hell that was supposed to mean I couldn't guess, but it looked poetic. Mendoza and I loaded our plates with a little of everything and elbowed along the terrace to a vacant table.

"This looks like a good place." Mendoza dumped her plate down and collapsed into a folding chair. "Nice view, breeze from the windows, close to a door for quick exit after the New Year strikes. I've gone as far as I'm going in these heels tonight, thank you."

"You said it, kiddo." I dove into my Theobromos zabaglione fantasia, and conversation sort of languished for a few minutes. With each passing moment, though, the ballroom grew more beautiful and the wan crowd of immortals livelier. King Pakal and his buddies struck up a medley of Cab Calloway hits, and a few Old Ones actually got out on the floor and boogie-woogied in their silk pants and hoop skirts.

"Say, Joseph, is that you?" Lewis wandered up with a massively loaded dessert plate and a dry martini. "And Mendoza! Good to see you again. Would you two mind terribly if I took this chair? My lady friend threw tact to the winds and locked herself in her room with a good book, so I'm going to spend my evening carping from the mezzanine and overdosing on neurostimulants."

"Sure." Mendoza speared a bonbon on her dessert fork and waved assent. "How the hell are you, anyway?"

"Just peachy-keen, thanks." He set his plate down and took a seat. Wriggling forward to the edge of it, he placed his fingertips on his knees. "And I've had the most splendid news. You'll never guess."

"What?"

"I'm being transferred!"

"No kidding? Where to?"

"England. The jolly old UK." He lifted a forkful of Theobromos torte and bit into it decisively. "Well, with a brief layover in Jamaica to build a cover identity. Oh, my, this has orange liqueur drizzled through it! Try some. In any case, I'm off next month. Hurrah!"

"England, huh?" Mendoza laid her fork down and frowned. "Well, you watch out, dear. It's a crazy place. Cold and wet, and dirty, too. I was miserable there."

She hadn't been miserable all of the time, as I remembered, but even under the cheery influence of the Theobromos I knew better than to say this. I just scraped my parfait glass clean and dug into the Theobromos pudding.

"Well, you were there in, what, the fifteens? This is a whole new era. London may be nasty, but there'll be coffeehouses and exciting literary parties. And, you know, I'm actually rather looking forward to getting my hands dirty in the field again." He raised his martini in a gesture of salute. I thought he looked as though he'd break in half if the dirt fought back with any determination, but then he was stronger than he appeared. We all are. Mendoza just shook her head.

"You take care, all the same. They're not a civilized people, no matter what they think of themselves."

"Oh, I know. I've some wild and woolly times to get through before Victoria toddles onstage. I'll be working out of the London safe house, though, so I shouldn't think there'll be too much cause for concern. Do you know London at all?"

"No." Mendoza sipped from her drink. "I was stuck down in Kent the whole time." I wondered why she was able to discuss England with everybody except me.

"Pity. Well, that's what access codes are for, though I always find personal recommendations helpful too. And! Even though my primary assignment will be coordinating arrivals and departures, somebody up there's finally remembered my literary training. I'm to collect rare volumes as they come off the presses and ship them off to 'specified locales.' What fun! Perhaps I'll run some cozy little anti-quarian bookshop in the West End. Assuming there is a West End yet. I suppose there must be." He carefully removed the nuts from a slice of Theobromos log before attacking it with his fork.

"You'll have a swell time," I assured him. King Pakal led a particularly raucous sign-off to the "St. James Infirmary Blues" and started in on some twenty-third-century neobaroque fusion stuff. I turned to stare at the ballroom, which glittered with movement as more and more people braved the dance floor. "Boy, look at the turnout. Is it like this every year?"

"Not so elaborate," Mendoza admitted.

"No indeed." Lewis waved his fork. "Look at all the slogans." I followed his gesture and realized that there were banners everywhere like the one above the buffet, with drooping gold script announcing such heartening sentiments as TEMPUS FUGIT, CARPE DIEM, WE ARE THE TICKING CLOCK MEASURING THE SOUL'S DARK MIDNIGHT, WE ARE DIANA'S FORESTERS, ALL GOOD THINGS MUST END, and TOMORROW AND TOMORROW AND TOMORROW.

"Nothing like wallowing in it." Mendoza shuddered.

"Well, it *is* the beginning of the end for this place," Lewis pointed out. "The Age of Exploration marches on, nipping at Houbert's heels. How he must dread the thought of all those earnest fellows in pith helmets searching for Lost Atlantis here. I must say I've been bored silly at old New World One, but I'll be sorry to think of the monkeys finally getting in."

"The human ones or the ones with tails?" Mendoza showed too many teeth in her smile. We all shared a brittle laugh and clinked our glasses, toasting nothing much.

The orchestra abruptly left off the fusion and struck up Mozart's "Chorus of the Janissaries" from *The Abduction from the Seraglio*.

"Whoops." Lewis and Mendoza got to their feet, as did everybody else who had been sitting down, so I stood too. All the Mayan waiters prostrated themselves. Base Administrator Houbert was borne in through the main entrance in a gilded sedan chair. He had on a getup of gold tissue and purple plumes, and wore a crown of violets. Big golden tears had been painted down his cheeks. I guess this was to signify that he was in mourning for the end of an era.

Lewis pressed his lips together, but Mendoza didn't even bother to conceal her giggles, until it became obvious that the chair bearers were taking Houbert on a grand circuit of the dance floor, past all the diners on the terrace. As he processed along, he dipped into a bag from time to time and tossed little round black pellets to the crowd. Black olives? Goat droppings? No, they were hitting with a sharp crack that made diners flinch and avoid them. The sound suggested a hard coating.

"Oh, God, they're *black* jelly beans this year," Mendoza muttered.

"Of course. The siècle is fin, after all," replied Lewis out of the side of his mouth. As the palanquin neared us, we gentlemen doffed our hats and bowed, which Houbert acknowledged with a graceful wave and a shotgun scatter of candy. I jumped up to catch one before it broke my margarita glass and popped it in my mouth. I was expecting licorice, but that would have been too pedestrian for Houbert; these jelly beans were flavored with Black Elysium liqueur. It figured.

I had drawn attention to myself with my leap, though, and Houbert's little eyes settled on me. There was a split second of recognition, then an icy stare, before he turned his face deliberately away. The sedan chair bounced on past our table.

"Well, that was as pointed a snub as I've seen in the last three hundred years," observed Lewis. Suddenly his face lit up. "Great Caesar's ghost, that story is true! You did electrocute his pet piranhas!"

"What!" Mendoza stared at me.

"They say he stepped into the damned breakfast-room pool and fried those fish with some direct current when they attacked him. Oh, well done!" Lewis applauded me.

"It was an accident," I muttered in embarrassment. "It was part of this dumb game he had me playing to find my access codes. I was coming down off a Theobromine high at the time, and I slipped."

"Ah. Plied you with Hell's Own Swiss Miss compound, did he? Serves the beggar right." Lewis resumed his seat and dug into a Theobromos napoleon with gusto. Mendoza collapsed into her chair, weeping with laughter.

"You of all people losing your stirrups. And I missed it? I'm desolated! I'd cut my own throat, if that would kill me! How, oh how did this happen?"

"Did you ever have the special stuff he serves his guests?" I said defensively.

"Oh, no." Lewis dabbed at his mouth with a napkin. "We've never been considered artistic or creative enough to appreciate it. We're mere bureaucratic cogs in the big chronometer of life, unlike you, apparently. No, old chap, you sampled a pleasure reserved for the elite few." He began to chuckle afresh. "That'll teach him!"

By this time Houbert had made a full circuit of the ballroom, and his bearers took him across to where a golden throne was just descending from the ceiling, its arrival on a raised dais timed to coincide with the end of the music. He dismounted from the palanquin and turned to face us all (except for me). A single pink spotlight hit him.

MY DEAREST CHILDREN! he boomed. We all winced, and he hastily adjusted his decibels. *Weep with me! Weep, oh weep! All weep!*

Nobody was weeping, and the Mayan waiters gave us some dirty looks. Finally there were some howls and boohoos of lament from the tables closest the dais. Houbert raised his big hands in seeming ecstasy, as though he were conducting an orchestra playing something slow and sublime. *That's it! Allow it to well up in your hearts! FEEL the sorrow of eternal life, the endless tragedy of the endless mortality in which we can never share! Let the tide of tears for all that you have known, and all that you can never know, wash into your hearts!*

"Have you heard about the latest nanotechnology they're allowing us in the field?" Lewis inquired of Mendoza. "There was a nice article in *Immortal Lifestyles Monthly*."

"No, I haven't seen this month's issue," replied Mendoza, draining her margarita.

For another day of reckoning dawns on the all-too-near horizon, my children! Once again the evil genius Time draws near with his hourglass and scythe, bringing destruction once again to a garden of paradise! Once again we poor deathless ones will wander homeless upon the face of the earth, as ruin devours what we once held dear! Houbert held out one palm and shimmied it slowly downward. He may have meant the gesture to be expressive, but it made him look as though he were shaking a tambourine.

"Well, it seems that someone's come up with a surveillance device of perfectly astonishing tininess, and here's the best part: it's packaged in miniature robots that look *exactly* like head lice." Lewis widened his eyes for emphasis.

"No kidding?"

Will no merciful God look down to stop the pitiless and eternally unfolding pageant of the years? Who among you but has fled weeping as barbarians despoiled Troy, or as fire and brimstone rained down upon Nineveh and Tyre? Who among you but has learned the bitter lesson that All Good Things Must Come to an End?

"As God is my witness. Even under a microscope, you can't tell, unless you know where to look for the manufacturer's mark. Plant one on a mortal subject, and you can hear every word that's uttered in a thirty-foot radius around him."

"The anthropologists ought to love that."

LAMENTATION is my theme this evening. Houbert threw up his beefy arms. *For this sweet utopia that will lie in ruins one century hence, and for us, poor creatures that we are, denied the blessed solace of eternal sleep, of kindly dust and gentle oblivion, of sharing the fate of those who have gone forever into that good night!*

"But! There's more. The article says that these are only the prototypes, and we can expect a whole new line of multipurpose lice. Tiny traveling cameras, for example. Lice that function as miniature hypodermics—" Lewis jabbed eloquently with his dessert fork. "One 'bite,' and your mortal subject is knocked out for hours, or inoculated with a vaccine."

"And the timing's so right, too. Just as the powdered wig is becoming *the* fashion statement," said Mendoza in admiration.

CHERISH the divine emotions that make you what you are, my children: the unnatural survivors of fragile humanity, from them but never again of them, watching eternally as human creativity is destroyed and yet eternally renewed, so that even as we unnaturals MOURN, we must unnaturally CELEBRATE!

"That's just what I thought, myself. Dare we take it further? Why not receivers as well as transmitters? Lice that pick up Company broadcasts of popular entertainment. Lice that store and deliver coded information. Think of the possibilities!"

"You know, I think I did see this article. Wasn't this in the issue with Alec Guinness on the cover?"

DO NOT shrug, as some will, and declare that weeds and death SHOULD conquer because the gilded and graceful SHARE the streets with poverty and disease. A glare in my direction left no doubt about Houbert's opinion of me.

"Yes, as a matter of fact, with an article on his postwar comedies."

"That's the one. I haven't read it yet. It's packed in my carry-on so I'll have something to read on the transport."

'Consider us here on this last night of a century, the deathless, the eternally beautiful, in all our comfort and felicity. Yet even WE shall scatter like leaves before the wind, and who can know when we shall meet again? This gorgeous pavilion will vanish with the dews of morning; yet our more PERMANENT halls shall prove no less insubstantial! Houbert buried his face in his hands, smearing his golden paint.

"Well, don't miss the 'Coming Attractions' section. Personally, I'm thrilled by the potential uses. I can just see myself sitting in some London salon with my lice-ridden peruke, eavesdropping on Doctor Johnson!" Lewis rubbed his hands together.

"How colorful." Mendoza moved her elbow as a Mayan waiter put down a silver ice bucket containing a champagne bottle. "What's this? We didn't order champagne."

"The Father of Heaven (who is, by the way, giving a beautiful speech to which everyone ought to be paying attention) gave orders that this beverage be served to all His immortal children," replied the Mayan primly. "Whether They deserve it or not."

"Oh yeah?" Mendoza glared back at him. "Well, you can go jump in the nearest fountain, pal."

Houbert continued: *Now, you will ask, my children: What are we to do? How are we to live, knowing that ALL beauty is ephemeral? And I shall tell you to dance! DANCE, and express the sorrow in your perfect and unfailing hearts! RENEW in your beautiful dance the pattern of the cosmos itself! Dance, my children, even as you hear the bell tolling, and know it shall NEVER toll for thee!!* And the spotlight went out, causing him to vanish.

"Certainly," said the waiter, drawing himself up in injured dignity just as the tolling of a very large, very loud bell reverberated through the place. "I'll obey the Daughter of Heaven immediately. I'll go right out to the nearest fountain, even in these clothes which require pressing and starching, and I'll just leap in." He turned to push his way through the crowd on the mezzanine, which had become pretty dense by this time, so I was able to grab his arm.

"What are you, nuts?" I demanded, and Lewis joined in: "Now, now, let's not lose our tempers."

"Look, you stupid bloody Indian—" Mendoza yelled in exasperation as a frenzied waltz began to play.

"Mendoza—"

"Why, of course this slave is stupid. But not so stupid that he has forgotten he's under oath to obey any order whatsoever given him by a Child of Heaven, no matter how unpleasant or irrational. But stupid most assuredly. The Daughter of Heaven has said so." The waiter jutted his ferocious nose in the air.

"Aw, come on, you don't have to go jump in any fountains," I told him.

"No, with all respect, Son of Heaven, I must obey."

"Not if both he and I countermand her order," Lewis proposed. "That would satisfy your oath, wouldn't it? Two Children of Heaven surely overrule one. We both order you *not* to go jump in the nearest fountain. Don't we, Joseph?"

"Yeah, we do, and not only that"—I looked sternly at Mendoza—"the Daughter of Heaven is going to reverse her order too. Aren't you, Mendoza?"

She got an evil gleam in her eyes.

"And she's not going to order you to do something painful and difficult with the champagne bottle, either!" I yelled.

"The Daughter of Heaven reverses her previous order," Mendoza enunciated clearly. I released the waiter's arm. He shook out his bar towel with a crisp snap, refolded it, and draped it over his wrist.

"Thank You. If You have no further orders, this slave is going to continue serving wine to other Children of Heaven, who have *also* disregarded the Father of Heaven's request to dance." And he moved away, back as stiff as a ramrod.

"Goodness, that was awkward," observed Lewis. "But

cheer up; soon enough we won't have passive-aggressive members of a vanished empire to order about anymore."

"Three cheers." Mendoza leaned back wearily. "And I'm not getting up to dance, even if a whole priesthood of Mayans disapproves of me."

"Good evening, all," said a voice, seemingly from under the table. A moment later our fourth chair was pushed back, and a little figure clambered up into it.

Lewis nodded. "Good evening, Latif. I assume you have permission to stay up this late?"

"Naturally." Latif settled back into his chair. The candy-box costume was gone; he wore now the school uniform for the neophyte class, with pleats pressed razor-sharp. "Any of you opening that champagne, by the way?"

"Oh, why not?" Lewis peered into his empty martini glass. He pulled out the drippy bottle and prized up the foil and wire with fastidious care. When the cork finally blew, he poured fresh drinks all around, and we sat for a while watching our fellow immortals dance.

Something I've noticed over the years: we don't dance well, on the whole. None of us are clumsy on the floor, or anything like that; just the opposite. We're too . . . smooth. Too perfect. Well, you can't avoid saying it, we look mechanical. Like big sharks gliding around and around. Never a missed step or beat. Mortals move with a difference, with an awkward something that makes their motion beautiful. Maybe it's passion. I don't know. I only knew one immortal who danced well, and she won't anymore. But maybe it's just the heels she wears nowadays.

As the level in the champagne bottle grew lower, Lewis began to look green.

"Oh, dear," he said faintly. "I don't think I ought to have eaten that last helping of Theobromos mousse."

"You were drinking martinis before the champagne, weren't you?" Latif pointed out in his bright little voice. "Theobromine and gin don't combine well, you know. Try metabolizing sucrose."

"I haven't taken in enough starches. Oh dear."

"Here." Mendoza pushed back her chair, and Lewis sort of toppled over into her lap, where she fed him sugar cubes from the little dish on the table. He lay there pale and wan. I ordered more champagne, which I shared with Latif. Mendoza just watched the whirling dancers as she stroked Lewis's limp hair, her face sad and cold.

Hmmm. I looked at them out of the corner of my eye. Had they had a relationship or something, at one time? Lewis was hardly her type. On the other hand, he seemed funny and kind. I found myself hoping she'd made at least one friend during all these years and realized I was in for a lot of trouble on this next job if I let myself worry about the state of Mendoza's heart. I looked away.

"You're a lot more presentable in the uniform," I told Latif. "How'd you get Houbert to let you out of the Hindu prince suit?"

"Nothing he can do." How could a baby grin wolfishly? "A communication came through this morning. It seems my timetable's been moved up. I'm to be posted to Labienus ahead of schedule. I leave day after tomorrow. Tell me, sir, have you ever been to Canada? Should one pack a heavyweight wardrobe?"

"Thermal underwear and flannel everything," I advised. "And plenty of blankets and waterproof shoes. They won't want you freezing if they're in such a hurry to get you up there," I told him. I wouldn't have put it past him to have intercepted and altered a couple of transmissions to facilitate things, and I wouldn't have blamed him either. What a cool little customer Latif was. Just like I'd been, once. What would he be like in twenty years?

"Well, we'll just see, won't we?" he remarked cheerily, and stood in his chair to pour us both more champagne.

Lewis felt better after a while and lurched upright, just in time to hear *La Valse* by Ravel pulse into its opening chords.

"I wondered when they'd play that," he groaned. "That's

Houbert's favorite piece of music, you know. After *The Phantom of the Opera.*" The lights in the ballroom deepened to an ominous and weird purple.

"Well, it's appropriate for tonight, anyhow," said Mendoza. "The way it evokes glittering empires about to crumble. Music full of death. God, that's spooky. Look at everybody!"

I peered out on the dance floor, and I swear I felt the hairs on the back of my neck stand. Houbert had worked some trick of lighting, some perversely brilliant special effect, that gave the illusion of death masks on each perfect clockwork dancer who skimmed the ballroom floor in time to that terrible, beautiful music. Swooping and circling, they moved, so many skeletons in satin clothes.

No, wait. They weren't *human* skeletons. Something was picking up the alloy frame in each of them, the machine that had replaced their mortal, breakable bones, the indestructible casing that held their brains and eyes. Was it some quality in the purple light that caused them to glow through the flesh?

No, not the light—or at least not the light alone. The champagne we'd all been given! He'd had it adulterated with something, some chemical harmless in itself, or we'd have detected it in the first taste. That was what was making our hardware glow.

Slowly I looked down at my own hands. Fine jointed mechanisms riveted to a pivoting frame that disappeared into my lace cuffs. I tried to look at Lewis and Mendoza without turning my head much. They were staring out at the dancers with haunted eyes; they hadn't noticed that they too were part of the show, a dapper gentleman skeleton machine and a lissome skull-faced lady machine. And Latif? Well, he wasn't glowing much, because less of him had been replaced, you see. Just a little machine, yet.

And as the music soared to its crashing close, a deafening chime was heard—two, three, four. The chimes kept coming, and the clock was striking midnight. Happy Hellish

New Year, 1700! Things like snakes began to fall from the ceiling, and of course they were only black streamers. Our Mayan waiters began to blow paper horns and crank noise-makers. The waltz ended, and the lights came up. "Auld Lang Syne" was playing, the classic soupy Guy Lombardo arrangement.

Lewis looked gray and tired. Mendoza was pale, shaking. I thought she must have noticed the ugly illusion at our own table—well, not illusion, after all—but she drew a deep breath and said very quietly:

"Oh, how I hate parties. Here we sit tonight, and do you realize how unlikely it is any of us four will ever be together in the same room again?"

Was it loneliness she was afraid of? I reached out my hand to clasp hers.

"Hey, kiddo, you'll see *me* again. We're going on the same assignment together, remember?"

She bared her teeth at me.

Chapter 10 ⚘

Bᴜᴛ ᴡᴇ ꜰᴏᴜɴᴅ ourselves on the same transport the next morning, strapped into our seats and watching New World One drop away beneath us.

"It was time for you to move on anyway," I told Mendoza consolingly. "It was stuffy. Decadent. Dull. Nothing should be decadent *and* dull."

"Your father was a Moorish groom and your mother performed circumcisions on sailors," she informed me.

"Hey, that's okay. I know you're not really sore. You're going to love it in California."

"I won't be able to get a cocktail there for at least a hundred years," she brooded. "And longer, for a Ghirardelli's hot fudge sundae."

"Well, you hated parties anyway."

She just snarled and opened her magazine, shutting me out. I didn't mind; do I ever mind? I'm only the guy who gave her eternal life, after all. I settled back in my seat and closed my eyes. Forty winks after last night's party seemed like a good idea.

I thought about Latif, the self-assured little administrator-in-training, all his buttons polished, intent on asking the right questions and making the right moves. Funny that he so worshiped my buddy Suleyman, who was anything but a bureaucrat. Still, when you're tiny and mortal and frightened, and this big god comes looming out of the darkness to offer you a hand—well, it makes an impression. I thought about what it must have been like, in the stinking hold of a slave ship, with all the comfort and safety you'd ever known lying beside you bewilderingly dead . . . and just as the loss got through to you, and the scream began to rise in your throat because you knew you were *alone,* just then the big man appeared and called your name.

I don't know how he knew my name. I don't even remember what my name was. But he was there, looming against the darkness, a god in a bearskin, and his axe and his hands were red. Lying around his feet were the bad guys, all smashed, the tattooed devils who'd caught my family away from the rock shelter. He didn't smell or look anything like anybody else I'd ever seen. He looked like a mountain and his brow was a cliff, with his pale eyes staring out from its shadow. He saw me where I was hiding. He put out his red hand and called my name, in his flat high voice. I went to him. He took me out of the painted cave and past the fires where his army was burning the bodies of the tattooed men. He explained that the tattooed men had to die because they were bad and made war. I was glad they were dead and burning, because it meant that I wasn't going to die.

He told me I would never die. He took me to the other place, where there were clean quiet people who didn't smell. They fed me, washed me, and put me to bed where it was safe. Later they made me immortal.

But I could never seem to get completely out of that darkness that was scary and smelled so bad. Then I was in the prison and staring through the doorway at the little girl who sat huddled in the straw, such a thin, sick little girl, her arms and legs like white sticks. All the life she had left was burning in her eyes, furious black eyes. I loomed against the light and put out my hand to her. She told me

to go to hell. I knew then she had to be immortal; you need
a tough will to work for Dr. Zeus.

"Hey." Mendoza shoved me. Light all around us, clouds
drifting past the window. "Wake up. We're over Alta California."

Chapter 11 ❧

CALIFORNIA.

Named after a queen, supposedly, and you could see why. She's the schizoid goddess Fortune herself: sometimes a smiling benefactress who gives mortals all they could hope for in life, sometimes a snarling bitch driving her children from her with a whip and a flail. The trick is, see, you have to know what you really want from her when you go there.

First we saw a pretty coastline: mountains that rolled back from the coastal bluffs, scored with deep valleys. Everything was green, but it was winter, you have to remember.

We saw a place where the land stuck out like a snail's head just emerging from its shell. That was Point Conception, our destination. No trees here: bare scrubby headland, and even from the transport you could see the bushes tilting sideways in the sea breeze. We felt the wind buffeting us as we sank toward the landing platform.

When we stepped out, wow. An ice-cold gale that made my eyes water. I noticed that all the field personnel lined up to greet us wore sunglasses, the wraparound kind like goggles. I hoped I'd be issued a pair. The winter sunlight was sharp as diamonds.

"Where are the palm trees?" said Mendoza through gritted teeth. "Where are the swimming pools?" There was the sea and a lot of bare rolling hills, and that was about it. We slogged across the platform, the wind whipping at the train of Mendoza's gown, and presented ourselves to the foremost of the goggled welcomers.

"Hi." I thrust out a hand. "Facilitator Grade One Joseph reporting to AltaCal Base."

"Good." The welcomer smiled, took and dropped my hand. "And Botanist Grade Six Mendoza?"

"Reporting."

"Good. This way." We followed him to our shuttle, which was a rickety car set to run on a wooden track held above the earth on cement piers. It looked like a roller coaster. It drove like one, too.

The wind would have torn our voices away if we'd tried to speak out loud, but the man made no subvocal communication attempts either. Nothing like *So this is your first time in California?* or *Wait'll you folks taste the abalone chowder we fix around here.* He might as well have been a mortal. Mendoza just stared off inland; God knows what she was thinking. I watched the blue Pacific glitter in the sun. It certainly was blue, I gave it that.

We rattled away north to a beach at the mouth of a canyon. The main base was here, a plain modular station backed up on its piers into the cliff at the south side of the cove; the kind of place that could be removed later and a judiciously engineered rock slide or two would hide any evidence it had ever been there. It was painted for camouflage, but otherwise featureless. Like the personnel. Everyone I saw was wearing Company base issue, which is blank utility clothing with a lot of pockets and no style. Houbert would have been appalled. Men and women alike wore the same one-piece garment. No lace, no padding, no embroidery. I'd worn it myself once or twice, back in prehistory, but I could see Mendoza staring at it aghast.

Or maybe she was looking aghast at the mortals, of which there were a surprising number among the base personnel. Not natives that had been fixed for maintenance labor like the Mayans, either, but actual officers. Kids from the future. It must have cost the Company a fortune to ship them all here.

Aren't those—she subbed at me, and I replied, *That's right.*

Our little thrill ride took us right up under the base, where at last the roar of the wind was shut out. Our driver popped the door open for us, and I ventured, "Lotta youngsters here, aren't there?"

"Yep."

"Real windy place, too."

"Sure is."

"I was expecting something a little more temperate."

"Yeah?"

"Say, you don't talk much, do you?"

"I'm busy." The guy half-turned. "Mr. Bugleg asked that you report to his office immediately upon arrival. Go up those stairs, and the admitting desk will direct you."

I figured it out at last. He was an immortal like we were, all right, but a recent recruit: probably born in the twenty-third century. So that's what they looked like in the future? Was *he* ever caught between two worlds.

We clambered up the steps with our luggage, and Mendoza growled, "Always the same damn story. I've never in my life seen an escalator in one of these places." She grabbed up her train with one hand and hoisted her suitcase in the other. I pushed my tricorne to the back of my head and followed.

At the top of the stairs we were met by a smiling mortal woman with a clipboard. She might have been good-looking in a silk mantle, with maybe a little lace apron. She wore the sexless coveralls, though, like everybody else we'd met so far.

"Um, welcome to AltaCal Base Eight. You must be Facilitator Joseph, and you must be Botanist Mendoza, am I right? Hello and welcome—"

"Yeah. Hi," replied Mendoza. "Look, that driver told us we've got to report directly to a meeting. Was he kidding?

Don't we get to see our quarters first, wash up a little? That's pretty inconsiderate, don't you think?"

"Oh, Mr. Bugleg wants to see you right away. It's very important." Rapidly the girl clipped little ID tags to us and our luggage. Her own tag read STACEY. I guessed she'd seen a few of us in her brief lifetime, but not enough to be cool about it. She was radiating discomfort. A little fear, a little more repugnance. I could smell it, and so, unfortunately, could Mendoza. "You can leave your bags here, and we'll deliver them to your rooms. Mr. Bugleg wants to discuss your mission over dinner."

"Great. Thank you very much. Where is the man?" I inquired, hurriedly because I could feel a confrontation building.

"Go through that door at the end of the hall," said the mortal girl, just before Mendoza said, "Did you know you've got an impacted wisdom tooth, Stacey? I'd have it checked out if I were you."

Stacey's hand flew to the corner of her jaw, and my hand flew to Mendoza's arm and I pulled her away with me down the hall.

"Mendoza, that was not nice. Scanning them without permission is impolite."

"I don't give a rat's ass! Did you smell the way she felt about us? If she's got a problem dealing with immortals, why's she with the Company? Nobody told me there'd be mortals crawling all over this place."

"Are you going to do this to me again? Don't do this to me again, Mendoza."

"What'd she think we were, for crying out loud? *Androids*?"

"You've never worked with any Company mortals, have you?" I paused, scanning the long featureless hall in confusion. What was that pinging noise?

"Sure I have." Mendoza turned her head irritably, picking up the sound too.

"I don't mean native busboys. I mean officers and shareholders of Dr. Zeus, from the future. We make them uncomfortable." I paused outside a door and scanned the room beyond. There was a mortal inside, interfacing with an entertainment console. That was it. Somebody was playing a holo game.

"But why? They made us, didn't they? We do exactly what they built us to do, don't we?"

"I know. I'm not sure what the reason is. Maybe some of them feel we're not much more than superpowered slaves and they feel guilty about that?"

She took that in for a minute, as we walked on down the hall.

"Well, that's just ducky," she hissed, and I knocked on Mr. Bugleg's door before she could tell me just how ducky it was.

We were let in by a mortal kid, I guess he was a junior clerk or something, and there was Mr. Bugleg standing at the other end of a table set for four. He'd put the table between us and himself, but otherwise you couldn't have told he was a bigot at all. Nice plastic smile like the girl Stacey. He was mortal too, of course. The food looked lousy. *Oh, boy, this is going to be some tour of duty,* broadcast Mendoza. *Shut up,* I broadcast back. She looked around the room, which was otherwise bare of ornament or furniture save for a plain day bed and a wall console with an enormous private entertainment center. Quite a change from New World One. Bugleg cleared his throat.

"Mendoza. Joseph. How are you? I'm Bugleg. Have a seat." His smile faltered off. He looked like a scared toddler at a birthday party. He was a thirtyish mortal, not quite beginning to sag yet, fairly pasty-faced, and his head was a funny shape. (But, then, all their heads look funny to me.) He wore the same drab clothing as his staff: no medals, epaulets, or gold braid.

"I'll ring for my aide now," he told us, and he did, and after an uncomfortable moment of silence a door opened and another man walked in. This one was an immortal and decently dressed, too, with a good wig and a spiffy brocaded coat. He had a black silk steinkirk knotted casually about his throat. To judge from the heels on his shoes, he wasn't any taller than me, but he strode up to us with authority. The man had style.

His eyes were gray and cold, and his grip was a little too firm as he shook our hands.

"This is Mr. Lopez, my aide," ventured Bugleg.

"Joseph. Mendoza. It's a pleasure meeting you. I'll be briefing you on the mission as we"—he paused significantly—"dine."

He pulled out Mendoza's chair for her. Bugleg sat down and watched in horrified fascination as Mendoza seated herself, settling her acreage of rustling silks less inconveniently.

"Why did you wear all those clothes here?" he asked. "You should put on clothes like we wear. You'd be more comfortable."

Mendoza was too surprised to say anything, for which I was grateful.

"You must remember, sir, that we field operatives spend our whole lives in the past," Lopez explained smoothly. "I've told you about this before. For us, the past *is* real time. We wear these clothes because they're what's being made this year, which happens to be 1700 A.D., by the way. Mortals would notice us if we dressed differently. Besides, if we wanted to wear clothes like yours, they'd have to be specially imported from the future, which would be expensive. It's much cheaper simply to wear what everybody else is wearing in this time period. In fact, we're quite used to these fashions. It may be hard for you to believe, but she's just as comfortable in her clothing as you are in yours."

"Oh," said Bugleg.

The food was just as lousy on closer inspection as it had seemed at first glance. At each place was a shaped tray with compartments containing various pureed or textured substances, brightly colored. We all made courteously exclamatory noises over it, though I noticed Lopez's elbow twitch as he stopped himself from reaching for a claret decanter that wasn't there. I lifted my plastic sipper bottle to see what our beverage was. Distilled water. Bugleg lifted his and slurped as happily as though it were champagne. He put it down and said:

"It's so great you're here at last. Now we can really get some work done. We couldn't start without you, uh, Joseph. What do you need to know about your mission?"

Mendoza raised her eyebrows, but I said, "Well, as I understand it, we're kind of lifting an entire biosystem off the face of the Earth in situ, right?"

Bugleg's jaw hung slack. *He doesn't know what the big words mean,* transmitted Lopez, and out loud he said, "Right. To be specific, we're collecting the Chumash village of Humashup. The people, the animals they hunt, the plants they gather, the fish they catch, their culture in its entirety, even samples of the local geology and seawater."

"Yes," affirmed Bugleg.

"No wonder you've brought so many specialists in on this," remarked Mendoza.

"Impressive, isn't it?" Lopez almost reached for the claret again. "You'll find access codes for all relevant anthropological information in your assigned quarters, and I believe you'll find the texts by John P. Harrington and Alfred L. Kroeber the most useful. To give you an overview, however: the Chumash are the aboriginal inhabitants of this region of the California coast. Our preliminary studies show a Neolithic level of technological development but an extremely complex social and mercantile structure. They're hunter-gatherers but also industrialists, if you can imagine that. They produce a wide variety of objects manufactured specifically for trade with other local tribes. They've developed a monetary system that other tribes have had to adopt in order to do business with them, but they've retained sole rights to the manufacture of the shell money they use. The word *Chumash* is a corruption of the name given to them by their neighbors, which can be roughly translated as 'the people who make money.' Which they certainly do, literally and figuratively. By local standards they're millionaires."

"Savages with an economic empire." Mendoza looked amused.

"Hardly savages. Their standard of living is quite high. Life is easy for the Chumash. They haven't had to develop agriculture or domesticate animals, because the wild food sources are abundant. The climate in the interior is temperate, so clothing is largely unnecessary, though they enjoy elaborate jewelry and hair adornment. And they bathe more frequently than contemporary mortals in Europe."

"Well, who doesn't?"

Lopez put his elbows on the table and leaned forward. "These people have saunas. They have municipal centers for organized sporting events. They have ballet. They have stand-up comedians. I think most people would define that as the Good Life."

"Sound like stereotypical Californians to me." I bit down on a hard lump of something. Analysis proved it to be an unrehydrated nugget of protein paste. I made it vanish discreetly into my paper napkin. "Do they have any less attractive qualities?"

Sighing, Lopez settled back in his chair and pushed his food away. "They have their problems. They seem to get most of their aggressions out on their neighbors by controlling commerce, but there is some territorial warfare. Their infant mortality rate is suspiciously high. Seems to be a high level of domestic violence, too."

"Nobody's perfect." I drank the rest of my water and looked around for more. Lopez's elbow twitched again. No crystal decanter to refill my bottle, and Bugleg seemed oblivious to the possibility that his guests might want more. Lopez and I both sighed. "So, what's their religion like? I understand I'm playing a god?" I continued.

"More or less. They're loosely pantheistic, animistic, and

their astrologers are quite accomplished astronomers as well. They do debate philosophy to some degree. Their principal semidivine totemic hero is Sky Coyote. You'll get all the available data on him when you access your orientation material, but he's your standard Trickster figure who's also the friend and helper of the human race. Hence our choice of him as our liaison."

"I don't know what that word means," complained Bugleg. The conversation came to a screeching halt, and we all stared at him.

"Which word, sir?" inquired Lopez.

"*Hence.* You went, *hence.* That's one of those old-time words."

"Why, yes, sir, but we're old-time people, aren't we, sir?" Lopez smiled at him with great effort. "So you mustn't mind it."

"*Hence* means 'So that's why,'" I explained. "Like, 'So that's why we chose Coyote as our liaison.' See?"

"Oh." Bugleg looked sulky. "Then you should have gone 'So that's why,' not that old-time word. You shouldn't use those old-time words. They're weird."

Lopez drew a deep breath. I began to have respect for the man. He rushed on: "You're going to make contact with the Chumash and persuade them to relocate. Then you'll keep them cooperative as we go through the subsequent stages of the operation. We're staging it now, because communication among villages is limited at this time of the year and we're aiming at closure within two months. In fact, we chose Humashup because it's comparatively isolated and word of our presence is less likely to spread. It's also the nearest community to Point Conception (known to the Chumash as *Humqaq,* or Raven Point), which was chosen as our base site because it figures in their mythology as the gateway to the next world. The locals avoid the area for that reason, making it an ideal place for our installation."

"And if anybody sees anything high-tech and strange, it can be explained away as spirits," I guessed.

"Exactly. Once we've collected them, all the villagers will be airlifted to Mackenzie Base for further study and assimilation."

"Sounds like I'll need to do some pretty fancy talking to get these people to go with us, if they have such a good life here," I said.

"The Company has every confidence in you," Lopez told me firmly. "You yourself are the product of a similarly primitive culture, after all, which ought to provide you with some insights. We're also fitting you with complex appliance makeup and biomechanical prostheses to turn you into their patron god. In fact"—Lopez took out an octavo memorandum and consulted it—"you'll report to suite A$_3$ at eight hundred hours tomorrow for preliminary fittings and tissue matching. Shower and shave first, please."

"Is this an uncomfortable process?"

"I'm afraid so."

"Oh, well. I guess I'll need every possible arrow in my quiver." I shrugged.

"You're not supposed to use arrows!" said Bugleg, in some alarm.

There was another pause. *I give up,* transmitted Mendoza. *Is the guy brain-damaged or what?*

He only speaks Twenty-Fourth Century Cinema Standard, explained Lopez.

But so do we!

Not exactly.

But we've read their books! We've seen their films! Charles Dickens! Somerset Maugham! Warner Brothers!

Those are mostly drawn from the few centuries preceding his time, Lopez told her. *In his era, most mortals find them too difficult to understand. Particularly technocrats such as our friend here. The liberal arts are consequently—how shall I say it?—rather suspect.*

Mendoza was stunned into silence. All of their conversation took about a nanosecond, so without even missing a beat I turned to Bugleg and grinned like his best pal. "Just a figure of speech, sir. A metaphor. You know."

He blinked.

"I won't really shoot anybody with any real arrows," I assured him. "Say, isn't this Proteus-Brand Synthesized Protein we're eating?"

"Yes."

"In béarnaise sauce. Well, well. You know, it'll be great once we're really settled in here at this base and your catering crew get their act together. Plenty of great stuff to eat in California, you know. There's abalone and swordfish out there in the sea. Venison's abundant in this coastal range, too, I hear. Swell fresh cuisine."

I swear the guy turned pale.

"We feel more comfortable with our own food," he said.

Okay. I got down the last of my foodlike substance and looked around longingly. No wine, no brandy, no liqueurs or coffee. No dessert either.

"What a great meal," I said. "Got any Theobromos?"

!!!!!!! broadcast Lopez. Bugleg looked shocked.

"Is that a joke?"

Whoops.

"Of course it is." I grinned most charmingly. "Take it easy. I guess you've heard us field operatives are a pretty wild bunch, but really nobody does Theobromos. Honest. just pulling your leg."

"Just—"

"I was only joking with you," I clarified.

"Oh."

I hope they don't search our luggage, broadcast Mendoza.

By that evening, as I reclined on my uncomfortable twenty-fourth-century mattress accessing anthropological data, I had Bugleg all figured out. You know those Victorian big-game hunters who'll insist on bringing all the apparatus of their civilization into the jungles with them? Formal dress for dinner, *London Illustrated News,* teatime?

Every little British social custom rigorously observed, so they don't go native? That was what was going on here. Bugleg couldn't have volunteered for this mission, he must have been horrified to have been chosen; and so he'd compensated by wrapping his whole sanitized twenty-fourth-century world and all its values around himself, and we were expected to conform, like native bearers obliged to wear white jackets to serve dinner.

What kind of rank did he hold in the Company, though, to have pull like that? It must have cost a fortune to ship a whole chunk of the twenty-fourth century here, just so he could cope. He seemed like such a moron.

The Chumash were a lot easier to understand. Even before I'd finished the material by Harrington and Kroeber, I felt I knew them. Everything Lopez had told me was true, and if you don't believe me, access the files yourself. They really did have an economic empire and a sophisticated lifestyle, for people living in a Neolithic world. To tell the truth, they were a lot more advanced than the tribe I'd been born into, back in France or Spain or wherever it had been.

I didn't think I'd have any problems, though. The truth is, *Homo sapiens sapiens* is pretty much the same the world over, regardless of skin color or technological development. Racists and provincial types have problems with this fact, but it is a fact. All mortals have the same potential, and only chance determines who's playing a spinet or who's clubbing dinner to death with a big rock. And, you know what? Mortals adapt to the environment in which they're placed. Switch babies between savages and technologicals, and nobody notices! I know, because I've seen it done. I've seen the son of a club-carrying cave dweller fuming because his accounting software wasn't quite adequate for his needs. All humans have the same brain package.

Nowadays, anyway.

Chapter 12 ❧

NINE HUNDRED HOURS, day two of my time in Alta California, and I was gingerly withdrawing my hand from a Fineplast casting. Matthias, the tech, nodded approvingly at the hole I'd made and handed it off to a mortal assistant. Matthias was one of our Old Ones, like me; except he had the big face and unflappable calm of the Neanderthals. I'd always gotten on well with these guys. Nowadays, of course, they couldn't work in the field much, due to the fact that the human gene drift had moved away from their kind of looks and made them really noticeable if they went out among mortals; but they seemed happy enough working as technicians and pilots around Company bases.

"Now, here's a model of the hardware we'll use for the paw prosthesis. It fits over here"—he took my wrist and demonstrated—"and we'll graft the implants here, here, and here. The nerves will run right down through the flesh frame to your own, so there'll be no loss of sensation and no lag time in response. The digits may look short, but we've practiced with a model and you can manipulate them perfectly well. You can eat, drink, take care of sanitary functions . . ."

"I'm so glad."

"Yeah, we thought you'd be." Matthias put down the skeleton model and took up a graphics plaquette. "Now, we have quite a few possible heads, here. We can go the full-head approach or we can go with appliances, which might be more comfortable for you but would have fewer effects. Your choice." He held up a series of sketches for my perusal.

I surveyed my choices. The full-head model was spectacular; on the drawing board it could do enough tricks to have me convincing Rin Tin Tin I was his brother. Still, I passed on it. I've worn prostheses with fancy effects before, and they never work right, no matter what the techs tell you. Besides, I'm a minimalist. A good actor doesn't need all that stuff to have mortals believe in him.

We settled on a combination of appliances I felt would work, and while Matthias was making notes, I inquired casually, "So, where do discriminating palates dine around here?"

Matthias looked into my eyes, glanced at his mortal assistant, and said:

"Petrie, I want a Fineplast five-eight, medium olive range." And when Petrie had gone off to make it, whatever it was, Matthias leaned close and said: "So far we've been able to have a couple of seafood bakes. There's a place farther down the beach, still inside the perimeter but out of sight from the base, and there's some shelter from the wind. If you can get away Saturday night . . . You like venison?"

"Are you kidding?"

"Okay, well, Sixtus brought down a buck last week and he's hiding it in the refrigeration module. It ought to be great by the barbecue. For God's sake don't tell the mortals, though. We'd never hear the end of it."

"I gather the administrative staff are strict vegetarians?"

"You can say that again," he said, shaking his head sadly.

"So, what's the deal, here?" I prodded. "I've never seen so many twenty-fourth-century bureaucrats on a mission in my life. How much did Dr. Zeus spend on this show, anyway?"

"Buckets of cash, from what I've heard," Matthias told me. "Apparently it's something political. I don't ask, friend,

I just do my job." He toyed with his stylus absentmindedly as he spoke, making it rotate over and under each finger in turn. You never see that kind of manual dexterity anymore; Cro-Magnons didn't have it, and it wasn't passed on to the hybrid *Homo sapiens sapiens.*

"There seems to be a lot of, uh, bad feeling between them and us," I observed.

"*You* try living with these people for six weeks," Matthias said with a sigh. "I've been here since setup, man, and I'm so sick of them, I could cry. I'm just hoping they'll transfer me back to Greenland when this job's over. Get you into your coyote suit and I'm out of here, with any luck. I can't believe the stares I get from these kids. I'm about ready to make myself up as a Cro-Magnon, just so they stop flinching when they pass me in the hallway."

He dropped his voice as Petrie came back and informed him that my five-eight was ready. It turned out to be the medium for my lower-body cast. Quite an experience.

Chapter 13 ❧

So HERE I am, Mr. Sky Coyote.

I like this role. Trot trot trot on my new feet, leaving strange prints along the creek bed. A seagull floating inland gives a high far-off cry, and I cock my ear most comically. Up the winding canyon, and any real beast meeting me here in the gloom under the oak trees will have the fright of its life. If I wanted to give chase, I wonder how I'd do? The muzzle points, the sharp teeth bare, and they snap and slash. We had to compromise on the tongue so I could still speak, but I've practiced panting in the mirror. I'm confident I'll make a good impression.

Once upon a time, see, the line between men and animals was a lot less clearly drawn. If you were out with your spear thrower on a summer morning in Spain a couple of hundred centuries ago, you might have met with a creature like me and been scared, yes; but not really surprised. Things were more fluid then. Perception wasn't the same. Mortals have since learned not to see what doesn't fit into the world pattern they're most comfortable with, so of course there are no human-headed bulls, no transparent women walking along the surface of rivers, no balls of fire that hang in the air and scream with human voices. Any time mortals live out in the open, though, it becomes harder for them to shut out the inexplicable stuff, so they have to develop some context for it. That's why they tell stories about creatures like me, with my teeth and my tail. That's why they'll accept me as Sky Coyote come for a visit.

Yeah, I'm pretty game for a guy walking into Chumash territory buck naked except for some prostheses and strategic fur implants. But, hey, I'm a Facilitator! We're more flexible than the Conservers or the Techs, psychologically, physically, morally. Disguises and intrigues are what we live for. And these really are the very best effects the Company can provide.

Let's try Angry Coyote. I crouch, and look at those ears go back, back, look at those hackles rise! I snarl, I sidle. Tail down like a broken plume.

Happy Coyote. Mr. Perky! Everything upright and bouncy! Whoops. Maybe too upright and bouncy, but what the hell, maybe the Chumash will think it's funny. Got to remember my cultural context here. I frisk. I frolic. I try a few yards on all fours and actually do pretty well. Could even run like this if I had to.

Anyway there I was, following the creek back into the hills, miles and miles of getting into character, and suddenly I picked them up about a mile ahead of me and fifty feet up the hillside to my left: mortals. Two males.

When you're going to impress somebody with your otherworldly godliness, it's better to try it from high ground. Silhouetted dramatically against the sky, like. Sprinting up the steep slope through the sagebrush or whatever it was, I thought of Warner Brothers 'toons and giggled. There was a nice outcropping of red rock just out of bowshot from where they'd pass. I got up there and struck an attitude. They were coming steadily nearer; they'd heard me crashing around.

In a moment I saw them, and they were buck naked too, literally, insofar as they both had on these kind of stuffed deer-head hats that Chumash hunters wore for camouflage. Pretty clever, if you're after deer. I was after *them*.

"Hello, nephews," I barked.

The little deer heads stopped bobbing forward. They rose

slowly, and we beheld each other, I and my two earthbound kin.

"You haven't caught anything today, I see," I observed, scratching myself with my hind leg. Sort of.

"It's Sky Coyote," one of them observed faintly. I cocked my ear at that.

"Well, of course I am. Why are you so surprised to see me?" They were more than surprised, actually, if the sudden reek of urine from downwind was any indication. I'd overdone it on the otherworldly-god bit, but I sure had made an impression. To keep them from running away, I continued with the conversation: "I've got some very important matters to discuss with you boys."

"Really?" replied the other of them, still trembling.

"Really. Very important. But excuse me a minute, won't you?" I cocked my leg majestically, hoping to damp down, as it were, their awe. They stared, and then one of them straightened up and pulled off his headgear.

"Oh, for God's sake, it's just a man in a coyote hat," he said in disgust. "Who do you think you are, mister?"

Time for action. I leaped down and landed in front of him. "Who do *you* think I am?" I retorted.

Up close, the whole carefully crafted illusion was undeniable. I watched his face as his reality shifted out from under him, never to settle back in the old way again. I seized his shaking hand and dragged it up to my ear. "Look. Feel. Pull it. Now do you know who I am?"

"My God!" he burst out. "You really are Sky Coyote! I mean—excuse me—"

"Why are you so surprised?" I repeated. "Haven't you been hearing about me all your life?"

"Well, yes—it's just that nobody's ever actually *seen* You. In our village, anyway."

"I don't get down to this world much lately. It's sort of out of the way. Nevertheless, I'm here, because I have big news for your village. I'm here to save you all!"

So they took me to meet the folks.

Their names were Kenemekme and Wixay, and they were upright, fit, and clean-limbed young guys, with nice clear skins. Gleaming white teeth, hair like black silk. Pretty much representative of their race. Kenemekme was tall and nervous. Wixay was sturdier; he kept exclaiming and smacking the earth with his bow as we walked along.

"I just can't get over this," he said excitedly. "You're really here! Sky Coyote, in the flesh! There are so many things I've always wanted to ask You."

"Such as?"

"Well, is it true that You wanted to fix it so we'd never get old and sick by letting us swim in the Lake of Youth, but the Earth Cricket voted You down in the Sky People's council?"

"It's true. He said things would be too crowded if men never died." I nodded emphatically. "And he was right, actually, but you can't blame me for trying!"

"And is that story true, how you were the referee when Hawk and Turtle had their race, back in the first days of the world?"

"That's right. And were they grateful for my honest judgment? I don't think so!"

"But this means it's *all* true, then, doesn't it? About the World above This One and the Sky People and everything?"

"Yes, nephew, it's all true," I told him solemnly.

"Wow." He shivered with pleasure.

"You're serious about this, aren't You?" Kenemekme studied me as we trudged along. I nodded. He bit his lip.

I didn't blame him for being uneasy. Mortals occupy a pretty low place in Chumash cosmogony. There's a principal supreme deity who's the Sun, usually, and there are a few subordinate deities who keep the universe running smoothly and punish their fellow supernaturals who get out of line. The only celestial big shot who concerns himself with the human race is Sky Coyote. He created men, he meddles in their affairs, he negotiates with the other spirits for good harvests and low mortality rates. Not all-powerful and not especially virtuous, either, but he's the only friend men have. Just the role for me.

Chapter 14 ❧

So HERE'S THE semigod or tutelary spirit or whatever he is, arriving in the valley of Humashup with two of his mortal nephews.

Humashup was not a big town, but it was a prosperous one. There was a residential district back in the oak forest, three or four broad streets lined with woven houses. Over on the west side was the big municipal sports field and beyond that the sacred enclosure and cemetery, tidily fenced. To the south a long thatched enclosure marked the village meeting house. Down by the creek I saw the communal acorn-processing rocks and, a respectable distance away, the private steam baths. The little open-air shrine I could see was in fine repair, and the altar pole was loaded with offerings. Times were good in Humashup, obviously.

We advanced from the west, through what you might call the industrial complex: a stone yard with stonecutters busily at work, a boatyard with canoemakers busily at work. Until they saw me, of course.

And then, hey, the people came out to look. The workers dropped their tools and stared; the women pounding acorns stopped in midpound and stared; the boys driving a hoop around the playing field stopped and stared, and the hoop went wobbling away unnoticed.

I waved. "Hello, everybody. It's Uncle Sky Coyote. Remember me?"

Now, these people were not idiots, and the first conclusion most of them came to was that I was a mortal man in some kind of coyote suit. Thank Dr. Zeus for high-quality grafts, implants, and appliance makeup. I think I'll just skip over all the times I had to have my tail pulled to prove I was real, likewise the times people said things like I've Heard a Lot about You but I Never Actually Thought I'd Meet You. Let's cut to the big meeting in the council house that night.

I had the seat of honor, on a boulder near the fire. Everyone else sat on mats on the floor, and the place was packed, more than packed; through every crevice and slot in the tule wall I could see a pair of eyes gleaming, from all those who weren't important enough to sit inside.

As soon as everyone had gotten comfortable, Sepawit, the chief, stood and cleared his throat. He was a thin man approaching middle age, with an intelligent face. Like most of the other men, he wore nothing but a belt and some shell-bead money, but his hair was long and arranged in an elaborate chignon with beautifully carved wooden pins.

"Well. Well, folks, I guess our distinguished visitor doesn't need much of an introduction to you all—" Scattered nervous giggles at that. I laughed, too, tongue lolling and fangs bright, to show I appreciated the situation and to show off some of my head's effects. "And though it's certainly been a long time since He's visited us, I'd say we're unanimous in extending a heartfelt welcome to Sky Coyote from the people and fraternal organizations of Humashup!"

There were polite nods and mutters of assent. The chief went on. "Uncle Sky Coyote, I'd like to introduce Nutku, spokesman for the Canoemakers' Union. Nutku is also First Functionary of the Humashup Lodge of the Brotherhood of the Kantap."

Nutku rose to his knees so I could see him. Powerful arms on this fellow, and he wore more strings of shell money than Sepawit did, and had a bearskin cloak over his shoulders too. His hair was done up with mother-of-pearl pins. I scanned him and detected mild arteriosclerosis, a touch of hypertension: he dined on lots of fatty red meat and made executive decisions. Introduced first, too. Important guy.

"And this is Sawlawlan, spokesman for the United Workers in Steatite." Another one wearing lots of money, with big hair and a sea-otter cape. "And Kupiuc, spokesman for the Intertribal Trade Council and Second Functionary of the Humashup Lodge. And this is Kaxiwalic, one of our most successful independent entrepreneurs."

"Pleased to meet all of you," I said, all benevolence. I had my audience pegged, now: here were the upper classes, wearing a certain hard and confident look, a can-do look, you might say, and across their chests the rolls of shell money rippled and clicked like backgammon counters. The nobodies were at the back of the room, with open, vulnerable faces like nobodies everywhere. I could play to this audience. I'd played to their like for more centuries than I remembered.

I got to my feet. My shadow loomed up behind me on the dome of the hall, unsteady in the firelight.

"It's good to be back in Humashup, children," I said, "though it's true I haven't been to see you in a few generations. But it's a long journey from here to the World Above, let me tell you, and I'm a busy god. I only found the time to come down now because I have very important news.

"Now, you all know"—I held out my strange hands to them—"how we play a game up there, the Sun and I, at midwinter every year. We gamble. We outguess each other, He and I. And you all know what the stakes are.

"Yes, I can see you do. It's your *lives* He wants, the Sun, because He's always hungry. All that burning, burning up in the sky, and how does He do it? He feeds on men. Your lives light the sky, heat the earth, and the only one who can keep Him from taking you all is me. If I didn't gamble with him to save some of you every year, you wouldn't be here now to listen to me, any of you. This fine hall would be dark and cold, and you'd all be in the cemetery out there.

"But don't worry: I'm a good gambler and I win often. When I do, the Sun can't take any of you but the old sick people. Better than that: He has to pay me in good things, acorns and fish, deer and geese in plenty, which I send down to you. I win you rainy seasons to make the hills green. I win you calm weather at sea and big runs of salmon. All these things come from me, because I'm your uncle and I look out for you.

"You know all this. And this is how things have always been, every year. But not anymore!"

Eyes widened at this, and there was some muttering. The mortals smelled afraid. I went on: "Last month was midwinter, and I went to the corner of the sky where I gamble with the Sun. And He was there, all right, and there were the dice ready for the cast, but I saw something else too: the Sun had a talisman around His neck on a piece of cord, and it looked like a canoe, only a *big* canoe with the wings of a white bird."

A few people exchanged meaningful glances.

"Anyway I settled down to play with Him, and I noticed that He took off His talisman and lay it down by His right foot. We cast the dice, the little shells spun around, and at first I won. Then my luck changed! If I called five, three came up. If I called ten, I'd throw two. I couldn't call a winning throw no matter how I shook the shells.

"This went on and on. I lost ten of your lives, ten of you here in this very hall. Whose lives do you suppose they were? Then I lost fifty lives. Then a hundred. Sun threw every number He called, but never me. So I watched closely, and I saw what was happening.

"There were little men hiding in Sun's canoe talisman, tiny men white as chalk. When it was my turn, they'd run out and bowl the shells along like hoops until they landed me a losing number. When Sun threw, they'd bowl and flip the shells so that He won every time. And more and more of you were dying, and not only you but all the tribes, the Yokuts and the Ohlone and tribes you haven't even heard of. Finally I threw my hands up and cried, 'Sun, You're cheating!'

"He just laughed and said, 'If you think so, call in Moon to judge between us.'

"This seemed all right to me, because, say what you like about Moon being changeable, She is a fair judge at least. She came in and watched us play for a while. You know how sharp She can be, especially at certain times of the month when She's in a bad mood! She spotted the tiny white men right away. She shook Her head in disapproval and said, 'You're right, Coyote, Sun is cheating!'

"Sun just laughed at us. He said, 'I became tired of losing to you all the time, so I got myself a little magic to change the score. I'll pay the penalty for cheating, but I'll tell you this: my magic can't be stopped. The white men in this canoe will collect human lives for me, all I can eat forever. You can't stop them. You can win all the good harvests you like, but who will you give them to? So hot, so bright I'll burn on all those lives!' "

Absolute silence in the meeting hall. I lifted my head and howled. I made it the sound of all desolation, and the naked little mortals sat rigid with terror.

"But!" I went on after a suitable pause. "Moon looked at Sun with blood in Her eye and said: 'You cheated at the midwinter game! Do You think You can get away with it? I'm going to fine You! Sky Coyote can have seventy years for his people before Your white men come for them. Also, if You eat all the people, the earth will go out of balance, and we can't have that. So here's a further penalty: Sky Coyote can take *four* magic canoes of his own and fill them with as many of his people as he can carry to safety. Those people You can never eat. Then, after seventy years, You are free to do Your worst to the people Sky Coyote leaves behind.'

"That was what Moon had to say. So this is what I've

come to tell you, my children of Humashup: I will not leave you behind. Because I love you the most, I'm taking all of you away with me in my canoes."

Silence. Then a babble of panicked voices, louder outside where people had been listening through the walls. Sepawit looked around at all the confusion and rose to address me.

"So . . . we're to interpret all this literally, then."

"Of course!"

"And not as a series of metaphors."

"What did you think, I came here to read you riddles?"

The chief turned and stared at his shamans, who looked uncomfortable. From the back of the room, someone cried out: "I've seen those big canoes with wings! They're sails! And they *do* have white men in them!"

"Like I said." I crossed my arms, or forelimbs, or whatever. Must have been some Spanish ships straggling north from Mexico that weren't making it into the history books. Oh, well. I'd known these people weren't stupid. It might be a good idea to ease up on the mythic style, though.

"You have to save us, Uncle Coyote!" cried the general mass.

"Now, everybody, calm down!" The chief waved his hands. "There's no immediate danger. Sky Coyote has already promised to save us. And we have seventy years— didn't You say seventy years?—yes, all right, He said seventy years before the white men even get here, by which time I'm sure we'll be long gone. So you see, there's no cause for alarm."

"I'd like to ask a few questions." The spokesman for the Canoemakers' Union got to his feet. He looked determined, though he'd gone pale like the rest of them when I howled the doom of everything he knew.

"Ask, nephew."

"First, the Canoemakers' Union would like to thank You for Your concern and Your timely warning. But we'd like to ask—could You be a little more specific about this white-men thing? What exactly is involved here?"

"Yes, the United Steatite Workers would like to ask that, too," chimed in Sawlawlan.

Coolheaded pragmatists, huh? All right. I addressed my words to them, but I spoke to be heard by the fearful unthinking masses at the back. "You want to know more? I'll tell you. The Sun hasn't got just one of those canoes with sails, He's got thousands of them. They'll bring more white men than there are stars in the sky, and white men, let me tell you, are the masters of invasion. Everything they touch dies, even their embraces kill, and you should see their weapons! Don't think they're just coming for a raid on you, either, don't think they'll take the sea-otter pelts and a woman or two and go to sea again in their big canoes. They're going to *live* here.

"This won't be your land anymore, it'll be theirs. You'll be their slaves, as long as you live. And you won't live long. But while you live, you'll do what they tell you to do, you'll eat what they tell you to eat, you'll think what they tell you to think. And after they've destroyed you, they'll start on the very earth. They'll remake it to what they think a land should be. No more oak trees, no more wild places.

"Don't you understand? As soon as the white men get here, that's the end of this world. It won't even be a memory, because there'll be none of you left to remember what this place was like.

"Only Sky Coyote can save you."

Just about had them. Their eyes were wide and staring now.

"All right." Sepawit swallowed hard. "But surely, Sky Coyote, this is a little sudden—"

"You don't believe me, do you?" I looked down my muzzle at him, severe now.

"We do, but—"

"You never expected me to visit you, did you? You didn't even believe in me. Even now some of you are thinking, Who is this Sky Coyote really? Does He have to disrupt our comfortable lives like this? Couldn't we just stay here and take our chances with these white men? Well, believe me, if this is too much trouble for you, I can go to some other village."

Some of them began to panic. Sepawit was sweating. "No! No, please, Sky Coyote, don't take offense. You must understand, this is all something of a shock to us. We need some time to take it in. To, er, discuss it among ourselves. Won't you tell us more about what you plan to do?"

So I unbent, and graciously told them. Not the whole story, naturally, but the usual rigmarole about giant sky canoes carting everybody off to a wonderful promised land where they wouldn't ever die, even after their present bodies grew old and passed away. And I told them about my spirit servants who were going to be visiting to collect samples of the local flora and fauna, so the rest of their world could be rescued, too.

And they bought it, pretty much. The chief was mortified at my anger and ready to do anything to show himself cooperative, but I could tell I'd still have some work to do with the businessmen. Probably with the shamans, too. Get them alone, personal interviews, wheedling and threats and a little sleight of hand, one on one.

The questions and answers went on until pretty late, and I was invited to stay overnight in the special guest quarters for visiting dignitaries. With me went a couple of young ladies, groupies, as it were, in otter-fur capes, who wanted a closer look at some of my effects. You don't need to know about this part, but the Prosthetics and Appliances Division of Dr. Zeus passed yet another field test with flying colors.

"Wow." Puluy leaned back dreamily into otter fur, carefully arranging her hairdo. She was the prettier and more poised of the two. "That was neat, Coyote. I've never picked poppies with a Sky Guy before. You're so, like, you know, *furry*."

"Dummy," Awhay told her scornfully, stretching out her legs. She was the plumper and more serious one. "Of course He's furry! He's Sky Coyote, okay? So anyway, Uncle Coyote. Did You, like, really mean that, about the white men coming and all? I mean, the end of the world is, no shit, really coming?"

"That's right." I tried crossing my forelimbs behind my head and found I could do it. "You can kiss this place goodbye."

"That is so weird." Awhay stared at the ceiling, thinking about it. "And I can't believe the first person You talked to was Kenemekme. That guy is such a *loser!*"

"Omigod!" Puluy started up on her elbow. "I've got my birthday party coming up next month! My dad's sent me some money and my grandmother's jewelry. Oh, shit!"

"Don't worry," I said with a yawn. "You'll get your birthday party. We won't be leaving right away."

"My dad lives in Nipumu." Puluy frowned slightly. "Are You gonna be rescuing his village too?"

"Can't." I shrugged. "I'm only allowed to take so many. Sorry, sweetheart." She considered that a moment before her face cleared.

"Oh well. At least he's already sent the presents. And it's not like he's even seen me since I was ten. Like he cares." She lay down again, perfectly content. Awhay turned on her side and regarded me.

"What was it like in the beginning, Uncle Sky Coyote?" she asked. "I mean, *really*. Forget the shit we're told by the priests. You were there! Was there actually a big flood and all that?"

"Sure." I wriggled around and pulled up a folded fur behind my head to get comfortable. "We used to live down here in the Middle World, but after the flood we decided to be Sky People instead. But somebody had to live down here, so we got together to make you guys. All the Sky People contributed different ideas. Humans were designed by committee, and that's why your bodies work so badly.

We mold-cast the first couple in parts, see? And I was going to give you all nice useful hands like mine, that you can dig with and run around on without hurting; but at the last minute Lizard substituted a cast of his hands instead!"

"I've heard that story." Awhay held up her hand and peered at it. "But it's weird, you know, because we *don't* have lizard hands."

"Well. They look more like a lizard's hands than mine," I improvised. "And anyway, this is Sky Lizard we're talking about, and he has hands just like yours."

"Oh. Okay." Awhay settled down, but her eyes were still on me. "Tell us more about what it was like in the old days?"

"Well, let's see." I accessed more files. "Did you ever hear about the time I rescued Eagle's daughter from the Sea People?"

"Uh-uh. Tell us."

"Okay. Way back when we Sky People used to live here, Eagle had a beautiful daughter. She was so lovely, golden light shone from her, and golden poppies bloomed out of her footprints. And everybody wanted her, because her beauty was famous all over the world; but Eagle decided to marry her to his sister's son, Falcon, who was chief over on Limuw Island back then. So he sent a wedding party, a bunch of people in canoes, with Pelican and Cormorant leading because they knew the way, and a big fancy canoe decorated with golden poppies with Eagle's daughter in it.

"But halfway across the channel, a bunch of swordfish came swimming up out of the sea and attacked the bride's canoe! They made it capsize, and Eagle's daughter fell into the water and sank like a stone and vanished from sight. So did the swordfish. The wedding party put about and searched, and Cormorant and Pelican dove down to see if they could find her, but it was no use.

"Boy, was there a to-do about that! The groom, Falcon, was crazy with grief. Eagle racked his brains to think of what he could do. But what could he do? The sea was a big place, and he had no power there.

"And so at last Eagle swallowed his pride and sent for me. There'd been some bad blood between us for a long time—in fact I hadn't even been invited to the wedding. But I didn't hold it against him when he sent for me and admitted that only I, Coyote, was smart enough to steal his daughter back. I especially liked it that he got down on his knees and begged me. So I said, 'Sure! No problem.'

"I got some magic stuff together in a couple of cane tubes, and I had Pelican and Cormorant take me out in a canoe to the place where Eagle's daughter had gone overboard. Falcon insisted on coming along, even though I figured he'd get in the way. So as we sat there in the canoe, I handed him one of the tubes of magic stuff.

" 'Okay, kid, stick that in your ear and keep it there!' I told him. 'It's dangerous where we're going, but the tube should protect you.' And I put the other tube in my ear and told him, 'Now, when we get where we're going, you let me do all the talking, understand?' He told me that he understood, real meek, so I grabbed him and we jumped overboard. I stuck my head up out of the water and told Cormorant and Pelican not to come after us, no matter what happened.

" 'No chance!' replied Cormorant. 'We'll stick around a day and a night, but then we're out of here.'

"So down we went through the water, Falcon and I. First the water was clear as glass, then a gloomy kind of blue-green, then dark as night. We could feel the water squeezing us and freezing us, and we'd have been killed if not for my magic tube stuff. At last, a long way down, we saw a golden light shining in the black water.

"When we got closer, we saw that the light was spilling from the door and the smoke hole of a house that had been built on the sea bottom. It looked just like the house we're in now, except that it had a whalebone frame instead of wood and was thatched with kelp instead of tules. We went to the door and looked in. Eagle's daughter was in there, and the golden light was coming from her. Poor thing, she was crouched on the floor grinding up snails in a mortar, just the way you'd grind acorns, only these were nasty slimy snails, and the whole house was slimy and untidy inside. She kept working, crying the whole time and wiping away golden tears.

" 'That's my bride!' shouted Falcon. I clapped my paw over his mouth to shut him up, but it was too late, the Sea People heard us.

"There was hissing laughter behind us. We turned around and saw them. They were evil, dirty old men, with long white beards and eyebrows, and every one had a sword in his hand. Quick as a flash I said:

" 'Hi there, Undersea Fellows. This boy here and I are travelers, and we'd like shelter for the night. Will you grant it?' And this really screwed them, see, because once I'd asked for hospitality, they couldn't attack us. They looked at one another with their cold eyes, trying to think of a way around the rules. At last one of them said, 'Of course!' grinning with his sharp teeth. 'Please enter into our house, and share our food and the heat of our fire!'

"So we went inside, and they crowded in after us, careful to sit between us and the door so there was no quick way to exit. We sat down by the fire, but it was an undersea fire: it burned cold and blue and made the place darker. The only real light came from Eagle's daughter, who looked at us hopefully but didn't dare stop pounding snails in her mortar.

" 'That's a pretty girl,' I said to the Sea People.

" 'She's all right,' said the oldest old man. 'It's been a long time since we had a slave who made decent sea-snail mush! Come, we were just about to eat our evening meal of whale meat. There's plenty for everyone. You'll insult us if you don't eat heartily!' They were trying to trap us, see, by making us insult them at their own hearth, so they'd have an excuse to kill us. But I said, 'Sounds great! Bring on the blubber!'

"So one of them went out, and after a minute he starts to pitch dead whales in through the doorway. Obviously this was a magic house, because it expanded as the whales came in, so that everybody was able to sit comfortably with a dead whale in front of him. 'I hope you don't expect such decadent luxury as *cooking*,' sneered the oldest Sea Person. 'We eat our meat raw under this roof, it's healthier that way.'

" 'Of course!' I answered cheerfully. 'That's how it tastes best!' I could see Falcon looking green, so I leaned over and whispered to him: 'Just pretend to eat. Cut off chunks and pass them to me.'

"Well, the meal commenced. You should have seen the disgusting table manners those guys had! Grease and blood and blubber all over their faces. Each one chewed down a whole whale all by himself. I ate up all mine too—but then, I can eat anything. Falcon couldn't manage more than a couple of mouthfuls, but he tore off big pieces and passed them to me under his thigh, and I gobbled them down so the Sea People couldn't say we were turning up our noses at their food.

"When the meal was over, I licked my chops and grinned. 'What a great meal!' I told them. 'Truly you Sea People are masters of hospitality.' But the oldest one just grinned like a saw blade and said, 'If you liked our meat so much, you'll have to try our tobacco. Our feelings will be very hurt if you don't like it!' And they handed around a tube of the awful stuff they use down there. It was like sticking a salted fish up your nose! I took a big helping, though, when my turn came, and signaled to Falcon that he do the same. Then, just like with the meat, he passed me his share under his thigh, and I was able to partake of it without harm, because nothing makes me sick. But I was getting tired of this, and besides the Sea People were still between us and the door, giving us no chance of grabbing

Eagle's daughter and making a break for it. So I said:

" 'You've been so kind in sharing your comforts here in your home, allow me to repay you by singing to you all!'

" 'All right,' said the oldest of the Sea People, not knowing what to expect. Now, personally, I think I have a beautiful voice, but all the other Sky People have told me they'd rather be dragged over hot coals than listen to me sing. They say I sound like wild animals being skinned alive. Anyhow, I began to serenade the Sea People in my own special way.

"Poor Falcon went pale, and Eagle's daughter covered her ears and cowered down. The Sea People made faces as though they'd just bitten into something rotten; but what could they do? I was hoping they'd leave, but they were so tough and ugly, even my singing wasn't too much for them. I sang and sang, love songs and lullabies, fishing songs and songs of war. A couple began to rock back and forth in pain, one of them clutched at the side of his head like he had a toothache, and the oldest one's nose started to bleed. But there they sat, blocking the way for us to escape with Eagle's daughter.

"I sang at them for hours, thinking they would at least have to go out to relieve themselves. But nobody was moving, even after that meal! Finally I realized they were going right where they sat, like fish! Their poop didn't have any smell, like the poop of fish or shrimp, but it gave me an idea.

" 'Excuse me a moment while I refresh my voice, won't you?' I asked, and I slipped the tube of magic stuff from my ear and poured a little into my mouth.

" 'Oh, please, don't strain your throat,' begged the oldest of the Sea People, wiping blood and tears from his face.

" 'Don't you like my singing?' I asked in an offended voice. 'After I've racked my brains for every tune I know, just to entertain you?' Because I could feel the magic stuff working inside me, you see. And the Sea People brightened a little at that, because they thought I was going to insult them and there'd be a fight, so they could kill me at last.

" 'Well, I guess I can tell the truth in my own house,' said the old one with a grin. 'The plain truth is, your singing is terrible and hurts our ears!'

" 'Oh yeah?' I retorted. Yes, the magic was working! 'And do you want to know what I think of your taste in music?'

At that every one of the Sea People grabbed hold of his sword. 'What?' they said in a chorus. 'What do you think of our taste in music?'

" 'THIS!' I replied, and let loose a thunderous fart. Now you know I'm an ancient and powerful creature, and I'd had a huge meal of rotten whale and magic powder on top of that, so you can imagine what happened. The whole house rose on its foundations and settled again in the crater my fart made. Eagle's daughter and Falcon fainted dead away. Over on the islands, people thought they were having an earthquake. When the bubble broke on the surface of the sea, birds fell out of the air like stones, and fish were killed instantly, and washed up on the beach for weeks. There were colorful sunsets for a year and a half from the poison in the air. But the Sea People got out of that house as fast as they could. They didn't even bother with the door—they jumped out through the smoke hole!

"I grabbed up Eagle's daughter and Falcon, one in either arm, and beat it through the door and swam up and up until I saw clear water above me and the face of the Moon, white with horror. She used to be red like the Sun, before that night when I farted. I broke the surface and found the canoe still floating there, though it was half swamped, and Cormorant and Pelican were lying in it unconscious. I tossed in Eagle's daughter and Falcon, jumped in myself, bailed out the water, and paddled us all back to the mainland single-handed.

"Eagle's daughter and Falcon recovered and were married, and lived happily ever after. I'm not sure if they had children, though. At least I wasn't invited to any naming ceremonies! And you can hang that story on the hook, because I'm finished telling it."

"God, Sky Coyote, that was *so* gross!" giggled Awhay, rolling close to me. "Did it really happen like that? Was that really the truth?"

"As much of the truth as I ever tell, child of earth." I grinned lazily at her.

"My mother used to say You're a truth made of lies. Maybe she was right, for once in her life." She snuggled closer. "You know what? I think Puluy's gone to sleep . . ."

When it got quiet at last, I lay there between the girls and watched the stars. From time to time a little wind moved in the oak trees, but mostly there was only the old sound, the oldest sound, mortals breathing slowly by their hearth fires, with now and then the whimper of a child or dog.

Sleep tight, children. Sky Coyote is with you.

Chapter 15 ෨෨

I SLEPT, AND saw all the terrible things I'd warned the Chumash about. From the sea came the white sails, and they anchored and the white men came striding up over the land. Their armor gleamed silver and their priests carried banners with crosses. My people fought and died, or turned to flee into the mountains. But from beyond the mountains came more white men, under a striped banner, bearing long rifles. What were my people going to do? Were we all going to die?

No! Because here they came, the Enforcers, heroes to save the day. Budu pointed at the Spanish and the Americans with his ax. He pronounced his sentence on them, as he always did: If you make war on other tribes to take their land, you must die. He gave an order, and the big men in bearskins moved, as they always had, like a wave rolling in to crush the guilty and protect the innocent. The Spanish cut them with steel, but they kept coming. The Americans shot them with bullets, but they kept coming.

Oh, it was wonderful! All the terrible things I'd prophesied weren't going to come true after all, no near extinction for the Chumash, no mission slaves, no conquerors! The Enforcers were seeing to it that life would go on in the ancient ways forever and ever, so that good people could sleep safely by their fires under the kindly stars. The problems with history being changed had all been smoothed over, somehow.

Now all the invaders seemed to be dead, and Budu was helping his men take heads. The bodies were stacked in heaps and burned. He was laughing his high-pitched laugh; his pale-blue eyes were dancing. The Chumash were bowing down to thank him. But then from the dead I saw a figure leap up, a priest who somehow hadn't been executed, a small man in a black robe. He slipped in under Budu's arm. He had a long knife in his hand. I tried to yell a warning but I couldn't, and anyway I recognized the man in the black robe. I saw myself running my knife in between Budu's ribs. No. No.

It didn't happen that way. I would never have done that.

Would I? If I'd been ordered to do it, would I have betrayed him?

I was shivering when I woke up, but the girls were hogging the furs. Growling softly, I nipped at Awhay until she woke up enough to relinquish some bed space to her principal divinity.

Chapter 16 ✍

IF THE CHUMASH had been impressed with me, I really made a sensational entrance at the weekly production meeting.

I had to open the rear seam of my breeches to let my tail out, and it stuck through the rear pleat of my coat. I had to abandon my wig, but my tricorne fit very tidily between my coyote ears. Yes, all eyes were on me during my report on Initial Contact and Preliminary Negotiations. I disconcerted Mr. Bugleg no end. I could tell, because he kept dropping his stylus. Then again, maybe he usually had trouble holding small objects. Anyhow I concluded my report and stepped down, and there was vast creaking in that prefab hall as fifty people shifted uncomfortably in their folding chairs.

"Questions?" inquired Mr. Lopez.

One of the administrative team put up his hand, an elderly mortal. He wasn't a scientist or anything; he was just some investor the Company had sent along on the trip so he could think he was helping to make decisions. He stood and frowned at me.

"I'm sure everyone at Dr. Zeus would like to thank Joseph for his report, and it sounds like he's doing a great job, but I don't see why he had to include in his report his adventures with the underaged native girls. I would like to go on record as protesting that."

"So noted," intoned Lopez, and I made my ears droop. There was a wave of subvocal giggling from the immortals in the hall. The old man glared around—you'd have thought he could hear us—and raised his voice as he continued:

"I would also like to go on record as protesting the choice of the Chumash tribe as preservation subjects."

"So noted," replied Lopez hurriedly, but the old guy went right on:

"I've been watching the preliminary field reports. These Indians aren't like the Hopi or the Navajo. Those were clean, peaceful Indians with an advanced society and beautiful mythology. They farmed and they built houses the way we do. These Chumash are different. They're dirty-minded, lazy, pleasure-loving Indians. They don't have anything important to contribute to human culture. I think it's a waste of Company funds to bother with them."

"So noted. Thank you," said Lopez.

"And they're not spiritual people at all! Their sexual habits are depraved. They're decadent. They remind me of those emperor people who used to lie around in togas— you know. What were they called?"

"Romans, sir," said Lopez faintly.

"Romans, right. The Company would be spending its time and money much better if it went after a nicer tribe. There are Indians down in Los Angeles now with much more meaningful lives. I saw a thing on the holo where they've even discovered monotheism and they have a prophet and everything. If *they* were the ones we were saving, I'll bet they'd develop into a great civilization."

Lopez cleared his throat.

"With respect, sir, we operatives aren't permitted to judge the quality of one mortal culture against another. You all have equal value in our eyes, regardless of your beliefs and practices. We simply follow the directives of Dr. Zeus, and in this particular case Dr. Zeus has decided that the Chumash are worth rescuing."

"Yes, I know all about you immortals and how smart you are. Well, I'm just an old man from the twenty-fourth century, but I'll tell you this: we should have programmed you with a sense of right and wrong. Because it sure seems to me that you androids don't have any." *Oooo!* What a faux pas. There was a real vibration of subsonic rage in the room from my fellow Old Ones. Lopez drew a deep breath.

"Sir, we are cyborgs. Not androids. There is a difference."

"Whatever." The old guy waved dismissively. "The point is that you people just don't have any values. So I want to go on record as protesting this Chumash thing. *And* the way Dr. Zeus is being run nowadays. I know I can't do anything about it, but I've been a stockholder since this company started, and I don't like one bit the way it's turned out."

"So noted," said Lopez. And over the red wave of immortal wrath that filled the ether, he broadcast: *Please, everybody, the old horse's ass is retiring next month.*

The meeting moved on to other topics, and afterward there were refreshments, if you found distilled water and little sea-algae crackers refreshing. I didn't stay.

I went back to Humashup by a path different from the one I took the first time. People are funny about their gods: might be one or two lurkers hoping to get off an arrow or two at me. So I went over the hills and just strolled in through the oak trees behind the houses, where there were some children running around. They didn't notice me. I crouched down to watch them.

Little brown kids, mostly naked, playing with some rocks by water. I'd been like that once: no bright electronic toys, and no possible way to understand one if I'd encountered it. That was before all the operations that turned me into a brainy little cyborg like Latif. Old Eurobase One in the high Cévennes in France, that had been where Budu sent me. They'd unloaded me, crying and airsick and disoriented, straight into the base hospital. When I awoke, my intelligence had been zapped upward a few million points, and I had the potential to become immortal.

The very first thing I remember seeing, in my new improved state, was a flat white wall on which images danced, a lot more colorful than my poor dad's bison and horses. There were other children lying in beds nearby, and they were giggling weakly at the bright figures. There was a little pink man with a weapon, and a rabbit and a duck; the duck was trying to get the man to kill the rabbit, but the rabbit was so clever, he managed to turn the duck's scheming back against him every time. The duck's bill was blown completely off his face. I laughed at that until I hurt.

Eurobase One was a lot more primitive than the deluxe private-school bases the Company built later. It was more like a military base with a school attached as a kind of afterthought, and we kids were used to seeing Enforcers go charging out to fight off the latest stupid attack by the Great Goat Cult. Bad guys were stupid. I remember a nurse sitting down on the edge of my bed and explaining this to me. The Rabbit was the hero, because he wasn't trying to hurt anybody, and he used his intelligence to confuse his enemies so they hurt themselves instead of hurting him. It made sense to me, and as a role model the screwy Rabbit was hard to improve on. Which was a good thing, since Eurobase One had a limited budget for teaching tools in those days.

I wondered how these kids would adjust to a new world, and to new heroes like rabbits and stuttering pigs? To say nothing of all the shiny educational toys the Company provided for its mortal wards. The kids wouldn't be turned into little geniuses like I'd been, but life was going to offer a lot more than the game of scrambling up on a high rock and stopping everyone else from getting up there too.

These kids seemed to be having a great time, though, getting muddy in a stream. Nobody was watching as one little guy, maybe fifteen months old, toddled away downstream and found a big pool of still water to stare into.

Something on its surface fascinated him, and, after watching awhile, he made a grab for it. He lost his balance and fell in. It wasn't all that deep, but he wasn't all that big, and once he'd choked and got water up his nose, he became panicky and uncoordinated. Facedown in the water, and somehow unable to climb out.

Now, I can watch human tragedy on the large scale and yawn. Nations fall? Big deal. Revolutions fail? So? Societies collapse? I'll join the looters. Most people have it coming to them. Their babies don't, though. So I sprinted over and fished the kid out before he could drown. At the sight of me he coughed up water and began to scream bloody murder.

The other kids paid no attention until one of them glanced over and noticed I was Coyote, and then they all came running. "Sky Coyote!" they all yelled, mostly in unison.

"Are You really Sky Coyote?"

"Are You going to take us away in a canoe?"

"Will You make some magic work for us?"

"Can I go up in the sky with You?"

"Look, whose baby is this?" I demanded, holding him out at arm's length because he was wetting all over the place in his terror.

"That's my little brother, Sky Coyote," admitted a boy about eight years old.

"Well, why weren't you watching him? He almost drowned," I said sternly.

He just stared at me.

"Where's your mother?" I barked at him.

"She's working in her house," volunteered another child.

"Well, where's her house?" Now they all just stared until I bared my fangs at them, and then they all took a step backward. One of them pointed to a house down the street.

"Over there."

"Thanks," I growled, and hauled the still-shrieking kid

in that direction. As I departed, I heard one of the group say:

"He's *mean*."

The only reason the baby's mother didn't hear me coming was that she was having an argument with a man at her door. She was a nicely plump lady in the two-piece outfit most of the working women wore, a woven tule skirt under a tabard of the same material, fastened at the shoulder with a feathered pin. The skirt was weighted at the hem with little plumb bobs of drilled stone to keep it hanging in dignified folds. This regal effect was spoiled a little by the fact that she was yelling so loud, the veins were standing out in her neck.

"You have to be crazy!" she was shouting. "I can't turn out three-color baskets that fast! Nobody can!"

"My other manufacturers do," the man said.

"Oh no, buster, no no no, you just said the *wrong* thing. Didn't you ever think me and the other ladies would get together and compare notes?" Her eyes widened in fierce triumph. "You've been using that line on all of us! And we found out you've been lying about a *lot* of things. Like the price controls on deergrass!"

He was withering under her assault when I barked, "Excuse me." She barely glanced at me, and then she and the man did a set of double-takes so classic, it put me in mind again of the rabbit and the duck. "This your baby, lady?" I held him out. She didn't take him, but he scrambled loose from me at last and ran to cling to her. "What's going on, here?" I inquired.

"Just a business discussion, Sky Coyote." The man held up his hands. I recognized him as Kaxiwalic, the one introduced to me at the town meeting as a successful entrepreneur. Not all that successful, to judge from his skinny appearance and the fact that he wore only a couple of strands of shell money. Right now he looked as though he'd like nothing better than to vanish silently into the sagebrush. "I'll see you later, Skilmoy."

"Hey, now here's somebody who'd be interested in your dirty tricks!" Grinning hugely, the woman grabbed him by the arm. "What do You think of smooth operators, Coyote? This lousy slave driver charges us extra for our materials and then gets a kickback from the Deergrass Gatherers' Union—" The baby's squalling threatened to drown her out. She leaned down and slapped him a good one. "Shut up! Kyupi, will you get out here and do something with him?"

An adolescent girl came out of the house. Her eyes got big when she saw me, but she grabbed up the baby and scuttled back inside with him. I could hear her rocking and shushing, rocking and shushing.

"These women are all lazy," said Kaxiwalic in a chummy way, evidently assuming I was a male chauvinist god. Skilmoy rounded on him furiously.

"Lazy! Sky Coyote, do You know how hard I have to work to feed all these miserable children? Do You know how much fish costs these days? I'm an *artist*—"

"Your baby almost drowned."

"He what?" Her face crumpled up. Tears came into her eyes. "How can I watch him when I have to weave baskets every hour of the day and night? The kids won't help me with him at all."

"Maybe you shouldn't have had so many," said Kaxiwalic, looking smug.

"I'd like to see you pregnant every year, you bastard, and count how many big basket deals you'd make—"

"Now, hold it." I stepped between them. "What's the point of all this? Weren't you listening to what I told you in the meeting hall? The end of the world is coming soon. What do you need all these baskets for?"

"I can sell them, Sky Coyote," explained Kaxiwalic. "I mean, wherever we go, people are going to need baskets, right? And wait'll they see my merchandise. I see the end of this world as an opportunity. Think of the new markets opening up in the next one!"

"I wouldn't count on it. Maybe I didn't make myself clear: you're going to a wonderful paradise. Do you think there are underpaid, overworked women in paradise to make baskets for you?"

"But that's exactly why I need a big inventory before we leave! I have to—" I took him by the arm. He flinched at the touch of my paw. I looked into his eyes and shook my head.

"Uh-uh," I told him. He stared at me.

"But if I don't have baskets to sell, I—"

"Uh-uh. You can't use World Below methods in the World Above."

He opened and shut his mouth a few times. He glanced quickly at the woman and then said to me, lowering his voice, "Can I discuss this with You later?"

"Anytime."

"Thank You. I have to be going now." He hurried off, doubtless to call an emergency meeting of the local businessmen.

Skilmoy had calmed down a little, but now she looked worried.

"Sky Coyote, are you saying Kaxiwalic won't need us to make baskets for him anymore?"

"Yes, my child."

"But he can't lay us off! How are we going to live, with no money coming in?"

"What will you need money for, in paradise? As far as that goes, why do you need it now? Don't I send you plenty of good food? Look at all the acorns there are, look at all the roots and seeds and bulbs. I haven't seen one starving person in this town."

"Well, so nobody's starving, but I have to pay the fishermen and the hunters, don't I? And I have to pay the fees to get my son into the Kantap Society, so he can go somewhere in life. For all the child support I get, my ex-husband might just as well be in hell, which is where I wish he was anyway."

"Now, now, my child." Boy, these people needed a social benefits program or at least a day care center, but that wasn't my job. I was only there to play God. "Don't you understand that all these concerns won't exist anymore, very soon?"

She looked at me with slightly narrowed eyes. "When You say we'll all be in paradise . . . You don't mean we'll all be dead or anything like that, do you?"

"No. You'll live long, long, and happy lives, and you'll never be sick or in need." And that was the absolute truth; the Company had great retirement plans for its mortal employees. "Then you'll move on to another plane of existence."

"That's just . . . that's too good to be true." She stared hard at me, wanting to believe it all the same. "No trouble? No bad luck? No work?"

"I didn't say there wouldn't be any work."

"Ha! I knew it."

"But it'll be easy work, helping the Spirits. You'll have everything you could possibly want. If you didn't have *something* to do, paradise would be a pretty boring place. But you won't have any worries."

"Well, no offense, Sky Coyote, but I'll believe it when we get there." She got an odd look on her face. "Coyote? Are You going to rescue the people at Syuxtun Township too?"

"No," I told her. "Only Humashup has been chosen."

She clapped her hands and let out a whoop of laughter. "My ex-husband and his girlfriend live in Syuxtun!" she cried in delight. I put my head on one side and regarded her. "You're a pal, Sky Coyote! Come in and have some food. Do You like roasted agave heart?"

"With cherry sauce?" I said hopefully. She looked coy, and I followed her inside.

The girl was still rocking the baby by the fire. As we came in, he pointed at me and began to scream again.

"Oh, shut up, stupid, can't you see this is Sky Coyote?"

Skilmoy went and rummaged among her kitchen things.

"Hello, Uncle Sky Coyote. He's too little to understand, Mama," said the girl.

"Hi there." I sat down on a tule-reed mat.

"Well, he'd damn well better learn to understand, if he wants to get anywhere in life," retorted Skilmoy. "Kyupi, where's the agave heart we had last night?"

"I had it for breakfast, Mama."

The woman turned and slapped her. "Didn't it occur to you that I might bring a guest home? I'm so sorry, Sky Coyote. Would You like some acorn porridge instead? Or— oh." She looked appalled as something dawned on her. "You don't want . . . ? I mean, I've heard stories that Spirits do lots of stuff backward in the World Above. I've heard that the Sky People eat . . . well, shit."

I'd encountered this quaint belief in a few other cultures. What a dilemma for a thoughtful hostess!

"Actually, acorn porridge will be fine," I assured her. I had no idea there was any difference between Spanish acorns and the New World variety, which are, well, an ac- quired taste. But after the first shock I choked the stuff down with a happy doglike expression. Laying the abalone- shell bowl aside, I looked around the room. Domestic chaos was everywhere, except for the corner that was clearly where Skilmoy worked. There were tidy bunches of deer- grass and split rush there, sorted for length and tied in bun- dles. Some of them had already been dyed assorted colors, reds and yellows and blacks. In a small woven tray were a few simple tools, a bone knife and an awl, a couple of spools of thread, and some bone needles.

"So this is your work?" I picked up a stack of baskets and examined them. They were so tightly woven, they could have held water, and so beautifully finished, you could turn and turn one in your hands without finding a loose end anywhere. The spiraling patterns were sophisti- cated and dizzying in their complexity.

"You like them? Yes, they're mine. I'm the best, even

Kaxiwalic admits it." She came and sat down beside me so her knee touched mine. "The ones with the colored patterns are the most expensive," she explained.

"I guess the colored dyes cost a lot, huh?" I turned one over and stopped cold. Worked into this basket was a pretty fair representation of the flag of Spain. There was no mistaking it; I've marched, ridden, and persecuted heretics under it enough times to know those little castles and lions when I see them.

"What's this one?" I said, when I'd collected my wits.

"That? That's a new design. Some strangers came ashore in a canoe at Syuxtun and bought a lot of baskets at Kaxiwalic's shop down there. They were such good customers, he copied some designs off their gear. The idea is, next time they stop there, he'll have a whole new line of merchandise to appeal to them. Kaxiwalic's a lying bum, but he gets good ideas." So much for the purity of Chumash culture.

"Well, you know—" I frowned, holding the basket up to the light. "It might not be a good idea to trade with those people. I'm pretty sure this is the tribal tattoo of the white men, the ones the Sun is sending? That must have been one of their scouting parties that came ashore. They may not be causing much trouble now, but soon . . ."

"Oh, Sky Coyote, how terrible." She looked into my eyes, and hers were wide with—concern?

"It was hard to hear You through the wall when You spoke to us the other night, but You looked so impressive, standing there towering above everyone else. Won't You tell me more about this? These white men you speak of frighten me." And she leaned forward. All those kids notwithstanding, she still had a figure.

"I think I'll go out for a walk," said the little girl, and she got up with the baby in her arms and took him outside.

It must have been the ears or something. I hadn't seen this much romantic action in a couple of centuries.

Chapter 17 🐍

"You know what you look like?" Mendoza peered at me from her beach chair. "Like the guy in that Beauty and the Beast movie. The one by Cocteau."

"Nah." Ashur paused as he moved from refilling her glass to refilling mine. He stood back and studied me. The campfire danced behind him. The surf boomed distantly; it was late, and the tide was way out. We were celebrating Matthias's upcoming transfer back to Greenland One, and the party had gone on too long.

"Wrong clothes," Ashur pronounced at last. "The one in that movie had a high lace collar. Remember? With this shirt he's more like the Beast in the Duvall version."

"I think he looks like Puss in Boots," somebody on the other side of the fire giggled. I glared across at her.

"You're all wrong," I stated. "I look like the guy in the Kracowiac ring holo of *The Isle of Dogs*."

There was silence and then a scattered chorus of agreement from my fellow Old Ones. "Except the costume's still wrong," amended Matthias. "That production was done in late-twenty-first-century dress."

Never play trivia games with immortals. Do you know how many movies we've seen?

"Henry Hull in *Werewolf of London*," somebody ventured, but he was drowned out by somebody else insisting, "No! No! Oliver Reed in *The Curse of the Werewolf!*"

110

"Ssh." Ashur waved his arms above his head drunkenly. "Keep it down. Wind's shifted and noise carries. Don't want the"—he jabbed a thumb in the direction of the base—"the New Kids to hear."

"Let 'em hear. What a bunch of snotty-nosed, puritanical brats they are, to be sure." Mendoza tossed back another shot of home-brewed aguardiente.

"They don't mean to be. We just sort of—" Sixtus groped for words.

"Gross them out?" I suggested.

"They're too delicate for this end of time, that's all. We see venison, they see Bambi. We see swordfish steaks, they see Friendly Flippy lying murdered."

"We see ourselves, and they see—" Matthias scowled into his drink. "Savages, I suppose."

"Don't take it to heart," Ashur said, patting his shoulder. "They're just a bunch of rude, racist, species-ist adolescents."

"Then they ought to get back to their own damned end of time and let us manage affairs at this end, like we've always done," growled a zoologist named MacCool.

"Even the abalone they get sentimental about," mused Sixtus. "Can you imagine? I don't remember any animated mollusk classics, do you?"

"Wrong. There was a whole French school of cinema d'abalone in the late twentieth century," I lied. Matthias gave a high-pitched giggle.

"No, with the abalone it's bacteria they're afraid of," Mendoza informed Sixtus, ignoring us. "They're positive everything here is contaminated. I tried to get clearance to put in a little vegetable garden on the leeward side of the base. You know, for fresh tomatoes and maybe a lettuce or two? You'd have thought from Bugleg's face I was suggesting we grow amanita mushrooms. What about the microbes, the man said. I don't know where he learned a big word like that. As though I couldn't spot a goddam pathogen a mile ahead of him any day!"

"It's because they can't see them that they're so frightened," pointed out our principal anthropologist. Imarte was her name.

"Yeah, well."

"They think germs are scary?" demanded Sixtus. "They ought to see some of the things we've had to fight in their service, over the ages. A damn sight nastier than microbes, most of them! Eh?" He elbowed Matthias. Matthias and I exchanged uneasy glances. Most of the younger operatives don't know about that particular episode in prehistory, and official Company policy doesn't encourage letting them in on the secret. Besides, Sixtus was wrong to assume Matthias was part of the operation. Full-blooded Neanderthals weren't drafted to be Enforcers. They were too short, and they just couldn't ever seem to get worked up enough.

"How on earth can they know what we've seen?" mused Ashur, belching gently. "We've made life in that precious future of theirs so safe for them, they can't even imagine what real danger is."

"They're ungrateful brats," MacCool said.

"I think you're missing the point," Imarte tried to tell him, but he rounded on her:

"Aren't you appalled by them? Weren't you brought up to see them as the wise and benevolent Masters of the bloody Universe? Remote figures in their twenty-three-hundred offices who Know It All? God help us if these people are representative of Dr. Zeus."

"Of course not. They're field lackeys, that's all."

"So why do we have all these geeks from the future on this job?" Mendoza wanted to know.

"Because this one is a big moneymaker for the Company," I said, glancing sideways at Matthias. "Or so the rumor goes. There's a lot hanging on this one."

"There's a lot hanging on every one," grumbled Sixtus.

MacCool flung a deer rib into the fire and watched it sizzle. "We've been running things for them for how many millennia now? Thirty? Forty? We were always good enough for the job before. This boy in charge can't seem to make up his mind whether I'm some sort of temperamental office equipment or belong in a cage next to the specimens I collect. Were they always like this? I can't ever recall being called an android before, can any of you?"

"We're starting to get close to their end of time," Ashur told him. "Only a few more centuries to go. Makes 'em nervous. Have little drink."

"It's all that processed food they eat making them constipated, that's why they're nervous," chortled Sixtus.

"And these are the cretins we're saving the world for." MacCool's eyes smoldered.

"You're-talk-ing-TREA-son," sang somebody from the other side of the fire.

"And if I bloody am?" He half-started up.

Matthias stared at him. "Boy, what's eating you? No need to fight about it, is there?"

"Sorry." MacCool raised his drink in a gesture of apology. "I've had this little spit-and-polish mortal jerk overseeing my project. He seems to feel that if he isn't right there to watch my every move, I'm going to club and eat all my specimens before they can be shipped. I thought of telling him about the times I've watched his ancestors clubbing and eating one another! Where does he get off thinking *I'm* barbaric, the chinless little twerp!"

"Okay, okay, mortals stink," agreed Ashur.

"Not the New Kids," said Mendoza in a thoughtful voice. "Have you noticed? They have no proper scent. They don't even sweat."

"I mean it!" MacCool turned slowly to stare at us all and settled his gaze at last on Mendoza. I should mention that he was a big good-looking guy with a black mustache that would have done an Armenian poet proud. She looked up at him. "What are these people? They don't watch their own movies, they don't read their own books, they don't listen to their own music, their art embarrasses them, and as far as I can tell they're afraid of one another. They stay in their rooms playing games! How in the living hell did they ever create us?"

I knew some answers to that question, but it didn't seem like a good time to give them, not with the mood he was in.

"MacCool, their lives are so short," pleaded Imarte. "They don't have time for anything. Why shouldn't they be frightened? What if you knew you only had two centuries of consciousness, maybe less?"

"Then I wouldn't waste it in a holo cabinet shooting at imaginary soldiers," snarled MacCool. He looked down into Mendoza's eyes. "Would you?"

She returned his stare with a flat, opaque look, but smiled and drew her shawl around her shoulders. "Certainly not."

"Is *that* what they do all the time?" somebody asked.

MacCool turned and said: "As God's my witness. When they're off duty, they hook up to a console and play holo games. They shoot at targets or collect little blue dots of light. That's all they do, for hours on end! Take a look at their entertainment programs sometime. Not one book or film will you find, and no music more than two years old their time. Nothing but games, and not even that many of them."

There was a moment of silence.

"Well, maybe they're exercising. Practicing reflex speed or something," Ashur suggested. "They have to operate a lot of machinery. Maybe in the field they don't want any other entertainment. They seem to be big on stripped-down efficiency. Function over form. Look at those god-awful clothes."

"They're more androids than we are," muttered MacCool.

"Although . . ." Mendoza said slowly. "They *do* seem to have a point about wearing simpler clothes in the field. I'm ruining all the stuff I brought up from New World One. It's hard collecting specimens in all that lace. I've broken three sets of heels climbing around in these canyons. I don't

know who I thought I was going to impress in my Madrid
fashions, because the sagebrush sure doesn't care. This is
stupid. I'm ordering more sensible clothes. Khaki. Low
heels. That kind of thing."

I stared at her in disbelief. MacCool put his hand over
hers.

"But the lace suits you, you know. Jesu, don't let them
persuade you to their notions of fashion. They *have* no
fashion."

Mendoza looked down at their touching hands. I couldn't
read her expression.

Was he thinking of putting the moves on her? He was
definitely her type, as I remembered her type: large, loud,
and physically impulsive. A crusader. I prayed to every god
I'd ever burned incense to that I wouldn't be treated to a
ringside seat as history repeated itself in Mendoza's love
life. Even a wimp like Lewis seemed far and away a safer
choice. But who was I to get involved? She wasn't a kid
anymore.

"It has nothing to do with the New Kids," she told him.
"Why indulge in vanities like fashion if simpler clothing
will make my work easier?"

MacCool reached out uncertainly and brushed her hair
back from her face. "I also like the way you look in white
silk," he added.

"Well, the Don Juan of the canid world has to get his
beauty sleep," I said loudly, briskly shaking the sand from
my tail. "See you guys in the morning. Don't forget to
cover the still and bury the barbecue leftovers. We wouldn't
want Bugleg to find out about these swell parties."

"Huh?" Matthias started up from where he'd begun to
doze.

"They know perfectly well what we do out here," said
Sixtus sullenly, staring into the fire.

"Probably, but isn't it fun to pretend? 'Night, all." Putting on my hat, I walked back down the beach toward the

lights of the base. There was salt in the wind. I turned up my collar. One thing you can say for mortals: when they get together at a party, they don't have the same damned conversation every time.

Chapter 18 🐍

"SKY COYOTE! DELIGHTED you could make it," Sepawit welcomed me from the doorway of the sacred enclosure. It was an impressive doorway, framed by whale ribs. Do you have any idea how big whale ribs are? I stepped up to go in, but he stopped me with an apologetic little smile.

"I have to precede You walking backward. It's customary. I know You probably don't demand anything like that, but the shamans are so set on protocol, and my Speaker is away on business for me, so if You don't mind . . ."

"No problem." I gave him a conspiratorial wink and let him back in ahead of me.

"Welcome to our house, Uncle Sky Coyote; welcome from the north, welcome from the east, welcome from the south, welcome from the west," he recited in a loud voice.

"Slower!" somebody hissed from inside. "Don't babble it like that."

"And the white wind welcomes You. And the red fire welcomes You. And the black earth welcomes You. And the blue rain welcomes You." Sepawit looked mortified. This might take all night. I put my paw on his shoulder and stepped past him into the enclosure.

"Thank you, all you directions and personified natural phenomena, your welcome is gratefully accepted. Well, well, and who do we have here?" I looked around at the religious dignitaries assembled before me. They looked

117

back at me, formidably. Time for a few good guesses. I bowed to one elderly gent, portly and very distinguished in appearance, with a nice mild face like the bishop of Madrid.

"My greetings to the astrologer priest," I ventured.

"Uncle Sky Coyote." He inclined graciously. "You are truly with us."

"So I am." I turned and bowed to two more gentlemen of the same august sort, whose feathered topknots poked at the ceiling. "Reverend sirs! May your divinations produce answers. May your sacrifices find favor. May your rituals go smoothly."

"Welcome, Uncle Sky Coyote," they fluted. That left a couple of lean men with staring eyes. These were the ones with tattoos, knotted hair, animal parts strung about their persons, and a general look of having partaken way too frequently of certain vegetable alkaloids.

"Learned doctors," I tried. "Best of luck in your pursuit of knowledge." That seemed to please them. They began to rock back and forth where they sat.

So far, so good. I whisked my tail out of the way and sat down casually. Their eyes all widened. I must have sat on something sacred. I checked over my shoulder and yes, I was sitting on some kind of intricately painted skin. Okay, I'd forge ahead.

"Now, naturally enough, you don't have to tell me why you asked me here. I can tell you. You want the truth about my revelation of the other evening. You're all initiates, and you know there's more here than can be understood by those who have not traveled the secret paths." Right? Right, guys? After a breathless pause Sepawit nodded.

"We knew that story about the white men was a cover for something. It's the Chinigchinix thing, isn't it?"

Who? What? I opened my mouth for a bluff while I accessed hastily, but was saved the trouble of some fast thinking by one of the shamans, who leaped to his feet.

"I am one with Sky Coyote and I speak for Him! I can tell you what is in His heart. The white men represent the followers of Chinigchinix who dwell in the south. Do they not paint their heads with white clay? And their Sun is not our own true Sun but an angry god who drives out all gods but himself and visits terrible punishment on unbelievers! Sky Coyote is trying to tell us that Chinigchinix is readying his people to invade us. So says Sky Coyote!"

There was silence for a moment as we all took that in.

"Thank you, Pahkshono." Sepawit gave a slight cough. "Now, Coyote—"

"No!" One of the priests jumped up. "My knowledge is greater than his! You only have to look at Sky Coyote to see the truth. Has He not sat in the midst of the sky map of the summer solstice? This signifies the intrusion of celestial forces into our Middle World. And does His tail not point in the direction sacred to the autumn harvest? By this, we may know the time of the divine invasion. Plainly, the Sun is attempting to kill us by sending a great drought which is to wipe out this year's harvest."

All this made me nervous. I crossed my legs.

"Liar!" shouted yet another shaman. "See how Sky Coyote has negated your specious interpretation of His revelation, which is utterly clear to anyone with any *real* hermetic training. By sitting on the sky map, Sky Coyote is plainly demonstrating His contempt for you and your dependence on astrology. Are not the stars celestial bodies like the Sun? We can infer from this that by 'white men' he means the stars. Sky Coyote warns us that dependence on the so-called wisdom of the stars will lead us to damnation."

"That is precisely what He is *not* saying," said the astrologer priest severely. "By sitting on the sky map, obviously Sky Coyote acknowledges that the same cosmic system supports those in the World Above as in our world. Even the Sun Himself must follow the preordained celestial patterns. If you think Sky Coyote came all the way down to Earth to overturn the existing order, you're vastly mistaken."

"And yet, isn't that what He's saying?" countered one of the priests. "The existing order is about to be overthrown by these white men, whatever or whoever they are. What we ought to be asking ourselves is, What is the reason? I think it must be that our people have strayed into evil ways and wrong thinking. The young have no respect for their elders, divorce is on the rise, and there is no proper respect paid to the sayings of the priests anymore. We have grown decadent. Do we not deserve this terrible punishment?"

"No!" cried another shaman. "Sky Coyote *wants* us to be irreverent. He is the spirit of divine anarchy! His message is that He will save us just as we are, in fact He will carry us away to a world of everlasting pleasure where we can sin more enthusiastically and reach ever wilder levels of chaos!"

"Now, hold it! Hold it! Hold it!" I interjected.

"Hold what?" they replied in unison.

"He said it three times," observed one of the diviners.

"So much for a message advocating anarchy!" crowed the astrologer priest. "By 'Hold it' Sky Coyote signifies that we must contain ourselves and our wasteful urges."

"You timid equivocator!" thundered a shaman. "He meant, 'Hold on to the concept of liberation through excess'!"

"Wait—" I said.

"For what?" demanded a shaman.

"How long?" inquired a diviner.

"Where?" asked the astrologer priest.

"Sky Coyote, I wonder if I might have a word with You outside for a minute?" murmured Sepawit. I got up and went out with him. Behind us a furious discussion of my posture ensued.

"Look, er, Coyote . . . I'm no theologian or anything, so I'm afraid Your answer might go right over my head, but I need to know: how serious is this Chinigchinix threat? Am I going to have to organize a war party? Because if I have to, it's only fair to tell You, we wouldn't have a chance. The Chinigchinix cultists are fanatics, and there are thousands of them. They keep growing in numbers, too, because they forcibly convert their captives. My Speaker isn't away on business—I've had him out gathering intelligence for the last ten moons, and what I've been hearing makes my blood run cold. The priests don't know. The people don't know. I'm the only one who's put all the facts together, and I don't know what to do. You must have come here to save us from them. Tell me, Sky Coyote, that's why You're here." The poor guy was shaking.

"You've worked hard for my people, Sepawit. Do you think I'd let you down?" I soothed him in the voice I'd used in confessionals in Madrid. "You don't have to worry about Chinigchinix. We'll be safely out of here before anything happens."

"But You have no idea how fast they move," he rattled on. "At least—excuse me, of course *You* do. It started down south among the Tongva, at a village called Yang-Na. They had this prophet who's supposed to have been born on Huya Island, who went around telling everybody that there's only one god and anyone who doesn't believe that will suffer horrible punishment. He convinced his people to fight for this god, and they've been taking every village in their path. All the tribes to the east have gone over, and most of the island tribes, and it's been spreading north. They're fanatics! They still trade with us because we make things they want, but in my opinion it's only a matter of time before they declare holy war."

"I know, my child," I told him. It was a story I'd learned a long time ago. Almost the first story I'd ever learned, now that I come to think of it; and later I'd seen it acted out in Egypt, and in Byzantium, and in North Africa. One man becomes convinced he's found a truth so important, the whole world must be forced to acknowledge it.

"And they always conquer." He looked at me with haunted eyes. "It's as though they really do have the most powerful god on their side. This prophet's followers aren't afraid of anything in battle—my spies tell me it's because they're all on drugs. And they say—" He looked away from me. "They say You're the Evil One. They say You used to be a servant to their god, and that You did something terrible and were cast down among the nunasis."

"Boy, that figures." I shook my head. "What do you think, Sepawit?"

"I know You're our uncle. I know You've always helped us in the old stories. But even in the stories You lose sometimes. What will happen if You lose now?"

"We won't stick around here long enough to find out. Sepawit, I think you're a brave man, and a wise man, or you wouldn't be so scared. Will you help me save our people?"

The sound of argument from inside the sacred enclosure grew louder. Sepawit glanced over nervously. It sounded as though somebody was throttling the astrologer priest.

"Of course I will. Tell me what to do."

"Just follow my orders. I really am going to get you all out of this, Sepawit, but you have to see to it that everybody cooperates with me. I don't want any more argument or second-guessing out of that bunch in there." I nodded at the sacred enclosure. "You're the chief, after all. They have to obey you, right?"

"Supposedly," he replied. "It would be a help, Coyote, if You could tell me which of them was right."

"All of them, naturally," I replied. "And none of them, of course."

Well, how else is a god supposed to answer a question like that?

It was a lot to think about, walking home. Isn't it funny how patterns repeat themselves? Unless you're immortal, though, you don't usually get a chance to appreciate just how often they repeat themselves.

I mean, there my people were, not bothering anybody, hunting and gathering like everyone else in 18,000 B.C.E., moving from a winter cave to a summer camp and back again as the seasons changed, regular as clockwork. The only thing we did that was in the least bit remarkable was paint on rocks and on the walls of our winter cave, and actually only my father did any painting. Aunt Druva did a lot of scrimshaw with mammoth ivory, of course, but that didn't count.

The paintings did count, because they were almost the first things the tattooed strangers noticed when they came walking into our hunting grounds. This wasn't a good thing, as it turned out. We had no clue why they started screaming and killing us, but I learned later that they had this god whose principal commandment was that every living soul on earth must be tattooed, or the universe would collapse. Anybody not submitting to mandatory skin art was guilty of not doing his bit to keep the universe in place and must therefore die. Anybody who lavished art on something other than skin was guilty of blasphemy and must also die. They had developed a lot of sound theological reasons for this, I'm told, and we'd have probably listened patiently to them as we submitted to being tattooed; my people weren't dumb.

Unfortunately the evidence that we were blasphemers was daubed all over the walls of the cliff we sheltered under in summer: leaping deer and lolloping bison in every shade of ocher and umber my dad had been able to mix. He'd been the kind of guy who just couldn't resist a blank surface, my poor dad. The tattooed guys never even tried to convert us to the Way; they took one look at those paintings and waded in to restore cosmic order with their hatchets.

My people would have been wiped out, as a lot of other tribes had been wiped out, if it wasn't for the big men in bearskins who appeared out of nowhere to smash the tattooed guys all to bits.

I didn't know any of this at the time, of course. It was only explained to me later how the big men had their own commandment, their own method of keeping the universe from collapsing, and it was a lot simpler than seeing that everyone got tattoos. They just went around killing anybody who tried to kill anybody else. It was okay for *them* to kill, because they were Enforcers, but nobody else was allowed to. They'd been after the tattooed people for a long time. Eventually they got them all, too.

Which was a shame, in a way, because then the real trouble started . . .

Chapter 19 ❧

LOPEZ WELCOMED ME into his quarters with a bow, and I bowed in my turn, sweeping off my tricorne.

"Nice place you've got here." I looked around as I straightened up.

"I like my comforts," he replied, going to a sideboard where a decanter was set up beside two fine glasses. I realized his rank must be pretty damn high too, to have his personal furniture shipped out to a base at the back of beyond like this one. I'd been a successful operative for longer than I cared to think about, and I didn't even *own* any furniture. So how had Lopez managed to hang on to those two comfy chairs, that carved walnut sideboard, that Turkish carpet? Not to mention the nice little Rembrandt study, looking sadly out of place on the gray prefab wall. Best of all, it was golden amontillado he was pouring into that Florentine glass. I nearly shed tears as he handed it to me.

"To the Company." We raised our glasses. He gestured me to one of the two comfy chairs and himself sank into the other one. We put up our feet in front of his heating panel. "That's more like it, I trust?" He sipped his wine.

"You can say that again," I sighed. Beyond the dark window a Pacific gale was howling in the winter night. I edged my feet a little closer to the panel. They were bare, of course, because I couldn't get shoes or stockings on my coyote hind paws. I guess they looked a little odd emerging from my red knee breeches, because Lopez casually remarked:

"The younger members of our organization just can't seem to get used to the sight of a coyote in a brocade coat."

"Yes, I'd noticed that." I cocked my ears and grinned at him. "The alternative is to go nude, though, and I think the New Kids would like that even less."

"I've heard they would prefer it if you wore Company-issue coveralls to clothe your nakedness," said Lopez mildly, and we both laughed, but it was clear he was dropping a hint. I narrowed my eyes. Not on his eternal life. I looked strange enough as it was.

"Poor future kids." I shook my head with an air of indulgence. "They're finding this mission a little hard on their sensibilities, aren't they? Things must be sort of rough compared with what they're used to up there in the Platinum Age."

"They find us outlandish," Lopez admitted. "Extravagant. Eclectic. Unfathomable."

"Frightening," I added. He smiled slightly and shrugged. "Distasteful," I went on. "They're barely polite to us. Not that I take it personally, I'm an open-minded kind of guy, but anybody else just might suffer some hurt feelings."

"Yes, I gather there've been some problems with morale," he mused. "Androids . . . ," he said, at the same moment I said it. He looked gently pained and shook his head. "That *was* unfortunate."

"I thought so." I looked into my glass. Drinking with this muzzle took a bit of concentration, but if I sort of made a long spoon of my tongue, I could get the sherry down my throat without spilling any.

"And so there have been a few late-night parties where some grumbling went on. A few ill-considered words. A few rash opinions."

Aha. Lopez was an attitude cop. He was sounding me out over discontent in the ranks.

So I relaxed and sank deeper into my chair, savoring my amontillado and letting it take me back to a certain garden in Madrid where the sun was warm, and just around the corner was a great little wineshop, and just next door to that was a really fine tailor's, and next to that a lovely old church whose bell sounded the Angelus sweet and mellow through the sleepy air, and if the wind was right, you could barely smell the heretics burning . . .

"Well, you know, Lopez, I think we all agree that what matters most is the Company. We all want this mission to succeed, we really do. But it's hard, meeting somebody like Bugleg, to feel confident that this mission is in the best hands. Now, you know and I know that, despite appearances, these mortals are perfectly competent guys." Boy, was I smooth. "So what if they're a little culturally limited? I'll bet they're swell at interfacing with information-exchange terminals. But some of our old field operatives have trouble appreciating that, you know? Especially with somebody like Bugleg. What's the story with that guy? Level with me. He's somebody's nephew, right?"

The corner of Lopez's mouth quirked, but his gaze remained opaque. "Now, now. He has his talents."

"I'm sure he has." Maybe the guy collected stamps.

"Joseph, I truly understand how you feel." He reached over for the decanter and refilled our glasses. *I'll bet you do,* I thought to myself. I accepted my drink, and as I took the glass, I looked him straight in the eye, sincere as hell.

"I'm an old, old agent, Lopez," I said. "I love my work. The Company is everything in the world to me. All I ask is to know for certain that Dr. Zeus is being run by people who'll treat it right." I practically had myself crying, but Lopez saw right through me. He leaned back, sipping his sherry, considering me with bland eyes.

"I feel I can speak frankly with you, Joseph. You're a Facilitator, after all, and you've been around long enough to know a few things the rest don't know. The conservationists, anthropologists, botanists, and others, they're not really designed to grasp the big picture. Are they? Too focused on their own particular areas of expertise. Only a Facilitator has the necessary detachment to view a political situation with any real perception. Only a Facilitator—well, an older one, you or I, for example—has the experience to act effectively in that political situation."

"Maybe," I said, shrugging, remembering that pleasant little garden where no one could provoke me into revealing anything. Lopez smiled grudgingly at my control.

"You'd be a fool if you weren't concerned about the future, and I happen to know you're no fool. I've read your personnel file, you know."

Hadn't everybody?

"It's an impressive record," he went on. "Only three disciplinary incidents in your whole career! And I was tempted to discount that last one. Tell the truth: weren't you taking the heat for that protégée of yours? She's on this mission, in fact, isn't she, the botanist Mendoza? Presumably she's older and wiser now. Let us hope."

"It was just one of those things," I said, trying to sound as though this was something I hadn't thought about in decades. "Kids! What can you do? They always seem to want to learn the hard way. She's straightened out, though. They always do, eventually."

"How true," he said, sipping his drink. "Setting aside the incident with the young lady, however—I was particularly struck by your ability to see clearly and function correctly in, let's say, personally complicated difficulties."

What did *this* mean? How far back in my file had he read? It can't have been easy to interpret my expression through all the appliance makeup, but he was managing. He smiled reassuringly.

"You've made some difficult choices, in your time, but you always chose correctly. That business with the old Enforcers, for example."

Yikes.

I let myself look sad and shook my head. "Poor old guys.

But, you know what they lacked? That same quality you were just talking about. Detachment. They were damned good at their jobs, but it made them a bunch of loose cannons in the end. I was really relieved to hear they'd been retrained before they could do themselves more harm."

His stare was like an icepick, but he wasn't going to pry anything else out of me. Not on this subject. He seemed to accept this and went on convivially:

"Your feelings do you credit, especially since they're tempered by wisdom. You know what I admire in you? Your ability to trust." I almost grinned, but he held up his hand and went on: "You've been able to understand that this operation—by which I mean the whole thing, from its beginning, before either of us was created—couldn't have been conceived, planned, or carried out by people who didn't know exactly what they were doing. You have never, for one moment during your very long career, questioned the authority over you. Not because you're a drone or a toady, either. You have always understood that, whoever might be running things, their plan was sound."

"Like I said." I lapped up some sherry to break the mood.

Then he truly surprised me.

"You know what you have to keep in mind, Joseph? They're children, the mortals. No more than children. Life is so simple in that bright future of theirs, they've never had to trouble themselves to learn how to do more than play. For some of them it's very, very creative play, mind you, but . . . it has a certain uncomplicated quality, shall we say. Because, like children, they're bored by complicated things. More than bored: they feel threatened. Give a child mashed potatoes and butter, and he's happy. He doesn't want to try the rich sauce with capers, in fact he'll cry if he's forced to taste it. You see what I mean?

"But, listen, Joseph. A child is easy to control. Keep him happy, and he'll believe what he's told to believe. The mortals believe that they're running the Company, that they make the decisions, that they have the ideas. The child believes the world revolves around himself. Nursie knows better, but of course she doesn't tell him so.

"Though," he added thoughtfully, "he will learn the truth, someday."

What was I to make of this? I took a gulp of wine and looked askance at him. He might be letting me in on some genuine secret politics, but on the other hand he might be baiting a trap for a seditious renegade.

Well, he was sounding out the wrong man. I've worked for the Spanish Inquisition, and this is one game where I know the rules, thank you very much.

I shook my furry head. "I'm afraid this is all too deep for me. I'm just an old field agent, and maybe I'm a little out of touch with the way my betters are running things these days. But, you know, I've always felt we operatives shouldn't trouble ourselves with that end of the business. If you tell me that whoever's in charge knows what's best for Dr. Zeus, why, that's good enough for me, and I'll take your word for it."

"You're an honest fellow, Joseph," purred Lopez. "You touch my heart. Another glass of amontillado?"

"Have some greens, Sky Coyote." Nutku passed me the dish. It was full of wild onions and miner's lettuce. The greens had been steamed limp and were getting limper in the stifling air of the sauna.

"Thanks." I helped myself, and he leaned back with a grimace.

"My personal shaman says they're good for me, but what does he know? It's my spirit I pay him to take care of, and at pretty damned exorbitant rates at that. What I say is, after working my butt off to get where I am, it'd be a fine thing if I couldn't eat steak when I wanted to."

"You've got a point," I agreed.

"Let's have a little more mist, shall we?" Kaxiwalic poured some more water on the hot stones. They hissed and sent up dense clouds, making it harder to see in the already blurry air. Not that my eyes gave me any problems, but I was praying that the fancy circuitry in my prostheses wouldn't be affected by all the damp heat.

"Now *thaaat's* more like it," Kupiuc groaned, easing his big body backward. Even here he'd brought his charmstone with him, a small polished artifact he had the nervous habit of rolling between his fingers. "What a day I had. What a day. My ex-wife is after me for child support again."

"No kidding?"

"The she-whale. She wants me to get all three boys into the kantap down there at Syuxtun. She's obsessed with status. What I say is, let the kids be fishermen or something. At least they won't have to put up with job stress the way their old man does. Anyway, she's wasting her time on the youngest one. He's a lousy little hoodlum; I had to beat him when he was up here last summer. Caught him stealing! It's a shame when you have to say it about your own flesh and blood, always assuming he is, of course, but the kid's just no good."

This met with frowns from his fellow sweat-lodge members.

"Huh." Nutku cleared his throat. "Kantap's a good start in life for a boy, though, you know. It might turn him around. He'd be running with the right crowd, too, not a bunch of losers like hunters. The kantap made *you* what you are, that's for sure."

"Oh, well, of course," Kupiuc hastened to say. "Don't get me wrong. But I'm not made of money, am I?" His charmstone was describing ever faster and tighter circles in his palm.

"Just don't put the kantap down," growled Sawlawlan, and went into a coughing fit that lasted two whole minutes. I scanned him idly. Twenty years of carving steatite had left his lungs lined with talc. He had hemorrhoids, too. Rich as he was, he must have been miserable most of the time.

"You've got to have a word with the boys up at Skax-pilil, by the way." Nutku splashed a little water in Kupiuc's direction. "It looks as though they've been letting redwood consignments through again. I think they're stockpiling. Might be time for a little Miwok lightning."

"Stockpiling?" I inquired.

"We've got an agreement with the towns up north, Sky Coyote. Don't You do this kind of thing in the Upper World? They hold back on their redwood export, and we can keep the price of redwood canoes nice and high."

"That's pretty clever!" I said ingenuously. "Of course, wouldn't that mean most people can't afford them?"

"Right, so they buy pine. Which means they have to get a new one every sixteen moons. Either way, big profits." Nutku looked hard at Kupiuc. "So any bastard planning to flood the market with cheap redwood had better have his inventory torched before he gets the chance. Understand?"

"Nutku, I've got it under control. Trust me." Flip, flip, flip went the charmstone.

"We may not be the dealers You guys are in the Upper World, but we know a few tricks, huh?" Nutku grinned at me. He leaned forward conspiratorially. "So, what about a little straight talk on this white men thing, Sky Coyote?"

"Straight talk?" I looked as innocent as I could. It's not easy with pointed ears and fangs.

"Come on, Sky Coyote, You can level with us. The metaphors are okay for the little people, but we're community leaders. We know how the game's really played. These white men, is that some kind of code phrase for the Chinigchinix crazies down south? You can't mean there's an invasion planned? Why should they invade us? They need us. They can't produce any trade goods worth mentioning."

"Stranger things have happened," I told him. "But, no. The white men are somebody else entirely, and they really are going to invade you. In fact, their advance forces have already been scouting your coast. You know those funny-looking canoes that landed at Syuxtun? The strangers you sold all those baskets to?" I leaned back lazily and smiled at Kaxiwalic.

As my words sank in, he froze in the act of pouring more water on the rocks.

"What?"

"Remember those fancy new patterns you had designed for souvenirs? Those people, remember? Didn't they look just the teensiest bit, oh, *white* to you?"

"Actually some of them were black—but—" His mouth hung open.

"So they're real?" Nutku looked grim. "Well, so what? They're only men like we are, then. They want to invade us? We'll see about that. Our war parties can kick ass like nobody's business."

"What's it going to take to get through to you guys?" I barked. "This is not just an invasion. This is a cosmic matter. There are Big Players in this game. The white men and the Chumash are just pawns."

Kupiuc stared. "So there really is a World Above."

"Do I look like I've come from the next village over? Of *course* there's a World Above. Look, I'll level with you. You all understand, I'm sure, that there are times when you have to let out information in a strictly controlled way. You're not lying, exactly. Just telling the truth strategically. You all follow me?"

They nodded tensely.

"All right, so we've been a little vague with you about Life Up There. It isn't all that different from life down here, if you want the truth. It's a power struggle. You have to play the game to win. You guys would understand that.

"Now, your lives are a commodity to us, like any other commodity. Some of us have vested interests in you. Others are more interested in controlling the rate of flow." I made my eyes mean and small. I canted the tips of my ears forward. "With you guys it's shell money. With us it's human lives. My stock goes up when there are a lot of you running around. But the other party—and you can go on calling

Him the Sun—does good business when lots of you die off.

"So I've had inside information on a move He's planning, this white-men business. If I can pull my capital—all of you, I mean—in time, I can protect most of it and transfer to a long-term investment. He'll flood the market with His invading force, and I'll take a loss, but I won't be wiped out. See? Then He'll have wasted a lot of His resources. I can pull back, draw on my reserves, and hit Him in the next game, and He'll be at a disadvantage because He won't know about my secret strategy this time around. And *that's* how the game is played by the Big Boys, nephews." Whew.

They sat there in shock a minute or two. At last Sawlawlan moved uneasily on his rock and said, "Well, I never thought the universe worked quite like that . . . But, you know, now that I think about it, it's sort of comforting. I mean, this is a system I understand, anyway."

"Yeah," said Nutku.

"And it's not like we were unimportant or anything," ventured Kaxiwalic. "We're vital parts of the big plan, aren't we?"

"Sure you are."

"Hell, yes, we must be, or Sky Coyote wouldn't be here! Right, Coyote?" Kupiuc looked narrow-eyed and astute. "The good-and-evil stuff is just a front. It's business up there just like it's business down here." He squeezed his charmstone tight.

"And you smart boys figured it out instinctively." I smiled with all my sharp and pointed teeth. "The priests are all chasing moonbeams, but leave it to the real leaders to understand the truth." They all basked in that for a moment, then Nutku cleared his throat again.

"So, um, Sky Coyote . . . what about *our* investments?"

"I knew you were coming to that."

"Kaxiwalic mentioned something about losing our markets . . . ?"

"I won't lie to you. Sure, you'll take a loss—but not the way everybody else will. So, where does that put you? Ahead of the game, right? Which will make you insiders when we get to where we're going. And, Kaxiwalic, chum: don't get too worried about our little conversation the other day. I mean, one of your producers was standing right there! Do you think I'd let one of *them* in on this?"

That lightened up a couple of faces, and I rushed on. "Plus—and listen up, this is a big plus—think of the aggravation you're leaving behind! Ex-wives. Fanatic cultist trading partners. Redwood overstock. Okay? And as for all your existing inventory, hey, all I can say is, sell out now. How, you ask, it's winter! Sea's too rough to go on the trade routes. Land's a mess with mud, and there's hungry bears and mountain lions on the trails. Well, I can bring in buyers who'll take it all off your hands! And at retail prices, too! Canoes, bowls, baskets, the whole works, AT RETAIL! You can liquidate all your assets, and when we get to the new place, you'll be the ones with the capital to get the ball rolling in the new game. And believe me, boys, it'll be a new game. There are easier ways to make a living than chipping stone bowls. Can you trust your Uncle Sky Coyote?"

Nutku clenched his fists. "You guarantee you can unload my inventory before we go?"

"I said retail, didn't I?" I replied cheerfully, leaning forward to slosh some hot water on the stones and cloud the issue. I didn't know where Beckman, our art curator, was going to get all that shell money, but that wasn't my department.

Chapter 20 ✆

As it turned out, all this had been foreseen, and Beckman had enough cash with him to buy a couple of museums, let alone a luxury canoe. If he'd worn all his money, he couldn't have stood upright, of course. Instead, he stood unburdened in one discreet but high-denomination strand of shells, a deerskin jockstrap, and green body paint, with the rest of the loot carried in satchels by a couple of burly techs.

They waited patiently with the rest of the salvage team in the icy breeze coming off the Pacific. I could see them waiting as I hopped out of my knee breeches. Actually, some of them weren't waiting so patiently.

"And here he comes! The star player! Yaay!" I went sprinting out to them. Fourteen freezing specialists and thirty security techs glared at me, and nobody cheered. With the goose pimples, green paint, and skimpy Chumash costumes, they looked like a bunch of avocados in a diorama.

"Does it get any warmer away from this goddam beach?" Mendoza wanted to know.

"Sure it does. This is California," I told her. "Now, everybody, probably we won't encounter any locals until we reach the village. I never give them any clear idea of when I'm going to visit them, so I don't think they'll shoot at you or anything, but let me go first and do all the talking.

Everyone accessed their language files last night, riiiight?"

"Riiiight," they echoed in sour unison.

"Heads up, everybody, here comes Bugleg," hissed MacCool.

Yes, here came our fearless leader, out to review the troops, shepherded by his faithful dog or puppet master, whichever view of Lopez one preferred. They emerged from the base, and Bugleg stood there blinking rapidly in the wind. I don't think he got outdoors much.

I saluted briskly. "Hello, Mr. Bugleg. Any words of inspiration for us before we hit the beach?"

"What did you say?" He looked bewildered. "This is the beach. I thought you were going to the native huts."

"Figure of speech, sir. Beach, front lines, salt mines, trenches. Engaging the enemy. Going off into the wild blue yonder. Beginning the beguine. Setting off on our mission." *Damn it, Joseph!* broadcast Lopez, and I gave him a coyote grin and responded, *Sorry, I've really gotten into my role.* Bugleg's face meanwhile was desperate as he dodged my metaphors and caught the only phrase he understood.

"Oh," he said. "Oh. I hope it goes all right. Okay? Be careful, everybody."

It was a wonder the massed wave of scorn projected at him through the ether didn't knock him off his feet, to say nothing of the silently transmitted raspberries. Careful? Mortal man, we're immortals! We tread water through the Great Flood! Ashur over there got out of Pompeii a month before things got hot, sold his house at a profit too: he could hear the mountain grumbling in its heart. Imarte can smell a Turk coming a mile away, was well clear of Byzantium before the fall. I saw the writing on the wall myself, at Tyre: never mind what it said, but I left on a fast horse the same day. Beckman's never booked passage for a shipwreck, or stood on a wobbly scaffold. Careful? Mortal, you don't know what careful is.

Though of course nobody looked scornful, because that would have been rude. Instead everyone said out loud,

"Thank you, Mr. Bugleg," in a quiet and nonthreatening way. He turned to me and complained, "They're all green. Why?"

"Local folklore, sir, remember? They're supposed to be supernatural beings."

"Oh." He nodded. I think he comprehended, even though *supernatural* is five whole syllables long. "And everybody is going in just like we planned?"

"Right. We have a zoologist, an art curator, a botanist, a marine biologist, a geologist, a, primary cultural anthropologist, a primary physical anthropologist, and six class-two anthropologists to work in teams with the other specialists."

"But what if the natives shoot at them?"

"Well, sir, that's what the security techs are for, isn't it? And they'll also help us transport artifacts." Bugleg blanked on that one. "You know, the things the Indians make. Beads and stuff? Souvenirs?"

"All right." He shivered. "You better get started. I don't like it out here. Too cold."

"Yes, sir, it's very cold."

"I'm going inside." He turned and left.

We set off, up the long canyon. Behind us there was a mortal face at every window.

"Symbolic, isn't it?" Beside me, Mendoza settled her pack.

"What?"

"Mortals behind us, mortals ahead of us. We're always in the middle, trudging up some blind canyon with our collecting gear, bare-ass naked."

"You're not bare-ass naked; you're in colorful local costume," I reproved. "I bet you're wishing you had your Madrid fashions on now, huh?"

"And how," muttered a dozen immortals.

But their spirits rose as we got inland, away from the wind. The sky was blue, the sun was warm, and nobody was shooting at us: basic elemental pleasures like that.

More, though: we were finally away from all the bureaucratic crap and going out where we could do some work at
last. We were on the job again. It produces a sense of eu-
phoria in us. We were designed that way.

And we certainly had time to do what we'd come to do.
Seventy years at least before Father Serra, bless or damn
his well-meaning soul as you like, limps up the coast to
found his mission system. Twice that long before the Yankee boys see Spanish estates the size of minor kingdoms,
all empty and pastoral, and decide these lazy *Gentes de
Razón* must be pretty damn dumb not to see the money
they could be making if they'd cut down the oak trees and
build towns. Two hundred years and then some before the
engineer Mulholland throws open the sluice on his new
aqueduct and yells, "There it is—take it!" as somebody
else's water cascades down to a host of real estate developers and orange growers. Putting in five words the creed
of everyone who'll ever lay eyes on this poor California.

Well. Come genocide, come developers, come pollution
and urban war. Let 'em do their worst: we can clone even
Eden, if we get there before the Serpent and take samples.

Chapter 21 ✺

I LED EVERYBODY up the back of the big hill that overlooked the village. We paused on the summit to look down at the little houses and work yards and the tiny figures going to and fro. "Humashup," I announced.

"Okay, we're fanning out," announced the head security tech, and he and the other members of his team vanished into the sagebrush, leaving their packs for the rest of us to carry. Within seconds even we couldn't tell where they were, but we knew they'd be down there doing invisible surveillance.

"It's *perfect!*" said Imarte, eyes shining. "Look, there are children playing the hoop game—and that must be the cemetery—oh my god, they're making canoes over there!"

"See the shell mound?" Beckman said, shading his eyes. "That's not a midden. Those are money shells. And that man's cutting abalone shell for inlay work . . ." The others crowded close to see, muttering excitedly. Only Mendoza stood apart. I looked over at her.

She'd barely noticed the village. She was staring beyond it into the land, green and rolling with huge oak trees like gods, rolling away to green and blue mountains. She was breathing in the scent of the aromatic brush on the hills, the sage and the agave with its white spires of clustered flowers. She was taking in the cloud shadows and the pattern the wind made coming across the savanna before it

140

funneled into the canyon and carried away the smoke from the cooking fires of Humashup.

I know it's pretty wild and empty, but it won't be so bad, I transmitted to her. No reply, but a sound I couldn't describe exactly, kind of a throbbing sound, kind of a storm sound. What was she tuning in to that I couldn't hear? She turned her head slowly to stare at me, and her eyes were a thousand years away. I shivered. Last time I'd seen that look, it was on a nun whose palms had suddenly and inexplicably begun to bleed. *You okay, Mendoza?*

Her brows drew together in a faint frown, as if she'd just noticed me.

"This is the most beautiful place I've ever seen," she replied. "How could anybody cut down those trees?"

I went and took her by the arm. "Nobody's going to start for a while, but you've still got plenty of work to do. Come on."

There's always a letdown after first contact with an endangered species. You get real moved at the thought of saving all those mortal lives, and then you actually meet the mortals and it's sort of a disappointment. Except for the anthropologists. They love mortals. Good thing, too.

In spite of my careful preparation for this moment, the people of Humashup did not take it well when they beheld a crowd of green beings descending the green hillside. Men stared and rummaged for their spears, women ducked inside their houses, children ran screaming after the women who had ducked inside the houses.

"Children! Children! There's nothing to be afraid of!" I barked. "Don't you know friendly spirits when you see them?" Sepawit had come out of the council house and was standing there with his mouth open, watching us approach. I caught his eye. He turned and waved his hands frantically.

"It's all right, everyone! It's only Sky Coyote and his spirits! It's *green* men, not white men! Come on back, all of you!"

Actually it took about an hour to calm down the populace of Humashup and entice them to an orderly assembly, during which time my fellow immortals stood awkward and embarrassed in their viridian near nudity. Except the anthropologists: they ran around with little cries of delight, taking notes and holo shots of everything.

"Thank you all for coming," I said at last, pacing before the silent and staring village. "You mustn't be afraid of my servants! Why, except for the fact that they're green, they look just like you, don't they? And you all know I'd never do you harm. I've brought them here to collect things. You see, I'm not just saving all of you, I'm saving this world. I'll want to build it again someday, so I'm having my servants collect a little of everything: the plants, the animals, the stones and shells. They're also here to collect wisdom, to collect your knowledge of these things. You must help them by answering any questions they ask you. Be truthful. Don't lie about anything. After all, if you lie, I might make some mistakes the next time I create this world."

The crowd took that in, and there were a lot of thoughtful nods as they accepted it. The concept of an infallible deity was going to be something new to the Chumash.

"I mean, you wouldn't want me to make a world where the creeks flowed blood, or the oaks grew bones instead of acorns, would you?" Scattered laughter and shudders.

"We do things a little differently in the World Above. When we spirits relax, we like to sit down to a big heaping bowlful of rabbit pellets with a few rattlesnake heads scattered on top for that extra burst of flavor"—screams of delighted laughter—"but somehow I don't think that would suit you folks very well. So it's very important for you to give good, truthful answers to the spirits. Otherwise, who knows what people could find themselves eating?

"Now, tell me: Who are the best hunters here? Who's the best at bringing down the deer, the ducks and geese?" Quite a few skinny guys stepped forth uncertainly. I nodded to MacCool and the anthropologist Giovanna. They advanced out of the group.

"Good! Now, this man is the Spirit Who Catches Animals. He needs to catch two of all the animals you hunt. That woman is the Spirit Who Collects Hunting Wisdom. All of you hunters go over there with them and talk for a while, all right?"

They went obediently, and I beckoned to Mendoza and her team anthropologist, Dalton.

"Now, who among you ladies is the very best at gathering roots out of the earth, or greens in the rainy season? You members of the Deer Grass Gatherers' Union, where are you? You herbal healers, you women of wisdom, where are you? Only the wisest, mind you."

A number of hefty dames pushed their way forward, elbowing one another out of the way. There was a brief nasty squabble about which of them was the wisest woman of wisdom, and in the end I had to promise them they'd all get a turn at talking. I sent them away with the Spirit Who Collects Plants and the Spirit Who Gathers Herb Lore.

The rest of it went pretty peacefully. There was the Spirit Who Fishes, and the Spirit Who Collects Dirt, and the Spirit Who Wants to Know about Your Sex Life, and so on. Various elements of the population went off to sit under oak trees and talk with them, until at last there were only Beckman with his satchels and me. My executive pals from the steam bath had been waiting in a group, eyeing the satchel.

Nutku put up his hand. "That's the Spirit Who Buys at Retail, right?"

"Yes! This is the spirit whose coming I foretold to you." I grinned, tongue lolling. They converged on Beckman like sharks on a swimmer.

"Hey, spirit. I've got canoes! Beautiful canoes, all redwood models, with every luxury feature. Retrievable paddles, spear racks, mother-of-pearl inlay, I've got two-seaters, three-seaters, hell, I've even got a couple of war canoes at prices you won't find anywhere else!"

"You want baskets? I've got the best. Two-color, three-color, even four-color, large and small. Unbelievable patterns, also custom work!"

"*No* finer pots and bowls anywhere, guaranteed not to crack, and they're fireproof! Polished, carved, and inlaid by the finest craftsmen. We also carry utility vessels, hand mills, storage basins, durable kitchenware in designs that'll grace the poorest camp or the richest house. Ask me about our line of novelties, too!"

So they bore him off, and I heard his voice lifted and the rattle of his coin.

Neat stuff was acquired and sent back to the base for storage every night, already tagged and context-catalogued. Chumash kitchenware. Chumash clothing. Chumash tools. Chumash medical supplies. Chumash sporting goods. Chumash diapers. Chumash birthday presents.

The anthropologists became great favorites, because they were so friendly. They recorded endless hours of Chumash voices speaking at great length on every conceivable subject. Their eyes recorded weeks of footage of Chumash life. Women pounding acorns. Men carving stoneware. A birth. Sports. A death. Courtship. Commercial fishing. They collected the people, too: DNA samples were taken, and each individual was catalogued and described under his or her entry by gender, age, profession, and genetic code. All two hundred and thirty-six or -seven inhabitants of Humashup, tidily listed for the big cargo manifest.

This is not to say that things went smoothly, however ... though the Chumash weren't the problem.

"A *feast?*" Bugleg looked blanker than usual. "At night?"

"Yes, sir. The Chumash would like to throw us a party." I pulled out a chair and sat down, since I hadn't been invited to. "They'd like to show off some of their dances and stuff, and the anthropologists are thrilled. It'll be a great opportunity to record cultural material actually on location, you see. Their ceremonies and rituals aren't just performed every day. They're making a special occasion for us."

"Rituals," Bugleg repeated. "Ceremonies. Is that the same thing as a *cult?* That sounds scary. They're not going to kill people, are they?"

"No, no, no," Lopez hastened to assure him. "This will be a peaceful celebration, sir. And though it does require that we relax our regulations concerning base curfew for one night, it should prove well worth it."

"Why do we have to do that?"

"Why, so the operatives can all attend, sir," I explained. "They've been working pretty closely with the Chumash, and if they didn't show up after being invited, it would cause hurt feelings. Plus, the operatives *really* want to go. So it'll be all those who have gone on the collecting trips and the security teams who'll guard the perimeter, and everybody'll be out all night. Now, to do this, we need you to sign your name on this plaquette that says it's okay, because the rules say officially we can't have that many base personnel out after dark at one time." And I pushed the plaquette before him and put a stylus into his nerveless hand.

He wasn't happy. "I don't know. It doesn't sound safe."

"Oh, no, sir, it's safe. I mean, what can hurt us? We're immortal, remember?"

"I know that." He pursed his lips. "I didn't mean for you. I meant for us. We'd be alone here with all the security techs away from us. What if the natives attacked? If they play their drums and dance, they might attack. What would happen then?"

"Oh, but sir, they won't do that," Lopez assured him. "The operatives will be right there with them. If the Chumash tried anything of the kind, they'd all be stunned into submission, you see?"

"Though they won't do anything like that, sir, honest," I stated. "They're nice people, when you get to know them. Really."

"But they have rituals and dances," said Bugleg in distaste. "And they catch animals and kill them." His eyes widened as a horrid thought occurred to him. "A feast is where they catch an animal and cook it on a big fire, isn't it? Are they going to do that?"

Lopez and I looked at each other.

"Well, only an animal that's already dead, sir," Lopez told him at last. "It's not as though it's being hurt in any way."

"But there'll be—bones, and muscles, and . . ." Bugleg's face was going pale, either with the slaughterhouse mental pictures he must have been forming or with the effort of forming them, it was hard to say which.

"It's true, sir, meat in its natural state does have bones in it," I agreed. "But the natives are okay with that, and so are we. We're used to it, remember."

"But I'm not!" He clenched the edge of the table. "This is gross. And I just thought of something! You're all, 'Only dead animals will be cooked,' but that still means somebody will kill the animals, doesn't it? And you can't do that! You can't have *rituals* and . . . and all that other stuff! I won't sign permission. It's too nasty and scary."

"Oh, we won't kill anything," I told him earnestly. "The Chumash will be doing the hunting. Honest."

"But they'll be killing animals and you'll eat them. No. Nobody in the Company can do this while I'm in charge. You Old People get away with a whole lot, but you can't do this." He folded his arms. "No weird rituals."

I gave Lopez a long, meaningful glance.

"Wait a minute, wait a minute, I know what the trouble is!" I slapped my brow. "You thought—but how silly—I somehow gave you the impression that there were animal sacrifices going on. Wasn't that dumb! No, no, sir, no actual real live animals will be killed for this feast. No, we explained to the Chumash our feelings about that. It so happens they've got an ingenious way of fabricating protein out of, uh, acorn meal and soya flour, which they then sculpt into the shapes of animals, and *that's* what's actually consumed at the feasts. See?"

Bugleg wasn't quite that dumb. "But you were all, 'Meat in its natural state does have bones in it,' " he quoted. "You said about eating blood and bones and muscles. I heard you."

"Well, sure, but not at a party," I explained. "Hey, I can't fool you. You know that savages eat meat sometimes, and you know we Old Ones do too now and then. But, my God, you don't think we'd do it where anybody else could see! At a *party*? In front of other people? Gosh, even the Chumash would think that was crude. No, seriously, sir, the only animals we'll be eating will be pretend ones."

"Oh. Okay." There was actual comprehension in his eyes. He knew about hiding appetites where nobody could see them. I wondered what the games in his private entertainment console were like. "I guess that would be all right."

"Thank you for understanding, sir." Lopez guided his hand to the signature line. "This will help ensure that the mission is a tremendous success. Your superiors in the Company will be very, very pleased with you."

"That would be nice," he replied, obediently signing. "But it's more important to be sure no animals die."

It dawned on me then that he was actually standing up for a principle here, not just being ignorant and squeamish. I felt bad about lying to him, for a second or two. Lopez caught up the plaquette as soon as it had registered Bugleg's signature. "Authorization cleared! Let the festivities commence."

Chapter 22 ❧

IT BROUGHT BACK memories, let me tell you, hurrying through the dark canyon to the distant lights, with smoke and excitement on the wind. Party time! Behind me on the trail, they might have been tribal members and not anthropologists, all giggly with anticipation. How often are you invited to go back to the first days of the world, when evening dress consisted of feathers and beads?

The Humashup Municipal Sports Field had been co-opted for the party, neatly swept and fenced around with woven tule screens to keep out the wind. Only the side facing the sacred enclosure was open, framed by a doorway of whale ribs painted red, and a big fire burned there to light the dancing ground. Outside the field were cooking fires where people were lined up for helpings of barbecued venison and abalone-shell bowlfuls of acorn mush. One or two from each family were sent on the line to get as much as they could carry back to the others, who had staked out places with picnic blankets and woven drinking jugs. Everybody stopped what they were doing, though, to stare as we made our entrance: Sky Coyote and his spirits!

I wore my usual fur ensemble, but the rest of the team members hadn't been able to bring themselves to tough it out in green makeup alone, so they were wrapped in an interesting assortment of capes and cloaks of European design. *Eclectic* wasn't a strong enough word for the combination of cottonwood fiber G-strings and Florentine velvet brocade.

"Children! Good to see you again." I held out my forepaws as we swept in. "I hope we're not late?"

"Not at all, Sky Coyote, not at all." Sepawit rose from his party blanket, handing off a greasy toddler with a half-chewed rib bone to Mrs. Sepawit. "Please! We've saved a place of honor for You, here by the banners." He stepped through the crowd, escorting us to our seats. People scrunched over to make way for us, and there were several admiring and envious comments on the fashion parade. "We've even set out a buffet for You, here in the corner. Plenty of venison and side dishes, courtesy of the ladies of the Eelgrass Gatherers' Union, and lots of jugs of manzanita punch and chia tea. If there's anything else we can provide, we've got servers ready to fetch it for you immediately."

What a fabulous view! Imarte rhapsodized. *Look at this, look, we're right in line with the sacred enclosure!*

"This place pleases us," I announced. "Be seated, spirits. Sepawit, have I got time for a whizz before the ceremonies commence?"

"Certainly, Sky Coyote. This way." Sepawit and I stepped away discreetly through a break in the screen wall to where a latrine trench had been dug, special for the evening's festivities. We faced out into the dark and addressed the trench.

"Looks like everybody's in a celebratory mood," I remarked.

"They're thrilled," replied Sepawit. "Nervous, You know, because this isn't like performing for some other village's visiting dignitaries. I'm sure You've seen better dancing in the World above This One."

"You'd be surprised." I scanned the dark in infrared, spotting our security techs silent and motionless out there in the night. "Some gods don't care much for fun. My group are all set to enjoy themselves, though!"

"I think they'll be pleased with what the kantap's pre-pared," Sepawit told me. "They're really quite talented, our guys, remarkable artists, considering they're businessmen too. Um . . . by the way, Coyote. I suppose You're aware of everything that's going on in this world . . . You'd tell me if we were in any danger from, ah, other tribes, wouldn't You? Like for instance those people we talked about?"

"The Chinigchinix cult? Of course. They can't hurt you, Sepawit, not with me here. What's got you worrying?"

"Oh, just that I'm overdue for a report from my Speaker. I sent him south to gather facts . . . He should have returned by now, that's all." Sepawit finished and stepped back from the edge. I felt bad for him. He was looking out into a darkness a lot blacker than the night, from the edge of a pit much deeper and filled with nastier stuff.

"I can't answer for your Speaker, Sepawit. You know that bad things happen. You've got my word for it, though: I'll keep *you* safe, you and everybody here tonight," I told him.

"I believe You," he sighed, rubbing where his ulcer was hurting him.

We went back in, and Sepawit picked his way through the crowd to the fire, where he raised both hands for atten-tion.

"Everybody? We're just about ready to start"—assorted cheers from the multitude, spirits and villagers alike—"so settle down and get comfortable. Before we begin, I'd like to remind all of you to thank the Civic Works Committee for the great job they did on fixing up the hoop field at such short notice. And let's not make their job tomorrow any more difficult by leaving trash around, all right? Wherever you're sitting, be sure to look around you when you leave and pick up any bones or leaf wrappings or what-ever you may have discarded in the course of the evening and make sure you throw them in the latrine where they belong. Agreed?" There were grumbles of assent from various quarters. Somebody far to the back yelled:

"We want a SHOW!"

"Yeah!!" shrieked one of our anthropologists gleefully.
I turned around with a stern look. Got to preserve cosmic
order, after all. Everybody took the hint and focused attention on the sacred enclosure, except for MacCool, who was
solicitously offering Mendoza a bowl of acorn mush. She
was declining politely, looking through him.

"All right, all right!" Sepawit looked toward the sacred
enclosure for a cue. "Just sit tight, folks, because I think—
are we? We are? Here we go!"

He stepped back into the shadows as a drumming ca-
dence began and was picked up by a shrill chorus of whistles. From an unseen place the music grew louder, until it
was an alert, a warning, like flashing lights. Someone invisible threw something on the fire, and colored flames
leaped up. Out of the darkness came a long low growl, a
sound to raise the hackles on an old operative who remembered cave bears. Hold on: where was it coming from? Was
it drooling out of the shadows behind us? From over here?
Over there? *Had something come down from the hills?*
Every member of the audience shivered and crouched
down, but nobody could look away from the leaping
flames.

There! It was a bear, shambling forward out of the enclosure. It was a grizzly, turning his head this way and that
to smell the air. He shrugged his humping shoulders and
muscled up on hind legs, weaving from side to side. You
could see the costume feathers and Nutku's face, you knew
it was only him, but there was another dimension here. In
cities, in theaters in Europe at this very moment, with carriages drawn up outside and grease-painted players on dusty
boards, it would be called suspension of disbelief. Here it
was something a lot more profound, and it tugged at my
heart painfully.

It was a grizzly, and it was the power in Nutku's shoulders, and it was the thing you *think* might be a bear when

you're all alone on the trail and you've caught a glimpse, maybe, of a profile in the trees. It was that thing in the wild that makes your blood run cold. Though it fascinates, too, because you can't look away from what might be—what is—Death Himself standing on hind legs.

And here came crouched things, moving slow, shaking rattles of turtle shell in perfect time with the weaving dance of the bear. First one, then another, then a third set up a droning hum, three harmonic tones blending in an eerie wail. It rose in pitch. It became a melody with chanted words.

> *Listen up now, listen for your life,*
> *Show's about to start, the star is here, I am here,*
> *Tooth and claw, Murder on two legs,*
>   *Murder on four legs!*
> *Am I man? Am I beast? I'm POWER in the flesh!*
> *Do you feel me stamping, feel the weight of my step?*
> *Do you see the torn earth, see tree bark*
>   *hanging in shreds?*
> *Do you hear that groan, that cough that means*
> *It's time to hit the trail? Can you outrun me?*
>
> *No, don't move! Watch now and pray.*
> *He grunts, up there in the trees where you*
>   *can't see him.*
> *Is that an earthquake, or just him coming?*
> *Last night he came to a house,*
> *They thought it was a thunderclap, that noise,*
> *Rocking wind and rattling hail,*
> *Even when the walls cracked and split,*
> *Even when the Night came in for them.*
>
> *Oh, get out of my way!*
> *I am the One with the Raking Hand,*
> *I am the Mountain Come Walking,*
> *I am Power and No Reason!*

Is there anywhere safe from me,
Any corner of the world I don't own?
Pray I don't walk on my two legs to your house.
I am Power and No Reason!

The words trailed away, but the tune grew louder now and the music stepped up its rattling pace. The audience was frozen in place, even we immortals, because Bear was pacing among us. We could see the glint of his little malignant eyes, and those weren't costume feathers brushing us but rank fur. The clumsy shuffle wasn't funny, didn't make you think of country fairs and fiddlers, oh no; it was scary as hell, because we all knew it wasn't old Nutku in there, it was a dark god.

The menacing flutes and rattles led him through us, in and out of the rows of people, slowly questing after a scent, turning and turning his head to sniff the wind. Just about at the point where the tension was becoming intolerable, the music changed. Or was it the wind that changed? A whole string of little high notes made Bear lift his head: he'd caught the scent at last. He began to edge his way back out of the crowd, following that shrill refrain, and you could smell the relief in the audience as he shambled with deliberate steps for the arch of whalebone. *Chac chac chac,* the rattles led him on; *chac chac chac,* he nosed the doorway; he was almost through, the whistles very faint now; then abruptly, the fire blazed up as he whirled to stand, silhouetted black, claws up and threatening, and the flutes screamed out, and there was a thundering roll of the drums.

And blackout!

I gasped, able to breathe at last.

What had happened was that the kantap's special-effects genius had thrown a cover over the fire, a big woven lid lined with wet moss, and held it there a second in the darkness and confusion while Nutku made his exit. Then it was yanked away, and there was a dim light from the rekindling flames and a lot of smoke and coughing. People were laughing or sobbing with the release of tension. Stiff limbs were stretched. Old grandmothers with apple cheeks and droopy breasts shifted sleepy babies, a bunch of adolescent boys near the front whooped with sudden laughter like honking geese.

When the smoke had cleared and the buzz of talk had died away, a figure was revealed sitting alert and upright in the whalebone doorway. There were a lot of shy giggles and sidelong looks at me, then, because it was Coyote sitting there. It was Kaxiwalic, actually, in an eared hood with a long dog snout tied on over his nose, and in a little fur breechclout with a long tail attached behind and a long stuffed-fur penis attached in front.

I just grinned and laughed. Kaxiwalic waited until the snickers had died down before speaking.

"*Eeevening,* neighbors," he whined. "Got any food?" Which was apparently an old routine, because with delighted yells the audience began to hurl garbage at him. Gnawed bones and mussel shells clattered through the air, and he made a show of scampering about on all fours to retrieve them. He had the dog moves down perfectly: I could have learned a thing or two from him, especially when he leaped straight up to catch a flying deer rib in his teeth. He got a standing ovation and applause from my fellow immortals for that one.

"Thank you, thank you." He waved the bombardment to a stop. "You're all so kind! And what a turnout we have tonight, huh? What a lot of distinguished visitors from the World Above. Or is that a forest of trees?" An unseen drummer struck a double note you'd have sworn was a rim shot. Kaxiwalic peered through the darkness at us, shading his eyes. "No, no—some of them have tits. Definitely not trees. And look! There's my very own old Grandfather Sky Coyote! Grandpa, how's it going? Long time no see! Mama says you can come home now, by the way—the girl's brothers have all died and the baby was born without a tail!"

Whoops of appreciative laughter. A young mother wiped tears from her eyes, giggling, and her nursing baby pulled loose to chortle in empathy and clap his little fat hands. Kaxiwalic watched us all with bright eyes, judging the timing before he resumed:

"All right! On that spiritually uplifting note, I'd like to introduce a powerful ally. He's one tough customer, but we owe him a lot for driving those herds of seals up on the beach every year. Ladies, gentlemen, sky spirits, let's give a big welcome to—Killer Whale!"

Blackout again, and when the light rekindled, we looked on a scene of roiling waves, or maybe they were woven tule screens painted green and white and being moved from side to side by unobtrusive, hunkered figures. But you could hear the sea, thanks to the *boom-boom* of the big drums and the rattle and hiss of the small drums and percussion. It set up a counterpoint roll of surging surf that would have put Debussy to shame; we were all swaying in our seats in time to it. A flute came in with a string of ascending notes that were Killer Whale rising up through the depths, and sure enough he appeared, with a leap that took him clear of the green mats and with a spray of water.

It was Kupiuc, smooth naked, his big humped body painted gleaming black and white. Only around his neck he wore the bony jaws of a real killer whale, and he made the sharp teeth clash with the music. His eyes rolled white as he tossed his head, as he leaped and thrashed to the pounding drumbeats. He was telling us he was a king in his country, a fearsome hunter, that he had wives and power, that he knew how to go where none of us could go: down into green canyons and forests of waving weed, without any fear of storm. He told us, in his dance, about the silver flights of sardine he'd taken, about the runs of red-fleshed salmon, about his wars with Swordfish.

He sported before us in the sheer ebullience of being himself, a fine sea lord, but then his dance took on a menacing quality: he began to wheel and cruise, seeking something. He was on the hunt. Gradually we saw his prey, revealed a little at a time by the waving screens: one sleek brown head, then a second, then a third. Big frightened dog eyes and blunt muzzles. The seal dancers began to sing:

> Listen! Listen! He's on the wild water!
> He is everywhere, behind us, all around us!
> Oh, Grandfather, get us out of here!
> Why, oh, why did we ever leave the land?
> Maybe he'll kill a shark, and not me.
> Maybe he'll take a salmon, and not me.
> How much farther till we reach the shore?

One seal moved to the foreground, the dancer under the headdress floundering like a clumsy thing in panic. Kupiuc danced in place, his body semaphoring triumph. The seal dancer cried:

> Look at him, painted up to kill!
> Look at him, so beautiful!
> How can my death be so beautiful?
> Here under blue air, with white foam flying,
> Green water crashing, how can I die?

Here came the second seal, bobbing forward, singing:

> I lived, I had a mate, I had children,
> And now I'm cold, I'm old, too slow,
> Too slow! Twenty long seasons since
>   my head was big
> At Tuqan Island, and how slow I am now!
> And look at my scars! And my teeth are broken!
> But my lord is fine in his black and white!

Now the third seal, a big seal, joined them:

> How well I've fed! Sardines fed me, salmon fed me,
> All the little perch and mackerel fed me,

Made me too fat to escape! What will I feed?
Oh, how unfair it is, when life is so good!
Sleeping in the sun, and mating.
Why will this lord take it all away from me?

They cowered down all three, as Kupiuc leaped high. An unseen voice chanted:

Who said life was fair?
You run before me like leaves on the wind
To your certain deaths: but listen, listen,
You who love me, you old one, you fat one,
I'm not driving you to hear you cry,
I'm not driving you for cruel reasons.
Look up on the beach
Where Coyote's children wait for you
With swift spears, with quick clubs.
I'm driving you for them,
Because I'm sometimes kind:
Poor naked creatures,
Aren't they cold without your fur skins?
Aren't they lean without your rich fat?
Here in the white water it all ends,
Here in the breaking wave it all ends!

And the seals moved in one synchronized leap of agony, straight at a painted mat that was flung up before them, where the stylized figures of men with spears leaned out. Men and seals vanished under the mat as Killer Whale curvetted and jumped his triumph, and the music rose to accompany his gradual return to the sea, through the green mats whose motion was slowing. At last he vanished, with a last jet of spray, and the lights went down.

Beside me, Imarte shivered in ecstasy. "I can't believe this," she whispered. "I've never encountered a society where the businessmen were also the entertainers."

"Hey, you're in California, remember?" I grinned at her and reached for a nice fat venison rib.

The lights were coming up again. Coyote came dancing out between the red whale bones, deliberately making his penis bob in time with his steps. When he threw out his hands and stopped, it kept dancing up and down as though it had a life of its own. He pretended to notice and did an elaborate double take. The audience tittered.

"Hey! What do you think you're doing? *I* stopped dancing," he admonished it.

"So?" it replied. "You think you're the only one who feels like dancing now and then?" This guy was some ventriloquist! "Why should the party stop, just because *you* get tired?"

"Because I'm the one in charge around here, that's why!" shouted Coyote.

"Oh really?" The penis craned up as though it were staring balefully at him. It was a clever puppet, it had to be a puppet, but I was damned if I could see how it worked. "So you're the big chief, huh?"

"That's right!" Coyote told it, backing up a little as though he were intimidated, but of course the penis stayed right with him.

"I don't think so," it replied.

"You what? You've got your nerve!" shouted Coyote. "I'm the one who decides where we go. I'm the one who decides when we wake, when we sleep, when we play. I'm the one . . ." But his penis was shaking its head.

"Suppose you're relaxing on a nice warm sandy beach, but I see a pretty girl and decide to go talk to her. Do you think you get to sleep in the sun? Uh-uh."

"Well, maybe, but—"

"And suppose you're hungry and digging for roots, but I see a pretty girl. You're going to go hungry a while longer!"

"Well, that's happened, but—"

"But nothing! *I'm* the one who calls the shots around

here. And from now on, I'm not just hanging around."

"Oh, yeah?"

"Yeah! I'm going to have my own social life. To begin with, I'm not riding around down here anymore, I'm going to perch on top of your head."

Coyote was aghast. "You can't do *that!* I'll look ridiculous?"

"You think I'm not tired of looking ridiculous? Now it's your turn. Besides, the brains belong on top! When I see a woman I want to talk to, no more arguments! We're going right to bed with her. Bear's wife, for example. Eagle's wife! We'll jump in the furs with her right away."

"We can't do that!" cried Coyote. "Eagle will kill me! Bear will too!"

"What do I care? Did you ever care what happened to me when you went diving in the cold surf?" The penis shivered dramatically. "If Bear or Eagle beat you up, too bad for you. We're doing things my way now!"

"We're not!" Coyote shouted.

"And another thing! I'm tired of being bald! I want a nice toupee of otter fur. The most expensive kind!"

Oh, the people were rolling on the ground, crying with laughter.

"You must be crazy!" Coyote yelled, after a pause to let them quiet down. "Where do you think I'm going to get that kind of money?"

"You just get it, that's all, or else!" The penis reared threateningly.

"Oh, yeah?" said Coyote furiously, glaring down at it. "Or else what?"

By way of answer the penis squirted a stream of water into his face. The audience roared. "Aaargh!" Coyote shook his head wildly, wiping his eyes. He took a swing at the penis, which dodged out of the way.

"Ha ha ha! See how *you* like a faceful of that stuff!" the penis told him. Coyote swung at it again, and it dodged the other way. Back and forth, back and forth it dodged as he tried to hit it. "Missed me, missed me!" it jeered.

At last Coyote mimed *I'll fix HIM* to the audience. He brought both fists up together in the air over his head, clasped them together as though he were gripping a sledge-hammer handle, and brought them down on his penis with all his might. BOOM, went the drums, and the flutes screamed once. Coyote froze, his face a mask of astonishment.

For a minute there was absolute silence, except for the audience, who were leaning and clutching at one another in their howling merriment. Coyote remained standing perfectly still, and then he began to blink very fast. Flutter flutter, went his eyelids, though nothing else moved. Then his toes curled.

The drums began a roll, building steadily to a crescendo, and at their height Coyote leaped backward, falling down and spinning wildly on his back. "YIPE YIPE YIPE! I've killed him, I've killed him, oh, help, somebody!"

"What's the matter? What's all the noise about?" A figure came running out between the whale bones. It was Sawlawlan, but judging from his little fur hat and the black paint on his hands and around his eyes, he was supposed to be Raccoon.

"I've, uh, injured myself," groaned Coyote.

"Oh, my goodness, how terrible!" Raccoon threw up his little black hands in dismay. "What did you do?"

"Well . . . I was asleep behind a rock on the beach, and my penis is so long, it was lying out along the sand, and some men came along and thought it was a redwood tree washed up. They tried to split it into planks, and now it's dead!" Coyote told him.

"Poor Coyote! It certainly looks dead." Gingerly Raccoon reached down and lifted it by the tip. He let go, and it flopped lifelessly. Coyote howled.

"Don't worry, Coyote! I'll get help. Everyone, call with me!" Raccoon implored us. "Call out like this: Help! Help! Coyote's penis won't stand up!"

"COYOTE'S PENIS WON'T STAND UP!" we all yelled. Coyote looked indignant.

"That's right! All together now! Coyote needs help to get his penis up!"

"COYOTE NEEDS HELP TO GET HIS PENIS UP!" shouted the reverend elders, and the fathers and mothers, and the bright-eyed children.

"Hey!" Coyote protested. "Don't tell people that. Call for help some other way. Tell them—I broke my fishing spear."

"If you say so. Help! Help! Coyote broke his fishing spear!"

"What's that?" Through the whalebone door came Kupiuc, still all black and white but with feather ornaments now, and a beaked mask instead of teeth.

"Oh, Cormorant, I'm so glad you're here!" cried Raccoon. "Coyote hurt his—"

"My fishing spear," said Coyote.

"His fishing spear?" Cormorant cocked his head and looked at Coyote out of one eye. "I didn't know you were a fisherman, Coyote."

"Of course I am! I'm a famous and clever fisherman, only I've broken my spear and I can't fish just now!" snapped Coyote.

"You look like you've hurt your penis, too," said Cormorant, moving his neck snakily, considering Coyote from another angle.

"Nonsense! Nothing wrong with it at all!"

"But—but—" Raccoon pulled at his ears in bewilderment.

"If you have got a spare fishing spear you could lend me, I'd be much obliged," Coyote continued, gritting his teeth.

"Certainly. Here you go." Cormorant held out a spear, and Coyote took it. "Going to go fishing now, are you?"

"Of course, of course, as soon as I've rested a little.

Don't let me detain you! Please go on and do whatever you were going to do. Bye-bye."

Cormorant shrugged and left.

Raccoon wrung his hands. "Coyote, are you crazy? What are you going to do with a fishing spear?"

"Here! Tie it to my penis!" Coyote snarled. "Maybe this will help make it stiff again. Ow! Be careful! Not so tight!"

"I'm doing my best!" fretted Raccoon.

"There! See if it will stand up now," Coyote demanded. Raccoon held it up again, but it fell over with a dismal flop, accented by a falling run of notes on the flute. Fresh gales of mirth from the audience.

"It's not working, Coyote," cried Raccoon. "Whatever shall we do?"

"What's all the noise?" came a wobbly falsetto, and out minced big Nutku in drag. He had a long gray wig of fiber cord and a deerhide cloak painted with a pattern of datura plants, big leaves and white trumpet flowers as fine as on a Georgia O'Keefe calendar. There were white flowers wound into his braids, too, and tucked behind his ears.

"Oh, Moonflower, we're so glad you're here," said Raccoon. "Coyote's hurt his—"

"Good heavens, Coyote!" exclaimed Moonflower. "Why on earth do you have a fishing spear tied to your penis? You'll never get a woman to sit on it like that!"

"That's not my penis," grated Coyote. "That's uh, my baby!"

"Your baby!" Moonflower whooped with shrill laughter. "Old woman as I am, I thought I'd seen everything! Your baby, eh? Why does the poor little one-eyed thing have a fishing spear tied to him?"

"He has curvature of the spine," replied Coyote with an attempt at dignity. "I don't have a cradle board for him, so I tied him to a fishing spear."

"No cradle board?" said Moonflower. "It so happens I have a spare cradle board here, one my grandson outgrew."

She produced one from under her robe. "This will fix his little back!"

"Er, thank you, Moonflower, but, you know—I think what he really needs is a dose of your special medicine." Coyote looked beguiling. "That wonderful elixir you serve, the one that kills pain and brings visions? Just leave some with me, and I'll administer it."

"To a baby? Don't be silly, Coyote. He'd get so stoned, he'd never be right in the head again," Moonflower chuckled. "Here, you just let an old woman who knows about these things see to him, eh? Come, poor little ugly baby, Old Woman Moonflower will bind you so you'll grow up right!" She proceeded to bind Coyote's penis to the cradle board, while he grimaced wildly in discomfort. "You have to tie them tight, that's the secret!"

"I think you're squishing his head too much—" gasped Coyote.

"Why, haven't I raised more children and grandchildren than I can count? You may have sired a thousand little yipping brats, but you know nothing about them. Now you just keep that poor little creature tied up nice and tight, and he'll be fine." Moonflower drew her robe about her and left.

Coyote gestured frantically at Raccoon. "Take it off, take it off!" he begged.

Raccoon clasped his hands, looking befuddled. "But, Coyote, don't you want your baby to grow up with a straight back?"

"It's not a baby, you idiot!" Coyote growled. "It's my penis, remember?"

Raccoon crossly crouched down and started untying the bindings. "First it's a fishing spear, next it's a baby. Really, Coyote, why you want to tell so many lies is beyond me! If you ask my opinion, I think we ought to call in Horned Owl."

"All right! All right!" Coyote was twisting on the

ground, pounding it with his fists, kicking his feet. "Anything!"

"All right, everybody?" Raccoon faced the audience. "Let's see if we can find Horned Owl. Is he flying around up there in the night? Everybody crane your heads back and see."

And while we were all staring up into the black night sky, past the fluttering banners at the million stars, there was a blinding flash of light from the whalebone doorway. All our heads snapped forward, and we saw a new figure standing there, wreathed in plumes of colored smoke.

It was Kupiuc again, wearing the astrologer priest's feathered topknot with two big feathered horns. He had a big medicine bag at his belt, and whatever trick of makeup Lon Chaney would use to give his Phantom of the Opera horrible lidless eyes, Kupiuc had figured it out first. What a wide, glassy stare!

"Yes!" he announced. "It is I, Horned Owl, the powerful shaman! Is someone in need of my services?" And he spread his arms wide, so the folds of his feathered cloak spread out.

Raccoon bowed and scraped, rubbing his hands. "Oh, yes, please, Wise One! You see, Coyote here has broken his—"

"Nothing serious, Your Grace, I've just suffered a slight fracture of my seed beater," interrupted Coyote, but Horned Owl drowned him out with a thunderous cry:

"Silence, dissimulator! By the position of the stars"—he turned his staring face to the sky—"and the augury of the sacred shells"—he threw a handful of clam shells on the ground, leaped into a crouch over them, and peered down intently—"I can see it is a penis and not a seed beater that has been broken!"

"All right." Coyote lay down flat and dejected. "It's useless to try to hide anything from a clever and powerful creature like you. I woke up this morning and found it had died in the night. I must have rolled over on it and suffocated it by accident."

Horned Owl sprang to his feet. "The sacred shells tell me that you yourself assaulted your defenseless member!"

"Oh no!" Raccoon threw up his hands in horror.

Coyote began to weep loudly. "It's true," he sniveled. "I struck it in anger, and now it's *deeaad!* Oh, please, great and ingenious healer, bring it back to life! Don't let my poor flute go tuneless the rest of my days—"

Horned Owl flung out his hands, fingers crooked like claws. "I can alleviate your distress, but an injury this serious requires tremendous effort! The very patch of universe we occupy at this moment in time must be realigned with the heavenly bodies!"

"Oh, my!" said Raccoon breathlessly.

"And so I must have SILENCE while I perform the sacred dance to manipulate time, space, and the material plane!" Horned Owl raised his hands, and he had silence, all right. Then the flutes and rattles began, and the action of the play stopped while he performed the sacred dance.

It was a bravura display of the kantap's secret special-effects craft. Horned Owl paced slowly. He stamped, and weird lights shone. Globes of fire came down and spun in the air like planets, scattering sparks as they rotated. Over beyond the sacred enclosure, spectral figures of gauze or smoke rose pale into the night, and the spooky music led them in a counterpointing dance. All very mysterious and scary. By coincidence, it was during this part that I picked up a sudden signal from somewhere out in the night, a strong flash of nearly hysterical rage and terror. Who was it? None of my Chumash, I could tell that much. I saw other immortals turning their heads in puzzlement.

Security? I sent to our big silent guys, invisible in the trees.

Acknowledged.

Did you hear that?

Affirmative. Investigating. Beginning perimeter sweep now.

Okay. Thanks.

And that was all. Meanwhile Horned Owl had made green flames rise in the central fire, and little things popped and chattered like ghosts speaking. The dance drew to a close with Horned Owl striking a dramatic pose.

"Unworthy creature," he said, "the spirits have spoken to me. In your vile act of self-abuse, you have unbalanced your own cosmic order! Your interior self is blocked. Its channels cannot flow, because of all the gross matter backed up there! Or, to put the matter plainly—"

"He's full of shit?" guessed Raccoon.

"It is so!" Horned Owl gave a dramatic leap. "And the spirits have therefore decreed that Coyote must have"—out through the whalebone doorway came bent figures carrying an enormous agave trunk with a wooden nozzle at one end—"an enema!" He seized it from them and brandished it aloft.

Coyote sat straight up as the audience rocked with laughter. "I'm feeling much better, suddenly!" he said.

"Silence!" shouted Horned Owl. "Your masculine apparatus yet lies lifeless before you!"

"No, really, he's fine now!" Coyote held up the limp head and waggled it to and fro. "See? He's standing up and waving hello! Complete recovery! Miraculous revival! Your lovely dancing must have done it, Your Reverence! What a genius you are!"

"Come now, it's for your own good, after all," scolded Raccoon.

"You think it's so great, *you* have the enema!" cried Coyote. He got up on all fours to flee; but Raccoon caught hold of his tail, and in a single flowing gesture Horned Owl pretended to ram the nozzle where it would do the most good.

"Whoops," quavered Coyote, frozen in midflight.

Horned Owl pulled the probe back, and Raccoon let go

of Coyote's tail. Yelping, Coyote began to race around in circles, dragging himself along on his buttocks at unbelievable speed.

"Is it supposed to have that sort of effect on him?" inquired Raccoon worriedly.

"In extreme conditions, the reaction is extreme," stated Horned Owl. "But even now I can sense that his channels have begun to flow."

The rudest noises now came from the musicians. Coyote pulled up sharp and began to flip and spin on his back like a break-dancer. "Gotta go, gotta go," he yipped. "Look out, everybody!"

He backed up to the whalebone arch. "Drop and cover your eyes!" cried Horned Owl. "Here it comes!"

With an agonized howl, Coyote fell forward on his face. From behind him a jet of flame shot up, and then some unseen device belched forth a fireball that rose and exploded. When we opened our eyes, we beheld Coyote with his tail on fire, rolling and whimpering. A front-row toddler hid his face in his mother's lap, wailing in terror. She rocked him but could not stop laughing.

"I bet he feels better now," said Raccoon.

"Ow ow ow! Oh, my poor tail!" screeched Coyote.

Horned Owl accepted a woven pail of water from one of the crouching figures and doused Coyote's tail. "Now then, Coyote, how do you feel?" he asked.

"I wish I was dead," whined Coyote, where he lay panting on his side in a puddle of water.

"And serve you right, too!" yelled his penis, jumping up between his legs. Raccoon clapped his hands.

"Hooray! Hooray! Coyote's penis is alive again! Let's all dance and rejoice!"

He began to do a little hopping dance of triumph, in which Horned Owl joined; the musicians struck up a lively syncopated air; and out came Moonflower, and the seals, and the various bent-over creatures that had facilitated the stage business. At last even Coyote struggled wearily to his feet, and they all did the Chumash equivalent of the Bergomask dance, with Coyote's penis bobbing along merrily.

> *Listen! Listen!*
> *We are the Kantap*
> *Of Humashup Village!*
> *Who say they're better*
> *Than we are, at magic?*
> *Other kantaps eat our dust*
> *When it comes to dancing, singing, or jokes!*
> *Have you ever had a night like this one?*
> *Have you ever been so scared, or laughed so much?*
> *Show us the pastime that can compare*
> *(Except for gambling, of course)*
> *With the entertainment we provide!*
> *Let anyone who didn't enjoy himself tonight*
> *Be eaten by nunasis on his way home.*
> *But all of you who had a great time,*
> *Let us know by cheering!*

We cheered and cheered. And had they known, those hardworking kantap guys, that cameras filmed them that night, and the whole bawdy, silly, terrifying show would be watched by scholars and analyzed long after they were dust, would they have been proud? In a way it was immortality, and yet I wondered if it would be the same watching the show in cold daylight, on a gray screen in a clean room. You wouldn't have the stars overhead, or the sound of the wind in the banners and the oak leaves, or the smell of wood smoke. And you wouldn't *know* the players, you wouldn't be thinking, Hey, there's old Nutku, there's Kaxiwalic, there's the rest of them, and the firelight bright on the delighted faces of the old people and the young people. It'd be like somebody else's family pictures, meaningless to your heart, and the jokes wouldn't be half as funny. We save so much for those future mortals, we preserve so much heritage they would otherwise lose; but in the end, maybe we can't really give it back to them. Not the part that matters, anyway.

Not that I was thinking anything so gloomy as I congratulated the performers afterward, standing around laughing outside the entrance to the sacred enclosure as the audience staggered away through the night to their beds— some to lie down on furs in tule houses and some on shaped foam in modular cells. A couple of mood-elevating substances were passed around, of which I partook like a regular guy, though they had no effect on me—other than maybe to paint a more brightly colored mental snapshot of Kaxiwalic half out of costume, laughing, his face shining in the firelight, or Nutku flouncing around and waving his wig, talking to it in his gravelly baritone.

I felt at home. When you're an old, old immortal, you've long since learned to make your home inside your unbreakable skull. You've learned to accept that the simpler time, the better time, the long-gone faces won't ever come back. So you make a village in your head. And that's where it's always that good time, with your people telling jokes beside the fire, with everybody happy and everything all right.

But warming yourself by an image of a fire doesn't satisfy when you see a real fire burning, when you have a chance to creep close to it and feel some real warmth for the first time in longer than you want to remember. It wasn't really my fire; but for a little while that evening it had almost been. My village and my dead were almost there with me again.

Anyway, eventually we looked around and realized that nearly everybody else had gone, except for one or two chat-happy anthropologists who'd found insomniac Chumash to talk to. So I made my farewells for the night and set off down the canyon trail that wound away to the sea.

It was late. Old stars had swung around to stare down disapprovingly at us unfamiliar wanderers in the night. I scanned and picked up the perimeter guard making an orderly retreat through the trees, and a long uneven string of

Old Ones winding their way back to the base along the trail.

In fact . . . there were a couple of operatives up ahead, formless moving shadows by starlight unless you looked at them in infrared, when they became Mendoza and Mac-Cool. They were going slowly because she was picking her way with finicky care. I could hear them, too. MacCool was saying:

"You know, what you want to do is ask one of the Indians to make you a pair of tule sandals. Then you can just stride along without worrying about rocks and thorns."

"Thank you, but I'm all right." I knew the expression on Mendoza's face without seeing it.

"No, really, they're happy to do it. Jacqueline got a pair, and they're quite well made, ought to last for years! Better than you'd get in shops."

"Mm."

"I'll ask for you, if you'd rather not talk to them."

"We'll see. Wasn't that a wonderful show tonight?"

"Best I've seen in centuries," he agreed. "But, can you imagine what our lords and masters would have made of it?" He laughed, and Mendoza chuckled along with him.

"I daresay they'd be horrified," she said. "At least the ignorant prudes they assigned to run this mission would be."

"Too right!" His amusement faded. "If the Company officers are the benevolent and all-knowing people we've always been told they are, why do they send a bunch of idiots to run a mission as important as this one is supposed to be? Tell me that. Rude idiots, too. If any of them had gone in to make contact with the Chumash, they'd have been massacred."

I heard Mendoza sigh. "That's why they had us do it, MacCool."

"Why, of course. We're their slaves, the builders of their empire, the ones who go in and do the hard things. Now that I'm actually seeing the inhabitants of the future, it's obvious to me why we were created!"

"To preserve life from death," Mendoza said with another sigh. "To save man from the consequences of his own destructive stupidity. To save the rest of the life on this planet from man."

"That's the official reason, but—isn't it convenient that we also give our masters infinite wealth and infinite power? All their platitudes about world conservation aside, do you think they'd keep us if we threatened their supremacy even once? Why do you suppose we're never given any information from the future after the year 2355? No books, no cinema, no history?"

"Well, that's the year all our work bears fruit, they say, the year the earth becomes a paradise again and we immortals can all rest and enjoy things firsthand. And of course nobody has ever believed that for a minute. Everybody knows there's some dark secret Dr. Zeus is keeping from us about 2355."

"I suspect that's when we all get retired," said MacCool grimly.

"Yeah, or there's a cosmic disaster and they ditch the earth (and us) and take off in a space ark with all the stuff we've saved for them. I heard all the theories back in school! Something big happens in 2355. Some say that's when we immortals rebel and take over at last. Some say there are factions among even us, twenty different cabals, each with its own plan to take over the world. Some say the Company has a self-destruct mechanism built into each of us that we can't detect, and that 2355 is the year they push its button. MacCool, who the hell knows?"

"Twenty cabals?" He sounded nonplussed.

"But, you know what? None of it changes the fact that we *do* preserve life. We *do* prevent extinctions and rescue great art. Whatever the truth is, we're doing the only work that really matters. Why should I care if that also means that some bureaucrat somewhere is getting fat off my labors? As if anybody could get fat on that atrocious food, anyway!"

"But doesn't it ever make you angry?"

"Angry?" She stopped on the trail and turned to him. "You can't imagine my anger. It's infinite rage; it's surrounded me so long, I no longer have any idea where it begins, where it ends. So what? I'm just a machine. You are too. What use is anger to either of us?"

"We're more than that," protested MacCool. "They're the machines. They have less human feeling than you or I do."

"Not me." Mendoza leaned toward him. "My human feeling is falling away, a grain at a time. Every year I find myself having less in common with mortals, even with my own kind, for that matter."

"You feel rage, but you work on. That's exactly the kind of attitude a good general prays for in a soldier." MacCool sounded weary. "That's what Dr. Zeus is counting on, don't you see? And don't you see that you should place that unshakable faith of yours in worthier masters?" He took her by the shoulders and looked down into her eyes.

She sneered. "Faith? You dope, that's resignation! I don't *care* how the Company's run! Are you actually promoting some kind of rebellion against those poor idiots? Do you think it'd change anything? Has there ever been a revolution that produced something better than what it overthrew? The only thing people learn from being oppressed is how to oppress others!"

She stalked ahead. He followed cautiously, and I followed more cautiously still.

"That's true of mortals, I grant you," he ventured. "But how can you think we'd do the same?"

"I'll tell you how." By infrared she was a figure made of flames, dancing on the path in her anger. "You think there aren't some of us who hate the goddam human race by now, after what we've seen? How long do you think it would be before we started rounding them up in camps for their own good? And we'd have to weed out the genetic defects, of course. And supervised breeding programs, we'd have to have those. We'd run things, because they're evil and incapable of learning, while we're these godlike superior beings!"

"And if it came to a time when we had no choice?" he demanded. "What if that's the only way to save them, in 2355?"

She threw back her head and screamed in silence. He moved toward her.

"You're shivering. That cape's no use here. Mine's wool—" He slung it off his shoulders, and the colors of his body changed instantly as the cold bit into him. He draped it around her shoulders, and I'm afraid she didn't even thank him. He drew a deep breath and said, "It could come to that, you know. Aren't they becoming less than human? And all the same, I'd rule with human compassion."

"And what makes you think you'll be running the show, you sap?" Mendoza paced back and forth in her agitation. "There are those among us smarter than you, my friend. I mean—here we are, eternally young, infinitely informed, and *designed to preserve ourselves at all costs*. Now, if we all suspect we're going to be terminated in the year 2355, doesn't it seem likely that some of us have already taken steps to make sure that that never happens? What if we're already running things? But if that's the case, we aren't exactly ruling mortals with human compassion, are we?"

"If that's the case, it's not our fault," replied MacCool. "The rule about being unable to change history applies to us as well. But we don't know what happens after 2355! If we move then, we might be able to make a new beginning for the world. Doesn't it make sense to start preparing now?"

"Stop this, MacCool!" She put her head down and started on up the path, but stopped and turned to him again. "Here's a thought for you. They (whoever they are) can hear everything we say to each other. All the electronic shit in our heads, you know? All those audio and video transcripts we record. You think we can't be accessed as easily as we ourselves access? Why bother with plots? They'll know." She turned to go again. He caught her arm.

"But don't you see? If they know what we're saying and not punishing us—then either we're already in control or they're hopeless simpletons. There's no risk involved, Mendoza!"

She ignored his hand on her bare arm. "How do you know you can trust *me*, fool?"

At this juncture Old Coyote—old Joseph too, for that matter—was wishing He could turn around on the path and go back to His children of Humashup, snuggle down beside their mortal hearths, listen to their sleepy mortal talk and snoring, and give advice on their little mortal concerns, such as how to get their daughter to stop dating that boy or whether to save up for a canoe they couldn't really afford.

"Because I know you, Mendoza. I know your history, what you've endured." MacCool's voice was full of compassion, but I cringed inwardly. He was treading on really dangerous ground with her; did he know it? He pulled Mendoza close to him. "Why would you serve mortal despots, after what you've suffered at their hands? You wouldn't betray me to them, not you. Not after what happened in England. You've been alone too long, Mendoza, but you needn't be!"

He didn't wait for her reaction, but bent her back in a dramatic kiss. That was enough for me. I decided to take an alternate path home and veered off uphill through the sagebrush, heading for the ridge route. As I did, though, I heard her come up for air with an infuriated yell of "Aw, for crying out loud! Was *that* what this was all about?"

I left them below me, climbing through the darkness until I made the top of the ridge, where I could look out across the folded canyons at the black night ocean. I needed to sit alone for a while.

It wasn't the embarrassment of being an inadvertent spectator to the seduction attempt. Mendoza appeared to have that particular problem well under control, and if MacCool was smart, he'd lay in some frostbite salve. Of course, he wasn't smart.

He was a lot more than not smart, and it had nothing to do with Mendoza. How can you work for the Company for however many hundred years MacCool had been around and not know how it handles little troubles that aren't supposed to happen?

We're going to have a flashback sequence now.

Chapter 23 ❦

I HAD COME a long way to find him, following rimrock trails through what would one day be the Italian Alps. He'd set up a base in a cave there, with his heroes around him. It was well below the snow line, but as far as the local mortals went, he was as safe as though he were on the moon; they knew his reputation.

You don't want to go up there! the village headman had signed to me. *Angry god up there. Really angry. Takes heads. You stay down here like us, don't make trouble, hunt for ducks or cut wood—no problem. You go trespassing his place, he kill you.*

I'll be all right, I signed back. *He won't kill me, because I have no weapon. He only kills men who go after him with weapons.*

The headman stared at me a minute, then slapped his brow to indicate that I was right. He'd never noticed it before, but the angry god did seem mostly to pick on people with weapons!

Isn't he a good god most of the time? I signed my inquiry. *Kills bears for you, keeps invading tribes out of your valley?*

I guess so, signed the headman, *but when we go out raid cattle from other tribes, he go after us too.*

Well, that's your problem! I explained.

176

The headman thought about that. *You mean we not supposed to invade anybody either?*

That's it.

The headman looked appalled as this sank in. Then another thought occurred to him. He looked at me worriedly. *Are you his priest or something?*

No, no, I assured him. *Just a friend.*

He stared after me as I went on my way, and when I had climbed so high that the little village looked toylike in its alpine meadow, I could still see him standing there, lost in thought amid the edelweiss. Or whatever those flowers were. I hoped I hadn't started a religion.

I kept climbing, and before long I saw a pair of the heroes, standing with their spears on either side of the path like towering menhirs. All they wore were bearskins. You have never seen guys that big and strong in your life, unless you're as old as I am, because they're all gone now.

Imagine immortals made from Neanderthals, with just a little genetic interference to give them some Cro-Magnon characteristics, like extreme height and the tendency to go crazy when they're excited. All the rest of their personal qualities were pure Neanderthal, though, the weight lifter's build, the helmet head, the big clever hands; also the courage that nothing could shake, and I mean nothing.

You want an example? When a guy in a Cro-Magnon hunting party fell into a bear den, his friends would step away from the edge and wring their hands. They'd compose sorrowful elegies about him afterward, or maybe horror stories about bears; but no way would they endanger themselves to get him out. When a guy from a Neanderthal tribe fell into a den, though, his friends wouldn't even stop to think: they'd jump right in after him and lay about them with their fists, if they had nothing else, until the bears stopped biting or their friend managed to scramble out.

Of course, it doesn't take a genius to figure out that eventually there were a lot fewer Neanderthals than Cro-Magnons, which meant that Neanderthals contributed a lot less genetic material to *Homo sapiens sapiens*. They contributed some, though.

"Hey, Big Nose, how's it going?" I greeted the one I recognized. That was only a nickname, his real name was Dewayne, but his nose really was this massive lumpy thing between his wide eyes.

"How's it going yourself, you little sack of shit?" he responded in the flat high voice they all had. He grinned, dropping to one knee. I went up to him, and we hugged hello, trying to make each other's ribs creak. Guess who succeeded. "Been a long time," he told me. "Look at you! Tailored skins and everything. How long you been a Facilitator now?"

"Since graduation," I told him. I was looking him over, too; almost no scars remained to give away the fact that when I'd first seen him, he'd been bleeding from a dozen wounds, including the stump of his neck. His head had been in a bucket between his feet on the stretcher. The medics cursed at us kids and told us to beat it, not to watch or we'd have nightmares the rest of our lives. I took somebody up on a dare later, though, and sneaked into the base intensive care unit to see the fallen hero in his regeneration vat. There he was, floating dreamily in blue solution; his head had been reattached, and his wounds were healing already. Little Preservers like me were programmed to avoid physical injury at all costs, but the big Enforcers were so brave, they didn't care what happened to themselves, so long as they did their job. That was why they were heroes. We were taught to admire them but never to imitate them.

"All grown up." Dewayne got to his feet. He giggled. "Though I'd be surprised if you hadn't, after seven thousand years. You here to see the old man, by any chance?"

"I'd like to," I replied. "I hope he'll see me."

"You? Why wouldn't he?" he said, and then his smile faded. "You're here on Company business, huh?"

"Kind of unofficially," I replied. "Where is he, Dewayne?"

"Well—"

It's all right. Send him up. The transmission came through loud and clear. Dewayne pointed up the trail and stood to attention again, resuming his unblinking watch over the valley below us. I passed through three other patrols before I came to the cave under the glacier.

He was sitting in the sunlight at the cave mouth, frowning slightly at the clouds that were massing in the northern quadrant of the sky. He lowered his head as I approached and smiled at me with his pale eyes. He didn't look surprised to see me. Budu never looked surprised. He surprised other people.

He was bigger and older and smarter than any of the other Enforcers, and even the people who loved him were frightened of him. I don't want to give you the impression I didn't love him. I've paid lip service to thin sad gods on crucifixes and bearded gods who flung thunderbolts and green gods all wrapped up in bandages, but the god my heart really believes in wears a bearskin, has bloody hands and a calm, merciless stare.

"What nice clothes, son," he observed, and I ran to him and we embraced. He still smelled the same: not like a *Homo sapiens sapiens* at all. I came up to his collarbone now, but I still felt four years old.

"Thanks. Look! Custom stitching!" I preened, trying to make him laugh. He did smile a little.

"Look at you, how grand you are nowadays. You must have risen high in the ranks," he remarked in his toneless voice.

"Oh, not all that much," I said. "Otherwise I'd have a nice soft desk job. I'm just a field operative, and they keep me busy, let me tell you."

He nodded. "Sending you on errands like this one."

I coughed a little at that. "They didn't exactly send me. I wanted to come, to talk to you myself There've been a lot of strange stories going around. I wanted to get your opinion on things."

"My opinion or my statement, child?" he said, and chuckled at my discomposure.

"You know what's been happening," I told him, deciding to throw circumlocution to the winds. "The war's over. It's been over for centuries, really. If there are any of the Goat Cult left anywhere, they're keeping to themselves, not bothering anybody. A lot of the Enforcers are balking at new assignments, though. They won't believe the Goats are really gone."

"They *are* gone," Budu told me.

"I knew you weren't one of the problem cases," I said, reassured. "So maybe you could tell me what's going on with the other guys, that they won't come back to the bases with their regiments? One or two have even refused direct orders. You'd think they'd be glad to come in out of the cold, after all this time!"

"And some have done worse things," he prompted.

"Yes," I sighed and looked down at my feet. "It's a pretty ugly story. Marco commandeered a mortal village and quartered his regiment there. Said his intelligence was that there were Goat spies hiding out with the civilians. He began interrogations."

"And it came to killing," Budu said.

"Yeah. But apparently nobody there had ever even heard of the Goats. A lot of innocent mortals died."

Budu nodded slowly. "Marco is a fool," he said. I was so glad to hear him say that! But my relief was damped down when he went on to say:

"He doesn't need the Goat Cult."

"*Nobody* needs the Goat Cult!" I agreed desperately. "And he knew that as well as you or I. He did his job so well, all of you did, that nobody will ever have to worry about the Goats again. All he had to do was bring his men home. And now he's facing a disciplinary hearing, when he ought to be retiring with honors."

"And is he sitting in a detention cell, awaiting trial?" Budu inquired.

"Well—not exactly," I admitted. "He's still out there. He says he's on the trail of a new Goat incursion. He's refusing to come in."

"How unfortunate," said Budu, "for everyone concerned."

"It really is. The rumors are that there were even women and children killed at this village," I went on.

"But we always killed them." Budu looked at me. "He-Goats, she-Goats, little Goats beside their Goat mothers. We spared only the infants. The indoctrination was too complete in the others. If you'd been crouching beside a Goat body instead of by your mother, I'd have knocked in your little head too, lest you grow up into a big Goat."

He watched my reaction with a cold twinkle in his eye. "Now you look shocked!" he joked. "Don't worry. I knew you were a good child when I saw you. But really, there was no way but to exterminate them wherever we found them, and they were everywhere in those days. Not now."

After an uncertain pause, I said, "So, have you any suggestion about what to do with Marco? I don't suppose you could talk to him?"

"I might," Budu told me. "If I see him. I could tell him he's wasting his time hunting for Goats."

"It would really, really be a good idea if you could," I told him. "It would ease a lot of people's minds at Company headquarters. Some of those committee members don't understand—well, no, they do understand what you guys have done for them. But they're getting a little scared, to tell you the absolute truth."

"They know they can't do much to stop us, if we refuse orders," said Budu.

"Exactly," I agreed.

A silence fell. I hurried to fill it in.

"Under the circumstances, you can see how the Company might be a little uncomfortable that you've chosen to postpone coming in, yourself."

"I've been busy," he replied.

"It sounds like you've been doing a great job with the locals," I said lamely.

"I've been busy thinking," he said.

"Oh. Okay," I said, and then he got up and paced out to the edge of the bluff, and I had to run after. He stopped and looked around him. You could see for huge distances in all directions, well into what would one day be different nations.

"You ought to look at this and think about it, too," he told me. "Look, out here. That will be Italy, one day. The little man Napoleon will come from there, and go over there"—he swung his big arm around in the direction of France—"to raise his armies, trying to be a god. Many, many people will die before he learns he's a man." He swung his big arm around. "And that will be Germany, where there will be a man so stupid, he doesn't know what happens when one group of animal breeds only with itself, or one family marries only its own cousins. You know what he'll do in the name of what he calls his race. How many will die? Ten million? And how many others will learn the idea of big murder from him, and do as he did in their own nations? And look out there," he went on, turning. "Spain. They will feed people to their god, and then go conquer a world, beyond that sea, where the rulers feed people to *their* god.

"Keep looking, Joseph. That will be Africa. Think of all those slaves dying for the wealth of nations, and the curse they fulfill. And there, in Jerusalem, three people of one book, children of one god, will tear one another to pieces. Farther, where you can't see, from the steppes, another little man will come, with his horses and his men, conquering with no other plan than to make heaps of skulls wherever he goes. British, Americans, Japanese, Russians. Look up at the sky, think of all those people burning to death on Mars. Big murder, son. You can't look in any direction without seeing a nation that deserves to be gelded."

"Well—yeah," I agreed. "That's why Dr. Zeus was

founded. Why we were made. To preserve the good part of humanity from all the awful things these people will do."

"That was why *you* were made, son." He turned to look down at me. "And since you were made to hide things away to keep them safe, it must have occurred to you how much simpler your job would be if we Enforcers were permitted to keep monsters from running loose in the world."

"Of course," I said uneasily. I could see where this was going. "But what can we do? Those people will have their time. Hitler, the Vikings, the Church of God-A. All we can do is work in their event shadows to make the best of things. We can't prevent their existence, however much we'd like to. We can't change history."

"How do you know, son?"

"Because it's impossible! Every one knows that. It's one of the first things we learn. The laws of temporal physics prove it," I stated.

"And you've made a study of temporal physics?" He put his enormous hands behind his back and regarded me.

"No, but I know what everybody else knows," I answered, feeling panicked.

"Because Dr. Zeus told you." His gaze traveled out to the world again. "Think about this, son. If the Company were lying to you, how would you know? And if the Company were lying, and history *can* be changed—would it be to the Company's advantage to change it?"

"Well, of course," I responded. "Except—well, wait. No, because the whole operation has functioned by using the event shadows cast by history as it exists. If history were changed, all those chains of connected circumstance would be broken. We don't know what would happen."

He nodded slowly. "The Company owns many fine things, saved from war and wickedness. But if there were no wars, no thieves and murderers, who would own those fine things? In the future there are wise and powerful men who send us our orders, you and me. If history were changed, would those men lose their power?"

The line of black clouds was advancing from the north, bringing a storm that couldn't be blown away or outrun. He sighed, watching it come.

"Maybe our masters are great and good and have told us the truth. But if they've lied to us—and how can we know they haven't?—then a thousand generations of innocents will die to make our masters rich."

"But we have no way of knowing that they've lied, either!" I protested.

He looked down at me and smiled. "No way at all," he said. "So I'll speak to Marco, when I see him. Tell me, do you know what they're going to do with us, my Enforcers and me, now that we have served our purpose?"

"You'll be retrained." That was what I had been told.

"Will we?" He held up his big hands and looked at them. "Will they make us Preservers, like you?"

"I—I guess so."

"Then we must obey," he said. "I wonder about something. When the year 2355 has come and gone, will the Company still need its Preservers?"

"Not as Preservers, no," I said after a moment. "The Company will have made a new civilization, one that's so advanced, there won't be wars."

"Or natural disasters, or accidents?" he asked. A breeze came out of the north, cold as ice, the outrider of the coming storm.

"Maybe they'll need us to preserve things from those, then," I said. "We have to trust the Company, Father! What else can we do?"

"I don't know," he told me. "But you should think about this, son."

I didn't want to. It was pointless. What could I do, even if he happened to be right? But I owed him a son's duty, so I told him I'd think about it.

I left him and made my way back down the mountains. Near the pass into future Switzerland, I encountered a mortal traveler swinging a nifty copper ax as he strode along.

Is pass open? he signed to me.

Yes, I signed back, *but you'd better hide your ax.* His eyes widened at that; he must have heard about the angry god. Hastily he slipped it over his shoulder into his backpack.

Thanks, he signed.

You should probably turn back, though, I added. *There's a storm coming.*

His gaze traveled off to where I was pointing at the wall of clouds. It had come a full third of the way across the sky. He evaluated for a moment and then shrugged.

I bet I make it.

I shrugged back at him and went on my way. If that guy got caught in the storm, he might be stuck up here until skiers found him in the late twentieth century; but it wouldn't be my fault. I'd warned him, hadn't I? Whatever doubts Budu might have on the subject, it was my experience, so far, that history couldn't be changed.

Chapter 24 ❧

ON THE OTHER hand, Budu had been right in his suspicion that the Company didn't always take the high moral ground where troublesome immortals were concerned. The Enforcers were gone now; I hadn't seen one in centuries. Were they really leading happy and productive lives somewhere? What happened to immortals who asked the wrong questions, like Budu? Or like MacCool, for that matter?

And what *was* going to happen in the year 2355?

I stood up slowly and looked out into the night. There were the lights of the base. No nice warm fireside for me; I had a berth among the other ageless, in a gray future room without decoration, where walls met floors and ceilings without molding or baseboard, stripped bare of decoration and other nonfunctional nonessentials.

Oh well. It would at least be warm and dry. I turned to head down the ridge.

What was *that*? There was that emotion again, that broadcast from somebody far out in the night. Anger, but with it a certain glee. Whoever it was had evaded our patrols. Great. Well, he wasn't close enough to do me any harm on my way home. I'd make my report in the morning, which it was already, actually. One of the really important things an immortal needs to know is when to go to bed.

* * *

I made my report, and the security patrols were stepped up. They found evidence somebody had been lurking around, all right; some Native American covert surveillance guy was peeping at us. Would he be back? It was anybody's guess, but the proper precautions were taken. Meanwhile, those of us working in the field tried to speed up the job a little.

I was watching Mendoza and Dalton at work. They were on their knees in a meadow, examining some plant with one of the wise women, who was pronouncing:

"Now, this we call *tok*, and it has many uses. The flower buds are good to eat—"

"*Asclepias eriocarpa*," said Mendoza under her breath. "Ask her if this isn't the same thing they use to make fishing tackle." She could speak Chumash perfectly well but preferred to let Dalton do the talking. With one memorable exception, Mendoza avoids contact with mortals.

"Don't you use this for fishing tackle, too?" prodded Dalton obediently.

"Of course! You see, you just cut the stems and peel them open . . ." Their voices faded into the background. Far but sharp, I heard a man weeping. I smelled mortal misery.

I scanned. He was a mile distant, but his emotional state streamed in the air like a banner, blue and purple. I focused in and could just make out somebody huddled in oak shade on a hill due west of us. Mendoza was too focused on what she was doing to hear, but Dalton sensed him too and glanced across at me, questioning. I got up and strolled away in a casual manner until I was out of sight, when I broke into a run.

No, no, this would never do. Everyone was supposed to be happy about leaving. Upbeat. Glad to be clearing out before the murderous white men or Chinigchinixians or whoever arrived. If one mortal sat down and actually thought about it and got sad, others might too. Mortals are like that, for all their lack of sympathy for one another. And unhappy individuals ask questions, which is never a good idea when you're trying to lead a people to a promised land. I had to find this poor wretch, whoever he was, and cheer him up. Or something.

Half a mile down the canyon, I could identify the guy: Kenemekme, the first man to speak to me. I'd got to know him, slightly, since. He seemed to be the loser my groupies had said he was: a decent hunter, but nobody much otherwise. Not wealthy. Once a husband and father, but something had happened to the baby and the wife had run off with somebody else. Nobody listened to him in the councils. I guess you might hide in the bushes and cry, if your life was like that.

By the time I got to where he was, he'd stopped crying and was resting his chin in his hands, staring at the far-off sea horizon. He jumped a little as I hunkered beside him.

"Nice view, isn't it, nephew?"

He looked down at his feet. "All right, I guess."

"Yes, lovely view. The sky is blue, the sun is warm, the salvation of your people is proceeding apace. So, why such a long face? You can tell your Uncle Sky Coyote." I put my head to one side, watching him.

He swallowed hard and at last replied, "I thought it would be different."

"What would be different, nephew?"

"Well, I thought—it's just that before You came, I had my own ideas about the way things worked. All that about Father Sun drinking blood and devouring corpses, like the priests told us—I mean, that *couldn't* be true. He's no more than a monster if He does things like that. I had Him pictured more like a kind of grandfather, loving but stern. Terrible to the wicked, yes, that I could believe. And . . . I thought some kind of higher order prevailed in the Upper World. But from what You say, things are just as bad up there as they are down here. Even God cheats." He gave a shaken little laugh that caught on a sob.

I sighed and shrugged. "Nephew. What did you think, when the priests and shamans told you about us Sky People? When you hear a story, do you believe only the nice parts? Truth isn't like a baked fish, where you can eat the flesh and leave the bones and skin. You have to eat it all."

"But if some of those stories are true, then worship is pointless, isn't it? Why worship beings like that? And all those rituals, all those kantap mysteries, why bother anymore? I mean, now we *know*."

"Well, the kantap's another affair. But—"

"And as for prayer, forget it. Why pray to a cannibal who cheats at dice, no matter how powerful He is? And why behave at all? You Sky People have Your nerve dictating rules to us, the way You carry on! When I think of some of the stories I've heard about You, Coyote—"

I hated to do it, but it was time to drag out my Spanish Jesuit training.

"All right. Think what you're saying, nephew. You don't like us Sky People, so no more moral restraints for you. You can lie, steal, and cheat, yes, rape and murder too, if you feel like it."

"Well, no, I won't, because—well, it's wrong, and if everybody did it, nobody could live anywhere, and—we have to have some way to protect people. And I won't be like You Gods!"

"I see. But doesn't that mean you're deciding to be good without anybody telling you to? Nobody punishing you if you sin, nobody rewarding you for virtue? Think of that, nephew."

He struggled with the idea. It scared the daylights out of him, of course. I've never met a mortal it didn't scare. So he said:

"Wait a minute! Why am I even listening to You? Of course! You're a liar! In every story I've ever heard, You tell the most outrageous lies!"

"So it follows that—?"

"Well, it follows that none of what You've been telling

us is true." He grasped at a ray of light. "And maybe things *are* like I'd imagined, and maybe Father Sun *is* loving and benign and cares for us . . ."

I shook my head. "You're forgetting something, nephew. I didn't tell you that Father Sun eats people. That's been said by your own priests, by all the reverend truth-tellers of your own village."

He stared at me and bit his lip. "Then maybe they don't know anything either . . ."

"Then figure it out for yourself! Here I come all the way from the Upper World to save my people from annihilation, and what happens? I get called a liar. Thank you *so* much." I rose as if to go.

"No! Wait, just this once, couldn't You tell the truth?" He caught hold of my leg in desperation. "The shamans don't know anything more than I do. They've never been to the Upper World, but You have! You're the only one I can ask! If You really love Your creations, why can't You at least tell us the truth about it all? Why do children die? Why doesn't love last? Why are our lives so short and miserable? Why do You allow evil? Isn't there *anywhere* things are the way they ought to be? What's the truth?"

"Is that what you're really in search of, nephew? Truth?"

"Yes! Truth!"

Hell, I hate to see people unhappy. "Then look into my eyes, nephew."

Truth is not all that hard to do, as special effects go. You just put mortals in a trance, scramble their brains a little, and invest some random object with Mystic Significance. It can be anything: a rock, a bush, a flower, a word. The tricky part is making sure your subject has a nice neutral Life-Affirming Experience and not a Call to Action. Otherwise he or she is likely to go out and preach that it's necessary to the world's salvation that (for example) everyone must be tattooed or the universe will collapse. Look at whoever this guy was down in Yang-Na.

Me, I'm a professional. I don't make that kind of mistake. When I blow somebody's mind, I empty the ammo chamber first. Kenemekme staggered back and shook his head. His eyes filled with tears.

"The beauty," he sobbed. "Oh—oh, the beauty!"

"Happy now?" I ventured. He threw his arms around me.

"Yes! At last, I understand! It all makes sense now and—what *beauty!*"

"Yes. But you can't put it into words, can you? That would be blasphemy."

"Oh, yes, You're right. How could I ever describe . . . How can I ever thank You?"

"And you won't try to go out and tell other people about it, will you? No preaching or anything like that? This is our little secret."

"Yes! Yes! Thank You, thank You, thank You!"

"Don't mention it. You run along now and be happy, okay?"

"Yes!!" he cried, and went away down the hill singing.

Piece of cake. His brain, I mean.

Mendoza paused, her spoonful of Proteus lifted halfway to her mouth. She frowned slightly.

"Are we having an earthquake?" she wondered. All over the commissary, immortal heads were raised, immortal brows creased in the same frown. There weren't any mortals in there with us except for the food servers, who weren't noticing. I shivered and grabbed my ears: all those long inner dog hairs had begun to vibrate unbearably. She threw her spoon down in disgust. "That's all we need. A goddam temblor."

But nothing was shaking or rattling, not anywhere in the room. We looked around at the other immortals. I shrugged.

"Something seismic somewhere, I guess, but not near enough to involve us," I told her. She shrugged too, picked up her spoon and went on eating. You could almost hear

the whirring in the room as twenty people accessed their
files on earthquakes in recorded history. It occurred to me
that we weren't operating in recorded history, exactly, but
I didn't say anything about that. Panicked immortals are
awesome to behold.

"Yeah, I remember now," I went on. "There's a lot of
regular volcanic activity a little way up the coastline. No
big deal. Lava pillows in the cliffs, hot springs in the interior. I bet that's what we're noticing."

"Hot springs, huh?" Mendoza looked mildly interested.
"No spas yet, of course. Funny your Chumash don't seem
to know anything about them. You'd think a hot spring
would be an ideal place to build a sweat lodge."

"Actually, they have." An anthropologist named Catton
leaned over the back of his chair. "Not our people here, the
tribe living up there. They even have a health resort, so to
speak, but they don't get many customers from other tribes,
because their rates are so high."

This brought a general chuckle from the listeners around
us. There were a few jokes about mints on pillows and
complimentary sherry in the rooms. God, I'd have liked a
glass of sherry right then.

Mendoza got up and went across the room to the cooler
for more water, all straight lines in her new field garb. She
hadn't been able to bring herself to adopt the space age
coveralls; her compromise made her look like a sensible
Victorian tourist in khaki. I leaned forward to speak to her
when she returned.

"Uh . . . say, I don't see that guy with the mustache and
the attitude. What's his name? MacIntyre?" I said, very
casually.

She gave me the look she usually gives at such moments.

"*Him.*" What a lot of contempt could be crammed into
one syllable. "The name you're straining after, not very
convincingly, I might add, is MacCool."

"The two of you have been seeing a lot of each other,
huh?" I said.

She stared at me, surprised, but only for a moment.

"What the hell is it to you?" she demanded in a savage undertone. "Are you all set to leap in and sabotage my little romance again?"

"Look, your private life is none of my business—"

"Gosh, thanks so much!"

"But—" I struggled to find a way to tell her the guy was bad news. "I thought . . . Weren't you and Lewis . . . ?"

For a moment she looked blank.

"*Lewis.* My God, what an imagination you've got! For your information, Lewis and I were very good friends and that was all, I can assure you. Do you think I'd ever in my life fall in love with anybody again, after what happened in England?"

"You might think it was safer, with somebody who wasn't mortal," I blundered on. "One of us, maybe."

"I might, but you know something?" Jesus, her eyes were hard. "I'm discovering I don't like the company of·my own kind much better than that of the mortal monkeys. I don't want the complications, the interference, the distraction. I have work to do! What's the point of sitting around with a bunch of millennial bores and listening to them complain about things they can't change? Some of us are just as stupid as mortals, if not more so."

"Glad to hear you say that," I ventured, meaning to go on with something complimentary about her work ethic. Before I could, though, she looked me in the eye and said quietly:

"Level with me, Joseph, for once in your life. You're older than most of the people in this room. I can't remember ever seeing you have a real emotion. You are one perfect Company machine. You don't feel a damned thing anymore, do you? No, please, I'm not trying to insult you. I just want you to tell me something.

"Our hearts, they do go dead after a few centuries, don't they? The human emotions stop bothering us."

I had to tell her some of the truth. So I said: "The game

is learning to avoid pain, babe. No more, no less. They told you that in school, didn't they? Look around you. The rest of these people aren't necessarily more successful at it than you are. I don't even manage it, all the time. It isn't getting free of your heart that saves you. It's your work that saves you, because it's the only thing that will never let you down. Okay?"

Her eyes bored into me a few seconds before she decided to accept that. She looked down at her plate, and I had the sensation of having a sword point lowered from my throat.

"I don't want a human heart anymore," she said quietly. "It's not a question of pain, either. It's . . . it's the scope of the work here. This country. These mountains. Those trees, Joseph, those magnificent trees. All the years wasted at New World One, when I should have been here! Parties and babbling and new clothes, all keeping me from this place. I don't want . . . people tugging my attention away from it now."

She was in love again, after all; but not with MacCool or anything human, mortal or immortal. I chose my next words very carefully.

"Exactly! You're focusing on your work, which is what you should be doing. I think this is great, Mendoza. You're instinctively choosing to turn your attention to the important stuff, and it's going to make you a lot happier than some people I could mention who spend all their time bitching about management."

"Like MacCool?" She looked up again, sneering. "Was that what was bothering you, the prospect of my falling for somebody like him? Well, don't trouble yourself, dog boy. That guy is a disaster waiting to happen, and I've had enough disasters, thank you very much. He smells like burning houses and screaming civilians trapped in wreckage. Wrong, wrong, *wrong* for little me."

"MacCool? He was transferred," said a geologist at a near table, leaning toward us.

"He what?" I started. Mendoza became perfectly still, staring at me.

"This morning. He was pulled for a special project elsewhere, or so I heard. His orders came through last night. I don't know where they sent him."

"Ah," I said.

Mendoza, still looking at me, was even whiter than she usually is. *Joseph,* she transmitted, *you're scared.*

You can tell that through the dog face? You're imagining it. I'm surprised, that's all.

You're scared. MacCool was shooting his big mouth off, and now he's been taken away, and you're scared.

I am not! But if he had to go to a disciplinary hearing somewhere, I'm damn glad you're not with him. He was stupid. We're not stupid. We keep our heads down and do our jobs, right? Because we know that whatever happens, in the long run the Company is on the side of the angels, or whatever there is up there. Years of habit kicked in, and I made the sign of the cross with my coyote paw. She did, too, shakily. Once a Spaniard, always a Spaniard.

And maybe that was why it was easier for her to accept the idea of people just disappearing, no trial, no trace. It should have been easy for me. It's not like I haven't seen it happen before.

Part of the trick of avoiding pain is to make sure that all the people whose personal misery can hurt you too are off safe somewhere, doing something that can't possibly screw up their lives again. If you can get them settled securely in some comfortable rut, you can go your own way without thinking all those creepy little thoughts that come to you in the sleepless night.

I had thought Budu was safe. Everybody knew that most of the Enforcer rank and file had been retrained as Preservers, but the Company had found what seemed like an ingenious solution for the best ones, the officers. Who has the most opportunity to plunge into the wreckage of war and take what would otherwise be burned or smashed? A soldier, right? And when you're an ex-Enforcer, you can do the job even better than an original Preserver could, because you're a really big, ugly soldier who can get away with taking loot or prisoners for himself. Your fellow warriors aren't going to argue the point. You can be a barbarian, mercenary, pirate, or legionary and be in at the kill as empires totter, as libraries and monasteries are sacked, and help yourself to what the Company wants.

And Budu and his officers did pretty well, for what seemed like a long time. They weren't kept together, of course. After *Homo sapiens sapiens* became the only game in town, a bunch of guys that big and that strange-looking would have drawn attention. Separated, they were less noticeable, especially in armies whose men came from diverse ethnic and racial groups, like Rome's. So they passed themselves off as Hyperboreans, later as Norsemen, and if the men they soldiered with hadn't ever actually been to Scandinavia, it helped.

Or so I heard. As the ages went by, I kept in touch less and less, because I was pretty busy. I knew that Budu had become a Roman legionary and loved his work: he found the ethics of the republic admirable and enjoyed fighting alongside all those hardworking enlisted men. That was the image of him I kept in my mind for the next few centuries, Budu happy and occupied, smashing barbarian skulls so that neat little garrison towns could be carved out of the European wilderness. Though I served as a centurion myself for a while, our legions were never quartered near each other, so I never had the chance to drop in on him.

Of course, if I'd let myself think about it, I'd have come to the uneasy conclusion that once the Caesar family got into power, Budu wouldn't find Rome quite so admirable. I didn't let myself think about it, though, because of my habit of avoiding pain. And after Rome fell, I just assumed

he'd switched sides and was helping to tear down what he'd
helped build.

But I never asked, never looked him up, because . . . why
because? Probably because deep down I knew what was
happening.

Chapter 25 ❧

I'D BEEN A spy for Alexis Comnene, one of his army of invisible men doing their quiet bit to keep the status quo in old Byzantium. Right now the best way to prevent the Basileus's boat from rocking seemed to be encouraging those reliable and dependable enemies, the Turks, to slaughter those worst of loose-cannon friends, the Norman knights. It was a political scene a million miles removed from armies on the Tiber and memories of Budu.

I saw him last in Antioch. That was where everybody saw him last. I was surprised as all hell to meet him there, too. He was sitting in a transport lounge placidly reading a magazine. The transport lounge was seven stories below ground level, the year happened to be 1099 and Budu was wearing the mail habit of a Crusader. The strange thing was that he sat between two nervous-looking security techs. I knew what had happened, but I wouldn't admit it to myself. I just smiled and advanced on him with my most innocent look of delighted astonishment.

"Wow, Father, what are you, under arrest or something?" I exclaimed.

He lowered the magazine and looked at me. "Yes," he replied.

He might just as well have thrown a punch into my solar plexus. I stopped dead and gave a weak little giggle. "You're kidding, right?"

But one of the techs stood up and placed his hand on my shoulder. "Sir, can we ask you to move on? This operative has nothing to say to you."

"I'm a Facilitator," I told him, remaining reasonable and calm. "It's okay. I have clearance for stuff like this."

The tech looked into my eyes. He was checking my retinal pattern, not my sincere expression, and after a second he nodded. "We're just his escort, sir. He's on his way to a hearing."

"Of course," I said with a nod, feeling queasy. "Look, can I have a few minutes alone with the old guy? Maybe I can learn something useful."

The tech didn't like that much, but my record was clean and my rank was high—higher than his, at least, which was what counted. "Go on, take your friend with you and have a couple of Turkish coffees. I'll bet I can get something out of him in the time it takes you to get down to the mud. Okay?"

"Okay," the tech replied, and nodded at his friend, who rose readily enough to go with him. I had a feeling they weren't enjoying this duty. Budu watched them go, shaking his head.

"Look at them, just walking away after a few smooth words from a stranger. If they were under my command, I'd order them both to step off a cliff."

"If they were under your command, they'd do it, too," I said, sitting down beside him. "What the hell's happened, Father? What are you doing here?"

"I refused a direct order," he replied.

I don't get caught flat-footed often, but that time I sat there gaping like an idiot. After a moment of my stunned silence, he decided to take charge of the conversation.

"I have something to ask you. Listen to me, son. How long has it been since you've seen one of my kind? Almost a thousand years, hasn't it? And yet there were hundreds of us. Where have they all gone? Do you know? Tell me if you know."

"They're—they're working on Company bases, or in military operations," I said. "Aren't they?"

"No, they're not," he told me. "I've been searching. I've seen classified information. Most of them were never retrained at all. Marco was never retrained. Where is he? And the rest of the commanders, the ones like me who were sent out to save with one hand and slay with the other, do you know where they are? I'll tell you as much as I know. One by one, as the centuries have gone by, the others have fallen in battle. Just as in the old times, Company medical teams have collected them and taken them back to the nearest base for repair and regeneration. *But they have never been released.* No record of reassignment for any of them, anywhere. I am the last."

"They must be on some base somewhere," I said faintly, but I knew he was telling the truth, as hideous as it sounded.

"No personnel list on any base on Earth carries their names," Budu told me.

Then he did something without warning, without asking my permission, taking advantage of the state of shock I was in. He reached out and set his index finger between my eyes and forcibly downloaded information to me, an encrypted signal bearing something I *really* didn't want to know about. I gasped and shunted it to my tertiary consciousness.

"No!" I clenched my fists. "You can't stick me with this!"

He just laughed. "You'll have to decode it, one day. You won't be able to resist. I wonder what you'll do then? I hope you can hide the fact that you're carrying a secret message, son."

"Why?" I looked at him, almost tearfully. "Why did you do this?"

He half shrugged. "Insurance. The Company won't retire you, son, you look too much like all the rest of them, and you're too good a liar to be caught. You may succeed in doing something where I fail."

"Thanks a lot," I muttered. He swept the transport lounge in a leisurely glance. The two security techs were still at the coffee bar.

"I should tell you what I'm going to tell the disciplinary board," he said. "When I was assigned to Jerusalem, it was the last indignity I could endure. I have obeyed orders and have asked no questions all this long while, as the Company's purpose has been repeatedly betrayed and degraded. The excuse given was always that history cannot be changed. Why did I labor for them to make Rome mighty, if all that power and order was to be handed to a family of monsters? Why did I lend my strength to drive the Saxons out of Britain, if Camelot was to fall in one generation? Once it was not so, but since history began, the Company's way is always to bring something great into being and then to let it die. They set me to kill, because I like to kill, and they think that my pleasure will distract me from the dishonor of these days." He held me silent with that pale-blue stare of his, so pale a blue, cold and self-assured, it was almost no color at all.

"Look now! Islam has brought order here, knowledge, tolerance. And I must wear this cross and wade in innocent blood, that I may get for my masters a box hidden under Solomon's temple. Do you know what some of these Christians have been doing? Eating human flesh. Moslem children. You remember what we would have done to mortals for such an offense, in the days of our power?"

I nodded, shivering.

"That's what I'll tell the disciplinary board," Budu continued composedly. "It may make some of them sorry for me. It won't change what they mean to do with me, but it may put them off their guard. Here come my little dogs."

The security techs were returning now. We watched them approach. Budu said to me:

"I could strike you, if you like. I could pretend anger

with you. It might help you disassociate yourself from me, if you're afraid of coming under suspicion."

"I don't want to disassociate myself from you," I whispered.

"Then you're a fool," Budu replied, and picked up his magazine again. "Goodbye, son. Access the code, if you dare. I wonder if you will."

I stood up and walked away from him shakily, nodding at the techs.

"That one's been in the field too long," I told them in an undertone. "I'll transmit my report this afternoon. Watch yourselves, guys."

But they didn't, apparently; or, to be more precise, they didn't watch Budu. He never got to that disciplinary hearing. I don't know why, I don't know what happened, I only know there was an extremely discreet all-points bulletin broadcast later, using a lot of euphemisms and addressed only to the attention of operatives with a certain level of security clearance. He got away somehow.

I've never seen him since. I haven't looked for him. He hasn't attempted to contact me, and I'm grateful for that. Maybe he was caught a long time ago; how do you hide, after all, from a Company with advance knowledge of every event in history? Though a lot of history is unrecorded, and who knows the event-shadow areas better than we immortals, who have to work in them so much of the time?

I've never accessed his message, all the same.

I've gone through seven centuries with this permanent Pandora's box in my head, and I have nightmares now and then, where I give in to temptation and decode the damn thing, and something awful always happens. Moaning and shuddering, I wake up with a start.

Chapter 26 ❧

I woke up on my Foamfill synthetic bed with a start. As my nightmare faded around me, I realized that my ears were doing that awful inner vibration thing again, and after a millisecond's analysis I knew why. You couldn't have seen me as I dove for the bag under my bed and fled through the doorway of my cubicle; I was moving too fast.

Out in the corridor, doors were popping open all along its length, and there was a white flurry of immortals in various kinds of eighteenth-century nightdress moving like wraiths—very, very fast wraiths—each clutching an emergency bag, rushing for the door at the end of the hall in an unstoppable torrent. But there was hardly a sound, and under the eerie calm of the blue hall lights it looked like a dream sequence from a film.

Down the stairs we went, with muffled thunder of bare feet and slippers, to crash open the ground-level doors and burst into the ice-cold night full of the noise of roaring black surf. Nobody stopped; nobody said a word; we kept going, plowing through the cold soft sand across the beach, gaining speed as we reached the solid ground and sped uphill for the nearest high place.

We'd found a good refuge around a rocky outcropping in seconds, and that was where we were assembled when the first shaking began. At first, vibrations only we could perceive; then the trembling that the base warning system picked up, causing it to emit the shrill bleeping signal that woke the mortals; then the steady *bang-bang-bang* of a fairly big one. It wasn't so bad where we were; a few pebbles went bouncing off the outcropping, and we swayed slightly and clutched one another. We heard the mortals screaming inside the base structure, which rocked and groaned on its pilings like an uneasy elephant. A couple of them came running down the stairs and then stopped in the lobby, staring out in horror at the floodlit sand, which was dancing as though it were alive, each grain leaping up.

"STAY WHERE YOU ARE!" cried one of us, his volume up to the maximum setting. I crouched down and grabbed my poor ears. Where was Mendoza? The shaking got harder; it was coming in waves now. The exterior floodlights flickered and went out, throwing the lobby into black shadow, so we couldn't tell if the mortals obeyed or not. Somebody—it was the geologist who'd spoken with me at dinner—pushed his way to the front of our group and stared down. He stretched out an arm, pointing and yelling, "Sand boil!"

And these things came spouting up from the beach under the moonlight, like jets of water but not glittering the way water would; no, these were liquefied sand fountains. We stared in fascination, swaying to keep balance, until somebody gasped, "Oh, shit, look!"

A sand boil had erupted right beside one of the base's support pilings. As we watched, the whole modular dome began to lean, tilt, as if the uneasy elephant had decided to kneel down, or as if a horseshoe crab had decided to bury itself in sand. There was one shocked outcry from us all, blended with profanity in dozens of long-forgotten languages and dialects, then silence. We watched motionless through the longest ten seconds I could remember in a while, as the base settled, and tilted, and settled. We heard things breaking. The mortals trapped inside were making the kind of noises that come to you in nightmares for years after. We didn't even notice that the shaking had stopped.

With a final groan, the base settled at last and didn't tilt anymore. The mortal crying—and it was mostly crying now, the hysterical screams had stopped—drifted up on the night air, faint as the sound of summer crickets. The wind and the surf were so loud.

"Six point two," announced the geologist.

"All right." Lopez pushed his way to the front of the crowd. He wore a long nightshirt with lace cuffs, and without his wig I saw he had a crewcut bullet head. "Security! Initiate damage assessment and rescue attempts." They saluted and filed away down the hill. "Idomenus?"

"Sir." The geologist stepped forward.

"What, in your opinion, is the least likely location to be affected by aftershocks?"

"This hill's pretty good, sir. Granite bedrock close under the surface."

"Good. We'll establish our emergency camp here. Operatives! Kindly open your emergency kits and prepare shelters and triage facilities. I assume we can expect aftershocks?" He turned to Idomenus.

"Oh, yes."

All around us, immortals were fanning out along the wide saddle-backed hill, and here and there tents were already popping open like mushrooms in the moonlight. Lopez asked me, "Can you estimate what effect this is likely to have on the mission?"

"I don't guess it'll bother the Chumash much, not physically—their houses are pretty earthquake-safe. They'll view it as a mystical event; they have an earth goddess named Khutash, and maybe they'll assume she's angry—" My ears began to go crazy again, and I grabbed them.

Lopez's eyes widened. "Operatives! Aftershock in five seconds!" he shouted. Sure enough, the earth gave a rolling tremor, and we braced ourselves. Fresh screams broke out down at the base. I realized I was getting motion sick. Lopez watched me with interest.

"God, that's useful. Your ears are functioning as an

early-warning system superior to ours," he said as the rumbling subsided.

"You wouldn't want it made standard issue, believe me," I said wretchedly.

"Perhaps not. Continue with your report, please."

"Uh . . . so, the earth goddess is mad about something. I'll have to come up with a reason. I can do that, no problem. As far as the rest of the mission goes, we won't know how it's been impacted until we get a report from security. Was our equipment damaged? Was our collected material damaged? That has to be determined."

"Yes, of course." He nodded thoughtfully.

"You want me to go help them set up tents now?" I looked around for a bush behind which I could throw up.

"No. Remain with me. You're too useful in detecting aftershocks, for the time being. Let's see: it's now oh five hundred hours precisely. As soon as the sun rises, you're to go to the Chumash and reassure them about the seismic event. Perhaps the earth goddess is angry with the Sun about the coming invasion?"

"Yeah, or something."

"Something to pacify them." He turned briskly and surveyed the eastern horizon, which was already a little paler than the rest of the sky. Low down, there was a spreading, rolling puff of what I would have thought was fog, only it was blood-red and blowing from inland out to sea. It was dust, from who knew how many landslides. I worried briefly about my Chumash, until I remembered that Humashup was laid out sensibly clear of possible slide areas.

"Looks like they're bringing out some stretchers," called Ashur, whose tent area had a good view of the base.

"Tsk. Operatives, prepare triage for incoming wounded! What is it, are we about to have another shock?" He whirled about in concern as I staggered for the nearest bush.

"Nope," I replied feebly, and whooped my guts up. "Well, actually . . . now we are."

"Aftershock!" he announced, and it came rolling through,

and we rode it out. "All operatives with medical training report to the triage area, please!"

"That includes me." I held up my paw.

He looked severe. "I rather think your appliances rule out your performing brain surgery at the present time," he told me. "Now, let's go see what's become of our mortal contingent. In the event Mr. Bugleg has deceased, you are second in command."

"Okay." Gosh, I'd made officer again. He strode away to the line of security techs that was just winding its way up the hill, and I wandered after him. We passed Mendoza, who was briskly setting up her tent like all the others. I waved at her. She looked up and grinned.

"Some ride, huh?" she shouted. I nodded and kept going. Nice to know she was all right.

The preliminary reports were: no dead; fifteen slightly injured, with assorted scratches and contusions; three badly wounded, two of whom had been in the lobby, because the glass doors broke when the dome tilted over; and two mortals with, respectively, one broken arm and one broken ankle. Not bad. There were people unaccounted for, but we were still evacuating them from the base, which had remained structurally sound despite its support failure. In the growing light, the base looked like one of those crablike things out of a Hieronymus Bosch landscape, gigantic and marooned on the beach, with tiny people crawling in and out of it. Obviously not a Houbert design. But the lead security tech was confident it could be righted with a day of heavy equipment work.

And I wasn't an officer again after all. Bugleg was escorted stumbling and weeping up the hill by two techs. Lopez and I both scanned him as he approached.

"Minor contusions on your knees and elbows, slight abrasion of your chin," Lopez diagnosed. "Very good, sir! You clearly did the sensible thing and stayed in your room during the shaking. The base modules are designed to provide maximum protection—"

"*You* didn't!" sobbed Bugleg. "You left us! You left us and ran outside!"

"Well, but that's what we were designed to do, sir. We left early so as to have nice shelters all prepared for you when the quake was over. See?" Lopez pointed. "Everything's ready: tents set up, triage hospital in operation, evacuation proceeding on schedule. You'll even have breakfast on time."

"But the base fell over and *you left us!*" Bugleg's voice rose to an accusatory scream. "You knew it was going to happen, you old-time people, and you didn't tell us!"

Lopez hauled off and slapped him in the face. Even I jumped.

"Stop that blubbering at once," said Lopez in a low, cold voice. "You'll frighten the others. Now, then. None of us operatives had advance warning from the Company of this, any more than you did. It's known that California has earthquakes, so precautions were taken, and they've paid off, I might add. None of you has been killed. But there is no written history for this particular region in this particular year. This is one of those dark zones we operatives have to contend with all the time in the field: times and places where anything might happen. You've just experienced a little of the danger we have to face continually.

"As for staying behind and getting you out of your beds, we could no more have done that than we could have told the earthquake to go away. We were designed with the irresistible compulsion to avoid danger at all costs, even at the cost of your lives. You designed us that way, sir, you and your associates, so you've no cause to complain if we perform according to specifications."

I don't think poor Bugleg was taking in half of what he was being told. He stood there in his jammies, shivering and blinking back tears. Lopez looked him up and down.

"Now, I suggest you retire to a shelter and calm yourself. We'll attempt to send a communication to the Company as soon as it can be determined whether or not our system was damaged."

"Okay," Bugleg sniffled.

"Come on, guy, there's a nice one all set up over here," I said, leading him by the sleeve to a minidome a few paces from Lopez's impromptu command center. He was so upset, he didn't seem to notice the physical contact, which would have had him recoiling at any other time. "Looky here! Protection from the wind, nice comfy air mattress, cozy Thermofilm comforter! Why don't we sit down in here and wait until Mr. Lopez gets everything under control, okay?"

"My clothes are dirty," he said sadly.

"Well, sure. That was bound to happen. They can be washed as soon as everything's back up and running."

"Lopez is mean." Tears formed in his eyes. "All you old-time people are mean. I wish I'd never made that pineal tribrantine three."

"Huh?" I gaped at him. Was he telling me he was the genius who'd invented PT_3, the stuff that keeps our immortal cellular clocks set at high noon? I was all set to blurt out the question, but at that very second my ears began to go nuts again. I clutched them and yelled, "Hey, Lopez! Heads up!"

"Operatives! Aftershock!" roared Lopez from where he was conferring with the security techs. The tent began to widgy back and forth, and Bugleg cowered, his eyes wide.

"It's okay! It's okay! Look! It's almost over. It is over, see? You're safe. Nothing can fall on you out here," I told him.

"I'm not safe!" he wailed. "It's cold. It's dark. We're out where animals and savages can get us! I left my sipper bottle in my room. And the rocks hurt my feet. And there's disease vectors and microbes, and the sun radiation will give us cancer. And we're killing the grass on this hill with these tents. And the shaking keeps coming. And . . . I have to be with old-time people." He wrung his hands.

"You don't like us, huh?" I studied him. He shook his head miserably. "How come?"

"You're weird and scary. You do bad things like kill animals," he gulped. The effort of answering a question seemed to focus him, calm him a little. "You chop down trees to make your houses and fires. And you smoke bad stuff and eat and drink bad stuff, even though you know it's wrong."

"Controlled substances." Like coffee, tea, chocolate . . . Boy, if our spartan little beach parties upset him, what would he make of a New World One? Did he even have a clue how Houbert was living down there?

"And you and the old-time mortals do all those rituals and superstitions. Lopez said you were a, a *priest!*" He mouthed the word in utter disgust. "And you watch those things where people kill each other. That's sick!"

"You mean . . . gladiatorial games?" I was mystified.

He shook his head. "No. The Agatha Christies. The Sherlock Holmes. You people *like* those. I know."

"But you guys play shooting games at your holo consoles."

"That's different." His voice dropped to an uneasy whisper. "That's to get out the bad thoughts."

"Bad thoughts?" I made a guess. "You mean, violent impulses?"

He stared at me, trying to decipher what I'd said. "Violents," he agreed at last. "People are bad. We're all bad. But if we play the games every day, just killing pretend things, we don't hurt anybody."

"So people are bad, and we have to keep from hurting anything," I prompted. "And that was why Dr. Zeus was founded?"

He nodded, wiping his nose. "People did war," he said. "Pollution. Killing things until they were all gone. We could stay inside and not hurt anything, but the bad things had happened already. We had to make them not have happened. That was why they made you old-time people, so

you could stop the bad things. But they made you wrong.
I don't like you."

"Okay. But you helped make us too, right? You helped
make pineal tribrantine three?"

"*I* made it," he corrected me. "I figured out how. We had
to make you fast and strong and not get old." And he proceeded to tell me how he'd done it, in technical language
that made my head spin, though the grammar and syntax
were stripped down to six-year-old level. Though I had to
access volumes to get even a grasp of the chemistry and
technology involved, it was obvious it was the simplest
thing in the world to him. Such was his concentration, as
he spoke, that he didn't even notice the next three aftershocks, or the screams of Stacey as she was having a piece
of lobby door removed from her leg.

"Only now I'm sorry I did it," he finished with a hiccup.
"I'm thirsty. Get me something to drink."

"Sure." I groped around and handed him a sipper bottle
of distilled water. He sucked on it contentedly as I stared
at him, trying to dope the thing out. Was he an idiot savant?
But the other mortals shared a lot of his attitudes, and many
of them were nearly as ignorant. Was he just an extreme
case of a future type, brilliant in his own field and proudly,
defensively moronic about everything else? It was a historical fact that after the Victorian era, scientists would become more and more specialized in their disciplines and
less informed about other fields, the opposite of Renais-
sance men. Would the trend continue long enough to produce *this*? And would ecological responsibility warp into
this bizarre self-hatred? What a substitute for a faith! Pu-
ritanism Lite! All the guilt without the God!

And yet . . . what did I want from the guy? He believed
it was morally wrong to hurt anybody or anything. He lived
by his principles and tried to make sure everybody under
his command followed them too, even if his command was
pretty much a joke.

It was sad that he was so terrified of the wild nature he

was trying to preserve, and so bigoted against the humanity he was trying to help. So unnerved, too, by the deathless creatures he'd helped create to do his work.

Jeez, he'd helped create *me*. Here I was, sitting in a tent, face to face with my creator. Or one of my creator's faces.

So I had a couple more pieces of that very big jigsaw puzzle I'd first sat down to twenty thousand years ago. Pieces of the edge, from the look of it. I was pretty sure that Bugleg and his peer group couldn't possibly be running things, poor little sanctimonious Victor Frankensteins that they were. They certainly would never have countenanced the creation of Budu and his fellow Enforcers. To say nothing of all the dirty-tricks squads that had operated for the good of the Company since then. Or Houbert's screamingly decadent parties.

Which meant that Lopez had probably been leveling with me when he implied that he and his cronies were the ones really in charge. It made more sense, and was in some ways a comforting thought. On the other hand, it meant that my kind were responsible for some pretty nasty work, including the betrayal of their own Enforcers.

On the *other* hand . . . you never have enough hands, you know? Look at it from the Company's point of view: here they are stuck with these enormously strong guys who don't even look human anymore, at least not by the modern definition, and as if that isn't awkward enough, they like to kill, kill, kill. Though only in the most righteous of causes! So to keep them happy, you have to keep finding evildoers for them to tear into little pieces. To make matters worse, the immortals are terribly cunning and now beginning to disapprove of *you*.

I would've started sweating, myself. And if there's this future of perfect peace and harmony coming in 2355, what place would soldiers have in it anyway?

I didn't see what choice the Company had. But the Enforcers couldn't have been done away with. They were immortal, after all. Probably they were hidden away somewhere having a nice long rest. Maybe being saved as some kind of special-unit ace in the hole just in case the future of perfect peace and harmony didn't quite work out. Yeah.

The awful bottom line, of course, is that if you're going to rule the world, you have to have absolute power, and everybody knows what absolute power does. Dr. Zeus set out to change things, to give the whole sorry history of the human race a happy ending. The Company discovered that it had to rule the world first; and then it turned out that nothing could be changed. As for that happy ending—we won't know until after 2355, will we?

So, really, what can one poor little coyote like me do about it?

You could decipher the message.

Bugleg began to snore. I scanned him and found that he had asthma, which the dust and spring pollen were probably aggravating. He couldn't even breathe the same air as us, poor bastard.

The east got brighter, and pretty soon my enemy the Sun rose, red and hungry. I got up and went over to Lopez to see how things were going.

He stood in the open air reading a transmission. Our communications system must be okay. He was still wigless, but somebody had fetched his tricorne out of the mess for him, and it threw a pointed shadow on the page in his hands.

"Want me to go check on the Chumash now?" I asked him, and he turned to me a face livid with rage.

"They knew," he said, "about the quake. In *their* time, their survey equipment is clever enough to read old strata like a book. Isn't that wonderful? Of course they had no idea it would be this severe, or that we'd be sitting right on top of it. They didn't tell us, because it would only have upset the mortals; besides, they knew we could handle any problems that might arise. Naturally. It's what we were designed to do, after all."

He crumpled up the paper and flung it into the sagebrush. I slunk away, my tail between my legs. Another round of motion sickness was coming on. Was it an aftershock, or all the shifting conspiracy theories?

You could hardly tell there'd been an earthquake, away from the base. Back along the trail everything looked just as normal and sunny as can be, with little birds singing and dew sparkling on the leaves. In a couple of places there'd been a minor landslide, a few bucketfuls of rocks and dirt fresh and dark on the path; that was all.

Humashup was busy as I walked in. Outside their doors, people were shaking ashes and charcoal out of their sleeping furs, or sweeping cold cinders into the streets. I let myself pretend for a moment I was walking into the old village I dream about, which was now probably buried under somebody's wine cellar in Spain or France. Sepawit, sluicing off ash with a basket of water, greeted me cheerfully.

"Hey, Sky Coyote, You should have been here this morning! We had quite a shaker!"

"Hell of a quake," agreed Nutku, beating his best bearskin robe until the dust flew. I was about to reply when a bizarre figure pranced by, decked in flowers and tootling away on a deerbone flute. It was Kenemekme; he had taken to doing things like that lately. We watched him in silence for a moment. Nutku sighed and went on shaking dust out of his robe, and I tried to remember what I'd been about to say.

"I know. Khutash is very angry. She found out about Sun's white men last night," I told them. They looked surprised.

"Khutash is angry? Is that what makes earthquakes?" Sepawit blinked. "Well, I guess You'd know, but we always thought it was a natural phenomenon."

"What?" Oh, boy, I wasn't at my quick-witted best today.

"We always thought it was the World Snakes down there

under the crust of the earth, the ones who hold everything up? We thought they just get tired every now and then and bump into one another," Nutku explained. "The astrologer-priest says they push the mountains up a little higher every year."

"Oh," I said.

Chapter 27 ❧

HUMASHUP WAS BACK to normal by midmorning. AltaCal Base took a lot longer to recover. Even after the techs had managed to right and reinforce the supports on the modular dome, we had trouble convincing the mortals to go back inside. They crouched in the pop-tents on the hill, shivering, and even when we explained that we could tell it was absolutely safe (hadn't they designed us to detect structural infirmity in any building we might enter?), they wouldn't budge. Finally I said I thought I'd seen bear tracks nearby, and that got them moving. Within an hour the corridors of the base were resounding with electronic beeps and blasts from all the reactivated holo cabinets, and another layer of mutual dislike and mistrust settled into place.

"So, can that thing see me all right?" Nutku inquired, peering into the holocamera lens. It was one of two reflective eyes in the face of a little crouching figure Jomo was carrying on his shoulder. The other two holocameras, similarly disguised, were arranged at the two other points of a triangle centered on Nutku.

"Just fine," Jomo assured him. Jomo was the Spirit Who Wants to Watch As You Build a Canoe. Chang, his team anthropologist, was excitedly talking to Nutku's apprentices where they were attempting to work. They were trying to be terribly cool and make it all look easier than it was. I sat in the shade nearby, glad I didn't have to stand in the sun in my coyote fur.

"All right. This is my boatyard we're standing in," said Nutku, gesturing around him. "Over there are my apprentices. Their parents are paying me plenty to take them on, believe me, because once you've joined the Canoemakers' Union and learned how to build fine-quality canoes, you're set for life. For an extra fee they can get their kid into the kantap, but only if I agree to sponsor him, and I only sponsor the really talented ones. Some guys will let any moron into the kantap if he pays enough, but not me.

"Where was I? So anyway, I've got them cutting up these logs." He walked over to the work site. The boys were hacking away self-consciously, trying not to look up at the camera. "Pine isn't your best material for canoes, but this is a midrange model with just a few luxury features—"

"Where do you get your wood?" Chang wanted to know.

"What?"

"Where do you get the wood you use?"

"Stuku the lumber dealer," Nutku replied, as though it were terribly obvious. "Except when we get some redwood from dealers I know up north, or sometimes we get lucky and a redwood log washes up on the beach. But we're talking pine right now, okay? So what I've got my boys doing is, they're splitting these logs up into planks. Show one for the spirit, Sulup."

One of the kids held up a plank that had been split off, rough and splintery, about an inch thick. He grinned at the camera. "Remember me, spirit! My name is Sulupiauset and my father's a rich man and I make the best canoes anywhere!"

"And you get tar detail, too, smart mouth," growled Nutku. "Pay no attention to these brats, spirit. Anyway, once the pine's all cut into planks, we adze them down until they're only about so thick." He measured a three-quarter-inch space between his index finger and thumb.

"What are they using, there?" Jomo asked, moving in for

a close-up. The boys gladly stopped working to turn to the lead camera and display their adzes, the various flint and obsidian blades in handles made of deer antler.

"Damned expensive tools, but their parents can afford the best. It's an investment, anyway," Nutku explained. "That black rock's imported all the way from the desert on the other side of Kuyam. Back to work, kids."

"Don't you find the flint lasts better?" I asked, surprised. My tribe had always preferred it. The camera wobbled over to focus on me for a moment—the heads of the two other little figures followed suit, turning silently—then swung back to the workers. Nutku stepped out of camera range and told me sotto voce, "Of course it does, but the kids love the way the black stuff looks, right? And it *is* sharp."

Chang meanwhile had become fascinated with the sight of the wood curling back from the planks—it looked so easy—and had taken up an adze himself to try a few tentative scrapes. The boys put their tools down and stood around to watch his efforts, very respectful. Jomo went for another close-up. After a couple of minutes Jomo set down his camera and reached for an adze himself.

"You're doing it wrong," he told Chang. The boys snickered and nudged one another.

"I don't think so," Chang replied huffily. Nutku turned and saw what was happening.

"What do you think you're doing, watching a race?" he shouted at the apprentices. "Get back to work! I want those planks cut and sanded by dinnertime!" He strode back and crouched down in front of the holocamera, which was still recording. "Can you still see me, little spirit? Okay, the next thing we do is cut the planks in the pattern for a canoe and drill the holes so the planks can be sewn and tarred together."

Jomo and Chang were still splintering away at their respective planks, so I went over and picked up the holocamera. "So, uh, what do you use for sanding? Sharkskin?" I inquired.

"What else is there to use? And don't think *that* doesn't cost plenty. Hey, do You use something else for sanding in the World Above?" Nutku stepped too close, and the frame filled with a picture of his chest. I set the holocamera on my shoulder and pointed it at the work team, trying to focus on the boys and not on Jomo and Chang.

"Well, we've got a few things . . ." I hedged, but Nutku pushed on:

"See, Sky Coyote, I've been wondering about something. I know you said we're all going to lose our markets in the World Above, but are You really, absolutely positive nobody's going to need canoes where we're going? What's Spirit Who Buys at Retail going to do with all those he bought, or this one?" Nutku gestured at the one that was being constructed for the documentary. "Maybe nobody uses canoes to get around up there, but couldn't there be some way to create a market? The spirits must go fishing once in a while. What if we came up with some sort of sales strategy, you and I, huh? What do you think?"

I was about to let him down tactfully, when an idea hit me.

"You know, it just might work!" I remembered Mac-Cool's comment about how popular Chumash woven sandals were becoming with our operatives. "Have you ever thought about diversifying?"

"What, make other stuff besides canoes? But canoe building is what I know," protested Nutku. He was clearly thinking about the concept, all the same, because a moment later he added, "Which is not to say I can't turn out wooden bowls and boxes, especially with inlay decoration."

"Even canoes, maybe!" I said, thinking about luxury bases like New World One, to say nothing of the Company's Day Six resorts for twenty-fourth-century tourists who wanted to go primitive. "You're right, spirits do go fishing once in a while. What I'm seeing here, though, is that you have a monopoly on a marketable commodity. Nobody else can make the things you and your people make, and as soon as the other Sky People see how beautiful your merchandise is, I'll bet it'll be in demand. If you organize with Sawlawlan and the others—I wonder if you couldn't start production again, once you're in the World Above? Some canoes, but also baskets, bowls, inlaid carvings, sandals, the kind of stuff people like to buy ready-made."

"Small items they could easily take away with them if they were traveling," breathed Nutku, his eyes lighting up.

"Things that would have a special value because they'd been made by you, the craft masters of Humashup, and wouldn't be available anywhere else," I suggested.

There was an outburst of profanity from Chang; the adze he was using had just broken. "See, if you'd been using it correctly, that wouldn't have happened," Jomo told him smugly.

"We'd have to make damn sure they wouldn't be available anywhere else," mused Nutku, rubbing his chin. "Some kind of bigger and better brotherhood system to put pressure on imitators, if you know what I mean."

"Hey! You wouldn't have to break a single arm," I told him. "We've got this law in the World Above about unauthorized use of somebody else's guild mark."

"Master Nutku?" One of the boys came forward tearfully. "The spirit broke my new adze! My father's gonna kill me—"

"Oh, shut up and take a new one from the basket," Nutku told him. He turned to grin at me. "The spirits are paying for it, after all."

Bit by bit, the town of Humashup began to take on an empty and untidy look, the way a house will when people are packing up to move. One day the chisels stopped ringing in the stoneworkers' yard: the last mortars, the last bowls had been made for the holocameras, and nobody would need any more. That ringing was subtracted from the sound of village life, but the subtraction wasn't noticed.

Next, the adzes stopped chuffing in the cured pine, the

last canoe was finished, and Nutku's boatyard was silent. The boys were glad to clean the pitch and the fragrant shavings off their fingers, glad to kick back and relax for a change. They were still thinking of the upcoming flight as a kind of vacation, nothing more. Only Nutku had grasped the idea that the rules of the game were about to change forever. You'd think that mortals would understand the end as a concept—it's what defines them as mortals, after all— but they never do.

It was my job, of course, to let them in on the truth and conceal it at the same time. I was sort of an anesthesiologist. I capered for the Chumash, I kept them laughing with funny stories, I diverted them with songs and sleight of hand (or paw). I came up with facile answers for the ones who asked awkward questions.

Mostly facile answers, anyway. Sometimes you have to come up with more.

We'd all gone down to the beach to watch the canoe launching—not the beach at Point Conception, where the base was, but the closer and convenient beach the Chumash frequented. It had turned out really well, that last canoe, that midrange model with spear racks (safety bladders optional), and, since people still had to eat until the day of our departure, the fishermen were taking it out to see what they could get.

Jomo had carefully positioned two holocameras on the beach and waded out with the third one for triangulation. Our other anthropologists had been thrilled by the news, and there were a whole bunch of them gathered on the shore, avidly watching-recording the ceremony. Nutku and three other guys were carrying the canoe on their shoulders, while the fifth waited, knee-deep in the surf, both oars over his shoulders.

"All right now!" hollered Nutku proudly, showing off for the spirits. "This baby's going to cut through the water like a Shoshone after a duck! Come on, boys, march! Give me some room!"

"Give me some room!" echoed his bearers.

"Don't give up!" Nutku sang out like a drill instructor.

"Don't give up!"

"We're almost there!" Nutku told them.

"We're almost there!"

"EEEE-ha!" Nutku charged into the water.

"Eeee-ha!"

They wrestled the canoe out through the surf, and the new owner waded uncertainly after them. I was cheering with everybody else, until the security tech appeared at my elbow.

"Jesus!" I leaped into the air. "Give a guy some warning, can't you? You're too good at your job, you know that?"

But he looked grim. Grimmer, I mean, than security techs usually look. "We've caught the intruder. Mr. Lopez said you were to deal with the situation immediately."

"Me? Is there a problem?"

"The Chumash know about it. Our rabbit just walked right into the village. We've got him isolated in one of their huts, but people are curious about him. He won't shut up, either."

I got a bad, bad feeling. Sepawit noticed me talking to the tech and approached hesitantly. "Has something happened, Sky Coyote?"

"Uh . . . the spirit tells me that a stranger has come to Humashup," I translated.

"Maybe it's my Speaker!" Sepawit's face lit up with hope. "Is he all right?"

I thought fast. "The spirits aren't clear about what's going on. I think I'd better get back there right away."

"Let's go." Sepawit sprinted ahead of me. How to tell the guy he wasn't going to like what he found, that he should leave this to old Uncle Sky Coyote? I couldn't think of a way, so I just dogtrotted after him. Halfway there, the tech and I caught up with him, and he limped after us into

Humashup, winded and puffing, holding his side.

Scared and curious Chumash were clustered a short distance from Sepawit's house, in front of which two of our security guys stood guard, tall, green, and impassive. From inside a voice was droning on and on in some kind of chant. Mrs. Sepawit (actually her name was Ponoya, I remembered now) approached us tearfully, leading their little boy by the hand.

"Sepawit, what's going on? Uncle Coyote, the spirits threw me out of my own house! They have a stranger in there, and they're not letting anybody see him—"

"Stranger?" Sepawit's face fell. "It's not Sumewo?"

"No!" she replied, as the security team leader came up to me and saluted.

"You'd better go in there, sir. He sounds like a spy. Potential compromise."

Sepawit pushed ahead of me, and what was I going to do, tell him to keep out of his own house? I did manage to get through the doorway at roughly the same moment, at least, so we saw our visitor at about the same time. I felt Sepawit's silent cry of disappointment. Myself, I was surprised.

After all, this was the guy whose rage I'd felt miles away, who'd been evading our patrols for weeks; I guess I'd been expecting some wild-eyed commando savage with dreadlocks. Not this little man. He wasn't Chumash; Shoshone, maybe, but there wasn't much identifying stuff like tattoos or ornaments, only a pattern of lurid purple burn scars on his chest. He was stark naked, in fact, but that was because the belt and pouches he'd worn had been confiscated. He was sitting on the floor, hands bound behind him, and he was chanting as we entered. Praying. I know praying when I hear it.

But he broke off when we entered, and stared up wide-eyed. He had an open, kindly face, mild of expression. When his gaze fixed on me, he gave a little gasp and a shiver, almost of pleasure. But he forced himself to look at Sepawit.

"Sepawit, my friend," he said in perfect, unaccented Chumash, and what a sweet, deep, authoritative voice he had. "I've come to ask you a question."

Sepawit stared. "What? How do you know my name?"

"Tell me, Sepawit, if you saw your neighbor's little child fall into water, and your neighbor wasn't there to see, would you rescue the child yourself?"

"What? What does that have to do with anything?" Sepawit's brow furrowed. "Who are you, and what are you doing here?"

"I'm trying to explain that to you. What would you do? Would you let the child drown?"

"Of course I wouldn't! Now, who the hell—"

"Who I am doesn't matter. *What* I am is His Voice. Now, follow my argument a little further. If your neighbor's house were on fire, and his women and children asleep inside, and he was with them and also sleeping, what would you do? Would you try to wake them by shouting? Would you try to beat out the flames? Failing that, would you go inside and try to pull them out, even at the risk of getting burned yourself?"

Sepawit controlled his temper with an effort. "Yes, I would. Anyone would."

"Of course you would, because you're a good man, Sepawit. Now. You should be able to understand my duty here. I too am a good man. I've been sent to pull you from the fire."

"In what sense?" Sepawit asked, eyes hardening. He was beginning to have some idea who his visitor was. "There's no fire burning here, stranger."

"You think not, because you are asleep. You've been lulled to sleep by the one who's set your thatch ablaze. You don't know what's happening. He came as a guest to your house, but he hasn't told you his real name. I know his name, however. He is the Great Thief and Cannibal.

He's come in all his evil to destroy your family, Sepawit, to take them off the face of the earth, and why? To prevent them from hearing the joyous Message."

"That's it!" Sepawit glared at him. "You're from Yang-Na, aren't you? You're one of the Chinigchinix priests."

The stranger beamed at him. "And, oh, Sepawit, I have got such good news for you. None of his threats are true! He's been lying to you all along. You've been lied to all your life! The Sun isn't your enemy, and there are no white men coming to do terrible things. All this was a stratagem of the Thief, here." He nodded at me, a little shy deferential nod, as though I were a celebrity.

I sighed and sat down. Talk about déjà vu. Why do I keep running into these guys?

Sepawit's voice was cold. "Uh-huh. I've heard your opinion of Sky Coyote. I don't care to hear more. What you're going to tell me is what's happened to Sumewo. Where is he?"

"Ah, Sumewo," said the stranger with a nod. "The one you sent to spy on us. He's safe; safer than he's ever been, in fact. He knows the Truth now."

Oh, Sepawit was afraid: sick afraid. I could smell it in the air. But he just nodded and folded his arms. "What's your business here, really? You're a spy too, I suppose."

"Sepawit, I meant it when I said I'd come to save you." The little man spoke softly, earnestly. "I really mean you no harm, not you, not any of the others. But when He told me I had work to do here, I must confess I had no idea you stood in such danger." The stranger dared a glance across at me. "We all knew the Thief had a grip on you up here, but I never thought he'd dare to walk among you all in his own flesh! How can you stand it? You must be able to see what kind of creature he is. And such a story he's told you! You must understand that it's not true, any of it. There is no evil old Sun who hates you. How can He be the sort of creature the Thief says He is, when all life proceeds from Him? Doesn't He warm you, doesn't He make food grow out of the earth for you? Do you think He'd do that if you weren't His beloved children?"

"I know your line," said Sepawit with admirable patience. "But if we're the Sun's beloved children, why does He let us suffer and die? Why did He beget us so weak and small? Why does He allow evil to trouble us? It makes no sense, and I don't intend wasting time listening to you tell me it does."

"But all the evil in the world proceeds from *him!*" The stranger gestured at me with a frantic nod of his head. "He's the one who gave the grizzly bear his cruelty, he's the one who stole the fire of eternal life from your homes! Oh, my friend, how he's lied to you all! You think the world is ruled by a host of petty little gods, more foolish and wicked than men are. I tell you it's not true! There's only One, and He's the Sun and the Moon both, the brightest Being in Creation! He may be terrible to the wicked, but not to those who believe in Him."

He had that professional magic in his voice that gets 'em up and storming the barricades. But Sepawit wasn't buying it—he was too afraid about the fate of his Speaker. He turned in disgust.

"What should we do with him, Sky Coyote? I've got boys who can get information out of him. Or do You think You can do something?"

"I'll talk to him," I replied wearily. I had the training, after all. "Go out and tell your people it's all right. Offer your wife my apologies. Oh, and send in one of the spirits, will you?" He nodded and stalked out.

The stranger watched Sepawit through the doorway until he was gone. Then he tried to focus on the ground in front of him, but he couldn't. I just sat and stared at him, and after a minute or two, he had to do it, he had to look up and meet my eyes.

"Hi there," I said.

He looked scared but joyful too, and I knew why. "I refuse you," he told me. "I reject you utterly."

"The feeling is mutual," I told him. This was the last place I'd expected to have this conversation again. I'd lived through so many miserable decades of standing over poor mortal bastards in dungeons, people who hadn't done anything to deserve what I and the rest of my pals in the Holy Office were putting them through. Every once in a while, though, there'd be somebody there on the torture table with the light of Revelation in his eyes, somebody who'd angled to die like a martyr. Mostly I deserved the names they called me, but it was hard not to lose patience with them. What kind of nuts were they, to thumb their noses at a power that could put them in a spot like this?

And you couldn't argue with them. Like this guy, they had all the answers. Like the Englishman had, the one who broke Mendoza's heart. What is it with martyrs, anyway? Are they so set on death because they can't cope with life? Or do they really believe that somehow at the last minute they'll escape by some mystical ladder to paradise? The big Englishman had. I remembered that flat certainty in his pale-blue eyes. God, I'd hated that man.

The security tech I'd requested put his head through the door.

"Sir?"

"Long-range broadcast to base. Give them a situation report. This is a spy for the Tongva, one of the Chinigchinix cultists. He appears to be operating alone. Could be advance scouting for an invasion. Could be a missionary. Interrogation is proceeding. Send instructions, if any."

"Yes, sir." The tech went out again. The stranger had watched us in fascination as we spoke, taking in every detail of the tech's green skin, of my muzzle and paws. When we were alone again, he cleared his throat. He would never for the world have admitted to himself that he was trying to get my attention, but I turned my head to stare at him again, and this time he stared right back, feasting his eyes on my strangeness.

"You're glad to see me, aren't you?" I remarked. "My

very existence proves something. Before today you believed what you believe on faith alone, but now you've seen proof with your own eyes. Of me, anyway. And if I really exist, then your Lord must, too, huh?"

"Even the Liar must tell truth when speaking of Him," he said. I had the feeling it was a quote from oral Scripture.

"You've done a pretty good job of evading my spirits. Why did you give it up? Why did you just walk in here and surrender?" I leaned forward.

"I had my duty to fulfill, and I'd waited long enough. At last, I saw no other way," he replied. "If I can't give these people the Message by my teaching, I can give them the example of my death."

"Nobody's letting you give them any examples."

"You think not?" He shifted, crossing his legs. "I've already planted the first seeds in Sepawit's heart. And all of them out there, Ponoya, Kaxiwalic, the rest of them, they want to know who I am and why you keep me prisoner here. I shouted no threats, I didn't fight your spirits; I let myself be led like a child to my prison. You think that hasn't puzzled them? I won't resist, either, when you have me killed; and you'll look brutal, killing a harmless little fellow like me, who's done nothing but testify to the Truth. And you'll have to kill me, or I'll keep talking to them, telling them what you don't want them to hear. Either way, His purpose will be served."

"Okay." I yawned and scratched my ear. "So let me see if I have this right. You've been sneaking around Humashup for months, maybe even before I got here, watching these people without their knowing it. You've learned their names; you know who's related to whom and all kinds of other little details about their lives. Whoever trained you did a great job. The plan was, when you knew enough, you'd just appear in the village one day, knowing things about people here you couldn't possibly know unless you'd been given divine knowledge."

"And if I scouted the place where I was to fight you,

Thief, who can blame me? Yes, I learned what I needed to know about these poor people. And I learned about you! I've seen your hive of demons over at Raven Point. I know all about what you're doing there!" His eyes were stern. "You've done your best to conceal what unnatural creatures you are, but you can't hide the truth from His Eyes."

"I'll grant you this, you're a pretty good sneak. So then, when you'd awed everybody with the confidence game, you'd start giving them the Message. Winning over converts and disciples to Chinigchinix. I'll bet you've been carefully trained in the right people to go after, too; the ones with power who are emotionally weak enough to listen to you, the ones you can scare. If that doesn't work, the alternative is to build up a convert base among the poor and dispossessed. There are lots of them, and they have nothing to lose by a change of government."

He blinked at me, saying nothing.

"Am I right?" I went on. "So, okay, the next step is invasion. If you've converted the rich, it'll be peaceful and gradual. If you've only managed to get the poor to listen, it'll be a civil rebellion, with lots of assistance from the Brothers in Chinigchinix down south. If you haven't won any converts at all, you'll still have enough information on these people to make an invasion force's job easy. And— worst-case scenario—if you're killed before you can accomplish any of the above, you've been trained to die well, and your martyrdom will confuse and intrigue everyone. Then another missionary will be sent to replace you. They'll keep sending little men like you until one of them does the trick."

He was trembling where he sat. I hated this. I didn't need his terrified expression to tell me I was guessing right; there's only one way to do a job like the one he'd been given, after all, and I should know. I've been a missionary myself. I've persecuted them, too.

"The only problem was," I continued, "nobody counted on my actually coming down here, in the flesh, with all my spirits, who hide in the woods and create surveillance barriers even the best-trained spies can't slip through. Suddenly you couldn't get close to these people anymore, that was one problem, and your other problem was that it was going to be a lot harder to sell your story to them with me here. You solved your first problem by letting yourself be captured. I don't think you're going to be able to solve the other problem, though."

"Wrong." The stranger swallowed hard. "I've told you. Sepawit is doubting you already."

"You wish. I don't think you realize that your people are building themselves a nasty reputation. Sepawit's heard of your tactics: why do you think he sent a spy to gather intelligence on you? And Sumewo wasn't the first one, you know. If you've killed the guy—and Sepawit is pretty sure you have—not all the sweet talk in the world will convince him to worship your god."

The stranger was silent for a moment before he shrugged. "Well. The Lord may have hardened Sepawit's heart for His own purposes. It doesn't matter. We *will* win here, you know that! We have conquered in His name everywhere we've gone."

"Everyone's a winner until he loses," I told him. "You've just had a long streak, that's all. Hey, why don't you tell me why this all-loving Father of yours would deliberately harden one of His children's hearts to *not* do His will? I've always wondered about that, myself. Think He's setting poor old Sepawit up for damnation, just to make an example of him? Sounds a lot like cheating to me. Almost like something a Trickster god would pull." I was getting angry; not a good sign for me. This was the place in the argument where I used to have to resist the temptation to give the wheel a little crank, just to wipe some of the smug self-destructive confidence off their faces.

"You're testing me." The stranger looked serene. "You're tempting me to doubt. Unfortunately for you, by manifesting here in earthly form, you have proved to me forever and beyond question that He is Lord. You yourself said it."

"Well, yeah, but I'm the Great Liar, ain't I?" I said with a grin. "What if the only thing my being here proves is that I exist? You can see me with your own eyes, but have you ever seen Him?"

"Everywhere," he replied with certainty.

I nodded grudgingly. "Nice. But not enough. Look, my friend, let's make this short and sweet. You're not going to teach anybody anything, and you're not going to win a martyrdom for yourself, either. I've worked too hard here for you to louse things up at the last moment. My friends the spirits are going to put you to sleep, and when you wake up, you'll be wandering along the beach at Syuxtun with no thought in your head but getting back to Yang-Na. You won't remember what happened here for months, if ever. I'm sure your god has a lot of fine qualities, but you ain't peddling him on this side of the street, not while I'm working it. Understand?"

He was opening his mouth to protest, when the tech came back in.

"Sir? Instructions from base. Prisoner is to be detained at all costs until the cultural anthropology team can get here. Do not, repeat, do not allow prisoner to sustain injury. This is a priority request."

"Huh. Okay." I turned to the stranger, hoping he couldn't read expressions very well. "And then again—maybe I will let you speak your piece. Not to these mortals, though. How'd you like to preach to my spirits? Think of it as a test. Can you convert one of *them?* I'll bet that'd win you commendation from your Boss, big time. Care to give it a shot?"

His face was something to see. Disappointment and suspicion and crazy hope. He leaned back against the wall.

"My faith is strong," he told me. "Do your worst."

*   *   *

My worst was sending him Imarte, who arrived in a flurry of field notes, dragging her little team pal Jensen with her. Imarte, by the way, was a good-looker of a type that doesn't pop up much in the gene pool anymore, Mesopotamian dusky with bright green eyes and an hourglass figure.

"I came the second I heard," she told me breathlessly. "I can't believe it! Until this time we've only had the Boscana manuscript as any proof this religion arose *before* the introduction of Christianity and not in response to it! What a fabulous opportunity to document a spontaneous monotheistic movement!"

"For you, maybe," I told her. "I guess you're going to interview him for the details. Will it take long?"

"Of course." She stared at me as though I were nuts. "You think I'm going to pass up a chance to study this man? He's a priest of a living faith, not some pathetic old mission wreck with half-forgotten traditions. Think of all he can tell us!"

"That's what I'm afraid of," I replied. "Look, I don't want to step on somebody else's discipline, but this guy's presence here is endangering my work. It'll be all I can do to keep the Chumash from killing him, let alone allowing him to live here while you pick his brains. You can't take him back to the base for study, because what will you do with him afterward? He's not going to Mackenzie Base with my Chumash, I can tell you that. I can't even guarantee he'll cooperate with you. You don't know these guys the way I do."

She gripped her notebook with both hands. "We'll manage. Joseph, we really have to do this! And you can bet that once the stockholders hear about this man, they're going to agree with me."

I threw up my paws. "It's your project. Don't blame me if things go wrong."

I led her into Sepawit's house, and Jensen followed us. The stranger had slumped down, but jerked up straight as

we entered. He had his serene and kindly look on again. It
slipped a little when he saw that his tormentors were to be
a lovely lady with big knockers and her mousy assistant.

"Hello." Imarte smiled at him earnestly. "I've come to
speak with you. Are you all right? Is there anything I can
get you?"

"The pleasures of love would be welcome, but will not
distract me from my purpose here," he replied, politely
enough. He looked at me. "What kind of test is this, Thief?
Am I to preach to *these?*"

"Oh, please do." Imarte sat down across from him.
"We've come to hear you speak, this spirit and I, and I
promise we'll listen respectfully. It's not our intention to
mock you in any way. You mustn't imagine we're servants
of Coyote!"

"Thanks a lot." I scratched myself. She gave me an impatient glare. The stranger looked from one to the other of
us, sizing the situation up. He leaned forward to Imarte.

"Listen to me, Beautiful One. If you will believe in the
One True God, even a creature like you will be treated with
mercy by Him. But I haven't come here to preach to your
kind; I came here for the people of this village. Let me go
out and speak to them! The Lord would look favorably
upon such an action on your part." His eyes were big and
appealing.

"Alas, Coyote has powerful sorcery and won't allow it,"
Imarte said with a sigh. "But tell me of this Lord you follow, for I know nothing of Him, and I want very much to
know." Her assistant began to record, unobtrusively.

The stranger knitted his brow. "What do you mean, you
know nothing of Him? You're a spirit. Of course you know
of the One True Lord. All spirits know of Him; they've
simply been wicked and disobedient since time began, and
refused to acknowledge Him."

"Well, but we don't know *much* about Him," Imarte temporized. "You see, um—Coyote has kept us ignorant." She
gestured dismissively at me. "But this I promise you, holy

man: if you will preach to us, this spirit and I will remember your words always, and we will tell them to other spirits. Now, wouldn't the Lord want that?"

He narrowed his eyes, I guess trying to figure whether she was lying. "How many other spirits would you speak to?"

"Through us, your words would reach more spirits than there are stars in the sky," she told him, more or less truthfully. "And everyone would know that you were the bringer of truth to the spirits."

Bravo, temptress! She hooked him with that one. No missionary born could resist such an offer. She knew it, too, from his expression, and pressed her advantage:

"What we would like to hear first is the true story of how the universe came into existence, followed by a description of Him and any earthly manifestations He may or may not assume, and then any notable miracles worked by Him or His prophet, and of course the body of His laws—uh—but why don't you just tell us in your own words? And please stop us at any time if you need a drink of water or anything like that. All right?"

"Very well." The stranger drew a deep breath, trying to ignore, the dazzling prospects opening before him—or maybe it was Imarte's bosom he was trying to ignore—and, raising his fine, loud voice, he began:

"In the beginning was Vacancy and Emptiness, but He was before the beginning.

"Then Vacancy and Emptiness became Pallor and Oblivion; but He was not pale, and He was conscious. Then Pallor and Oblivion became Explosion and Falling Outward, but He did not move, He was in the still center. Then Falling Outward became the Night, full of stars; and the Earth was in it, and He looked upon the Earth.

"And He saw her bear many children, but they followed no Law. He was angry with the children of Earth for this, and so He came to Earth and was born as one of her children too. He was more beautiful than the Sun, but He was so terrifying to the guilty children of Earth that she had to hide Him at first. Still He was like a fire shining out of a grave, and made His Law known to them.

"Earth taught all her other children to worship Him. Now, those who obeyed, He spared. But to those who would not worship Him, His avengers came, bringing terrible torment; the Bear to bite, the Scorpion to sting, the Rose to grieve, the Rattlesnake to poison . . ."

I sighed and left as discreetly as I could. The missionary ignored me and kept going, and Imarte listened, rapt, stars in her eyes, drinking in his every word. It wasn't that she hadn't heard the same old spiel, as I had, in a hundred ancient tongues, in a hundred different centuries; but this was her line of work, and it gave her as much delight as rare maize cultivars gave Mendoza or fake temples gave Houbert.

Not to knock the guy's religion or anything.

And speaking of religion, here was my own little prophet of Revealed Truth waiting for me just outside the door! Kenemekme pushed a chaplet of flowers up from where it had slipped over one eye and looked at me terribly earnestly.

"Is it true what they're saying, Uncle? Is that one of Your enemies in there? Why don't I just go in and explain about how nice You are?"

"Thanks, nephew, but I have my spirits in there working on him." I took him by the arm and led him away.

"I could play some music for him," he offered. "I composed the most beautiful song this morning, all about the light and how it shines and shines."

"That's just wonderful. Say, I'll bet the sea would like to hear your song, don't you think so? How about you run down to the beach and play some tunes to the waves?"

"What a beautiful thing to do!" Kenemekme looked enchanted. "I'll go right now." He ran away, breaking into his weird little dance as he went.

"Sky Coyote?" Sepawit was pacing nearby, looking unhappy. "How long am I going to be kept out of my house like this?"

"Not much longer, Sepawit, I promise." There had to be a more convenient place for Imarte to conduct her researches. "I've got my spirits on him now, softening him up. They'll get him to talk in no time."

"Sounds like he's talking well enough," Sepawit said with a scowl. He was right; the stranger's trained voice was carrying right through the walls, so that all Sepawit's neighbors were getting an earful of the Youthful Miracles of Chinigchinix. He had reached the part where the Boy Divinity takes His elderly blind aunt digging clams and tricks her into entering a sea cave, which He then walls up so she drowns at high tide, which is okay (as He explains to His disconcerted family) because she's really a sorceress, only nobody but Him knew.

"The spirit is letting him think he's converting her. Lulling him," I explained. "Once she has his confidence, she can trick him into revealing the invasion plans."

"If You say so." Sepawit looked down and sighed. "I don't suppose You could try to find out what became of my Speaker?"

"Sumewo. Right. She'll ask, but . . . the Tongvans had to have captured him, Sepawit. How else would the guy know to come straight here, to this village? And they had to have made him talk, and to do that . . . well, the outlook isn't good. I'm pretty sure he's dead, Sepawit."

Sepawit turned his face away. "I thought he must be." After a moment that wasn't enough, and he covered his face with both hands, and drew a deep breath and held it. Finally he managed to say, "But I have to know, Sky Coyote. You understand."

"He was your son, wasn't he?" I guessed. Behind us the droning voice went on, describing the birth of a prophet to a young girl who had never slept with a man. Sepawit nodded miserably.

"Not Ponoya's. My firstborn. From a long time ago. He

was a brave boy . . . would have made a great chief. He became my Speaker when he was only sixteen." He choked off. "He volunteered—oh, Coyote!"

I sighed. So many old masks to try and fit on over this coyote face. All afternoon I'd been wearing the Persecuting Inquisitor; now I had to put on the kindly Father Confessor.

"You know what happens to a soul like that, when it leaves the body? Flies straight over the rainbow bridge to paradise, straight as an arrow," I told him. "After all, this wasn't a boy who died in a stupid accident, or in a fight over a woman, or of illness. He was willing to risk his life for his people! And a strong soul, and a good soul, comes back sooner, because it has the most work to do in this world. You'll see him again, Sepawit."

"Will I see him where you're taking us?" he asked, without much hope.

"Well, no, because you won't be dead. But there are higher paradises, and you'll move on to them eventually, and he'll be there."

"If he's dead." Sepawit turned his head in the direction of the house, where the stranger had begun to sing a hymn. "There's always the chance, of course, that he isn't. It's not knowing that's killing me. Maybe the Tongvans aren't as bad as we think, maybe they've treated him well. What if he's alive, and we leave here, and we leave him behind us? What if . . . it makes me afraid to go, Sky Coyote, white men or no white men."

"No. You wouldn't want to fall into the white men's hands," I said emphatically. "I didn't tell you as much as I could have about them, you know. Your people would have been too scared. South of here, way south of here, they came for a tribe that was bigger and richer than you could ever imagine. Only a handful of white men against this powerful tribe, but you know what happened? They walked right into the biggest village and took their chief prisoner, without striking a blow. That tribe are all slaves now, the ones left alive. And you and I could walk south right now,

Sepawit, for only a few moons, and you could see with
your own eyes the graves of their babies stretching to the
horizon. You think that doesn't make me sick with fear for
all of you? And they're coming for you, Sepawit, don't kid
yourself. They're creeping up on the Tongvans just as
surely as the Tongvans are creeping up on you."

"Maybe the white men won't last forever," he sighed.
"Maybe there'll come an age of the world when they've all
gone away and we can be born again back here. And then
I won't ... then my son can be the chief he would have
been."

"Of course he will," I said. "But meanwhile your other
son will grow up free and happy, and he'll never have to
watch his mother being raped by conquerors, and he'll
never be sick a day in his long, long life. And why? Because you'll all be safe with me, in the place I'm taking
you. Think about it, Sepawit. You don't really have a
choice here, do you?"

"No, of course not," he replied. His gaze wandered to
the house again. The stranger was singing:

> And he told her, the priest said to the girl,
> To the girl white with anger,
> To the pure girl in her robe of honor,
> The priest fell to his knees and said to her,
> "O young girl! you are most fortunate!
> For you have been the one to bear the child
>   of the clouds,
> The son of the dead, the hungry one,
> The prophet of justice,
> The Sun in his person, the Moon and Stars
>   in the flesh!
> Here on this island of the blessed,
>   you will bear him!"

He had a beautiful voice. All of Sepawit's neighbors
were coming out to listen.

Chapter 28 ❧

I TRUDGED WEARILY back to the base by my devious ways and had myself a sponge bath. It didn't do much toward taking away the psychological stench, but not even peeling off my skin would have done that.

I used to soap up in various wooden or tin tubs after a session in the dungeons of the Holy Inquisition. Anybody in his right mind would have bathed, the places were so foul. The worst part wasn't working in the questioning chambers; it was being sent to fetch prisoners from the filthy cells where they'd been sitting forgotten for weeks or even months. Worst of all was opening a door and seeing a buzzing mass of flies whirl up from something that wasn't going to have to worry, ever again, about whether or not it was Jewish. Or maybe it was worse to open a door into darkness and meet the stare of a child, alone there, forgotten by everybody except some rabid priest who'd authorized red-hot pincers for her mother.

Maybe that was my last straw, maybe that was the moment I finally came to the place Budu had been when he watched Christians eating Moslem corpses. Not that I hadn't seen children die before. Maybe it was the cumulative effect of seeing them die over centuries, being able to rescue only the perfect few for immortality. Maybe it was just my amazement that the kid never cried.

She didn't cry once while we were interrogating her. She

was so angry. Her anger fascinated me; there wasn't a doubt in my mind that she'd refuse to break. Even when we began to wear her down, when she was terrified by having been shown the torture chamber, when she was confused and exhausted, she didn't cry. I think she was four years old, at most.

And she'd fit all the physical parameters. With an iron soul like hers, I thought she'd make a great Facilitator someday, so I spirited her off to the hidden lab where Marigny and I ran the rescue operation. I couldn't believe it when he came out later with that look on his face.

"What do you mean, she's not up to specs?" I hissed. "I scanned her myself. She's optimum for augmentation, for Christ's sake!"

"She scored high on everything, but that's the problem," he muttered, not looking me in the eye. "She's a Crome generator, Joseph. Not much, maybe only force two, but the readings are there. Look at the brain imaging, if you don't believe me. Any score above .009, and the Company doesn't want them. You know that."

I knew. Some mortals generate Crome's radiation spontaneously. Actually everybody generates some, under sufficient stress, but mortals who produce above a certain amount tend to do flukey things like levitate small objects and see the future. If it were controllable or predictable, the Company could make use of it; but it isn't, so we don't. And when you're transforming a mortal into an immortal, you *really* don't want anything uncontrollable or unpredictable in the equation, because any mistakes you make aren't going to go away. Ever.

But what was I going to do, send the little girl back to her cell to die? One more lousy deed in my life that was becoming an unending string of lousy deeds, just so I could occasionally get a good deal on something or someone Dr. Zeus wanted.

She's stressed, I told Marigny subvocally. *That's why she's scoring so high. So, you know what you're going to*

*do? You're going to fudge the test results so they read
under .009, and nobody's ever going to know you did it.
I've already forgotten what I just said. You owe me, Marigny!*

Out loud I said, "Well, you'd better go back and double-
check to be sure. Did you remember to factor in the med-
ication I slipped her?"

"Oh, my gosh, that totally slipped my mind!" exclaimed
Marigny. He wasn't as good a liar as I was, but he was
good enough. "I guess I'd better go back in and take another reading."

So he did, and this time Mendoza scored nice and low
on the Crome test, and we shipped her off to Terra Australis
Base to be processed for immortality. I couldn't believe it
when I found out she'd become a botanist. I'd been certain
that the kid was Facilitator material.

Then again, would I want a daughter to have to do the
kind of work I do?

"Are you out of your mind?" I took off my tricorne and
flung it down on the conference table so hard that papers
fluttered everywhere and styluses rolled off. "This guy is
poison! He already has my people arguing. Everything
we've done so far could be jeopardized. All that coopera-
tion, all that trust could go."

"With respect, Joseph, you're overreacting." Imarte kept
a tight hold on both ends of her stylus. She looked de-
murely down the table at Lopez. "You should see the man,
sir. He's no warrior, not by any stretch of the imagination.
He came on a peaceful mission to evangelize for his faith.
While I agree that he mustn't be allowed to do that, for the
sake of our own mission, we have an incredible opportunity
to learn from him. And we certainly can't mistreat him in
any way! Not only is it in violation of our code and everything we stand for, it wouldn't give the Chumash a very
good impression of us."

Lopez sighed and drummed his fingers on the polished

synthetic substance of the tabletop. "Joseph's not asking that we kill the man, madam. You simply want him removed from the village, am I right?" He turned his head to me. Beside him, Bugleg watched us uneasily.

"That's all. Put him in a holding cell here. Conduct your interviews with him as long as you want, but in a place where my people won't have to listen," I implored. "The guy can project like a stage actor! And my poor chief would like his house back."

"I'm sorry about that," said Imarte, looking away. "We can try to make arrangements for Sepawit. But we can't move the man here, not to this alien environment! Don't you understand the importance of obtaining such material in context? Right now, his beliefs are intact. Even meeting you and me, disguised as we are, has reinforced his world picture and his belief system. The minute he's exposed to *this*—" she indicated the base with a sweeping gesture that took in the four long walls of the gray conference room—"the material will be compromised. His belief system will change."

"So dress up your quarters to look like the inside of a tule house," I snarled. "Don't let him see any plastic while he's here. Whatever. But I want him out of Humashup!"

"And we'll get him out," Lopez agreed. "I'm certain there's a way to accommodate everyone, Imarte. Our first priority must be the Chumash rescue, however."

"But they're as good as rescued. We've learned nearly everything we can from them. What can happen now?" Imarte said. "And this man is such a valuable source of information, it would be criminal not to learn as much as we can while we have access to him. Besides, not only would he speak differently here in this strange place, I'd listen differently. There's a mind-set that goes with hearing such stories seated on the earth, under a wooden roof, where I can smell the cooking fire and see the artifacts of ancient life around us. All that would be lost here."

"Look, you may be grooving on the primal ancientness

of it all," I said, "but in the meantime this man presents a real danger to everything we've accomplished. And the Company has a low, low tolerance for people who endanger our work."

"And if the Company knew what's at stake here?" She leaned forward. "You know how some of our stockholders feel about monotheism. They'd want him saved at all costs, you know they would! What if they put it to a vote?"

"What, indeed?" said Lopez calmly as he poured himself a glass of water. "They might just do that, if they knew about this man. They don't, however. Someone here did try to tell them; I intercepted an unauthorized transmission only last night, in fact."

Imarte gulped. My ears went up. "Of all the under-handed—" I began, but Imarte cut me off:

"We don't need to contact the future for a directive, any-way. There are enough representatives of the future here for a vote right now, if you call a meeting. Call that meet-ing, Lopez!"

"Unfortunately, madam, that authority does not lie with me," said Lopez, and took a sip of his distilled water. A silence fell. We looked at Bugleg, marooned as usual on his island of incomprehension.

"Sir." Imarte got up and went to him. "Surely you un-derstand. This mortal has information on a lost culture, on a faith that would have transformed the world if it had been given the time! The loss to human civilization is, conse-quently, incalculable; but we can change that. This is com-parable to finding Saint Paul or Mohammed and being able to record his actual doctrines in their purest state, not just the edited and half-obliterated translations that have been preserved. More so, because the ideologies of those relig-ions employed scriptural text and have thus survived as cultural influences. Not so with the Native American faiths. We came here to ameliorate that tremendous injustice, sir, and what we've done so far on restoration for the Chumash has made a good start. But we'd be betraying our purpose if we didn't utilize all our resources to record everything we can about this visitor from an equally significant civilization, given the remarkable opportunity we have to do so."

She leaned way over to emphasize her point with her cleavage.

Bugleg fiddled with his stylus. "Um—" he said.

"Sir, I implore you. This situation must be brought to the attention of the stockholders here," she told him. "Call the meeting. Let's have a consensus."

He looked horrified. I sat down and leaned back in my chair.

"You need to know some stuff, sir," I told him. "This man is a religious fanatic. He belongs to a cult. They do sacrifices and rituals."

"They do?" His eyes darted to my face.

"Yes, they do. And you know how we've been saving the Indians, and it's all been going really good? You know how we're going to take them off to a base where they can stop doing savage old-time stuff and live just like you? Well, this man wants that not to happen. He wants to make them belong to his cult. See, he's one of those guys who thinks it's okay to kill people who don't do rituals like he does. He's a priest. I used to be a priest, and I know what they do. I was part of that Inquisition thing. You know about that, don't you? That was where those bad old guys would torture people to make them join their religion. This guy is doing the same thing. We Old People learned from you that bigotry and intolerance are bad, but *he* doesn't think so. In fact, he wants to start a war over it that will kill lots of people. I bet lots of animals get killed, too. You don't want that, do you?"

"No!" cried Bugleg. He turned accusing eyes on Imarte. "You were all, 'He came on a peaceful mission'!"

"He *is* a man of peace, sir. You don't understand—it's not as simple as Joseph is making it sound." She looked at me furiously. "Yes, he comes from a religious group, but

you were the ones who decided that all mortal cultures have
equal value. You were the ones who thought everything
was worth preserving. I'm simply following our Greater
Mission Statement!"

"You know what he believes about his god, this guy?" I
said with a yawn and stretch. "That He sends animals to
attack anybody who laughs at Him. Hey, and you know
how she was all, Saint Paul and Mohammed? You know
who those guys were? They started religions that got billions and billions of people killed fighting one another in
wars. They said they were men of peace, too, but look what
happened. This is the same kind of guy. Now, she wants
to listen to his talking, and she wants to do it in the Indian
village, and she doesn't think it matters if my Indians hear
his cult ideas. I say it's dangerous. What if they listen to
him and turn into cultists? He's like a microbe, this guy,
he's like germs. Okay? And if you let her have her meeting
thing, and her consensus thing, the germs are going to
spread. Do you want that?"

"How can you *do* this?" Imarte had tears in her eyes.
"Joseph, you of all people should know what's at stake
here!"

I knew better than she did. Bugleg was shaking his head
obstinately. "No, no, no. You can't have a meeting. This
man sounds really sick. No sacrifices and no wars."

"Let's compromise, shall we?" said Lopez, who had been
watching us, chin on fist. "We'll have a replica native
dwelling built nearby. This man can be brought in—perhaps at night or while he's unconscious—and you can continue your interviews there, madam. Minimal loss of
context, and he won't be exposed to anything alien enough
to affect his personal mythology. Will that do? He won't
disturb the Chumash any further, and I'm sure you can
invent a plausible reason for his disappearance, can't you,
Joseph?"

"Sure! Sounds great." I got up and collected my hat.
Imarte stared down at the table with big soulful betrayed

eyes. Bugleg looked at us, from one to the other, still outraged.

"No meetings!" he said sternly.

"Nope. You did good, sir," I told him. "That was smart, giving that order. It'll save the mission from those nasty cult guys. You should be proud of yourself." But he shook his head again.

"Being proud is wrong," he told us.

The long walk back to Humashup wasn't all that comfortable, with Imarte sniffling and refusing to talk to me. I was sorry I'd had to play hardball, but this wasn't the first time somebody's enthusiasm for his own little line of work had made trouble on a mission. Sometimes you have to take people's toys away.

The sound of very loud prayer drifted to us from Sepawit's house as we approached. Was it my imagination, or were the people standing around eyeing me with a certain amount of fear and suspicion? The security tech guys stood stolid and silent outside the door. A lady named Anucwa, one of the bossy wise women, approached us cautiously.

"Uncle Sky Coyote, I think you'd better kill that prisoner. He's saying some terrible things about you. I don't believe any of it, of course, but people are starting to talk."

"Yes, I thought this would happen." I looked sidelong at Imarte. "What is he saying, sweetheart?"

"Oh, all sorts of nonsense . . . that you're the king of the nunasis, for one thing. Which is ridiculous, of course; but he knows a lot of other things that are true. He was sitting in there all night yelling about you, and about all of us here. Calling for people he's never met, but he knows their names and all about their families. We're all wondering how he knows so much about us. I told everybody he must be a sorcerer." She looked at me expectantly.

"Good for you!" I patted her on the behind. "You guessed right. Will you be a love and go tell the rest of them that? And not to worry about the things he says. He's just trying to scare everybody. I'm taking him away from here today."

"I'd better go in and talk to him," murmured Imarte, which was as close to an apology as I was going to get from her.

"You do that, babe." I watched as she and Jensen slunk away into Sepawit's house. Sepawit, right. Must talk to him.

I found him sitting outside Kaxiwalic's, where he'd been staying with his wife and the baby. The kid was crawling around on his lap, eating most of his breakfast for him. He didn't seem to mind. But when he looked up to wish me good morning, even he had a different took in his eyes.

"Has he told You about Sumewo yet?" he asked.

"I expect to find out today," I temporized. Damn, I'd forgotten to ask Imarte about that. Well, I'd go ask the guy myself. "You're getting your house back tonight, too."

"Oh, good," he said listlessly. "The baby's already broken a couple of Kaxiwalic's belongings. He's a bachelor, You know, so he leaves things lying around . . ."

"I'm sorry." I sat down beside him. "I'll pay for any damage." The baby offered me a grubby fistful of acorn mush, then changed his mind and ate it himself.

"Oh, that's all right," Sepawit said. He was a million miles away. "You don't suppose . . . What if he is still alive, Sky Coyote?"

"Does that seem real likely to you?" I asked him.

"No, but . . . that man has been going on and on about what a loving god Chinigchinix is, as long as you don't cross Him. He explained that Chinigchinix doesn't want everybody killed, just made to worship Him. He says his people haven't been making war on the other tribes. They've just been making them see the truth—His truth—and as soon as the other tribes accept that, then they all live like brothers. Not that I believe a story like that for a minute, but there might be some truth in it. It wouldn't make any sense to kill off all the other tribes you meet—I mean, who would you trade with?—and you can only take so many slaves. I just don't see what the point is of this insisting that everybody believe in the same god."

"He's a jealous god, that's all, and He doesn't want any attention paid to anybody else," I explained. "Children are like that, sometimes. New baby gets born, big sister wants mother to pay attention just to her and not to the new one. You can't give in to gods when they demand crazy things of you, or there'll be no end to the things they expect you to do. You know that tribe down south I told you about, the really rich one? They hooked up with a god who told them they had to give Him human hearts to eat, every day, and blood between meals."

Sepawit shuddered. "What an awful god! What did they do?"

"Well, they sure as hell didn't want to tear out their own hearts to feed their god, so they had to make war on their neighbors all the time so they'd have captives' hearts to feed Him. Pretty soon all their neighbors hated them. Also, they had dead bodies piling up—which they took to eating, because, well, there the bodies were, and how are you going to go hunting deer when you have to make war all the time? And the laugh was, their god dumped them in the end. He just let the white men come marching in and didn't lift a finger to save his people. Talk about ungrateful!"

"Well, if you behave like that, you deserve what you get," remarked Sepawit. "No, what I don't understand is why this Chinigchinix should want to bother *us*? We're good people. We know it's wrong to steal, lie, and murder. What did we do to get this god on our case?"

"Well, you're my children. He doesn't like me, as you may have noticed," I said with a rueful grin.

"It *is* true that You lie sometimes. And steal," Sepawit ventured, looking uneasily at me from the corner of his eye. "At least, the stories say so."

I shrugged. "I did stupid things when I was young. Didn't you? As it is with you men, so it is with us Sky

People. I think Chinigchinix must be a very young god, or crazy, to be so selfish."

"Maybe." He nodded. He was still watching me. "But, You know, that man seems so friendly. So calm. If they're all like him, maybe they're not so bad. Maybe they didn't harm Sumewo after all."

Okay: if you had your choice between believing that your son had suffered a horrible death by torture or believing that he was perfectly all right with good, humane people, which would you rather believe? And if the enemy is good and humane, maybe they're telling you the truth when they say that your kindly old Uncle is actually the Lord of the Flies Himself. And if that's the case, what's your next move?

I didn't know how far he'd gone along this path of reasoning, but he wasn't going to travel any farther.

"This isn't fair. You shouldn't have to suffer the suspense." I jumped to my feet. "I'll get an answer for you, Sepawit. You need to know, one way or the other."

"Thank You," he called after me.

Chapter 29 ✇

OUTSIDE THE HOUSE I could hear the stranger's voice raised in earnest entreaty.

"No! He will preserve you against harm. It's only the unbelievers upon whom He looses his avengers. You have only to agree to this, and I will initiate you into the Hidden Mysteries."

Imarte's voice was strained but courteous. "Please believe that I have nothing but the greatest reverence for your sacred stories. Myths tell us many beautiful truths about ourselves—"

"They are NOT stories!" shouted the stranger. "They are Sacred Truth! Can't you understand that if you deny them, you will be damned for all time?"

"He wants you to convert, doesn't he?" I said, ducking in through the doorway. "Hell, honey, go along with it. He'll be a lot more cooperative."

"I won't insult him by lying to him," she replied stiffly. In Chumash, she told him: "Sir, I want to know more of what you have to tell me. But you must understand that I am only a vessel of the truth. My personal faith is not the issue here."

"Yes, it is." He was staring at her with the most betrayed expression—where had I seen a face like that recently? "If you yourself have no faith, you can't carry it to others. I can never reveal what is hidden to the likes of you! You are hollow!"

"Never worked with one of this kind, have you?" I said, crouching down across from her. "True believers aren't real receptive to the idea that what they're telling you is just mythology. Doesn't matter how appreciative of their culture you are, Imarte. You want my advice, you'll fall down on the floor this minute in a foaming-at-the-mouth screeching fit of revelation from Chinigchinix Himself. Otherwise you're not getting a step further with this guy."

But it seemed my advice was badly timed. The stranger turned his head to stare at me, and he was wroth.

"Now I see the trick!" he hissed. "You've wasted my time with this woman, when I might have been out doing His Will! Oh, Thief, you are pathetic. Do you think a few hours' delay will prevent me from accomplishing what I set out to do?"

I had a snappy comeback on the tip of my tongue, but the guy vanished before I could use it.

It seems that all the while he'd been praying so loud, in there by himself, he'd also managed to free his hands. Then (so far as we could tell later) he'd managed to make a hole in the wall directly behind him, and cover it again with tules so it wouldn't show. This was Super Commando Missionary, after all. Since he'd fixed himself an escape route he could have used at any time, it must have been only the prospect of converting a couple of spirits that made him stick around.

"Oh, no!" Imarte sobbed, but I was out the door ahead of her.

Security! Your rabbit's loose and running! I broadcast. *Contain only! No force! Do not lay hands on the guy!*

Shocked affirmatives bounced through the ether. The missionary was going for his martyrdom, I'd bet. However things turned out now, nobody could see me or mine so much as touch him, or I'd be playing into his hands. He was running ahead of me, dodging and feinting, and he was quite a little sprinter; but he hadn't played for the Black Legend All-Stars like I had. We paralleled each other all the way to the sacred enclosure, with the astonished Chumash watching us. Some of them took up the chase. Oh, great: now he'd have his audience. In front of the whale bones he pulled up, daring me to come closer and prevent sacrilege. I kept my distance, but an outraged priest came out to see what was going on and caught him by the arm. He whirled and struck the reverend gentleman hard. The priest oophed and dropped to his knees, clutching his stomach.

"You see, people of Humashup?" the stranger cried. "It is a sign! The Thief has not caught me, and your own priest kneels to my Lord! The One True God has sent me as a friend to you, to tell you the danger you're in! Coyote told you a story about invasions, and persuaded you to go with him to an unknown place, lest you all be destroyed—and all the while *he* has destroyed you! Look around at yourselves! What's become of your village? Where are the things that made you what you are? You've sold them all to spirits! You are as naked as corpses, without even gifts to take into your graves! And make no mistake about it, people of Humashup, you're going to your graves. Do you know where he's taking you? I have seen the place! He's taking you to Raven Point, where the spirits of the dead travel! Let him deny it, but I've seen his spirits preparing the place!"

Sir? Containment achieved.

Gosh, thanks a lot. Are you in range to try a disruption?

That's against the code, sir—

Heads were turning, people were staring at me. "Of course we're going out on Raven Point," I replied. "That's where the Rainbow Bridge is. You know any other way to get to paradise?"

"But he's not taking you over the bridge!" riposted the stranger. "You'll all go down under the water, where the Lord's avengers will tear you to pieces, flesh and souls!

Don't let him do this to you, people of Humashup! There
are no white men coming! At Syuxtun, at Humaliwu, at
Muwu, your neighbors are living in peace, preparing to
receive the Glad Truth of the Lord! They aren't uprooting
their lives and casting off their property, like people about
to die!"

Nobody was looking at me now, they were staring at the
ground or looking at one another with fear in their eyes.
There were murmurs.

*I'll take responsibility. I don't want you to kill the guy,
anyway; just give him a seizure. Grand mal, preferably.*

On your order and under protest, then.

What a bunch of Goody Two-Shoes. The old Enforcers
wouldn't have blinked at an order like that; but then, they'd
never have let the missionary escape in the first place.

Fine! Wait for my signal—

"People, don't worry about it," I told the growing crowd.
"He's crazy, that's all. Listen, guy, who's going to believe
a little runt like you? Can your god come down and talk
to these people the way I have? You're only a man! Why
should they believe you instead of me, anyway?"

If everything had gone as I planned, he'd have fallen
down then in a fit, a clear sign to anyone watching that he
most definitely did not have God on his side. But Sepawit
pushed through the crowd, carrying a stone cooking bowl.
I swung to point my muzzle at the stranger.

"And another thing!" I barked. "You serve such an angry
god: why don't you tell us what fate befell the boy these
people sent out to spy on you? What did His avengers do
to Sumewo? What awaits those who defy Chinigchinix?"

"Hideous death!" The fool couldn't resist scaring them
with hellfire and damnation. "See the consequence of being
His enemy? The spy could not hide his presence from us,
and with coals and scorpions his tongue was loosened, with
the flaying knife his soul was liberated! But he was more
fortunate than you shall be, for at the end he accepted the
Lord, and so his spirit is at rest. You will envy him, when

the avengers come for you! And they will come—"

But the crowd gasped.

"Sumewo is dead?" Anucwa put her hands to her mouth in horror, and somebody else said incredulously, "Little Sumewo?" and there were moans of dismay, and a couple of people burst into tears. The missionary must have thought he'd hit the mark big time.

But Sepawit stumbled forward, unable to take his eyes off the stranger's face. "You did kill the boy, then," he stated.

"Not I, but the wrath of the One Lord!" shouted the stranger in his triumph. He made no attempt to dodge the stone bowl as Sepawit smashed it down on his head. *Sickening crunch* is a cliché for the sound it made, but an apt cliché. He dropped. There were brains in the dirt. Sepawit sank into a crouch and covered his face with his hands.

I went to him and knelt beside him. "Sepawit. I'm sorry. I told you about these people."

"I just bought that bowl," he said in a stunned voice. "Kaxiwalic won't want it now." He began to shake, and finally burst into tears. He threw his arms around me and wept his heart out, as unashamedly as though I were a sympathetic dog.

"Let's get this trash out of here and burn it," said Nutku grimly. He and a couple of other men took the stranger's body by the heels and dragged it away. People drifted off like ghosts, unwilling to intrude on Sepawit's grief.

Chapter 30 ✎

THERE WERE CONSEQUENCES, of course. There was a whole inquiry and report. Imarte made one hell of a scene, but the final ruling was that if she hadn't been such a fatuous ass, the situation wouldn't have deteriorated to the point it did. Interestingly enough, none of the Future Kids was particularly shocked at what Sepawit had done. After all, he was only a savage, wasn't he, and didn't they do things like that all the time? And maybe the mortals from the twenty-fourth century were still human enough to wonder what they'd do if they found out that one of *their* children had been tortured to death.

But my fellow immortals were mostly on Imarte's side. I had set in motion the chain of events that led to the death of a mortal; and while the older operatives understood that this had been necessary for the good of the mission, they were a little disgusted by the debating trick with which I'd beaten Imarte. None of them were Facilitators, naturally. The anthropologists, of course, were outraged and horrified at what a slimy little guy I was. The younger operatives agreed with them.

Except for Mendoza. She'd barely noticed any of it.

I was sitting in splendid isolation at my table in the commissary, pretending not to notice as people avoided sitting near me. Not that I blamed them; I wouldn't want to watch me eat, either, with this coyote muzzle. Mendoza came in and got a bowl of soup and some crackers. She carried them straight to my table and sat down across from me, to my surprise and shock. I looked up at her to see if she was maybe expressing a comradely solidarity. I should have known better; she was staring absently into space, crumbling crackers into her soup in a way that suggested she'd forgotten how to eat.

"It's tomato bisque today, you know," I told her.

"Uh-huh."

"With real synthetic cream."

"How gross," she said, but not as though she meant it.

"So, how's it going lately?" I inquired. "Haven't seen you in the village much, now that the operation's winding down."

"I've been in the field, doing a survey," she said, bringing her stare back from a great distance and focusing on me at last. "I went for a walk. I was gone seven days and seven nights, and never stopped walking. I went a long way up this country, Joseph, more than a hundred miles. You wouldn't believe the things I've seen."

"What did you see?" I leaned forward. She leaned forward too, and there was a warmth in her eyes for the first time in a long time, but it wasn't for me.

"I saw a high desert, a bitter, chill place with no water, a desolation of spines. But one night of rain, and there were flowers there stretching for miles, rolling away in every direction: violet, blue, crimson, and every shade of gold, pale gold like the morning or saffron yellow, and green-gold like brass. They just swept on forever, and the color pulsed and flickered like a bed of coals. There were clumps and stands of boulders rising from the desert floor, and they were *pink,* Joseph, like strawberries bleeding juice into cream, colors of the strangest innocence for that place of death.

"I turned my face north and went on, and looked down out of the mountains into a valley floor. It ran five hundred miles, with a river winding down it, and was so wide, a mortal wouldn't have been able to see across, and on the bottom was a lost sea. Only salt marshes left, marooned in the land, and cracked earth white with salt and bleaching bones. There was still a smell of the sea in the air, which was hot as a furnace. I walked across the valley and found mussel shells in the rocks. Condors drifted in the thermals over it, and dragonflies mottled green and orange, big as birds.

"I walked up that valley, following the edge of the hills, and crossed over west into the green coastal range. North of here, Joseph, are oak forests that run on unbroken for miles, every kind of oak tree, every species that exists! Some are so old, so huge, one tree might shelter a whole valley in its shade. But you should see the redwoods!

"Where the mountains fall steeply into the sea, that's where I found the best ones. You've never seen trees so tall, not even you, and these are so old, they might have taken root when you were young. They make a darkness like night down in the canyons, cold as night, heavy with shadows and incense. Around their roots, even the little growth is ancient: horsetail rush and fern, living fossils. It might have been a million years ago; I felt I had fallen into the past there, with not a human sight or sound for miles. It's all alive with its own life, Joseph, nothing to do with us!

"I went north until I saw a mountain of marble, like a white pyramid, and that was where I turned back and followed the coast down. It was like a garden! Madrone trees all along the ridges, standing like queens, the leaves every pastel shade, the blood-red bark peeling back from the branches that might have been smooth-cast in copper. Silver-barked alders following every little stream down to the sea, and buckeyes just beginning to put out big sprays of pink-and-white blossom, fragrant as almond oil. Tiny meadows a thousand feet above the sea, talk about your hanging gardens!

"And there's a place, Joseph, where a vein of green stone

works its way through the side of a mountain and down into cliffs that stand above the sea, and the trail to the beach winds over boulders like raw emeralds. The beach is all dark-green sand, and the water's clear and green like rolling glass. Not one human voice to hear, not a breath, not a heartbeat, not a cry! Only the sound of the sea booming in the green caves.

"I could have stood there on that headland forever, perfectly happy, until the green lichen had grown over me, until the long mosses trailed from my hair. I never wanted to move from that spot again. You must have found places like that, in all your centuries. Haven't you ever wanted that, Joseph, just to let go of your humanity and let the sunlight flood in on the black place where it once was?"

She looked so happy, and I was losing her, losing her into that wilderness. But the ice was melting, the stuff that had locked around her heart on the day the Englishman died.

I smiled my most sincere smile, coyote teeth and all, and said, "It sounds swell, honey."

"Oh, there's so much work for me here," she went on, her eyes intense. "The Spanish will graze cattle and work unthinkable changes on the environment, but what the Yankees do in their turn will make the Spanish look like conservationists. There will be mass extinctions of the native plants as species are introduced from Europe and go wild. There are endemics growing here that are found nowhere else, Joseph, plants that evolved on their own in some fabulously distant time, maybe when this whole range was an island to itself. Did you know it was an island once?"

"I'd heard that."

"The geology bears no relation to the mainland of America. This whole place just drifted in on the continental plate, appeared on the Pacific horizon like a cloud, and came to rest here. It will move out to sea again one day, tearing loose from America with enough seismic force to level the cities. Paradise on the move once more, and the angel with the flaming sword back in residence." She looked wistful. "Perhaps the people will all be gone by then. The trees will still be here, though, if I do my work right. Do you think I have a chance of staying here, Joseph, if I put in a request with the Company?"

"You might," I replied, knowing I would have to pull in a couple of favors again. "I don't see why not, if there's as much botanical work as you say. They need somebody here, and it might as well be you."

"Exactly. This was what I did my graduate work in, anyway, you remember? The particular botany of the New World. This was the place I wanted to go, when I started out. Isn't it funny how I was right about this, all along?" Resentment flashed briefly in her eyes. "Why on earth didn't the Company send me here first, instead of Europe? Think how different my life would have been!"

No denying that. "But you'd never have scored that *Ilex tormentosum*," I reminded her. Then I wished I hadn't, because such a bleak look came into her face, I wanted to lift my muzzle and howl that I was sorry, I was sorry, I was sorry.

"Damn you for the memory," she said. "Oh, hell, what's the point in denying it happened? It would have all been ended by now anyway."

"I tried to tell you."

"I know. And I never believed you, even after he was gone." Cold sorrow in her white face, all the happiness pale ashes again. She gave me that look like steel, straight into my eyes. "Do you know when I believed you at last? In 1596, when Sir Francis Drake died. There was quite a lot of chatter about it, you know, because he was a sort of anticelebrity down there in New Spain. Houbert held a big mourning party—all in fun, naturally. There was an enormous dessert, a ship, the *Golden Hind*, sculpted in Theobromos. Everyone was supposed to come dressed up as pirates, I remember. People were swaggering around speaking in terrible English accents, and the sound of those voices again—well. That was when it struck me, you know, that I'd been away from England for forty-one years."

She was looking past me now, out the commissary window at the dark Pacific. Her voice had grown cool and distant. "He'd have been an old man, my Nicholas, if he'd lived. I didn't dare try to imagine what he'd have looked like. How could time wreck that well-made body of his? Stupid question, since fire did the job in half an hour. Anyway I sat there at that table with Houbert's damned orchestra playing *Fifteen Men on the Dead Man's Chest,* dropping miserable tears into my rum cocktail, and that was when I knew you'd been right."

"As I sat there, a kind-hearted stranger saw me crying and brought me a handful of cocktail napkins so I could blow my nose. That was how I met Lewis.

"He was so kind to me, Joseph, that day I knew that you'd been right. It would have come to grief in the end no matter what Nicholas and I had done. You were right after all."

"I was hoping you'd forgive me eventually," I said.

She brought her gaze back to me with a snap. "I didn't say I'd forgiven you," she said. "You could have saved him for me, and you let him die."

"Baby, I couldn't have saved him! You know that. There was no way he was going to let us rescue him."

"Maybe," she replied. "But I know that if there had been, you'd have killed him just the same. He'd seen too much; he knew about us. That made him a security risk for the Company. He had to be silenced, and you were all ready to do it. It was simply your good luck he was so set on his martyrdom; saved you the trouble of injecting him with one of those nasty little drugs you used to carry around with you."

What could I say? We both knew it was the truth.

She put her head to one side, considering me. "No lies, no denials? Well, good for you. Listen, don't feel too badly about this. I can't forgive you, but I do understand that you had no choice. You're a Company man, and you had to do what the Company wanted. You always have; you always will. I don't hate you for it." She reached out and patted my paw absently. "There's not enough of *you* inside there to hate, is there?"

Maybe not.

I said nothing—what could I say?—as she got up and walked away. The soup she hadn't even touched sat there at her empty place, getting cold.

Chapter 31 ❧

THE LAST DAYS of Humashup were now drawing to a close. Nutku and his cronies had liquidated their assets and closed out their books. The priests had stripped their holy places of sanctity and shut them down. Streets and houses took on an eerily clean look, because what hadn't been packed up for travel had been sold to the Company. People had nothing to do but eat and talk to one another. We had come to the dangerous days, the time when second thoughts occur; and while the missionary had failed in his effort to convince them that I was Evil Incarnate, maybe some of them were now a little shaky in their confidence. Not Kenemekme, of course; nothing could upset him; he just danced his little dances and played his little tunes and was happy with me as he could be. But other folks were getting restless. Other folks were thinking about friends or relatives in other villages who would be left behind. Other folks were beginning to realize this was not a game.

How would I handle it? How would I keep them from contemplating the end of their world?

Try this some time and see if it doesn't work for you, when you're having problems with your Chumash.

"Sorry I'm late, everybody," I puffed, sprinting into the clearing where everyone had gathered at my request. It was just getting dark, so the white sheet I was carrying shimmered ghostly in the twilight.

"We're all here, Uncle Sky Coyote, like you wanted," Sepawit told me, looking uncertainly at the techs who'd come with me. They ignored him as they proceeded to set up the primitive battery-powered equipment they'd brought. Some of the people turned and stared at them; others watched me as I got busy tacking up the sheet between two oak trees.

"I can see you are, and I'm very pleased," I said. "I worked hard to get this treat for you tonight, I'll have you know. Had to send off all the way to the World Above for it!" Which was close to the truth; New World One was a tropical paradise, wasn't it?

"A treat? That's nice," said Sepawit, turning to let everybody know, but most of the village had heard our conversation and were murmuring to one another. When I turned to face them all, they looked up at me with bright anticipatory faces, the young people and the old ones, the shamans and the hunters and my pals from the kantap. I could see that the techs were just about ready, so I threw up my arms in a gesture of welcome. The white spotlight hit me, and there were cries of astonishment.

"My children!" I cried. "I hate being bored! Don't you? Doesn't everybody? Even spirits get bored, you know. We were sitting around in the Sky talking about what a great show the kantap put on for everybody, and the spirits were saying they wished there was something they could do to repay you all for the wonderful time they had that night. So I said, well, why don't we work some magic for them?

"And they agreed that was a great idea, so here we are. Tonight, I'm going to tell you stories the way we tell them in the World Above. Before we do, though, I have to show you my special hunting medicine."

There was a flash and a click as the first of the slides was inserted, and on the sheet an image appeared: a red cylinder as long as a man's hand, with a piece of cord protruding from one end and a little flame licking at the tip of the cord. I pointed to it.

"There. That's my Fire Flashes like Lightning. If I want to kill something, all I have to do is throw one of these babies and wait for whatever I'm hunting to run across it. It's better than a harpoon, and not only does it kill what I'm hunting, it cooks it for me on the spot! Like it?

"But look at this one!" The slide changed, and there was a bigger red cylinder, and this one had a stick protruding from one end and a cone-shaped head on the other. "This is my Flies like a Goose! When I want to go somewhere in a hurry, I just climb on its back, tie myself on with some cord, and hold a little fire under its tail. You should see me go!"

There were gasps of wonder. I could see Nutku and the others from the kantap sitting forward, peering hard at the screen to figure out how the hell I was achieving this illusion. I let my tongue hang out and grinned.

"Here we are. This is Pulls through the Air," I continued, pointing at the next picture. It was a figure like a red U on its side, and the tips of its ends were dull silver. "Whenever I want something to come to me, I hold this up, and it attracts it! Well—most of the time, anyway.

"Now, this is only some of my hunting medicine. Whenever I need more, you know what I do? I put some shell money in a pouch, and on the pouch I inscribe this." On the white screen the word ACME appeared. "This sign is the most powerful medicine of all. I can get anything I need with this sign. Yes, folks, that's my secret! Now you know how I became the powerful and successful hunter I am, and now you'll be able to enjoy the hunting stories I'm about to show you." I stepped forward, picking my way through the seated crowd, and sat down between the kantap and the other notables. "Roll it, guys!"

The equipment began to whirr, and there was a burst of sound that made everybody jump. A blurred image appeared on the screen, which resolved into a pattern of red concentric circles as a jolly little tune announced itself.

"What's that, Sky Coyote?" Kaxiwalic leaned over to ask, shouting a little above the bouncing music.

"It's the tribal tattoo for the World Above," I told him He nodded thoughtfully, and then his attention was seized and held by the bright figures that leaped into view. His cry of astonishment was echoed by most of the people of Humashup. The audience fell silent as they leaned forward and stared openmouthed at a brilliant world of red mesas, yellow desert, blue sky. Across this landscape a streak of dust was moving at high speed, emitting a high-pitched double cry.

"Hey!" said Sawlawlan abruptly. "I know where that is! Isn't that down at Sespe?"

"Who cares, you idiot?" growled Nutku. "Don't you want to know what's making the painting move?"

"Well, sure, but—"

Conversation died as the dust streak halted in its rush and everybody gaped at what had been emitting the strange cry.

"Is that some kind of bird?" Sepawit inquired politely, just as it began to move again. Close behind it, here came a second speeding blur. I elbowed Kaxiwalic.

"You'll appreciate this," I told him, just as the blur froze to reveal—

"COYOTE!" cried the whole village, nearly in unison.

If they'd been interested before, they were spellbound now. The people of Humashup watched intently as the hunt progressed, scarcely drawing a breath until the first time the coyote turned full-frontal to glare at the audience, inviting them to share his frustration at the unstoppable speed of his adversary. There were some horrified mutters from the priests and shamans, but they were drowned out by a wave of tittering. Kaxiwalic guffawed outright.

"All right, all right!" I said good-humoredly. "I'd had a little accident when these pictures were painted, okay? It grew back later."

The laughter never really stopped after that, even when their mirth at a coyote with no penis died away, because here was the first stupid blunder with the hunting medicine: Coyote trapping the damned bird under a tub and throwing one of his fire-sticks in after it, then waiting expectantly for the explosion that never came. Half the people in the audience groaned and howled warnings to Coyote as he couldn't resist peering under the tub to see what had gone wrong, then crawling inside the trap himself to investigate. Of course, the bird had magically escaped, and it looked on brightly as the explosion came, blowing poor Coyote sky-high.

No, they couldn't stop laughing at poor old Coyote, through his misadventures with the ACME hunting medicine that never worked right, through his collisions with inescapable red boulders and cliff walls, through his doomed stares at the audience as he free-fell down, down, down some red canyon, so far down that he disappeared before the tiny puff of dust below signaled his impact.

They had no problem at all understanding the humor. I needed to explain that the long gray stripe with the white line that wound to the horizon was a game trail, and that the wheeled things that charged along it blaring before they flattened Coyote were a kind of high-powered nunasis. Most of it they figured out for themselves, though, even the fiendishly clever contraptions of levers and springs that always failed to function until *after* the bird sped by, even the rocket-powered shoes or mail-order wings that invariably flew Coyote straight into rock walls. And how they laughed and laughed, including poor gloomy Sepawit, who hadn't smiled since the day he'd learned his son was dead.

Mortals are funny about their gods. My people were reassured: this was the Coyote they'd always known, this clever loser, always starving, never quite able to do anything without taking an ignominious pratfall. Who could imagine me as a demon of darkness now? When you laugh at something, you don't fear it anymore.

I sat there among them and wrapped myself in their happiness. Good old paintings: you can't beat them for a teaching device, whether they're bison that seem to dance on a rock wall by the flickering light of a tallow lamp or rabbits that caper on a white sheet suspended before a projector.

Once upon a time I'd been the rabbit, hadn't I? The rabbit who always won, who might drive the mean-spirited duck or the little pink man crazy with his tricks but who was never mean-spirited himself. That had been my favorite role for years and years, clever immortal guy outwitting brutish mortals but never doing them any harm.

Gradually the world got darker and smaller, and my job got a little dirtier. So I told myself I was the man who had to go down the mean streets, though he wasn't mean himself. I was still the hero, even if now and then I had to hurt somebody. And if it was kind of lonely sometimes, well, that went with the job. Philip Marlowe never got the girl, did he? He always seemed to end up alone in his rented room, no company but a bottle or a chess problem, until the door should open and another desperate soul ask for his help.

You really have to lie to yourself sometimes, if you're stuck with eternal life.

But there would come a point where it was just no use anymore, not with the things I had to do in my line of work, and I couldn't seem to find the role. I was the secret good guy on the bad-guy team, right, playing the Company's hand, not really a member of the Inquisition. But for every Jew I smuggled out of the dungeons because his genetic code was unique and the Company wanted it passed on, I had to watch as twenty were burned. Hell, I helped burn them. Being able to play the sinister Spanish devil, a good meaty part, wasn't much compensation.

I'd been playing Coyote for years now, really, hadn't I? No hero at all, and lately not even much of a villain. God knows I did what the Company asked of me—what else could I do?—but nowadays most of my jobs seemed to consist of catching anvils with my head. How far down was I going to fall? How far before my own personal little puff of dust signaled to the chuckling gods that I'd hit bottom?

Well, no way of knowing, and no point in wondering. I was immortal; no accident was ever going to set me free. Like the silly bastard in the cartoon, I'd just drag myself out of the hole I'd made and limp on to the next job, whatever it was.

Chapter 32 ✑

OH, THE CHUMASH loved those cartoons. They couldn't get enough of them. I had to order more from New World One. Imarte issued a snotty formal protest about it—supposedly I was wreaking havoc with their cultural myth sphere—but she'd said it herself, we'd garnered about all we could of their culture. Besides, as soon as we took them away, they were going to be exposed to a lot stranger things than coyotes on rocket roller skates.

So I showed them the stories about the rabbit and the hunter and the duck, and while I had to do a lot of translating, they found them as funny as I had, long ago. They were so enthusiastic, in fact, that I went ahead and gave them the stuff they really had no context for, like the duck and the pig and the Martian, or the rabbit and the hunter singing opera, or the furious little man with the six-guns. It took a few screenings for them to figure out what was supposed to be going on, but once they'd grasped it, they laughed twice as hard and clamored for more. The kantap began having intense discussions about devising new shows with a whole new cast of characters and new and improved special effects. Imarte was furious.

Not a day too soon, the personnel transports arrived.

I was screening a matinee in the meeting house at the time, so I didn't find out about them until they'd been there six hours. I was on my way back to the base for a nice hot sponge bath, when I saw Mendoza standing motionless on the hillside above me. She was staring intently out to sea. *Something going on?* I broadcast in inquiry. She glanced down, located me, and responded, *The ships.*

So I went trotting up to see and, by golly, there they were: four gleaming transports hanging far out above the water, waiting for nightfall so they could come in.

"Well, finally," I said. "I was running out of party tricks."

"Now you can give your mortals their ride in the chariots of the gods." Mendoza pulled her cloak closer about her. The wind battered at us, up here. My skimpy fur stood on end; Mendoza's hair streamed out like fire. I did a little dance, partly to express joy and partly to keep from freezing.

"This means that this time next week I'll be out of here!"

"Just when I'd got used to you with a tail," she remarked, actually smiling.

"Oh, I won't be out of the dog suit for another six months, believe me. I have to help the Chumash settle into their new lifestyle. Boy, will I have some explaining to do."

"You'll manage," she said. She was still smiling. I looked at her closely. As usual, the smile had nothing to do with me.

"You look happy," I observed.

"The Company approved my request, Joseph," she said. "I've been reassigned. I'm staying here in California."

"Congratulations," I said, mentally thanking the people who had owed me favors. "So you're going out to the base at Yosemite?"

"Out there? No. Though I'll certainly visit it when I get the chance; those sequoias are supposed to be amazing. No, I'm on my own recognizance. I'll be scouting with a complete field kit and sending stuff in as it's acquired. I thought I'd make myself a base camp in the coastal range hereabouts, just me and my credenza for company."

"You're kidding." I stared. "Mendoza, there's nothing here!"

"There's work, Joseph. There's enough work to keep me busy for years and years. No miserable departmental dinners. No social life. No *people,* very nearly. Only the land. Only those forests."

What reverence in her voice, talking about a bunch of trees and seismic zones. She had the answer, all right; she had found the True Faith, and she was as certain about it as the damned Englishman had been about his. She looked out at the ships and finally said, "I'll say this much for New World One. With all the luxury and all Houbert's silly rituals, all the conversation and busyness, there wasn't much time to think. That was a good thing, for a long while."

"Well, but what about your work? Your maize cultivars, that big project you've had on the burner since forever?"

"I have all the time I need for that," she said serenely. "I'm immortal, aren't I? Besides, I was about ready to settle down for a long spell of analysis of the hybrids I'd produced, and one can do that best inside a credenza anyway. Without all the distractions, I ought to make some real progress for a change."

She was already gone, settling her pack on her back and disappearing into the green leaves without a trace. I had to make an effort, all the same.

"But, Mendoza—you have no idea what it'll be like. I've been on field assignments in real fields, baby; there are no shelters, no generators, no emergency backup. You live like an animal in the woods, and you can lose yourself."

"God, I hope so," she said softly. I didn't know what to say in reply, so I didn't say anything. The big ships hovered out there, silent, waiting to take me away.

Chapter 33 ॐ

THE DAY OF the sky canoes.

Old Coyote went prowling back to the town in the dim hour before dawn, and as he stood on the hill above them all, he thought the place was already a dream. Not a soul to see, not a sound to hear: the houses looked transparent in the bleak air. Some cameraman somewhere was about to turn a rheostat, and they'd all fade out, shadows on a screen in a darkened room, no more.

I put my head in through the chief's doorway.

"Sepawit? It's our big day. Wake up your people."

A mound of furs on a sleeping platform stirred, and the chief emerged. He stared, half-asleep. Ponoya was a smooth curve behind him; between them sprawled the baby. "I saw the white men," he said thickly. "The trees died where they came."

"That's right, Sepawit. Wake up."

Back and forth between the houses I flitted, just like a real coyote hoping to find garbage. Or a loving father waking his children on Christmas morning. I guess I was somewhere in between. Young and old I woke them up, rich and poor, and one after another they emerged from their houses and stood blinking in the light.

"All right, everybody!" I jumped up in the air and waved my paws. "Come on out to the playing field, all of you! I have big news!" I loped away, and most of them followed me, except for one or two who weren't facing the day without breakfast even if it was the end of the world. They turned right around and went back inside, and soon you could see the smoke of their cooking fires.

The others milled around on the open ground, and I capered and frisked before them. "Now!" I barked. "You'll never guess what I saw this morning, out on Raven Point!"

"White men?" somebody ventured fearfully.

"No!" I replied, though it was true.

"The spirits of the dead?" tried somebody else.

"No! No, my own dear nephews and nieces, I saw not one, not two, not three, but four big sky canoes! The very same sky canoes that are going to carry us away from here!"

This made for general excited babble from most of them, though some thoughtful souls fell silent and stared. I raised my paws again.

"And they are *beautiful* sky canoes too!" I went on. "Wait till you see them! They shine like polished abalone shell. They're bigger than the council house. They're all enclosed, so the wind won't blow us overboard on our journey. The sea won't even splash us. There are fine seats inside these canoes and, best of all, they have what you have never, ever seen in any other canoe in your lives: latrines!"

This impressed everybody.

"You mean—"

"Yes! No need to worry about falling off while the canoe is moving. No need to cross your legs until you reach your destination. A beautiful private room instead, with a door that closes and plenty of hygienic accessories!"

"How do you get all that in a canoe?" demanded Nutku, clearly taken with the idea.

"Sky Magic, friend. So! My Sky spirits are waiting for us out on Raven Point. Each of you needs to go back to your house now, and pack a bundle for traveling. Yes, you can eat breakfast first. But don't bother to wash dishes, don't worry about banking the fire, don't even stop to fasten shut your doors when you've finished. Just grab those bundles and be back here in an hour!"

It took slightly more than an hour, but they did it. In the time between, the security team from the base arrived, sent by Lopez for crowd control in the event of panic. I can't say I wasn't a little annoyed by this: I mean, I'm a persuasive guy and I know how to do my job, right? But they did look impressive lined up behind me, I had to admit. A whole squadron of immortals as green as trees, as silent as a forest at my back.

When finally the whole population of Humashup had returned with their luggage, I cleared my throat and barked: "Let's all line up now! Families first. I want all the families in groups. Next, the single or divorced men. Single or divorced women next. Ladies, that's so you can watch their behinds as they walk!"

With a little help from the security teams, they were lined up in no time. I took my place at the head of the line and turned back to address them.

"Are we all ready? Good! I've composed a little song in honor of the occasion, and we'll sing it as we march along, all right? Here we go!"

Put all my sorrows in a basket,
I sing quietly as I go out upon my journey.
Farewell, Raven.
A woman stays awake to greet me,
She is sweet as honeydew.
Farewell, Raven.

In this place there are no shamans to assist me,
Only people who want to talk
About their own misfortunes.

Pile furs on my sleeping platform,
*   put wood on the fire,*

I will come home when the stars have faded.
Raven, farewell.

So that was the way they walked out of time, my people of Humashup: singing, and they never looked once behind them. But I kept my eyes on the village as we went along, walking backward most of the way, and I swear I saw the thatching on the houses blow away, their upright poles collapse, everything crumble. The ghosts took it over. My village died again, the old life died again. It was the year 1700, and time was running out for the old ways, the little tribal villages under the trees. A couple more centuries, and there wouldn't be any Stone Age left anywhere, would there? Except in my memory.

Then the town was out of sight, and we climbed up a canyon and wound across the green hills in a line, and the hard spring wind came up off the ocean and buffeted us all.

Sepawit strode at their head, holding his child tight in his arms, staring into the uncertain future. Ponoya trudged beside him, carrying the pack with their belongings. After him came a few married couples and several old folks carrying grandchildren, teenaged aunts and uncles pulling toddlers by the hand, big sisters or brothers carrying tiny babies, thin wary children on their own. Yes, there was little Kyupi lugging the baby I'd saved, with the two young boys tagging after. Farewell, Raven, they sang.

In the next group came the rich men, Nutku and Kaxiwalic and the rest of the guys, and their cloaks were made of otterskin and they hefted skin bags full of money. Bracelets of money rattled on their arms, money swung in pendant loops about their throats, and they shuffled with careful steps so they wouldn't lose any. I wondered if they'd packed their makeup and ceremonial costumes. Then came the shamans and priests, decked out in their feathers, bodies painted with signs to keep the world in balance, searching the sky for trouble. Last came the plain men, hunters, fishermen, and laborers, ragged or naked. Farewell, Raven, they sang.

The women came last. The well-born ones were skirted in deerskin, the poor ones in woven plant fiber, and all carried their lives on their backs. Some few carried infants. Some others wore a little money of their own. There were my groupie cuties, Puluy and Awhay, carefully dressed for the occasion, thrilled to trade the past for a new scene. There was the artist Skilmoy, angry about something again, and there was Anucwa, sagely giving her advice on what to do about it. Behind them they were leaving a hundred tasks undone for all time. Raven, farewell, they sang.

Get a good look at them all, because they're going away forever.

They stopped singing when we came in sight of the ships, and some of them stopped in their tracks. There was the holoproduced vision of the Rainbow Bridge, arching above the transport pad, its other end vanishing into a golden cloud far out over the sea. Some of my Chumash looked scared, but the security teams closed right in to push them along.

"Look!" I barked, prancing, frisking in circles. "Look at the lovely ships! Not only does each and every one have its own latrine, but we'll all get delicious food and drink on board, served by beautiful Sky Ladies who will wait on you with smiles. I can hardly wait, can you? Come on!"

So I led them at last to the transport pad, where the ships sat like silver ducks. Here were the anthropologists, out to meet us with open arms. Green arms with goose pimples, but open anyway.

"Look, spirits, I have brought my nieces and nephews for a ride in the Sky Canoes!" I saluted them.

"Welcome, Children of Coyote!" they cried. But the people hung back, staring up at the gleaming ships.

"They don't look like canoes," ventured Sepawit. "They look like that flying tube the War Helmet Nunasis had." He meant the Martian from our latest matinee. "Are you sure they're safe?"

"Of course they're safe! I'm going with you myself, aren't I? Would I ride in them if they weren't safe? You've all heard stories about what a coward I am." Inspiration hit me. "And, you know what else? There's *heating* inside those canoes."

This brought a look of longing to many faces, including the anthropologists'. Nutku pushed through the line.

"Well, I'm through freezing. I want to see what it's like inside one of those things," he said. That got them moving, because of course his fellow kantap members had to come too or lose status, and naturally the priests and shamans couldn't appear afraid, so they pushed forward up the boarding ramps, and as the leaders went, so went the townsfolk.

I breathed a sigh of relief. Backing around the side of a ship to get out of the wind, I bumped into someone. A cup of something hot was pressed into my paw. I gulped gratefully. Black coffee laced with aguardiente, wow.

"Swell!" I gasped, handing the cup back to Mendoza. "Burns all the way down. Say, what are you doing up here?"

"Turning to ice, same as everybody else. Came up to watch the end of it all." She had the hood of her cloak pulled so tight about her face, she looked like a nun.

"No, no, it's a new beginning!" I cried cheerily, overcompensating because it didn't feel like one. "The good people of Humashup are out, they're filing up the ramps, my bags are already packed and on board, and I know for a fact that the commissary at Mackenzie Base serves great food. Little Joseph is a happy Sky Coyote!"

Right on cue, it came into our line of sight, a canoe negotiating the surf and boulders below us to strike out into the open sea.

"One of your Indians appears to have changed his mind," observed Mendoza delicately.

It was Kenemekme, the poor dope. He was leaning way forward, inexpertly paddling a dugout he must have made himself, it was so crudely chiseled out of drift log. He was naked. All he had with him besides the paddle were flowers. Some kind of yellow flowers, he'd picked hundreds of them, they filled his canoe and hung over the sides, and a few bobbed yellow in his wake, floating in the sea foam. My muzzle hung open in astonishment.

"*Coreopsis gigantea, Eschscholzia californica,* and— let's see, that's *Oenothera hookerii,*" Mendoza said, peering at him, shading her eyes with her hand. "He must have been up all night gathering those. Shouldn't you be raising some kind of alarm or something?"

On one particularly enthusiastic backswing he noticed us, and stood up to wave. The canoe nearly capsized, but he steadied it somehow and gave us a crazy smile. He was shouting something. Mortals couldn't have heard him through the distance and the wind and surf, but we received him clear as anything.

"Uncle Sky Coyote! I'll meet You there! Don't worry, I know the way! But the beauty is shining out there, shining and shining beyond the world, can't You see it? I have to go find out what it is!" he cried. Then he plopped himself back into his canoe and went paddling on out to sea.

"If I remember Company policy correctly," Mendoza continued, watching me, "you're supposed to sound an alarm so the security teams can decide whether they'll go with option one, which is to rush out there and recover the escapee, or with the never-talked-about option two, which is to have a sharpshooter pick him off and thereby eliminate any loose talk or loose ends."

"I think I'm going to make an executive decision," I found myself saying. "I think I'm going to let that one get away."

"But heavens, whatever shall we do? He is already in the catalogue. Ah, but we've taken samples of what matters of him, so I suppose that doesn't pose a problem after all.

Perhaps you think he won't survive to tell anyone about us, in that wretchedly unseaworthy boat? You may be right. I estimate his chances of not drowning in the next three hours at seven hundred and fifteen to one. Though if the prevailing winds let up, he may have a better chance, and *might* make it to one of those islands out there in the channel. On the other hand, some of those islands are inhabited by worshipers of Chinigchinix, who are, as I understand, religious fanatics. If he lands on the wrong island, babbling about visions he received from Coyote, he'll be killed as a heretic. Though if he lands on the *right* island, he might be hailed as a new prophet and tell all kinds of tales we don't want him to tell. What does a Company man do in a situation like this, I wonder?" She watched me, coldly amused.

I yawned a wide coyote yawn. I shrugged.

"Hey, he won't last an hour in that thing."

"And if you send out an emergency team to pick him up, it'll delay takeoff. Sound decision, I guess . . ."

"I think so. Anyhow, you know what I always say? In a hundred years, who's gonna care?"

She was still laughing at that as I took back the coffee and had another hit. "Mm, good. Whoops—there go the boarding lights. Time for me to beat it. Well, Mendoza, it's been truly great working with you again after all these years. Keep in touch, okay? Vaya con Dios."

Chapter 34 ❦

I WAS KEPT busy in the next few minutes explaining to the sixty-five Chumash on our ship just how safe things were. When I was finally able to buckle myself into a seat and look out a window, I saw the base personnel assembled to watch the takeoff. There was Bugleg, eyes streaming with tears from the cold air and the pollen count, looking on unhappily as Lopez gave firm orders. Only the brass and the specialists were there, of course; all the techs were busy packing up equipment or dismantling the modular dome. Nobody was staying a second longer than was necessary, except for Mendoza. She was still standing there sipping her coffee, but she was staring away, fascinated, at the wild mountains of the interior. She looked up and raised her cup in a farewell gesture as the ship began to rise. I felt the climb speed up, and she seemed to sink into the earth as California dropped away below us. And there, quite a ways out to sea, I saw Kenemekme still bobbing along in his canoe full of flowers.

It really would have been more trouble than it was worth to go after him. Would he really have been happy at Mackenzie Base? He had his quest to find the beauty that was shining beyond the world, and he was sure to enjoy it more than orientation seminars and learning to drive loaders. The plain daylight around him was probably the closest he'd

ever come to his mystical goal, but maybe he wouldn't live
long enough to realize that.

Though I once knew a lady of a metaphysical turn of
mind who'd have argued that the plain daylight *is* the mystical goal, that God or whatever, being everywhere, *is* the
ordinary world all around us, and our quest is not to arrive
where He is but to notice Him right in front of our faces.
If she was correct, Kenemekme wouldn't be disappointed.
She died a long time ago, though, so I couldn't debate the
point.

But it made me feel good to see him paddling along
happily into the unknown. One little bit of Humashup was
being left behind, one tiny fragment of the lost world, and
maybe something good would come of it. Sort of like Pandora's box, you know? Shut in there with all the evils and
sorrows of the world was Hope. The rest of the people were
being taken away to a bright future, and Kenemekme was
being left in the dark, but maybe he'd brighten up the darkness a little while with his songs, with his crazy dances.

Chapter 35 ⨺

THE REST OF the story's pretty funny. Want to hear?

The people of Humashup did just fine at Mackenzie Base. Massive culture shock at first, of course, but they picked up on the delights of technology right away. More cartoon matinees! Food you didn't have to pound on a rock! Toilet paper! Not to mention lifetime jobs with the Company doing things like cleaning fuel tanks and working in processing plants. Menial work, but they were unskilled, after all, and it paid well. Great medical benefits, too. Most of them lived to see a third century.

They weren't allowed to breed anymore, of course, but that was okay with them, because most of them felt that parenting was a real pain in the ass. They happily donated sperm and ova to the Company freezebanks and let the anthropologists continue to pick their brains, though of course the longer they were exposed to a foreign culture, the less accurate their memories were about their old ways. They lived out long and comfortable lives eating Company food, buying Company merchandise, and vacationing at Company resorts.

Did I mention that Nutku and his fellow kantap members went into business? Their shell money was traded for Company scrip as soon as they figured out the exchange rate, and with it they bought the plant that manufactured the BeadBucks used at Company resorts for minor purchases like cocktails, appetizers, and beach-chair rentals. They parleyed that into a number of Authentic Chumash™ handicraft stands at Company bases all over the globe. Sepawit's kid grew up to become one of their CEOs, in fact, an executive with amazing vision. Numbers of ladies like Skilmoy supplemented their paychecks by producing Authentic Chumash™ baskets and other stuff in their spare time, which they had more of, now that they didn't have babies every year, and eventually banked enough to open their own, competing line. There was a real trade war that went on for years. Eventually they all died of old age, rich, and that was the end of them.

A long, long time later, the Chumash nation was reborn. Not the real Chumash, of course; the ones we left behind had long since died of smallpox or interbred with their invaders to the point that they ceased to exist as a culture, except for one determined tribe that ran a gambling casino somewhere.

No, the New Chumash were mostly Caucasian members of a religious group in the Federal Republic of Santa Barbara. Their spiritual leader had this vision that declared that he and all his followers were reincarnated Chumash. They believed the Chumash had spent all their time swimming with dolphins and getting energy out of quartz crystals. Nobody thought to ask the casino owners whether or not this was true, because running a casino didn't seem a very spiritual thing to be doing.

So the New Chumash bought up all this land north of the republic (pretty close to where Humashup had been, as a matter of fact) and declared it an ecological preserve and spiritual sanctuary. They were able to do this, despite the astronomical price of real estate in California, because they were stinking rich, being a very successful religious movement. The Reformed Church of Chinigchinix, by this time a toothless and benign old faith, gave its blessing to these fellow Native Americans by adoption.

And they had a lot of healing seminars and ate a lot of whole-grain carbohydrates on the sacred ground, but most of them felt that something was missing. Maybe it had something to do with the fact that the sacred ground, like most of California after half a millennium of over-development, was so chemically poisoned it looked like the back of the moon. All the whole-grain carbohydrates and the woven baskets they were served in had to be imported from Nigeria. Anyway, the reincarnated Chumash weren't quite happy.

It chanced that one of them, being a stockbroker, was at a dinner party with a lot of other rich and powerful people. There she met a friend of a friend who had connections with Dr. Zeus. She did a lot of wistful talking over her nonalcoholic Chardonnay; so did her money. One thing led to another, and within two weeks the New Life Chumash Nation had placed its order with the Company. As the Company had known it would.

Bring the Chumash out of the past for us, they said. Give us back our traditions, our ancient ways. We want to dress up in Chumash robes. We want the total Chumash experience. Spare no expense.

And with those magic words, Dr. Zeus got to work. From their labs they got out all this Chumash genetic material that they, uh, just happened to have. They brought out all the carefully propagated flora and fauna of the Chumash ecosystem from their botanical and zoological gardens. They brought from their records every possible detail of Chumash folkways and culture, and boy, they sure had a lot of material.

The sacred ground was detoxified and bulldozed back into its original contours; it was replanted; it was restocked with animal life. Cleaning and restocking the adjacent ocean floor was harder, but, you know, they'd said to spare no expense, and who was the Company to argue? There was some outcry from historical preservationists when the picturesque old oil rigs off the coast were dismantled. Cash donations shut them up. When everything had naturalized, Humashup was rebuilt down to the last woven hut, and the New Life Chumash Nation moved in.

The next step was making more Chumash. This posed a slight problem for the New Lifers, because they were all sexually dysfunctional in one way or another. No problem, said Dr. Zeus. We've got genuine Chumash sperm and ova here, and they can get it on in a petri dish as well as anywhere else. The ladies of the group coped admirably with the in vitro transplants; they drank raspberry leaf tea for nine months and found childbirth a very spiritually fulfilling experience.

But they were kind of disappointed in the resulting children, who didn't seem to share their values. And, let's face it, life on the sacred ground under the ancient oak trees was, well, *hard* and smelly, and there turned out to be absolutely no psychic contacts with dolphins. The tribe running the casino could have told them that, if anyone had bothered to ask them.

Eventually most of the New Chumash got tired of it and went off to be the other people they'd been in their past lives. Dr. Zeus got custody of the Chumash children, and the children inherited the ecological preserve. They had to be taught how to live on it, though, so the Company sent in all these anthropologists made up as Sky People to instruct them in their ancient culture. Including a Sky Coyote, but not me. That was some other Sky Coyote. I was somewhere else by then.

When they grew up, the Chumash took a good look at the world around them and decided they wanted out of the Stone Age. But these Chumash had been inoculated against diseases, and there were no Spaniards around to beat them up, see, so things turned out a little differently this time.

A couple of generations, later, genetic descendants of Nutku were the stockbrokers drinking Chardonnay at dinner parties in Santa Barbara. They still had their language and culture intact, which helped them become the most aggressive import-export entrepreneurs on the Pacific Rim. Many of them moved down to Hollywood, where they revitalized the entertainment industry to such an extent that there were soon dark mutterings in certain quarters about the town's being run by Indians.

They did have a problem with juvenile delinquency, however. Chumash gangs became the latest scourge of the venerable Republic of Mission Revival. The same intact culture that made them good businessmen also made many of them lousy parents . . .

But it was *their* culture, and at least they got it back, which is more than some people get. And, all things considered, they're doing okay. You should see how the Etruscans Nouveaux turned out!

Happy endings aren't so easy to come by when you're an immortal, because nothing ever quite seems to end. Well, things do; we don't, which is part of the problem.

New World One Base was closed down, right on schedule before the century ended. Deliberately ruined and abandoned to the jungle, leaving not a rack behind for Colonel Churchward or any of those guys to find. Houbert had decamped by then, with an entourage that included his few surviving Mayans. His next paradise was a château on the Loire, where I understand the Mayans refined the science of haute cuisine to an art before they, too, eventually died. Houbert was moved on to Monaco—it's one of those places the Company practically invented—and created another little celestial world on the Riviera. As far as I know, he's still there at the safe house, dispensing his own special syrupy wisdom to adoring mortal servants and unlucky subordinates.

Latif grew up into a superbly competent executive administrator, all brass and flash and hardball, and got the shock of his young life when he finally pushed through his assignment to North Africa and was reunited with his hero Suleyman. It took him a while to realize that sly, courteous old Suleyman was also a superbly competent executive administrator, and actually knew a few tricks Latif didn't. Eventually the student settled down at the feet of the master, and the two of them became legends in that part of the world.

I was thrown back in the arms of Holy Mother Church once I got out of makeup, but somehow my descent into darkness eased up for a while. I'm not sure why. Maybe because I was sent in as a jolly Franciscan instead of a villainous Jesuit. Maybe it was because the murderous power of the Inquisition—and the Church, too—had begun to wane at last. Less and less of my job had to do with the scourge and the branding iron, more and more with protecting lovely old religious art treasures from an increasingly rapacious secular world. Nice work, if you can get it, and I got it for a while.

But I go where the power is, and there was a new religion coming, a new force to hold people spellbound and visit them with dreams and terrors, to unite them with a common point of view and common assumptions about what life is and ought to be. It packed them into its pews every single night of the week without even one commandment, and Hollywood was its holy city. That was where the Company sent me, practically on the day Cecil B. DeMille rolled into town. I've been in the entertainment industry ever since, in one capacity or another. It's better than the Inquisition. Usually.

Lewis wound up in Hollywood too, for a while, as film scripts took on historic value of their own. He really did get work stunt-doubling for Fredric March and Leslie Howard, as it turned out. We occasionally had lunch at Musso & Frank's Grill and talked about old times over gin gimlets made with Rose's Lime Juice. We never discussed Mendoza, though.

I don't know where Mendoza is.

This is not to say I don't know what happened to her,

or at least that I haven't made a few good guesses; but I don't think about her much.

She was okay for a while. She did vanish into the coastal range of Central California, and really did all that good work she'd been so confident she could do; in fact, she won a few commendations. I saw her now and again, when she had occasion to stop by some mission where I happened to be portraying a kindly friar. But she was nervous and irritable in human places; she couldn't wait to finish whatever business had brought her there and disappear again into the wilderness. Just about the only times I ever saw her smile were when she'd turn for a goodbye salute before fading up some canyon, into some drift of coastal fog.

I played that game again: I told myself Mendoza was doing just fine and put her out of my mind, and if I thought about her at all, it was only in the context of how happy she was in some redwood forest somewhere, so I didn't have to worry about her.

Something happened, though.

I never saw her again after the middle of the nineteenth century. She just wasn't there anymore, and some other Company botanist had been assigned to that region. He had his work cut out for him, too, because suddenly there were Yankee homesteaders and miners all over the place, clear-cutting, burning, and grazing their cattle even in those precipitous ranges. Mendoza would have been so furious.

Maybe what happened to her had something to do with that. I'd know for certain, if I were to access the official notification the Company sent me. I never have.

I only read enough to glimpse her name and some mention of a disciplinary hearing before I filed it away, unwilling to integrate the rest of the information it contained. That was in 1863, and to this day there it sits on some buried level of my consciousness, right next to the access code that Budu forced on me. I've never found out what that says, either.

I did *think* I saw her, once, in the early years of this

century. That was a hallucination, though; had to have
been. She couldn't possibly have been sitting at that table
in the Hotel St. Catherine in 1923, and even if she had, she
couldn't possibly have been sitting with the other person I
thought I saw there. Anyway, by the time I managed to
push my way from the crowded bar to the place where I'd
seen them, the table was vacant, two wineglasses empty,
the terrace door open. Had they run away? No. They'd
never been there at all. Mendoza was somewhere else, I
knew that, stashed away in some secret Company place
because of something that would probably turn out to be
my fault.

But they can't have done anything too terrible to Mendoza, because she was a good operative, she did good work.
It's not like they could kill her, anyway, right? She's an
immortal, after all, as indestructible as I am. She must be
out there someplace.

Budu must be out there someplace too.

The year 2355 approaches, though, and not one of us can
hide from it or outrun it. I guess I'm going to have to access
Budu's message eventually, decrypt whatever it was he
wanted me to know. I'll probably read that memo on Mendoza then, too. I have a feeling that I'll find a new role to
play after that, which is okay. Between you and me, being
a minor studio executive with a leased sports coupe is beginning to pall a little.

"A Memo from Dr. Zeus, Incorporated."
by Kage Baker

DR. ZEUS INCORPORATED AUDIOMEMO:
  6 JUNE 2351
SPEAKER: J. BUGLEG
RECEIVER: J. RAPPACINI
CLASSIFIED! YOUR EARS ONLY!

Um . . . I don't think it's on. No, the little light didn't
come on when I pushed the button. No! See, you have to
push right there and—oh. I did? Okay, go away now. This
is classified. No cyborgs allowed. (Long pause.) Rappacini, the new stuff didn't work. I put it in his drink and he
drank it but nothing happened. You have to make something stronger. I'm starting to get a little scared we can't
do this. Gradenko showed me the numbers this morning
and I was right, there are almost as many of them as us
now.

We shouldn't have done it. They're too smart and I'm
scared they'll find out about this. If only we hadn't made
them immortal . . .

MEMO TO: ERESHKIGAL, FACILITATOR GENERAL
   ASIA MINOR
FROM: AEGEUS, EXECUTIVE FACILITATOR
   WESTERN EUROPE

Reshi darling, you were right; the pathetic creatures are
plotting again (see the above communication we pulled off
their "secure channel" this morning.) I suppose it isn't quite
time to tremble in our shoes, but I do agree we'll need to
keep them under closer supervision now through 2355. Really, the presumption!

But we must remind ourselves that for every treacherous
little idiot savant like Bugleg there are dozens of mortals
who are quite clever in their varied ways. What would we
do without their splendid poets, their painters, their sous-
chefs and all the others who make our eternal nights gra-
cious and our eternal days less tedious?

We must bear this in mind when we put them in their
place at last.

Lunch at Cesare's Biarritz on Wednesday?

TO: N
FROM: L

See the above. Aegeus wins my vote for Most Compla-
cent Ass of the Millennium. He simply cannot grasp that
the monkeys will persist in their efforts to unmake us.
Hasn't he ever accessed *Frankenstein*, for heaven's sake?
I look forward to teaching him a few painful lessons
when . . .

But in any case, if he can't be bothered to do something
about this latest covert act, we certainly should. It will
eventually sink into their tiny minds that someone is punishing them for Wrong Thinking. What would you say
would be appropriate? An outbreak of Marburg virus in

metropolitan Paris? Another suborbital flight disaster? Something less drastic but just as amusing? I'm always fond of anonymous Holo of the Month Club subscriptions, myself, mortals get so terribly irritated trying to send back unordered holos and never seem to get the return addresses right . . . endless fun!